W9-AFV-166

Praise for *More Than We Remember*

"A beautiful page-turner full of depth and hope. A reminder that faith and friendship can see us through even the most impossible situations. Don't miss this gift of a story."

—Catherine West, award-winning author

Praise for *If We Make It Home*

A *Library Journal* Best Book of 2017
and a 2017 Foreword INDIES Book of the Year

"Nelson's fiction debut is a tension-filled tour de force of suspense and human emotions. Fans of Cheryl Strayed's *Wild* and Jon Krakauer's *Into the Wild* will love this."

—*Library Journal*

"If you love discovering new authors with lyrical, literary voices, then you're in for a treat. If you like those voices to also deliver a powerful, engaging story with true emotional depth, then you're in for a feast. Highly recommended."

—James L. Rubart, bestselling author
of *Pages of Her Life*

"I turned the final page of *If We Make It Home* with a sigh of satisfaction. Christina Suzann Nelson is a writer to watch! The adventure these three friends found themselves on had me wide-eyed and holding my breath, but their inner journeys were even more breathtaking. High stakes for each of the characters, yes, but a payoff that is so worthwhile."

—Deborah Raney, author of *Chasing Dreams*

"*If We Make It Home* is a powerfully well-written novel layered with complex characters, witty dialogue, and superbly plotted collision courses of divine destiny. . . . [It] moved me with its gut-wrenching honesty and profound wisdom. . . . Christina Nelson has created an absolute must-read masterpiece."

—Camille Eide, award-winning author of *Wings Like a Dove*

Praise for *Swimming in the Deep End*

"An exceptional read and one that will live with me long after I close the book."

—Jaime Jo Wright, Christy Award–winning author of *Echoes among the Stones*

More Than We Remember

More Than We Remember

Christina Suzann Nelson

BETHANYHOUSE
a division of Baker Publishing Group
Minneapolis, Minnesota

Published by Bethany House Publishers
11400 Hampshire Avenue South
Bloomington, Minnesota 55438
www.bethanyhouse.com

Bethany House Publishers is a division of
Baker Publishing Group, Grand Rapids, Michigan

Printed in the United States of America

Library of Congress Cataloging-in-Publication Data
Names: Nelson, Christina Suzann, author.
Title: More than we remember / Christina Suzann Nelson.
Description: Minneapolis, Minnesota : Bethany House, a division of Baker Publishing Group, [2020]
Identifiers: LCCN 2019040450 | ISBN 9780764235382 (trade paperback) | ISBN 9780764235504 (cloth) | ISBN 9781493422692 (ebook)
Subjects: LCSH: Female friendship—Fiction. | Life change events—Fiction.
Classification: LCC PS3614.E44536 M67 2020 | DDC 813/.6—dc23
LC record available at https://lccn.loc.gov/2019040450

Cover design by Kathleen Lynch/Black Kat Design

Author is represented by the Books & Such Literary Agency.

20 21 22 23 24 25 26 7 6 5 4 3 2 1

To my husband.
A man worthy of my trust.

The perp was a mama raccoon.

Deputy Emilia Cruz turned her sheriff's department SUV onto the highway connecting her county to the rest of the world. Her foot pressed the gas pedal a little harder than usual. Thirty minutes of road twisted between her and West Crow, where she might actually do some good. Again, she'd been relegated to pest patrol. That was the problem with city people deciding to throw off their urban ways for the quiet life of the country: They tended to call in the police, taking time away from actual crimes to investigate any number of sounds or concerns that turned out to be wildlife.

Emilia opened her window. Cool summer night air drifted over her arm and woodsy scents floated in as the highway curved around the side of a towering hill. For a moment, she permitted her worries to blow away on the wind.

The last bit of turn gave way to a straight stretch, and in that fraction of a second, tranquility shattered as crumpled metal burst into view. Emilia slammed her foot on the brake, coming to a stop behind a blue Maxima. Dust still hung in the air, as if she had only just missed the moment of impact. She grabbed her radio. "This is Deputy Cruz." Emilia thrust the door open.

"I've got you, Emilia. What do you have?"

"Looks like a two-, maybe three-car collision on the Darlington-West Crow Highway, six miles from the northern county line."

"I'll get help to you as soon as possible."

Emilia flipped on her flashing lights, then stepped out of her vehicle. She shook off the immediate shiver of dread crawling up her back, replacing it with her most professional demeanor.

She approached the Maxima. The dome light shone, but the doors were closed. Emilia knocked on the driver's-side window.

Two girls, both appearing to be teens, startled.

"You two all right?"

Their heads bobbed with tiny nods.

"Could you step out of the car, please?"

The driver's door squeaked open, and a girl with long straight brown hair, approximately five foot five and slim, stepped out, eyes rounded. Her mouth hung open, but she didn't say anything.

Emilia ran the flashlight up and down her. "Were you injured?"

The other girl, a much taller blonde, came around the front of the car. "No, ma'am. We witnessed the accident, but we weren't part of it."

"Don't leave the site. I'll need your names and information." Emilia didn't wait for them to respond, doubting the first girl would even be able to speak in her shocked state.

A red Jetta lay on its roof, steam billowing from the engine crushed into the remains of the car's body, the back tires still spinning while the front seemed to have disappeared into the accordion of metal.

Emilia bent down and shone her flashlight through the broken glass on the driver's side. Scarlet blood pooled along the pavement, the stench almost more than her stomach could bear. Popping open one of the compartments on her belt, Emilia yanked out a pair of latex gloves and snapped them onto her hands. She tugged loose glass until the victim was clearly visible.

The assessment was immediate: This woman had not survived. Emilia pressed the button on her radio as she rose to check the other car. "Claire, it's Emilia again. We have a 12–16A. See if you can get the major traffic collision team from Benton County over here."

"Copy that. Ambulance is eight minutes out. We have fire and rescue en route from Darlington and West Crow."

Glass and plastic fragments crunched under Emilia's boots as she jogged across the highway to the green pickup pressed into the side of the hill. Her stomach wobbled. The image of the woman from the first car was tattooed on her brain for life. Hardened against scenes like this? Never.

Emilia looked down the road, willing help to arrive before she reached what remained of the passenger door, but the accident was nearly the center point between Darlington and West Crow. Eight minutes would tick by slowly.

The deflated airbag blocked the remnants of the passenger window. Emilia swiped her light beam under the vehicle and found no trace of gas. Then she clambered into the pickup's bed, retrieved her baton, and punched a hole in the back window. Once the glass was cleared away, she pushed close, the light illuminating a man with a long laceration to the scalp.

Blood flowed over his right eye and down his jawline. It didn't look good for him, either.

A moan cracked through the silence.

"Sir? This is Deputy Cruz. Can you hear me?" She reached her arm into the opening she'd made earlier and touched his shoulder, careful not to move him.

Another moan, but no words.

Emilia spoke into her shoulder mic. "Claire, advise responders we have one alive. Looks to be a man in his mid-thirties to early forties. Severe laceration to the head."

"Got it."

Emilia cleared a larger hole, then pressed her arm and face into the cab. It smelled of perspiration and chemicals from exploded airbags. "Sir, we have help on the way."

The man's body lurched, and he retched onto his lap, his head collapsing on the steering wheel.

A familiar stench filled the air.

Emilia jerked back.

This man was no victim. He was drunk.

EMILIA GAVE THE side of the ambulance two firm smacks before it left the scene, carrying away the deceased body of Georgianna Lynn Bosch. No sirens. No need for speed. Georgianna's life had poured out of her purse like the synopsis of a book. She was a single mother of three boys who, from their pictures, looked to be high-school age. A work ID showed she was a nurse with the local hospice agency. There didn't seem to be any other family, at least not close enough to warrant photos.

Emilia rubbed circles into the tight muscles along her neck. A hospice nurse. No doubt Georgianna had sat beside countless patients, easing them from this world with as much peace as she could manage. How gut-wrenching for those who loved her that she had died alone in a senseless and violent collision.

Once again, life wasn't playing fair.

Tucking loose strands of hair behind her ear, Emilia made her way to the unaffected car, where the two girls remained as ordered. A line of vehicles waited on the Darlington side for the lanes to be cleared on the route to West Crow. They'd be better off taking the detour even with the additional half hour on gravel roads. This wasn't going to be a quick investigation or cleanup.

Both girls sat so still, their heads resting together, that Emilia wondered if they had dozed off. She tapped the window with her knuckle. Two sets of eyes shot their gazes toward her as the girls startled to attention.

"I'm going to need your statements." Emilia spoke loudly to be heard over the rumble of fire truck engines and rescue workers.

The teen behind the wheel opened the door.

"Could you both step out for a moment? I want to go over what you witnessed tonight." Normally, she would have gotten to this questioning earlier, but they were short on deputies with Chadwick in Florida on vacation. That gave her little wiggle room and would keep her at the station late doing more than her share of paperwork.

The blonde was around the front of the car before the smaller girl even stood.

Emilia flipped open her notebook. She should really conduct these interviews separately, but it was well past midnight, and the brunette looked like she'd burst into tears if the other girl was taken away from her. In the distance, metal cried out as the hydraulic ram pushed the front of the pickup out of the rescuers' way, allowing access to the trapped man.

A deep voice carried over the noise. "We're thirty minutes into the golden hour, people. Let's move."

The girls leaned their backs against the side of the Maxima.

"Can I get your full names and identification, please?"

"I'm Harper Jane Hampton." The blonde reached into the purse strapped over her shoulder and handed Emilia her driver's license. She pressed her fingers into her collarbone. "And this is Ivy Lenaya Smith."

Emilia looked to Ivy for confirmation.

The girl nodded as she handed over her identification, but her eyes kept flicking to the scene where the fire department continued their attempt to free the man from his crumpled truck.

"Don't worry about what's going on over there. These people know exactly what they're doing. It's your job to tell me what you saw so we can handle the part that comes next."

Ivy's eyes pooled with tears. Flashes of red and blue from the emergency vehicles colored her face. "I . . ." A tear cascaded down her cheek. "Is . . . is the other driver . . . dead?"

Emilia cringed. This could be her own little girl in just a few years, scared and away from her mother when tragedy crashed in. "Have you contacted your parents?"

They nodded.

"It happened so fast." Harper put her arm around Ivy, pulling the other girl into her side. "The truck crossed the center line and ran smack into the car."

"What happened next?"

Harper shook her head. "It was loud. . . . I may have closed my eyes. I'm not sure."

"Did you notice anything about the way he drove? Anything unusual prior to the collision?"

"No. It was very sudden. Maybe he fell asleep or something."

Ivy started sobbing into Harper's shoulder. She would be little help tonight.

"You're from Darlington, but you were heading away from there. Where were you two going?"

Harper pulled Ivy closer. "Ivy forgot her sweater at our friend's house in West Crow. We were heading back to get it."

"You were going all the way back for a sweater? Ivy, is that right?"

The girl's eyes were swollen and red, yet tears flooded her cheeks like there was an endless supply. She turned toward

Harper, resting her forehead on the taller girl's shoulder, and gave a slight nod over her shaking.

"Do you have someone who can pick you up?" Emilia closed her notebook. "Ivy is in no condition to drive tonight."

"It's fine, ma'am." Harper ushered Ivy around to the other side of the car. "I can drive us home. Our parents said I should. They're waiting. We promised to come back as soon as we'd spoken to you. And no cell phones or anything. You know."

"Please let them know I'll be contacting them tomorrow. We'll set up a time for a formal interview."

Harper paused with her hand on the door handle. "Is that necessary? There isn't anything to add."

"It's procedure in a case like this. Drive safe." Emilia held a hand up to the line of waiting cars.

Harper took three tries to get the car turned around, then drove off along the empty lane and around the wide corner decorated with flares.

Three victims and counting. Those two would never be the same after what they'd seen. And neither would Emilia Cruz. This guy was going to pay a heavy price for his night of indulgence, and she would make sure he produced every single cent.

Emilia hollered to one of the volunteer deputies, whatever the guy's name was. "Hey, get these cars out of here." She motioned to the line growing around the corner. Why were so many people out on the highway in the middle of the night? West Crow and every town within a hundred miles closed down when the sun set.

The back of the second ambulance was open, a stretcher waiting for the moment they moved the man from the truck. A minute later, they eased him out, strapped securely to a board, then set him on the stretcher.

"We have a wallet here." A firefighter climbed from the open truck cab.

"I'll take that." Emilia stretched out her hand, then pulled it back when she recognized the face below the yellow helmet. A new wave of disgust washed through her.

"Em. I didn't realize you were out here." David took a step closer, opening the wallet and retrieving the driver's identification. "Whoa. That's Coach Kilbourn."

Coach Kilbourn? A town like West Crow wouldn't take kindly to having their hero prosecuted as a drunken murderer. And a final blow, the man delivering the message was her husband's former best friend. Emilia couldn't fault him for abandoning Roger. She'd been tempted to do the same.

"I've meant to come by." David had the good conscience to avoid eye contact. "It's been busy, you know, with Barbara and the kids. Maybe this weekend."

The back of the ambulance slammed shut. "We're good to go," the driver interrupted.

Emilia took the wallet from David and tossed it to the driver. "Make sure I get toxicology screens. I'll be at the hospital after I finish up some other details."

The ambulance driver nodded, then switched on his sirens, speeding off toward Darlington.

The night promised to be a long one, and Emilia didn't have energy to make nice with one of Roger's many friends who'd found it too *difficult* to be around her husband since his injury. Emilia and her daughter didn't have that option.

"Don't worry about it, David. Roger has a full weekend." Emilia checked in with another officer before returning to her car for the first time in nearly an hour. Now came the hard part. She'd have to deliver the news to Georgianna Bosch's family. She'd send another officer to notify the Kilbourns.

2

A twin bed was a tight squeeze for Brianne Demanno and her puppy, Chester. At twelve weeks, the dog was at least twenty pounds heavier than Brianne had anticipated. The Humane Society guessed him to be a quarter heeler and half border collie, with at least a quarter unknown. The math didn't add up to the beast of fluff with the lazy brown eyes of a Saint Bernard currently pushing her over the edge of the mattress.

Brianne sat up and reached for the jar of water, twisting off the lid and taking a couple gulps of room-temperature liquid. She'd learned the hard way about open containers near the bed. Chester got thirsty at night. The dog's first choice was her cup, then the toilet. If both of those were covered, he'd resort to his bowl.

When she'd moved back into the house where she'd grown up, Brianne had brought her queen-sized bed. But once she'd assembled it in her room, she could barely walk between the walls and the edges of the bed frame. After a couple of banged knees, she'd pulled the queen into the master bedroom and gone back to the lumpy twin from her childhood.

She could have settled in the room that had been her parents' until they had relocated to Arizona, the land of heat and grandchildren. But something about taking over the place where her mom and dad had slept for thirty years felt . . . wrong.

After nine months of home ownership, Brianne was still a visitor.

Refreshing coolness touched her feet as she made her way along the hardwood floor toward the bathroom. The rumble of an engine stopped her. No one came this far down the lane, especially in the middle of the night. The only neighbor beyond her parents' house—her house—was a cranky old woman who rarely had visitors.

Brianne eased back to her room and retrieved her robe. She shook Chester, but the dog she'd adopted for her protection was apparently only on duty during the daylight hours. Even then, he refrained from barking at anything or anyone other than the gray squirrels who lived in abundance throughout Oregon's Willamette Valley.

She reached under the bed, her fingers locating clumps of dust and dog hair, then finally the item she needed—her older brother's trusty baseball bat. Living alone wasn't something Brianne had aspired to. Five years as a clinical social worker had destroyed her fairy-tale thinking. Bad things happened. And some people were meant to be alone.

Brianne wrapped her fingers around the wood, squeezing until her knuckles ached with the tension.

A knock, more like savage pounding, sent her heart rate toward numbers she didn't reach during all-out sprints. Maybe fear was a superior source of aerobic exercise. But running was what she did to get away from the memories that truly scared her.

The light from a vehicle lit the living room, stealing the advantage of darkness. Brianne crept to the front door, questioning why her father had never installed a peephole. She knew the answer. He was a man ruled by trust. He trusted his neighbors, his community, his God. Brianne's trust had died with one of her favorite clients, Amanda Tanger.

Rising on her tiptoes, Brianne peered through the three small windows along the top of the door. She could just catch a glimpse of a police-blue baseball cap. Her breath caught. Police at the door. Middle of the night. Never a good thing. Her parents? Her brother? His family?

Or could it be another client she'd failed?

Brianne leaned the bat against the wall and unlatched the deadbolt, the click echoing in the space that felt too cold. She turned the knob and pulled, hinges crying out, until she stood face-to-face with Deputy Seth Wallace, the man who'd been there the last time tragedy hit her like a brakeless train.

"Brianne?" His eyebrows rose.

They'd spent years in the same high school, but she felt a twinge of surprise when he remembered her name. She'd been invisible back then, a book nerd hidden in the pages of a novel while Seth was the pride of West Crow, a town that took its sports as seriously as its public health. Probably more so.

"Hey, Seth." She ran her hand over sleep-crazed hair. "What's wrong?"

His head tipped to one side as he took her in like he was seeing something completely new. "Does"—he tried to look around her—"Coach Kilbourn live here?"

She crossed her arms in front of her chest. "You came by at this hour to ask if I'm having an affair with a married man? Of course he doesn't live here. What's this about?"

A blush spread over Seth's neck. "I'm so sorry. I didn't mean to imply anything. I was surprised to see you, is all. I thought maybe the coach had bought your parents' place." He flipped open his notebook. "There must be a mistake. Maybe I wrote it down wrong."

"The coach and his wife—I can't remember her name—just moved in with his mom, Caroline." Brianne stepped into the chill and pointed up the lane to the next house. In the distance, a faint light glowed from the front window. What were they doing up in the middle of the night? They had kids, but Brianne didn't remember any of them being babies who would need to be fed and changed at this hour.

"I'm sorry I woke you." Seth turned to walk away.

"Wait. What do you want with Caleb?" It wasn't any of her business, but this was a small town. If the gossip was juicy, she'd have no way of not hearing it three times before dinner tomorrow night. A five-minute run through the grocery store is all it would take. She might as well know now.

Seth stopped with one foot on the top step of Brianne's porch. He looked back at her over his shoulder. "You might want to get some clothes on and head down there. The family will need some support."

The words ripped through Brianne's heart. She'd heard them before from this deputy. *"The girl didn't make it. The mom will need you for support."*

Her mind raced over every interaction she'd had with Caleb Kilbourn or his family since their move into Caroline's house. There'd been little more than occasional nods or waves, nothing that should give Brianne a wash of guilt like the last time. So why did she feel as if she'd done something wrong? "I'll get down there as soon as I can."

Seth seemed to hesitate; then a small but sincere smile grew. "You're just the right person for this. Thank you."

Brianne leaned on her back foot, a strange shiver prickling her skin. She watched him all the way to his patrol car before closing her door as he drove away toward the Kilbourns'.

Heat warmed her cheeks. The Kilbourns were in the middle of some crisis, and Brianne had the gall to linger over the words of a man like Seth, who, though attractive, clearly had issues. No good-looking man in West Crow remained single into his thirties unless there was something seriously wrong with him.

Brianne flipped on the light, illuminating the long, narrow living room. Even now, something felt eerie, like she'd snuck out of bed and was wandering the house while her parents slept. She took two steps closer to the tiny hall with a bathroom and her parents' bedroom. After all this time, she still expected to hear the rattle of her father's snore through their door. There was nothing now but silence and memories. The same things woke her every night.

She entered her own room to find Chester awake but still claiming most of the mattress, his tongue hanging from his mouth as he yawned. The moment she threw her robe on the floor and grabbed jeans from a pile in the corner, Chester knew it was time to eat and walk. There was no stopping the day now. Three in the morning. Eight in dog hours. She sighed.

Chester bit into the hem of Brianne's pants, tugging her toward the kitchen.

She managed to throw on a long-sleeved T-shirt while hobbling down the hall. "Chester, we don't have time for this."

He released her and positioned himself in a perfect sit, eyes directed toward his source of food.

Brianne opened the door, but Chester didn't move. She tugged at his collar, but his heart and body were set on breakfast. His bladder wasn't a priority. Brianne wrapped her arms around the dog's middle and hefted him up, carrying the whining dog outside to the chilly front yard.

Chester looked around, then back at the door. He made a move for the house, lunging past Brianne and taking up his position in the kitchen.

Brianne rubbed her hands over her face before scooping food from the bin into his bowl. "Don't make me regret this." While he ate, she slipped her feet into tennis shoes and tied the laces. "Okay, buddy, I'm going to need you to hold it while I'm gone. It shouldn't be long. Just checking on the neighbors."

A string of drool slipped from his mouth and dripped on the edge of the chrome bowl.

"Sometimes I really wonder if you're listening." Brianne eased out the door, hoping he wouldn't realize she was going on a walk without him.

Oregon summers could be boiling hot during the day, but the night often cooled enough to cause shivers. Brianne hugged herself and increased her pace toward the Kilbourn farm.

Moonlight guided her down the gravel lane. Trees that colored the roadside in bright shades of green during the day seemed to reach dark arms toward her now. She quickened until she was at that awkward gait, too fast to walk, too slow to run.

Reaching the Kilbourn driveway, Brianne began to jog. As she approached the familiar farmhouse, Seth raised his hand to knock.

If the absence of her husband next to her hadn't woken Addison Kilbourn, the mattress spring digging at her left kidney would have. She reached across the space his body usually inhabited and plucked her iPhone from the nightstand. Holding it out as far as her arm would stretch, she strained to focus the numbers without her reading glasses. A little after three in the morning. Where was Caleb?

Addison climbed to the outer edge of the full-sized torture device and settled her bare feet on the cool wood floor. Caleb had met an old high-school friend for burgers. She'd expected him to wander in about the time she got the kids to bed, but he hadn't shown. They'd exchanged texts, Caleb saying he and Jeff were enjoying the opportunity to reminisce. But until this hour? That seemed excessive. And off. Something was off. She couldn't put her finger on the very thing, but Caleb had seemed tense before leaving, as if this reunion wasn't something he'd wanted.

A shiver ran through her body. Something wasn't right. She clicked on the bedside lamp, illuminating Caleb's childhood bedroom, complete with cowboy wallpaper. They'd been guests in her mother-in-law's home for only two weeks, but it felt like years.

Addison found her glasses and sent a text to Caleb. *Where are you?*

The pounding of her heartbeat accentuated each second as she begged God for Caleb's reply.

Nothing.

Wrapping a robe around her, she started for the stairs. Maybe he'd fallen asleep on the couch while watching ESPN. It wouldn't be the first time she'd had to rouse him and usher him to their room. But their room didn't exist here. This wasn't their home, no matter how many times Caleb claimed it was.

The lamp beside the threadbare couch still glowed, waiting for Caleb's return. Above the sofa, an old family picture hung. An image of Caleb with his brother, Wyatt, and their parents. Only half of that family remained. Addison shook her head. If she'd had loving parents like Caroline and Charles, she never would have left. Wyatt didn't know what he had.

She ran her hand over the rough sofa, vacant of any sleeping form. She'd seen this very piece of furniture in other pictures from Caleb's youth. Vintage, in her mind. She checked the front door. No one had locked it. She stepped outside and found the place between the house and shed where Caleb parked his truck. Empty. In the distance, a vehicle's headlights shone down the gravel lane, drawing closer. But that wouldn't be her husband. The lights came from the wrong direction.

The vehicle turned onto the driveway. The beams bounced as the car bumped along the ruts.

A line of lights topped the car.

She inched back into the house, closing the door.

Addison shook her head. *No. This isn't happening.* One of her worst fears had crept into her subconscious when Caleb hadn't been home at bedtime. She'd told herself she was imagining things.

She stepped backward until she bumped the wall, her head displacing a framed photograph that slid to the floor, its breaking glass shattering the silence. Blood pulsed in her ears. *Wake up!*

Outside the window, she watched a silhouette come up the front walk. Suddenly, the most important thing in her world was keeping her children asleep, adding precious time to their lives before whatever tragedy took over. She raced to the door, throwing it open before the deputy could knock.

His hand covered his weapon as if she were going to attack. "Ma'am? Are you all right?"

Tears pooled in her eyes. He was the one who had the answer to that question.

"Are you Mrs. Kilbourn?"

Her mind flew to her mother-in-law, the woman she'd always associated with that name. She nodded.

"You're Caleb Kilbourn's wife." His chin dipped.

He hadn't said *were*.

Addison pulled the robe tight around her middle, her face prickling, hands shaky. "Yes."

"Ma'am, your husband was in a serious accident tonight." He looked over his shoulder as if expecting backup. "An ambulance took him to the hospital in Darlington."

A tear slipped down her cheek. "Is he dead?"

"No, ma'am." He reached toward her but didn't make contact. "Do you have someone who can drive you to the hospital?"

"What happened?"

His face stiffened. "He was involved in a head-on collision traveling toward West Crow from Darlington. If you'd like, I can take you to the hospital."

Head-on. Did people come back from head-on highway collisions? There was urgency in the air between Addison and the deputy. Maybe he wanted her to say good-bye, to let her husband slip out of her life.

Her legs buckled, sending her to the floor, the rough doormat etching into her knees. So much pain. The fear arced across her chest, a monster ready to strip her of the man who'd given her all she'd longed for—a true family.

Someone knelt next to her, a gentle arm covering her shoulder with warmth. A woman cupped Addison's head in her hand and rocked her back and forth, the way a mother should.

"I'm so sorry." The voice was familiar but distant. "What can I do to help?"

Addison looked up into teary blue eyes. It was the neighbor. The one who jogged by with the fluffy dog. *Brittany. No . . . Brianne?* "I need to tell Caroline; then I'll go." She bit her bottom lip. Even in tragedy, asking a favor from a near stranger jarred her conscience. "Could you stay with my kids?" She couldn't leave them with their grandmother. Caroline had drifted from quirky to unstable.

"Of course." The woman stood and helped Addison to her feet. "You should probably change your clothes too."

Addison looked down at the short robe that covered her summer pajamas. "Thank you . . ."

"Brianne." The neighbor picked at the skin along the edge of her finger. "I'm the next house down." She pointed.

Determination came like a swelling wave. Addison had to make a plan. She needed to focus right now, for the sake of her husband and her children. She looked to the deputy. "Give me two minutes. That's all I'll need."

As if she'd downed a pot of coffee, Addison's veins hummed with purpose. She knocked on Caroline's door, the only bedroom on the first floor of the hundred-year-old house. When the knock wasn't answered, Addison opened it and stepped in. Light from the hall illuminated her mother-in-law, her arms laid wide across the mattress, her jaw slack. If not for the rumble of intermittent snores, Addison would worry Caroline was more than asleep.

"Caroline. Wake up. There's been an accident."

Nothing.

"Caroline?" She didn't have time for this. Addison nudged her shoulder, shook her arm.

The woman continued to snore as if she were sedated for major surgery. Addison had never seen anyone sleep this soundly.

After another try—hard enough to bounce Caroline on the bed yet with no sign of waking her—Addison crossed her arms. "Fine then. I'm not waiting on you. The neighbor can tell you about your son."

Addison rushed from the room and up the stairs. She threw on a light sweater and jeans, then grabbed her purse from the top of the chipped dresser, dropping a brush in it as she moved to leave.

"Mama, can I sleep in your bed?"

Addison froze, staring at her six-year-old daughter, her blond ringlets framing her face.

Lilly padded to the bed and climbed under the covers as if the question had been answered. Within seconds, her breathing slowed.

Addison tucked the blankets around her daughter's shoulders. She couldn't bear to tell the kids what had happened. Not now, when she didn't have the answers to the questions they'd ask.

Emilia sank into the patrol car. Light had begun to illuminate the world, as if today were just another peaceful summer morning. As if she hadn't, only moments before, spoken the words that would change three lives forever. Even through their tears, the young men spoke of their mother with deep respect. She had made them proud. Not an easy thing to manage with teens.

The ache of those boys' grief weighed heavier on Emilia than the twenty pounds of equipment strapped to her waist. They'd never again hear their mother nagging them to settle down, to do their homework, to clean up after themselves. Had their mom given them what they'd require to make it in the world? Would they become the kind of men society needed?

Moments like this were the nature of the job. Emilia would probably never know what happened in the lives of Jesse, Jordan, and Jared . . . unless their lives intersected with the law.

Crimes like the one that caused this mother's death could not go unpunished. Too many people walked around without facing the consequences of their actions. Those repercussions found homes on the backs of their victims' families.

Not this time. Caleb Kilbourn would pay the price for killing Georgianna Bosch, and Emilia would be the one to lock him up.

Deputy Wallace escorted Addison into the emergency room waiting area, handing her over to the receptionist like one would drop a stray dog at the pound. Had she even gotten his first name?

Addison's finger traced the sharp edge of the business card in her pocket. She wasn't being fair. The guy was doing his job, and he'd gotten her here. No one expected him to be her personal guide through this tragedy.

"Mrs. Kilbourn, someone will be right out. We're going to have you wait in the family room upstairs." The woman stood, her pink scrubs stretched too snug over her middle. "Do you have anyone coming to be with you?"

Chills spread down Addison's arms. She pulled her sweater tight. "It's just me. I'm . . . alone." Maybe she should call someone, but who? They'd lived in West Crow for such a short time. The idea of begging support from any of the women she'd known before the move felt like a step toward failure. She'd been a mom who knew the other moms, but they weren't friends outside of that shared identity. Friendship took investment. It meant opening oneself up to the potential of embarrassment and rejection. And who had the time? Addison's family was where she placed her value, not fitting in with the mom clique. It took an emergency to show her the importance of that missing asset.

A boy dressed as a medical professional appeared from a door in the back. "Mrs. Kilbourn, I'll take you upstairs." A badge hung from the pocket of his shirt, giving a morsel of credibility to his baby-smooth face.

Addison followed him down an empty hallway thick with the scent of antiseptic. Was this the place her carefully knitted life would begin to unravel? She'd gotten lax, drifting on a flimsy wave of security. It was her fault. If she'd been more watchful, guarded her family . . .

The elevator door slid open, the young man holding one hand on its edge as he waited for her to enter. Each step was like pulling her legs through knee-deep mud. Closer and closer to what was coming next, to news she'd never be able to forget.

Addison grasped the railing with both hands, her fingers clenching the metal as if it had the power to stop the elevator's movement.

"You probably don't recognize me."

Addison looked up and met the young man's eyes for the first time. There was something familiar there, hidden by a few years. She took in the name on his tag. Kevin Beck. Memories came flooding back. "Kevin. You've grown."

"Yes, ma'am. It had to happen eventually." His smile reminded her of all the times Caleb had spoken of the boy with all the heart for the game of basketball, but none of the height or athletic ability.

The elevator stopped, sending a wave of motion through Addison's body.

"I sure hope Coach is okay. I'm not supposed to mention knowing patients, but Coach is special. I'll be praying for him." He stepped into the hallway and motioned Addison through a door labeled *Family Waiting Room.*

Addison let her hand cover his wrist. "Thank you, Kevin." She blinked away a stubborn tear. "I appreciate that."

Kevin nodded, then turned away, letting the door swing shut and leaving Addison alone in a place where countless others had waited for news of their loved ones. What were the odds she'd be the one to get the good word?

A vase of silk flowers sat on an end table at the edge of a neutral tone couch. Magazines were fanned out on a polished wood coffee table. The room was like a staged replica of someone's living room, as if that would lighten the stress hanging in the air like a toxic cloud.

Addison lowered herself onto the corner of the sofa and pulled the throw blanket from the back over her lap. She fingered the edge of a pillow before bringing it close, hugging the plush material tight to her middle.

A large clock ticked on and on, a reminder of how alone she was. Her only ICE—the person she had listed to call "in case of emergency"—was Caleb. What would she do if he didn't make it through this?

Sounds from somewhere beyond the closed door caught her attention. Addison stood too quickly, and the room began to swim. She braced herself with one hand on the arm of the couch.

Any hope she still gripped washed down her body and onto the floor as the door opened and a deputy stepped into the room. No compassion softened the woman's hard face and no-nonsense eyes. She stole every ounce of confidence from Addison with one glare.

"Mrs. Kilbourn, I'm Deputy Emilia Cruz. I'd like to ask you some questions about your husband."

Addison turned to the window. Bright sunlight creeping over the mountains gave the hospital grounds a warm glow, even as Addison's skin tensed in the cold of the waiting room.

"Ma'am? What can you tell me about your husband's drinking problem?"

The question sent Addison's heart racing. She turned. "You've got the wrong man. My husband's not a drinker."

Officer Cruz dropped her shoulders. A smile spread across her face, sweet and artificial enough to be an ad for Splenda. "I'm really sorry for all you're going through. I'd like to get my information as quickly as possible. It makes it easier for everyone to move forward. I'm sure you want that as much as I do."

Addison tugged at her long hair, now twisted into a loose braid over her shoulder. There was never an easy way out of a mess. The one thing she knew for absolute certain was the fact that tragedy grew before it faded, and each incident left another scar on the lives it cut. "I can't think of anything that would help you."

"Where was your husband coming from when he was in the accident?" Officer Cruz took a step closer, that sticky smile still smeared on her face.

Addison shook her head. "He had dinner with a friend, Jeff. I don't know where."

"Interesting."

"Why is that?" Addison crossed her arms.

"Can you give me Jeff's last name?" Her pen was poised over the notebook, as if this information was somehow significant.

Addison shook her head. "I can't remember. We just moved into town. I haven't gotten a chance to meet many people."

The door opened again, and a surgeon walked in, her shoes still covered with paper booties.

Deputy Cruz snapped her notebook shut and exited the room without so much as an apology. As the door clicked shut, a small breath of hope returned to Addison.

The surgeon introduced herself, then led Addison back to the couch. "Let's go over what we've found so far."

Addison laced her fingers together, pressing her hands into her chin. "He's alive?"

"Absolutely. Your husband is a fighter. He's also my nephew's basketball coach." She winked. "We need to get him back to work."

Addison relaxed into the cushions. "So he's okay?"

"I believe he will be. Your husband suffered some serious injuries." She held an electronic tablet between them, a picture of a detailed skeleton on the screen. "The impact pushed the front end of the vehicle practically into the driver's seat. Your husband sustained deep lacerations, as well as two bone fractures in his right leg." She tapped the area of injury on the screen, then looked up. "I've seen much worse. I'd say he was pretty blessed the leg wasn't further damaged. We'll need to have the ortho guy repair the break. But first, we need to wait for Caleb to stabilize."

Tears stung Addison's eyes.

"We've stitched up a pretty significant laceration on his forehead. There doesn't appear to be any bleeding or swelling in the brain, but you can expect him to have significant concussion symptoms for at least a few weeks." She blew out a deep breath.

"There's more." Addison rested her head on her hand.

"A bit more. We found some bleeding from a tear in his liver. We've corrected that." The doctor set the tablet on the table, then folded her hands. "Caleb's blood was positive for a small amount of alcohol. Not enough to suggest impairment. But we also found oxycodone. The combination of the medication and the alcohol is a serious concern. I checked through his medical records, and I didn't find anything about a prescription. Has your husband had an injury we're not aware of?"

Cold tingles swam over Addison's skin. "That can't be right. Caleb is the healthiest person I know. He won't even take cold medicine. He always says the body knows how to heal itself."

"I had the test run twice. I'm so sorry."

Addison stood. "Can I see my husband?"

"Soon. He's waking up now. They'll come get you once he's in a room."

Brianne woke with a kink in her neck and a child staring down at her. She sprang from the couch, her feet hitting the floor, her hands rubbing at aching muscles.

The little girl tipped her head to the side, wrapped a finger in the silk edging of her worn blanket, and smoothed the fabric across her cheek. "Who are you?"

Brianne blinked and tried to get her bearings. Last night wasn't a dream. She sifted through the haze of memories, placing them back into a kind of order in her mind. "I'm the neighbor. I . . ." She didn't want to say too much, but finding a stranger asleep in your living room was a surprise that needed an explanation.

"Breakfast." Caroline's voice broke the tension as it drifted in on the scent of bacon and coffee.

"Grammy says we have to love our neighbors." The girl's mouth twisted. "Is that why you're here?"

"Your mom had to go out. She asked if I'd stay."

Caroline entered, wiping her hands on a towel tucked into the belt of her apron. "Let's not have this grub go cold now." She motioned for them to follow.

Brianne rubbed her hands over her face. Addison must have called and spoken with Caroline. Otherwise, the older woman would have been shocked by Brianne's appearance here too.

Brianne followed the child into the large kitchen, with a table and chairs at one end. Bright yellow walls gave an air of cheeriness. Copper pans shaped like chickens hung on either side of the sink. On the corner of the counter, a cookie jar squirrel watched the whole scene.

Caroline pointed a crooked finger at her grandson, the middle of the three Kilbourn children. "Connor, get your mother a cup of coffee."

Brianne's heart thudded. She swallowed.

A girl who looked to be a very young teen took in Brianne from over the top of a thick novel.

"Grammy." The youngest child tugged at Caroline's apron.

"What is it, Lilly?"

"That's not Mom." She turned Caroline toward Brianne.

Caroline shook her head. "Of course not. Good morning, Britta. Do you like cream with your coffee?"

"Yes." The mistaken name hung in the air. If Brianne corrected her, it could take on power in the form of the woman's embarrassment in front of her grandchildren. Surely it was just a slip of the tongue. Caroline Kilbourn had known Brianne since she was a toddler. "Cream would be wonderful. Can I help with anything?"

"Don't be ridiculous. You're our guest this morning." Caroline poured coffee into a mug, returned the carafe to the maker, then paused, staring into the black liquid.

"Where did my mom go?" Lilly turned around in her chair, one leg dangling on either side of the back.

Brianne held her tongue, waiting on Caroline for the answer, but the older woman had shifted her gaze to Brianne as though she waited for the response with as much interest as Lilly. "Didn't she call home?"

Caroline shrugged, rolling a dish towel between her fingers. "Maybe when I was out with the critters. I figured she and my boy went on an errand or something."

Awkward wasn't a big enough word for the position Brianne was in. She eyed the back door as if running from the house would fix everything. All eyes were on her now, waiting for Brianne to choose between her two options. She could give them a watered-down version of last night's ordeal, or she could give the dire and serious version.

She trained her eyes on Lilly. "Your daddy had a bit of an accident last night. Your mom went to make sure he's okay.

She'll call any minute." Brianne looked at the silent phone on the wall, willing it to ring.

ADDISON RUBBED THE heel of her hand against her eye, curbing the burn for a moment. She hadn't been this sleep deprived since Connor's colic-filled nights.

Caleb's face was pale, other than the purple bruises spreading across his right eye and cheek. A bandage covered the gash on his forehead, but swelling made the seriousness of the cut evident.

Addison pulled a chair close and slipped her hand into his. She leaned her forehead against the cold metal rail.

"Addy." His voice rattled like a handful of pebbles in an old coffee can.

"I'm here."

He moaned. "What happened?"

"You were in an accident. Do you remember anything?"

"No. Just packing." His eyes were thin slits. He pushed up on one elbow and winced. "Where are the kids?"

Pressing a hand gently to his shoulder, Addison guided her husband back onto the mattress. "The kids are fine. They're at your mom's." She prayed that the neighbor would still be with them. "Packing? You remember moving there, right?"

His lips tightened. "I remember the plan. Packing. But not getting there."

"We've been in the house for two weeks." She looked at the man in the bed with the rough cheeks in need of a shave and the gentle eyes that brought her so much comfort. Thank God, he'd survived, but he would need a long time to recover. The entire construction season—not that she really cared about their new house now. Caleb's injuries brought her priorities into realignment. There were countless hurdles coming his way, but Caleb didn't need to know about any of them now. It could all wait.

Tears glistened in his eyes. "No. We haven't loaded the truck yet." He lifted a hand to his head. The beep of his heart rate escalated on the monitor.

So many questions swirled around Addison, but evidently Caleb wouldn't be able to answer a single one. Where had he been? What took him out on that curving highway last night?

"I need to get out of here." He pulled on the guardrails, inching his way to the edge of the bed. Caleb's right leg, bound tight in a temporary brace, nearly slid off the mattress. He flinched, his face tightening with the shock of pain.

"No. The doctor wants to keep you here a few days." Addison stood, holding him back.

His breathing came in ragged puffs, like a man who'd climbed a mountain. "This isn't right. I have to go. They're telling you lies."

"What are you talking about? No one is telling me anything." Did he somehow know about the allegations? Did he remember more than he was admitting? Addison removed one hand from her husband and pressed the call button.

His hands tightened into fists, his shoulders raising toward his ears.

"Hey now." The nurse came around the other side of the bed. "What do you think you're doing? You have fresh stitches and a liver that needs mending, plus that leg."

Caleb eased his head to the side, his gaze crossing over Addison, then the nurse.

"Press that call button again, please." The nurse nodded her head toward the edge of the bed.

Addison punched it five times.

Seconds later, another nurse came through the door.

"Henry, can you get something to help Mr. Kilbourn settle down? The doctor put in orders."

A moment later, Henry was back with a syringe. He plunged the needle into the IV line and forced the liquid into the tube.

Caleb's muscles softened, and the three of them repositioned him in the bed.

Addison groaned. "He seems so confused. So agitated. He doesn't remember that we moved recently."

"Sometimes temporary memory confusion happens with concussions. And there can be a significant change in personality for a time. It's nothing to worry about."

Addison nodded, holding back the waves of tears that pounded behind her eyes.

"It's probably a good time for you to head home and take a break. He'll be out for a few hours."

Addison squeezed her fingers around Caleb's warm hand. His chest rose and fell, each time feeding her a morsel of comfort. Walking away from him now was like turning her back on the man who'd given her a life and a family. But the kids were waiting at home. They knew nothing except that their father hadn't been there when they woke up. And a woman the kids had only seen from a distance was there in their mom's place. Addison needed to be the one who guided them through this, and she definitely needed to talk to Caroline. Why hadn't Addison been able to wake her last night?

Another layer of concern piled onto the bonfire growing in her chest.

Emilia tapped send on the final email. Her shift had officially ended at eight a.m., three hours earlier, but time didn't slow just because a drunk took it upon himself to extinguish the life of an innocent mother. In the hours since the accident, Emilia had seen to the rescue efforts, informed three young men they were on their own in the world, collected evidence to use against Caleb Kilbourn, and filed so many reports, she wondered if she should have an honorary journalism degree.

But even with all of that, her biggest challenge still waited at home. At least this was her last graveyard shift. Cline was back from vacation, allowing Emilia to return to the day shift.

She tossed her sheriff's department jacket over her arm and stepped into the already hot day. Instead of feeling revived by the sunlight, Emilia's body softened into a sleepiness she'd have to fight as she drove home, and likely much longer.

Her job wasn't the day-after-day mountain of satisfaction she'd imagined when she started at the academy, but it paid the monthly bills and sometimes, when she got overtime, it made a dent against the loss of income they'd experienced since Roger landed on disability.

Emilia climbed into her Honda Accord. The day lay over

her like a lead apron, her feet throbbing from hours on the clock in a pair of not-yet-broken-in boots. But going home only meant the grind would begin. She took her time starting the car, even if all it bought was a moment or two.

She drove through town with the radio off and the windows down. Air laced with the remnants of outdoor cooking and the delicate scents of summer flowers made her miss her childhood. She'd been free to roam this small town without much worry of danger, but big-city problems were leaching into this once safe place. Meth laced almost every legal issue in the county. And now heroin was making an appearance.

When would people stop finding new ways to destroy their lives and their families?

A few children rode bikes and played ball in the streets, but fewer than there'd been even five years earlier. Emilia kept a tight rein on her own thirteen-year-old daughter, not allowing Tally to loiter where anyone suspicious could approach. She kept Tally safe.

A boy Emilia saw regularly waved as he pedaled his bike along the sidewalk. Maybe he'd grow up to have a happy family, but even the most carefully planned lives could be stripped away in a minute.

After a couple of turns, she pulled her car to the curb, inching forward to leave room for the garbage truck that would rumble by sometime around noon. Curtains moved in her daughter's bedroom. Tally would be a welcome sight against the cracked paint and lopsided porch. But the girl, the very core of Emilia's heart, was already becoming one of those kids who rarely left the perceived safety of her room. Privacy was the word of the month. A few years back, Tally had been a different child, open and the center of their family's attention. But none of them looked the way they had back when the house was truly alive and filled with laughter.

After stepping from the car, Emilia reached into the back

seat and hefted the loaded laundry basket onto her hip. She'd washed the clothes last night at the laundromat before starting her shift, but the fresh scent of fabric softener still clung, bringing back delicate memories of her grandmother. Nana had been gone twelve years already, but Emilia still missed her like she'd passed away only the day before.

The front door swung open, the screen snapping against the pocked siding. Roger, a mug in one hand, glared over the neighborhood.

Her husband's overgrown eyebrows pressed closer to each other, a sure sign today would not be one of his good days. "I'm half starved, and as usual, there's nothing to eat in this place. How am I supposed to get over these headaches and get a job if I don't have a decent meal?"

Emilia eased forward. "There's no rush on the job. The doctor said it would take time." She came a little closer, resting one foot on the bottom step. The shape of his head was forever changed with the deep scar from where a beam had nearly crushed his skull. It was no wonder he still suffered from blinding migraines. The doctor had said it could be a life sentence, but couldn't God grant Roger back his personality? Lately it seemed to be slipping away faster and faster.

"Easy for you to say. You get out of this dump every day. You get to work and have fun with your friends. Me, I'm here drowning in pain meds and watching Netflix. They should have let me die." He scrubbed his fingers into the back of his scalp, a shudder running over his still-broad shoulders.

Emilia slipped past him without making contact. "Come on in. I'll make you some breakfast." As much as Roger's dips into depression scared her, these were better days than the ones fueled by rage. "How about some French toast?"

"How long?"

"Twenty minutes by the time I get everything straightened out." She held back a yawn.

Roger's head fell forward. "Forget it. I'm going back to bed." He shuffled down the hall, his shoulders slumped. A moment later, their bedroom door clicked shut.

The last bit of Emilia's energy drained out with her released breath. She dropped onto the sofa. Fun-sized candy bar wrappers were strewn across the floor. No fun for the one who pulled clean-up duty. Two empty bottles sat along the coffee table's edge. The television droned in the background, the theme song for their pathetic reality. That and yelling.

If even the tiniest amount of fairness existed in the world, Emilia would be able to lie down on the couch and sleep for at least an hour. But she still had a daughter in the next room, a mess to pick up, bills to tackle, and food to prepare.

Somehow, she'd have to find the strength for another attempt to connect with Tally before Emilia allowed herself to doze on the lumpy sofa.

Emilia pushed herself up with the same grunt her nana used to make. Emilia was years ahead of her time.

In the kitchen, she found an even bigger mess than the disaster in the living room. For a man who grumbled about needing work, Roger sure wasn't managing to get much done around the house.

Emilia piled the dishes from the sink onto the counter, then filled the basin with warm water and a squirt of blue dish soap. When the waterline had reached the halfway point, she put the dishes back in to soak.

The next task to tackle would be the moody teen.

Music with questionable lyrics pounded through Tally's thin door.

Leaning her head against the wall, Emilia pleaded with God to give her back all the things she'd lost with Roger's injury. Five years ago, she was a mom whose life had been perfected when she met the man of her dreams, a man who loved her daughter and wanted to be a family with both of them. Every day was a gift from a loving Father, until a falling beam stole the blessings she never should have taken for granted.

Tapping the wall outside Tally's room, Emilia waited but didn't hear an answer. Finally, she turned the knob and pushed. The door bulldozed against discarded clothing.

Tally sat on her bed, her ears covered by headphones while music inexplicably also poured from the speaker on the desk. With her feet pulled up and knees tight to her chest, her daughter still looked like the little angel who loved to sit on her mother's lap and create storybook adventures.

Emilia and Roger would spend the rest of their years dealing with the fallout of someone else's irresponsibility, but Tally shouldn't have to. She was innocent.

The bed sagged under Emilia's weight, its firm support something enjoyed by the original owner years ago.

Brown eyes, oversized, as if Tally hadn't quite grown into them, looked up at Emilia. For a slight moment, she saw the little girl in her daughter, but then a glare took the place of the innocent shine.

"What?" Tally pulled off the purple-and-white noise-cancelling headphones her grandmother had thought would make her happy. "I'm trying to read."

Reaching out, Emilia switched off the desk speaker. "Do you really need both of those on?"

"It keeps me from hearing *his* complaining." She cocked her head to the side.

"That's not fair, and you know it."

"It's not fair that I have to live like this." She crossed her arms tight against her chest.

The urge to yell pressed at the corners of Emilia's jaw, but she held it back. She wouldn't add to the situation by cutting into her daughter. "Tally, I understand your frustration. Trust me, this is no picnic for me, either, but it isn't Roger's fault. He's doing his best under the circumstances."

Tally held up a hand. "Spare me the traumatic-brain-injury speech. He's not getting any better. I don't understand why you stay with him. You could get a divorce, if you cared about my life."

Tension piled onto anxiety, forcing Emilia's shoulders to relent. "You know it's not that simple. Roger put everything aside to give us the best possible future. Don't you remember how he loved us unconditionally? Why can't you understand that he deserves the same devotion? Love is not meant for only the good times."

Tally's head tilted so far to one side, her ear nearly touched her shoulder. "Are you telling me it's love when he yells at you? What about when he threw that plate against the wall? Was that love? Is that what you've decided to teach me?" Her lips twitched into a scowl. "Nice parenting, Mom."

The tight balloon in Emilia's chest sprang a leak, leaving her struggling to remain upright. Was it even possible to be a good wife and a good mother at the same time? Not under these circumstances. If it came down to a choice, she'd choose her daughter. Tally had always counted on her. But now, so did Roger.

The opposing sides raged a fierce battle in Emilia's heart. She gave Tally's knee a quick squeeze. "I'm making breakfast." She turned to leave, her gaze catching on the devotional she and Tally had been working through together before the accident. It sat on the shelf, untouched for all these months. Emilia placed her hands over her heart and took a deep breath. She missed those times. The longing for the way things had been weighed down on her, and she walked out the door, shutting it behind her before allowing tears to spill over her cheeks.

6

Well, I've got chicken business to tend to." Caroline rose from the table, lifted her coffee mug, and downed the last drops.

"Oh no!" Brianne gasped.

All eyes turned her direction.

"My dog. I need to go let him out." Her stomach, stuffed beyond full with bacon, eggs, and pancakes, wobbled. How could she have forgotten about that poor pup's needs?

Connor shot up, his toast dropping to the floor. "You have a dog?" He grabbed the bread and shoved it into his mouth.

"Yep. He's a puppy, really."

"Can we go see him?" Lilly scooted off her chair and slipped her bare feet into bright red rubber boots.

"Fine with me." Brianne's kinked muscles ached for a shower and a long nap, but today didn't look to be heading that way. Addison's call during breakfast tied Brianne tighter to the kids rather than relieving her of the duty. "Caroline, do you mind?"

The older woman was already on her way out the back door. She looked over her shoulder at Brianne, her eyes unfocused.

"You go on now." Maybe the news of the accident had hit Caroline harder than she let on. People could hold a lot of fear and grief under wraps when children were present. Brianne had seen it over and over in her work—her past work, that is. But the truth always came out, and often the children were hurt more than necessary in the end.

Connor was out the door before Brianne could get the dishes to the counter. "Hannah, are you coming?"

She set her book down on the table. "I guess."

They walked down the gravel lane, Connor and Lilly up front, turning now and again, their expressions begging Hannah and Brianne to pick up the pace.

"Do you like living here?"

Hannah shrugged. "It's all right."

Connor and Lilly stopped at the waist-high gate to Brianne's front yard. A pathetic whine echoed from behind the door. Brianne pulled the gate open, and the two younger kids jogged through the yard and up the steps.

Brianne smiled. The kids would make up for the neglect Chester was surely holding against her. "Go ahead and open the door."

Connor didn't hesitate. He turned the knob, and in a flash, Chester was out of the house, jumping and licking every face he could get access to, all while spreading a puddle of piddle with his spastic tail.

"That's disgusting." Hannah took a step back.

"I love him," Lilly squealed. She slung her arms around Chester's neck as the dog licked every inch of her exposed skin.

Connor found a stick in the yard and threw it for Chester, who lunged after it like the wood was a cut of beef.

Brianne looked at the oldest of the Kilbourn children. "Come on in, Hannah. I'll show you my books. You're welcome to borrow any of them you want."

They stepped inside, where the living room was an embarrassment of shredded newspapers and doggy toys.

"I left in a hurry this morning. I should have put Chester in his crate." Brianne scooped up an armful of paper and deposited it in the recycling bin.

"What's this?" Hannah stood next to the dining room table, a place Brianne used for everything but eating. Artwork in all stages of design lay spread over the wooden surface.

"It's called photo fusion. I take a picture, layer the image with colored pencil, and bring out the vision I originally saw in nature."

Hannah's face brightened with a smile, coming alive like the photos did with the addition of the added color and depth. "It's beautiful."

"Would you like me to show you how someday?"

She looked straight at Brianne for the first time, her ocean blue eyes shining. "I would. Is my dad going to be okay?"

Brianne's pulse throbbed in her ears. Her life used to be a series of very similar questions from children who'd seen and experienced so much worse than the one in front of her now. Her old stock answers felt foolish; Brianne had no way of knowing what would happen next for the Kilbourn family. All she had was the truth, or the truth as she saw it in this moment. "I don't know." She braced herself for Hannah's tears, but they didn't come.

"Thank you for being honest. Can we see the books?" Hannah turned away from the table.

"Of course." Brianne opened the door that led to her parents' old room. "I keep meaning to get these up on shelves." Cardboard dust twirled in the air as she tore the tape from a box. The contents brought a peace with them. They were the places Brianne had explored as a child, her wildest dreams and greatest adventures.

Hannah reached in and pulled out a copy of *The Magician's*

Nephew. She turned it to read the back cover. "This looks amazing."

"It really is. You should borrow that one right away. It's one of my favorites."

"Thank you." Hannah held the book to her chest as if it were already a good friend. "I'll read this next."

Foot thuds echoed through the house, coming to a stop at the bedroom door. Lilly fisted her hands, pressing them into her sides. "Connor is hogging the puppy."

Brianne tried to hold back a smile. "I think I have something in here you might be interested in." She got to her feet and pulled a large plastic tub into the center of the room. "Take a look."

Lilly let her angry stance soften and peeled the lid off, uncovering Brianne's favorite therapy toys: a castle, furniture, and a family of small dolls. "Whoa." Lilly dropped to her bottom, examining each piece carefully before setting them at her side. She reached in and came out with an envelope, Brianne's name printed on the front. Lilly didn't give it a second glance, just tossed it to the side.

Brianne's chest started to burn. There was something familiar about the hesitant handwriting. She took the discarded letter and walked out of the room, leaving the distracted girls. In the kitchen, she ran her finger under the flap and tore open the seal.

> *You've been a good friend, but I've done something really bad. My dad's in jail for something I don't think really happened. I did this. Please make it right. Tell him I'm sorry.*
>
> *Amanda*

Brianne held the letter to her heart, feeling the pounding through the fragile paper. Her mind reached for the memories of her last meeting with Amanda. She'd seen this girl as a client for years, and they'd developed a bond. She'd thought she'd known how to help her.

What did Amanda say that day? What did I miss?

EMILIA RECOGNIZED THE car the teenagers had been driving parked outside the Hampton residence. Hopefully that didn't mean Ivy was here now. Emilia needed to conduct her follow-up interviews with the girls separately, though nothing new would likely come from this trip to Darlington. The testimony of Harper Hampton and Ivy Smith would be the ink the jury needed to sign Caleb Kilbourn's guilty verdict. The drive time was worth it to put a killer away. Enough with these *accidents*.

A hook-shaped door knocker hung underneath a peephole. Above the framing, a camera was mounted. Emilia gave her ponytail a yank, tightening it to her scalp. People who took home security seriously were easier to respect than those who left their safety to chance and 911.

Emilia rapped on the aluminum door with her knuckles. Behind the barrier, a dog yapped.

"Just a moment, please." A woman's voice floated from a speaker in the corner.

Emilia turned her back to the door and looked over the well-to-do neighborhood, with its nice cars and upscale homes. The lawns were manicured and free from rusting yard art. Maybe she should look at changing jobs, see if there was anything she could get in Darlington. Maybe security work.

A year ago, the thought would have turned her stomach. But life changed. Her work didn't hold the pride it once had, and reviving her community one small step at a time now felt more like a giant waste of time.

The door clicked as the locks were opened, drawing Emilia's attention back to the job at hand.

"Good morning." A woman wearing cream slacks and a light pink blouse greeted Emilia as if she'd come for a social event rather than on official police business. "Please come in. Harper will be out in a moment." She led Emilia down a hall and into a bright room. A table was set with cups and plates. Even the scones on the center platter seemed to be organized in order of shape and size.

Emilia fisted and straightened her hands. She didn't much care for the clutter accumulating at her home, but this was unnerving. "I'm Deputy Cruz."

"Yes." Mrs. Hampton indicated Emilia's nameplate attached to her uniform. "Please have a seat."

A man in a polo and khakis stepped into the room. "Looks like we're ready to get started." He held his hand out to Emilia. "I'm Ken Hampton. Attorney."

Though his lips smiled, Emilia sensed the familiar threat lawyers wore like too much cologne. "Nice to meet you." She shook his hand, then pulled out her notebook. "I'd like to get started as soon as possible. I have another stop this morning."

"At poor Ivy's house, I assume." Mrs. Hampton shook her head. "That sweet girl. She's so sensitive. Her car has been here since the girls got back. Her mother says she doesn't want to drive it home." She pulled out her chair and waited for the others to do the same.

Emilia looked over her shoulder before taking a seat. Their daughter was nowhere in sight.

"Please help yourself to scones and tea. I can get coffee if you'd rather."

"No, I'm fine. Would you mind getting Harper out here, though?" Emilia resisted the urge to check her watch. Efficient, these people were not.

Mr. Hampton typed something on his phone, then stuffed it back into his pocket.

A moment later, Harper came into the room, yawning. Her hair was pulled up into a messy bun, and her makeup looked like it was freshly applied, but she wore pajama bottoms and a T-shirt cropped high enough to show a strip of skin. She dropped into the chair between her parents and set her cell next to her plate.

"Good morning, Harper." Emilia slid her business card across the table to the teen. "I just need to take your statement and maybe ask a few questions. That's it. Are you ready?"

Harper snatched a scone and tore a chunk from the corner, plopping it into her mouth as she nodded.

"Okay. Please start from the beginning." Emilia poised her pen above the notebook.

Harper blew out a sigh, as if this was the last thing she wanted to be doing. "Ivy forgot her sweater, so we were going back to get it."

Emilia made a notation. "Where were you going?"

"Just a friend's house. We'd been there earlier."

"Can you give me the name of the friend?" Emilia looked up to gauge Harper's willingness.

The teen hesitated. "Chase or Chance . . . I don't remember. He's just a guy we met at a game. He was having a bonfire and Snapped us, so we went."

Emilia held back the lecture she wanted to unleash on the girl but gave her parents a stare she hoped would pass on her concern.

Mrs. Hampton ducked her chin, then poured tea in Harper's cup and her own.

"The guy turned out to be kind of a creep. We didn't want him thinking we left the sweater on purpose or anything, so we went to get it." Harper dumped three spoons of sugar into her cup.

"What happened next?"

"It was fast, you know. The truck went into the other lane, and bam, that was it. Maybe I'm just in shock, but the accident is kind of a blur. And Ivy is a mess. I don't think she'll be much help." She grimaced and lifted the cup to her lips.

Mr. Hampton blew out a huff. "Harper. This kind deputy came all the way over here for your statement. Sit up and give her the information she needs."

Harper rolled her head around from one shoulder to the next, then began again. "Ivy Smith and I were heading west on the Darlington-West Crow Highway at approximately 12:10 a.m. The vehicle in front of us was a large, dark pickup. Its driver veered into the eastbound lane and collided with a car moving east."

With academy-learned skill, Emilia managed not to allow her mouth to drop open. Harper had been trained well by her attorney father.

Mrs. Hampton held up the teapot, as if asking Emilia a question that didn't require words.

She lifted her cup and allowed the woman to fill it with steaming tea, then brought it to her lips. Grass. Just like she expected, the tea tasted like water filtered off a pile of yard clippings. No matter how many times Emilia tried this stuff, it was always a variation on the same thing. "Tell me about what happened a few minutes before the accident."

"I don't recall anything unusual. There was nothing until he cut over into the other lane. Maybe he just fell asleep."

Mr. Hampton cleared his throat.

Harper cocked her head. "But of course, that's conjecture."

"Of course." Emilia snapped her notebook shut. "I may need to contact you again, and if charges are filed in this case, the district attorney may ask you to testify."

"We understand, Deputy Cruz. Thank you for coming all the way out here." Mr. Hampton rose, his hand extended for another shake.

There were few things Emilia cared for less than being dismissed . . . by a lawyer.

7

Addison pointed down Caroline's driveway. "That's it."

The backwoods definition of a taxicab, an old family van with the back seat removed, turned toward the farmhouse. Up ahead, Addison's kids were nearing the house on foot, the neighbor walking along with them, Lilly dressed in her favorite fairy wings and rubber boots.

Bruce, the man she'd been assured was the safest transportation in the county, parked his vehicle in the wide-open area between the front porch and the shed. "That will be twenty bucks." He ran his tongue over what remained of his top row of teeth, making a sucking sound.

Addison dug in her purse, finding a twenty and a five lined up in her billfold, nothing else. She handed the two bills to the driver and stepped outside into air that wasn't scented by mildew and stale cigarettes.

"Mommy!" Lilly leapt into Addison's arms. "How's my daddy doing?" She peeked around her mom at the van windows. "Did you bring him home?"

"Not today. He needs a bit more time for his bumps and bruises to heal." She kissed Lilly on the cheek, then set her down, holding tight to her little hand while the van backed up and turned around.

Hannah and Connor drilled their gazes into Addison. "We want to know what's going on." Hannah tucked a book under her arm.

"And you will." Addison pulled them toward the porch. "First, I want to be clear that everything is okay."

Hannah's eyes rounded, and her face paled. "That's what people say when everything is absolutely *not* okay."

In the thirteen years of Hannah's life, she'd never experienced trauma. That didn't seem to stop her from having eyes always on the lookout for tragedy's attack. Maybe she was more like her mother than Addison had realized.

"Your father was in an accident last night." Addison resisted the urge to shiver as cold washed through her veins.

"We already know that." Hannah's face was hard. Sure, maybe she was old enough to hear about her father's injuries, but she hadn't matured to the point of understanding that her siblings weren't.

Addison bit her lip. Now wasn't the time to reprimand Hannah for her disrespectful tone. She looked to Brianne, hoping for some help from a perfect stranger.

Connor took a half step back, his eyes shiny with tears, then ducked his head.

"He's going to be okay. Really." Addison touched her son's arm. "But it will take some time. His leg is broken, and he's got a pretty good bump on his head. And they fixed a cut inside his tummy."

"Like a stab wound?" Connor's lip curled up in dismay.

"No, more like a tear." Too much television for that boy. She'd told Caleb that their son was too young for movies like *Star Wars* and those about Indiana Jones, but her husband saw them as rites of passage. Or maybe that was an excuse.

"What's all this ruckus?" Caroline rounded the corner of the house, a pointed shovel resembling a tool from the pioneer era clutched in her hands. Dark dirt drew a line down her temple and along her jawline. She grinned. "I didn't expect you so soon. Guess the day got away from me."

Addison took a step closer. "You remember I was at the hospital, right? With your son?"

"Of course. That boy gets himself into more scrapes." She shook her head, but a slight smile deepened the lines on her face.

Lilly pulled loose of Addison's hand and ran around the house.

Addison picked at a fingernail. These were the exact kind of odd behaviors she'd witnessed in Caroline recently, the reason she'd been very clear with Caleb that she didn't ever want her mother-in-law solely responsible for the kids. "What are you up to, Caroline?" She tipped her head toward the shovel.

"Just digging a grave. I found Ann murdered this morning." Caroline leaned her tool against the siding.

The color drained from the faces of Addison's town-raised children.

"I must have forgotten to close up the coop last night. It's all right. Ann was a real bugger. She bloodied up Howard something good last week. Downright emasculated that poor rooster."

Addison gave Connor and Hannah what she hoped was an encouraging smile. "Do you need a hand?" She braced herself for the answer.

"It's done. Said a quick prayer and covered the bird. A waste of good meat." She stomped the dirt from her boots.

Hannah's eyes bulged.

That would do it. The girl would never eat chicken again.

Caroline was as tough as jerky. Addison half expected her to punctuate her sentences with a well-aimed shot of spit. It was like she'd come from a different place and time, an old woman who could hold her own in a fight yet loved her family with great affection. Addison had always admired Caroline's confident demeanor. She was the mother Addison wished she'd had. Maybe that was why she pushed so hard now to find out what was changing this woman. She couldn't let it just be age. She wasn't ready to have Caroline slip away like that.

Lilly bounded back around the corner, pulling a pygmy goat by a leash. "It's time for me to take Clarice for her walk. She needs the exercise. Just look at her belly."

Addison rubbed circles into her temples. Whatever was causing the older woman's quirks looked to be contagious.

Lilly stopped by the front porch, tied the leash around the railing, then shimmied out of her wings and slipped them onto the goat.

Had it really only been thirteen days since they'd moved from Brice? All of Addison's beautiful memories of their previous residence—moving in right after she and Caleb married, bringing her babies home from the hospital, watching them grow—had taken place in the rental house they'd left behind.

Why had they thought this move was a good plan? If they moved into Caroline's house temporarily, they reasoned, they'd save rent. They could be there to support Caroline through the grief of losing her husband. And they'd be right there to oversee building their dream home on the other side of Caleb's childhood farm. The kids could have the summer to explore and adjust to their new home, and Caleb wouldn't have to continue his long commute to his job as a teacher and coach at West Crow High.

But in December, their thoughts had been blurred by the sweet coziness of Christmas. When the world was lit by Christmas lights, it was easy to look past reality and see the beauty of possibility.

Six months later, life had gotten real. Caroline's mind was failing, yet she wouldn't acknowledge the changes. Caleb was seriously injured. Their dream house would have to be put on hold. This wasn't the kind of scene one would find in a snow globe.

"She's really something." Brianne looked toward Lilly.

Addison blinked, her body heavy with exhaustion. "Thank you. I don't know how I can ever repay you for what you've done."

Brianne waved the comment away. "It's nothing. We're neighbors. That's what neighbors are supposed to do."

"And love each other." Lilly's voice carried from the porch. "Love your neighbor."

The child had ears like a bat. Caleb and Addison had learned early on that they had to be extra sneaky when the conversation wasn't suited for six-year-old ears.

"When this is over, I'll have to find some way to make it up to you."

Brianne squeezed her arm. "Really, it was my pleasure."

Maybe West Crow would be okay. So many of Caleb's accomplishments as a teacher and a coach were rooted here. His childhood memories were tied to West Crow. Shouldn't they raise their children where the concept of *family* had a pleasant meaning? Even if Caroline's mind was beginning to go, she had a wealth of knowledge she could pass on to her grandchildren.

They'd be okay.

The scent of jasmine blossoms drifted on the breeze. It wasn't the Hallmark movie Addison had dreamed of in December, but it was their life, and for the time being, her family was safe.

She had this under control—or at least she would once she had a shower and a long nap.

Brianne returned to her house hours later than expected with an orange Tupperware bowl filled with leftovers packed by Caroline. Sometime during the day, the older woman's memory had seemed to come around. She started calling Brianne by her actual name and even mentioned a few memories from Brianne's growing-up years.

Entering her house, Brianne flopped onto the couch.

Chester took her lead and dropped to the floor, his chin curled onto his forelegs.

In the months since leaving public employment, Brianne had become comfortable with, almost addicted to, time alone with no one to perform to. She was no longer suited to the act of carrying conversations and the balance of small talk.

She breathed in deep, cherishing the subtle peach scent that clung to this house long after her mother had left. No matter what was going on in her life, that smell had had a way of conquering her fears and failures—until Amanda, that is. No amount of pleasant childhood memories could sway the heartbreak of losing that girl. And no amount of sweet fragrance in the air could ever dilute the sour taste of Brianne's failure.

For the last few hours, she'd pushed back the emotion boiling in her middle as she helped the Kilbourn family through their own struggles. Suddenly, being alone wasn't the paradise she'd been craving.

Brianne rolled to her side and pulled the envelope from her back pocket. She traced her name in the print of a girl who hadn't yet settled into her own style. And she never would. Amanda had given up the chance to become who she was meant to be. Suicide was such a final decision, an end that could never be undone, rethought, or healed.

It had been Brianne's job to see this coming. She was a mental health professional put in a place of authority. She should have seen the signs. She should have stopped Amanda before it was too late.

She slid the paper out of the envelope, a single lined sheet torn from a spiral notebook, ragged edges still hanging from its side.

Amanda must have stuffed this into the toy bin that day she showed up without an appointment. After five years of seeing Amanda off and on, Brianne had felt like she could read the girl well. But Brianne hadn't given her much time that day. She had a mother coming in who'd just left her abusive boyfriend in hopes of getting her daughter back from state custody. That case had trumped Amanda's seemingly casual visit.

Had there been clues to the tragedy that was to come?

Brianne shuffled through her memories, stretching for something that might not be there, starting to remember snippets of conversation, only to wonder if they were real or just something she needed so much that her brain created them to maintain her sanity.

Emotion pounded behind her eyes, and tears dripped from her jaw as she perched on the edge of the sofa.

The first time Amanda was brought in to see Brianne, it was by her mother, and Amanda had been eight years old, yet immature even for that age. It had been early in Brianne's career. She had only returned to West Crow the month before, accepting a job with the county to provide mental health treatment and counseling.

The memory of the little girl with the sparkle in her eyes and the perfect ringlets in her hair was not hard to retrieve. That image was so clear, like Amanda and her mother had come in only days ago.

Amanda's letter said she'd been wrong to make the allegation. She'd come to Brianne with that suggestion before, but Brianne had pushed it off as regret or guilt that her father was in prison. What if she *had* missed something? What if Amanda was right, and the abuse never happened?

She sprang to her feet, catching a toe on Chester and stumbling forward. During her graduate work, she'd attended a seminar about memory. The speaker claimed memories were the least trustworthy in terms of evidence. Brianne had to go back to facts—her documentation of Amanda's early sessions.

While she'd done the necessary electronic paperwork, Brianne still had an old-fashioned streak. Maybe it was from her experience as a homeschooler through middle school, or maybe it was a connection to her grandmother, a woman who documented everything on paper. Brianne kept detailed handwritten notes on sessions, a personal journal—even her calendar was kept in a large planner. Not that she had much to write down these days.

And Brianne still had all of her records. She was required to keep them for six years, but indefinitely was the recommendation.

She charged into her parents' old room. Tiny king and queen figurines were set up at a miniature table, little teacups in front of them, as though they'd been sharing a meal and conversation until the moment Brianne stepped in.

In the corner, a stack of four blue-and-white boxes stood, all that was left of her short career. Somewhere in one of those boxes was documentation of every meeting she'd had with Amanda and her mother. Somewhere in one of those boxes was the paperwork to pinpoint where Brianne had failed.

A chill moved across her skin. She'd have to do the thing she'd been avoiding. Brianne had to look back into the past if she ever stood a chance of moving forward.

No one could hold a longer sulk session than a middle-school girl. Yet at the same time, Emilia couldn't measure the greatness of the love she had for her daughter. Tally was a large piece of her heart, and though she often found herself frustrated, she would gladly take a bullet for her kid. Emilia reminded herself of that the next morning as she pulled to the curb in front of Tally's school and turned to talk to her daughter.

Tally pressed her lips together so tightly, the skin on her chin puckered. She huffed her good-bye and slammed the car door.

Tension filled Emilia's stomach. She pulled in a deep breath, mentally counting to five as she exhaled. Tally could shake her up faster than any crook in the county. Good luck to the day camp director. She'd need it.

In her rearview mirror, Emilia watched a plume of black exhaust bellow from the back of her car as she hit the accelerator and headed toward the sheriff's office. If she were in uniform and the car belonged to someone else, she would have pulled them over.

Before Roger's injury, she'd loved everything about her job.

It was a dream come true, her childhood goal attained. But now, the day-to-day task of cleaning up other people's messes seemed pointless and unending. Her job had become as rewarding as doing laundry, and the three minutes it took to drive from Tally's school to work were not enough to shrug off Emilia's foul mood.

Inside the office, she was greeted by Meredith, the longest-running member of the West Crow squad. Meredith handled the phones and dealt with the occasional visitor. At nearly fifty, she kept the department organized, all while maintaining vampire-length fingernails and a ratted one-sided ponytail. If Sheriff Commons would allow it, she'd probably come to work in one of those torn, bare-shoulder neon sweatshirts. The 1980s wouldn't die on her watch.

Meredith wiggled her finger in Emilia's direction. "How are you doing today?"

The kindness given through a look of complete sincerity was too much for Emilia to handle. She nearly crumpled when someone took the time to truly ask how she was.

Emilia lifted her chin and forced a smile. "Same old, same old." She picked up her speed and ducked into the back room before Meredith called her out on the lie.

She and Meredith had attended church together, working as a team on special ministry projects. But it had been over a year since Emilia's family walked through those doors. Roger's change of personality was too shocking for people. Many seemed to think this was his true nature all along, that the brain injury gave him permission to express his frustration in public.

They were wrong.

The man Emilia had married was kind and soft-spoken. He cared more about others than himself. His faith was strong, and his devotion to the community, powerful. Roger had been a real-life superhero.

As a firefighter, Roger had been used to risking his life for others, and Emilia understood that devotion. Her career wasn't much different. Yet the day of that final fire had started with an argument. It wasn't anything important, only a disagreement about the negative influence of Tally's best friend. By the time Emilia had arrived at work that day, she knew she'd been the one in the wrong, and she'd planned to tell him over dinner.

But there was no family dinner that night. There hadn't been one that resembled those of their old life in thirteen months now. Rather, they continued to fly farther off course as Roger became more unfamiliar each day.

"There you are." Bill Lineman strutted into the break room, still adjusting his belt. "Looks like you may be on swing for another week or so while Preston is out on baby-daddy leave."

"Why me?" She braced for a fight. Working night shifts on three hours of sporadic sleep—at most—was killing her.

His eyebrows bobbed. "You wanted to be treated like everyone else, remember?" Lineman's chest expanded, his posture rising as he looked down at Emilia.

"Of course I do. No problem." She held her mouth tight, keeping the bitter retort locked behind her lips.

Lineman didn't think a woman was qualified to be on the force, and he didn't hide his opinion unless their sheriff, another woman, was within hearing distance.

"I'm getting sick of traffic duty anyway." She turned her back to him before panic could make its way to her face.

Working into the night was torture with both Roger and Tally to care for. Sometimes Roger woke in the dark hours, raging for no reason. If only Emilia's grandmother were still alive, everything would be different. Emilia would have someone to love her, to give her a pat on the back and a change of the guard.

This kind of life was too much for her to handle alone. She thought she could do it, for better or worse, but maybe sacrificing her daughter's well-being was too high a price to pay.

Undersheriff Barkley walked into the room, dropped a file on the counter, and poured black coffee into a cup. "Hey, Cruz, I got your reports about the collision. Not sure if we have a case, though. I'm heading over to the hospital to question Kilbourn."

Her pulse buzzed. "What do you mean, no case? The guy was drinking and taking prescription meds. A medication that, from what I gathered, he didn't have a scrip for. Not to mention the woman he killed." She crossed her arms against her chest. "Don't you think the victim's sons deserve some justice? Or is this one of those boys' club things? Can't make the award-winning coach take responsibility?"

Barkley turned and leaned back against the countertop. "I'm just messing with you. The doctor said Kilbourn's out of the woods and I can talk with him. Come along with me, will you?" He chuckled. "Sometimes it's too easy to get you fired up. You know I can't resist that."

Emilia scrubbed her hands over her face. She'd walked right into that one.

ADDISON APPROACHED CALEB's hospital room, weaving her way past a tray of covered plates and a couple deep in discussion. The woman's eyes were rimmed in red. That could have been Addison. She'd never again doubt how fortunate and blessed she was, even if life became a tangle of unwelcome details.

Today was taking care of itself, one moment at a time. Brianne had volunteered to stay with the kids, allowing Addison the time to visit Caleb and not have to worry about Caroline's ability to keep them safe. Hannah and Connor were plenty old enough to be left alone, but Lilly was only six, and the farm had sprinkled more than a dose of fairy dust on her imagination.

Brianne's kind offer both gave Addison freedom and tied her down. In the game of friendship, Addison was not likely to be picked first for a team. She hated owing anything to anyone enough to generally avoid the back-and-forth favors common among girlfriends.

She gripped the handle, took a deep breath, and eased the door open, careful not to disturb Caleb.

"Sir, as I said, you are not under arrest. We need to understand what happened the night of the accident so we can put all the pieces together."

The voice hit Addison with the force of a hurricane. That deputy. Of course she'd come while Addison was away. Wasn't there some kind of law about messing with an injured man? If there wasn't, there should be, and maybe Addison would write one herself. She straightened every bone in her body, then walked into the room where her husband *should* be able to recover in peace.

Not a single eye glanced her way.

Addison cleared her throat at an impolite volume. A man in street clothes stood next to the deputy, a badge visible on his belt. "Deputy Cruz," Addison said, "we are not interested in helping you with a bogus investigation. And like I said before, my husband rarely takes a drink and doesn't touch prescription medication."

Caleb's chin shot forward. "What are you talking about? What kind of prescription?"

The plainclothes officer nudged Cruz toward the door. "You'll have to take that up with your physician. We'll get back to you soon."

Addison pushed the door shut, nearly clipping Deputy Cruz

on the heel before she turned back to her husband. "They certainly have a lot of nerve! Where do they get off questioning you when you're barely out of surgery? I should file a formal report with the sheriff's office and the hospital." She marched to the window and crossed her arms. "That woman gets under my skin. I'd like to see what she'd do if she were on the other side of this mess."

Caleb regarded her, a glint in his eye. "Looks like we're actually alone. Come sit with me."

Despite everything, a smile broke the surface. "This does not count as one of our twice-yearly dates. No way you're getting off that easy."

He extended his hand toward her. His face was a series of scrapes and bruises, but those eyes that had drawn her in on their first date still sparkled.

Addison took two steps, then slipped her fingers between his.

Already flowers and get-well balloons decorated every flat surface in Caleb's room. The floral scent almost obscured the lingering smells of cleansers and hospital food. *Almost.*

"Snuggle up. We'll watch the news and have Jell-O." He winked.

"Dinner and a movie, huh?" Addison eased onto the bed, careful not to bump his leg, stomach, or head, knowing the visible wounds covered deeper injuries. She lay her head on the pillow next to his and turned up the volume on the television mounted to the wall.

"The Corban County sheriff's office has released the name of the fatality in last night's head-on collision between Darlington and West Crow." A picture of a middle-aged woman with soft brunette curls popped onto the screen. "Georgianna Lynn Bosch, forty-two, was a hospice nurse and single mother of three sons. A GoFundMe campaign has been started to help care for her boys." Addison's heart hammered.

Her throat constricted. Three boys without a mother. Where would they go?

Caleb's hand trembled in hers. "Was that the same accident? Did I kill someone?" He pulled away, cringing at the pain.

"Don't say that." Addison sat up and trained her eyes on her husband's banged-up face. "This isn't your fault. Accidents happen all the time."

"Then, why did the police come to question me? That doesn't always happen, does it?" His words shot out, anger mixing with hurt.

Addison bit her cheek. "I have no idea, but we'll find out."

"I need to know what happened." He grabbed the hem of her shirt and squeezed the fabric.

Addison took a step back, untangling herself from his hold.

"Which side of the road did the collision happen on?"

"I don't know that, either. Honestly, Caleb, all I know is that you're alive, and I'm very grateful for that." Fear invaded her body, adding a chill to her blood.

He pulled his hand out of her grip, leaving cold air to take its place, then pressed both palms over his eyes.

Shivers ran across Addison's skin. Something horrible was coming. Like a sudden change in the weather, she could feel it, but how could she stop the storm before it crashed down on her family?

She searched for a way to ease into what had to be said, but she couldn't find one. "Caleb, we need to get an attorney and do our talking through him." She paced. "We can't do this on our own. Have you started to remember anything from the accident?"

He shook his head, his face still covered.

"The doctor said you had alcohol and some kind of medication in your blood. Was that a mistake?" She cupped one hand over the other and brought them, thumbs together, to her mouth. What other things didn't she know about her husband? If he couldn't tell her where he'd been that night, then Jeff would have to fill in the missing hours.

Addison's stomach pitched and swayed. Too much was missing. Too many details. Her skin continued to shiver while a fire raged inside her. The confidence she'd learned to feign was crumbling. When would she be able to move on and stand on her own strength?

"I don't need a lawyer. I'll face whatever the consequences are." There was a hardness in his tone, one she'd never heard from him.

Addison dropped into the chair and stared at the clouded eyes that only resembled those of the man she'd married.

He turned his face toward the door.

The heat in her took hold. "That's just great. Be the martyr. But you have three children at home. Don't forget about them. You have to remember what happened, and you have to figure out how we're going to move on from this, because I can't be a single mom."

"Georgianna didn't get to put up a fight. What about *her* three kids? Who's going to take care of them?" He clawed at the blanket draped across his lap. "I can't live like this. It would have been better for me to have died there too."

"How dare you say that? Are you going to look Lilly in the eye and tell her you'd rather not be alive to see her grow up? Are you going to tell Connor being his dad isn't enough for you? What about Hannah? Can you imagine what would happen to her if we lost you? She'd disappear inside herself. How can you wish that on your family?"

"I don't." The words were nearly a whisper. "I don't want that, but how can I live with this?"

"I don't know." Her heart hammered, but she kept her face neutral. She couldn't think about the woman who'd died or the children she'd left behind, because giving them even a tiny thought would break Addison's heart. She didn't have the luxury of feelings right now when she had to keep her family together. "I have to get back to your mom's house. Brianne is watching the kids again. I may need to bring our children with me next time I come see you. And your mother wants to come as well." She stood, leaning close. "You're going to have to hold it together for their sakes. Do you understand?"

Caleb's head nodded. "Maybe you should wait another day before coming again." His face twisted in an agony that seemed unrelated to his physical pain. "They don't need to see me like this."

Cold washed over her face. She was being dismissed by the only person who'd never done that to her. Was he trying to hide something?

EMILIA WAITED OUTSIDE the sheriff's office door, shifting her weight from one foot to the other. This was the time and the place to make her request, but another letdown was sure to follow.

The door swung open. "Emilia, come on in." Sheriff Commons, a woman only a few years older than Emilia and in far better shape, scooted around her desk and took a seat on her high-backed desk chair. Behind her, the taupe wall was lined with pictures, diplomas, and awards. Sheriff Commons could work in any county, but she chose to stay here, where her roots were. It was an act Emilia could respect. "What did you want to talk about?"

Sweat tickled Emilia's head where her ponytail had been bound too tight. "Ma'am, I feel I've been a solid team player on the force. I work the night shifts when asked. I always stay late, and my paperwork is thorough."

"That's true." The sheriff nodded and leaned back.

"I'd like to take point on the Kilbourn case. I was the first on the scene, and I think I understand it better than anyone. I've passed the detective test, and I've been waiting patiently for an opportunity like this. I'm not asking for a raise, just a chance."

"Emilia, don't sell yourself short by negotiating before you know the answer." She pulled open her top drawer. "I'm aware that you're interested in moving up. You've been on my radar for some time. But I have one concern."

The air seeped from Emilia's lungs. "Yes, ma'am."

"Will you be able to handle this case from a purely unemotional perspective?"

"Of course."

"Don't answer so easily. You've been through a lot this last year. Trials like the one your family has faced can put a bitter edge on how we see ourselves and others. And this case is sensitive. Potential charges could come down on a man who's a community hero. Prosecuting the basketball coach and favorite high-school teacher will not make you a popular person. And that's *if* you can convince the district attorney to go forward with charges."

"I'm aware. But it's my opinion that a person's standing in the community should not determine culpability. Georgianna Bosch is dead. Her boys are without a mother. It's not fair to them if we let this go because everyone likes Caleb Kilbourn."

The sheriff's mouth hinted at a smile. "All right. It's yours. Report to me regularly. I want to know what you have before you go to the DA."

Inside, Emilia itched to jump up and throw a fist in the air. This was her chance to prove herself. Finally, a break, and if she did well on this case, then she could request a raise based on merit. Investigations also meant no more patrolling during the night shift. And for once, Emilia would see the offender pay for his crimes, rather than hear later about the technicalities that let criminals back on the streets. Yes, Caleb Kilbourn would pay . . . unlike the mom who, thirteen months ago, had fallen asleep drunk and lit her house on fire with her own cigarette. She'd been rescued and so had her child. Both at the expense of Emilia's husband and daughter.

Brianne's camera hung from the strap around her neck. With spring moving into summer, the last couple of months had given her so much to photograph. Flowers were the best subjects she'd found for photo fusion. Caroline's yard should have kept her clicking, but thoughts of Amanda dulled the colors.

How many times would she tell herself that Amanda had been wrong? Children didn't lie about molestation. How would she have even known how to make up something like that?

A squeal brought Brianne back to the present. Lilly had the sprinkler turned all the way up. She and Chester were running through the spray of water reflecting the sun, a rainbow sparkling in the mist.

Brianne pointed her old camera's one hundred–millimeter macro lens toward the action. She experimented, moving from side to side in a way that changed how the sun filtered through a tall pine tree. The result of the rim lighting was a slight flare over Lilly's profile and the glint of the rainbow ending in the mist. Brianne snapped a few more pictures, knowing she'd never capture the fullness of the moment.

Lilly caught sight of the camera and twirled and danced

in the sparkling water, a smile stretching across her face as Chester bounded circles around his new best friend, his thick fur now flat and dripping.

Brianne stepped into the shade to examine the images she'd just shot. She scrolled through, deleting five or six that didn't justify the time it would take to polish them.

She could hear a page flip from where Hannah lay in the hammock, hung between two black walnut trees, but Hannah didn't look up or even acknowledge Brianne, who stood less than ten feet from her.

Slowly lifting the camera, Brianne took a few pictures of the beautiful teen, so lost in the story on the pages before her that she had no idea she was the perfect model.

If Brianne could bring out that lovely blush in Hannah's cheeks, the hint of a smile she probably didn't realize she had, and the depth of her ocean blue eyes, maybe she could get Hannah to see herself the way Brianne saw her, without the insecurities that inflated imperfections.

Hannah turned the last page, then laid the still-open book on her chest as she gazed up through the leaves.

When was the last time Brianne had been that content? Probably a year ago. She'd been seeing a nice guy, attending a weekly Bible study, and cherishing her job. Then Amanda died. Jaxon was suddenly not the man of her dreams. He'd probably never been that man, but she'd kept dating him in hopes of a deeper relationship.

She left her position a week after the funeral, and the Bible study about the same time. It was too hard to explain to the group of well-meaning women why she'd made what might look like a rash decision. For a single woman to walk away from a paycheck and try to support herself with meager art sales didn't make sense to anyone, even Brianne. Especially when the electric bill arrived on the fifth of each month.

Brianne found a lawn chair near the house, at a safe distance from the water and Chester, and set her camera down on it. She walked over to the hammock and eased herself onto the cool grass, her back against a tree, and faced Hannah. "Was it a good book?"

Hannah nodded. "A modern-day retelling of a fairy tale." The magic of the story still shone on her face.

"I'm impressed by how much you read."

She shrugged. "My mom says I need to get out in the real world and make friends."

"Well, that's good too." Brianne picked at the worn hem of her jeans.

"I don't see what the rush is. I'll have to deal with other kids when I start school. Why not enjoy the freedom I have now?" Hannah closed the book, keeping her palm flat on the cover.

"Interesting that you use the word *freedom*. Does it feel like a chore to be with other girls your age?" A bit of the counselor was sneaking in.

Hannah shrugged. "It's not like they're bad. Well, not all of them. I just like to read my books and maybe do some art stuff. And . . ."

Brianne bit the inside of her bottom lip, forcing herself to wait out Hannah's hesitation.

"I guess I'm afraid." She cocked her head to the side, as if trying on the concept for the first time.

"That's normal." Brianne put her hand on Hannah's ankle. "But it's a dangerous thing to make decisions out of fear. Fear can stop us from seeing the wonderful adventures and people who are waiting for us to show up."

Hannah's eyebrows narrowed. "I've never thought of it as fear. I guess I just thought I didn't want to, but I didn't know why." Her head bobbed. "I'll think about that."

Brianne gave Hannah's leg a pat. Her own advice was drilling a hole in her walls. Was fear behind the decision to leave her job, and was it fear that kept her isolated from other people? It was certainly fear that kept her from opening Amanda's case file.

ADDISON'S PLAN OF attack was mapped out in various colored inks in her planner. She'd taken each of their current hurdles and formed detailed responses, from meals to medications to maintaining normality for the children. With bullet points, goals sheets, and menu planning, she'd manage every moment until they found themselves back in balance.

"Are you sure you can make a meatloaf?" Caroline opened the oven again to inspect Addison's blob of meat mixed with vegetables chopped so small the kids couldn't pick them out.

"Yes. My meatloaf is quite good." She held back a yawn. "Give it a try. If you don't like it, you can make the next one." Addison filled the mixing bowl with hot water and soap.

"I don't think I'll be here for the grub." Caroline quirked her lips. "Too bad. I was really hoping to give your attempt a try."

Addison brushed loose hair out of her face with wet fingers. She'd made meatloaf at least a hundred times before, and no one had ever gotten sick or complained.

"I think I'll head over to the hospital and visit my boy. He could probably use a comforting face about now." She crossed her arms and breathed out a sigh.

In the sixteen years Addison had known Caroline, she never would have described the woman as hypercritical or harsh. Not until the last couple of months. At first, Addison had assumed the change in personality had to do with the loss of her husband. Charles had fought cancer's hard and long battle. Along with the potential savings in rent, his death last fall had pressed Caleb and Addison to the decision to move here early.

Addison cut into a red pepper, scooped out the seeds, and

set the emptied shell on a wooden cutting board. "If you'll wait until after dinner, I'll see if Brianne can come over, and I'll take you to see Caleb."

"Nothin' doin'. I'm a grown woman, and I can drive myself to see my boy. Brianne's done far more than her share around here." Caroline dug around in the back of the junk drawer. "I don't understand why Hannah can't take care of the younger ones. My mother had me caring for babies by the time I was six. Hannah's, what, eleven?"

"She's thirteen."

"Okay. That makes my point."

It's not that Hannah hadn't asked the same question. And Caleb too. But Addison couldn't do it.

Hannah possessed a maturity beyond her years and could handle the job. She was far more capable than Addison had been at that age, and still Addison had managed to take care of her little sisters while her mother swung between partying and being bedridden with depression. Addison's children would have a childhood, though, not be forced into living as miniature adults, with all the responsibility but none of the control.

She'd made promises like this to herself long before she knew what a healthy family even looked like. Addison was determined to be the turning point. Her children's growing-up years would not have even the slightest thing in common with her own. "I know she can handle it, but it's not time yet. I'm not ready."

Why can't you come to the hospital when I'm already going? Voicing the question in her mind gave Addison enough relief to form a slight smile. "I know I've said this before, but I'd love to take you with me. I'm going back first thing tomorrow."

"A mother knows when she's needed, and my boy sounds like he needs me. That won't wait until morning."

The knife chopped through the pepper, smacking hard

onto the wood below. Caroline was an adult. She didn't need permission to drive her own truck. However, the woman had the attention span of a puppy. That didn't seem like a good thing to combine with traffic. "Actually, I really need your help with something."

"What's that?"

"Caleb is having trouble putting together some of the details from the night of the accident." Addison shifted the clear salad bowl to the side and leaned against the counter. "Do you remember Jeff? He went to school with Caleb. I think they graduated in the same class."

Caroline wrinkled her lips into a twist, then released them with a sigh. "A name has come to me. I'm pretty sure that was Jeffrey Dahmer."

Addison's hand covered her mouth a moment too late.

"What's so funny? That's the name."

"Jeffrey Dahmer? You're telling me that Caleb went to school with Jeffrey Dahmer?"

Caroline's chin rose. "They called him Jeff."

"Jeff Dahmer was a serial killer." Addison looked more closely at her mother-in-law's confused expression. "I'm sure I would remember if Caleb's friend shared the same name."

"Suit yourself. I'm heading out."

"Caroline, wait—I didn't mean to be rude." *Oh, Lord, please stop her.*

The older woman waved off the comment.

"Let me take you to the hospital in the morning." Addison sniffed the air. The meatloaf smelled about as done as it could stand. She pulled out a drawer and grabbed two oven mitts.

The screen door slammed shut before Addison came up with a way to stop Caroline from going. She pulled the meatloaf out and set it on one of the back burners. Through the window above the sink, she could see Caroline throw her purse into the pickup's cab, then hoist herself in. The engine roared to life.

Addison opened the back door and found Lilly on the bottom step. "Stay right here while Grammy backs up the truck."

Her daughter looked up from the stuffed animals she'd put in line along the narrow sidewalk. "All right."

Lilly almost hadn't existed. After Connor was born, Caleb and Addison had decided two was a perfect number. They had a boy and a girl. What more could they ask for? The little oops sitting before her was one of the greatest joys in Addison's life. How close they'd come to missing out.

As they'd packed for the move, Caleb teased that maybe one more would make their family even better. Addison had caught herself contemplating this until the accident took away that tiny possibility. With Caleb's injuries, they'd be lucky to still get the new house built by spring. At least the doctor expected a full recovery. That should be enough to give her peace, especially when Mrs. Bosch's children had lost so much more. A summer to recover and delays in the building schedule—Addison could live with that.

A resounding crunch and thump shook her from her musing. She placed a hand on Lilly's head as she stepped around her daughter and toward the front of the house.

Dust and exhaust clouded the air. Caroline's back tire on the passenger side spun about a foot off the ground. The rear axle was wedged on a small boulder that had been along the edge of the driveway for as long as Addison had been part of the family.

By all appearances, God had come through on this one.

10

Emilia pulled up to the wrecking yard and unbuckled her seat belt as she rolled into the space reserved for police vehicles. She'd been on duty for two hours already that Tuesday, but by the time Sheriff Commons finished the briefing and Emilia had completed a list of tasks assigned to her, it was well into the morning.

On television, suspicious vehicles were kept in secure locations. Corban County was not like typical entertainment programing. The truck and the car from the collision had both been towed to the wrecking yard, where they were behind a padlocked fence, but a good lawyer could probably cast plenty of doubt as to the security of evidence found after transport to the impound lot.

Regardless, Emilia intended to search that truck from license plate to license plate. It wasn't an easy task to bring someone to justice for killing a woman with his truck, especially when that someone was a winning coach.

Earlier that morning, a fellow deputy had suggested she "let this one go and call it the accident it was." Not a chance. Maybe some people were willing to look the other way, but she wasn't one of them.

Every day she lived with the consequences of drug and alcohol abuse. It wasn't fair the criminals weren't the ones who paid the price. Their children and victims dished out for that bill.

Emilia went through the entrance to the office. The smell of dirty oil permeated every ounce of space, as though the very molecules were attaching to her exposed skin the moment she stepped inside.

Behind the counter, a man with black-ringed fingernails and a smudge of oil across his forehead stood near a computer that must have been one of the first small enough for home use. He tossed a look her way, then rolled his eyes at the guy he was helping.

Not even her uniform scratched the surface of chauvinism in this place.

"Be with you in a minute."

Emilia straightened her shoulders, forcing her face into a neutral position. Letting these guys see her squirm was an invitation to harassment. And if she allowed herself to get into it with them, it could end with her hauling this guy to the station. *That* she'd never hear the end of. No, he wasn't worth the time. Caleb Kilbourn, however . . . That man was going to see exactly what she was capable of.

"Listen, I'm here to see the Ford that came in early last Wednesday morning. Point me that direction, and I'll be out of your way."

"It's not that easy. You'll need an escort. Let me finish up with Bobby here, and I'll take you out myself." He again raised an eyebrow to his customer.

"I know my way around." Emilia adjusted her belt and took long strides through the room and out the back door that led to the yard. Two teens looked up from the dash of an old Chevy Nova, nodded, then went back to work. They didn't have an escort.

Around a corner, Emilia approached the location of the rigs not yet evaluated by insurance or owners. The Ford sat in the corner, framed on two sides by metal fencing woven with white strips of plastic. Usually, she'd need a key to get in, but the top of the truck had been peeled back to retrieve Mr. Kilbourn.

Emilia settled her belt back onto her hip bones, then climbed into the bed and looked down on what remained of the leather bench seat. Such a shame. This had been a nice truck. Of course, the death of his victim was a much bigger shame. A loss that couldn't be repaid with any amount of money or time served.

The puddle of vomit had spread and dried, leaving a flaky brown mess that curdled Emilia's stomach. After threading latex gloves over her hands, she felt in the grooves of the seat, looking for any little thing that would help lock the cell door on Caleb for many years.

A McDonald's toy was wedged behind the seat—a plastic princess. Emilia swallowed hard. More victims. She couldn't think of Kilbourn's family. It wasn't her job to consider them. Caleb was the one who'd let them down. Still, the thought had her blinking away tears, the consequence of having a child of her own.

With her belly laid over the seat, Emilia reached for the glove compartment and popped it open. Car manuals, insurance information, and maintenance records. Nothing unusual. As she was about to push herself up, her vision landed on something in the edge of the floor mat. Emilia strained, finally getting her fingers on the white oval pill. Swiping her hand under the seat, she retrieved a snack-sized baggie, another pill inside.

People with legitimate reasons to use narcotic pain relievers kept them in their original bottles, not plastic bags.

Coach Kilbourn had a little secret. But not for long.

Addison stepped out of the hospital accounting office with a better understanding of their meager insurance policy than she'd ever wanted. Every extra cent they'd saved over the last fifteen years had gone into their dream house account. By living with Caroline, they'd had just enough to complete the project and move in sometime before Christmas. But this accident was going to eat away a chunk. And if charges were ever filed, or the Bosch family sued, they could lose it all.

Today, there was a good chance the doctor would release Caleb. Her husband could be coming home—another step into the insecure future. Relief and trepidation flew at her with equal force.

Without thought, she stepped into the coffee line at the kiosk near the cafeteria. The man in front of her paid his bill and sidestepped to the right.

"What can I get you?" The barista pulled a Sharpie from the cup on the counter.

Addison's gaze drifted over the options. She was about to speak when she noted the prices. Her chest ached under her collarbone. "I'm sorry. I've changed my mind."

The girl behind the counter quirked an eyebrow, giving Addison a condemning look.

Addison held tight to her purse and stepped away, not making eye contact with anyone else in line. Maybe it was the stress of Caleb's injuries, the new living situation, and the finances, but it seemed as though everywhere she went, people were watching her, waiting for her to mess up.

No. She wouldn't let herself go down that path. This was a trial, one she would gain control over. She had three children to raise—three children she'd do anything to keep from facing the same neurotic worries she'd had to live with.

Addison took the stairs instead of the elevator. She forced herself to jog up the five flights, gasping for breath, her muscles burning, until the physical exhaustion stopped her mind.

She hit the door to Caleb's floor with both hands and stood in the hallway, puffing for oxygen.

"Mrs. Kilbourn? Are you okay?" Caleb's doctor evaluated Addison as carefully as if she were the patient.

She forced a smile. "I'm good. Just needed to get my blood pumping."

"I've been in with your husband. Do you have a moment?"

Addison straightened. "Absolutely."

"I'm very happy with how he's healing. The fact that Caleb was in such great physical health before the accident has made a difference in his recovery."

Maybe so, but Addison was looking at Caleb's healing from another angle. "He just doesn't seem at all like himself."

The doctor crossed her arms. "That's to be expected. Concussions can have personality-altering consequences." She reached out and placed a hand on Addison's shoulder. "It's unlikely this will be permanent. We'll keep an eye on his behaviors, and if he continues to seem depressed or angry, we can look at medication and therapy as well."

Addison's stomach soured. Her husband was an optimistic man, the one who always assumed circumstances would have a happy ending. She was the doubter, the worrier. They'd weathered the years together with this understanding.

The doctor let out a breath. "Listen, I know you're both under a great deal of stress. Watch him closely. If you see signs of severe depression, perhaps questioning if he should be alive, let me know."

Heat rushed through Addison's face as cold flowed through her arms. Caleb's words after discovering the accident had resulted in a fatality—had he been serious?

Shaken, Addison nodded.

"I'm going to sign the release papers. One of the floor nurses will be in soon to go over the discharge instructions. You can call and talk to a nurse anytime, day or night. And please"—her eyebrows lifted—"let your friends and family help out. You can't do this all on your own."

Addison swallowed. "Thank you."

The doctor didn't know her. Addison *could* do this on her own. And she would. She wasn't a stranger to hard times. It just took organization and a strong will. Fortunately, she had both.

This was her mission, her new purpose. The house of her dreams wasn't likely to be built that summer, and her husband would need care, support, and a good push to get back to the man he really was. But she'd pulled herself up before, and she was very capable of pulling her husband up too.

Addison shook out her arms, straightened her spine, and stepped into Caleb's room.

EMILIA CLIMBED OUT of the sheriff's department SUV, an evidence bag containing the pills from the crime scene in her hand. The meds found in the truck wouldn't hold up as evidence in court, but they could lead her to information that would. There was only one pharmacy in town, and if gossip hadn't traveled yet, she should be able to get a fair interview from James Schneider.

Inside, the discount drugstore smelled like a brothel, with every sample perfume getting plenty of use. She walked through the row of cosmetics and hair dyes. The pharmacy sat at the back of the store. Schneider's workstation was built up a couple feet, as if his degree gave him the right to look down on the people who came for his services.

Emilia went to the counter. A girl who didn't seem much older than Tally popped up from behind. "Can I help you?"

"Actually, I'm going to need to talk with your pharmacist, if that's okay."

"He'll be glad to give you a consult once your prescription is filled. I can take care of that for you." She held out her hand.

As if Emilia would ever want this kid knowing her personal business. This was one of the many reasons they used a mail-order service for all but emergencies. "Actually, I'm not here for myself. I'm here for work."

The girl gave Emilia's uniform a quick up and down look, her eyes going wide. "Yes, ma'am." She disappeared through the swinging door behind the register. A moment later, she reappeared with James Schneider, king of the pharmacy, walking behind her.

Emilia shook her head. She'd known this man since before either of them could spell their own names. Small towns were like that—people trying to gain respect in a crowd who could easily remember every bump and bruise they'd gotten along the way. "Jimmy. I need a minute. Could we please talk in private?"

That should give the girl plenty to text her friends. It would probably be all over town before Emilia even left the building. Let it. Sometimes rumors could work to the authorities' benefit.

"Emilia, my goodness." James flung open the door to the elevated station and stepped through. It swung back, cracking into the wall. "Do you have to make such a scene wherever you go?"

"When you stop acting like you're the keeper of the town gold, I'll stop putting you in your place."

He smiled. "I can't for the life of me figure out why, but I like you. What's the big deal you have to drag me out here for?"

She was pretty sure the only thing James Schneider liked about her was the fact that she was the only girl who wasn't interested in him in high school. His cockiness hadn't come with his diploma. James Schneider had been full of himself since kindergarten.

Emilia set the plastic bag on the counter between them. "You know what this is?"

"May I?" He nodded at the bag.

"Yes. Just leave it sealed."

James picked up the plastic and dropped his glasses into place. He turned the pill over, bobbed his head, and returned it to the counter. "That's oxy. No doubt about it. A pretty good dose too. That would make a woman your size pretty loopy if she wasn't used to taking it."

"You know anyone around here who takes this dosage?" She was fishing in the deep end here, but James had a way of needing to show off. It wouldn't be her fault if he slipped up.

He crossed his arms. "No way. That violates HIPAA privacy laws, and you know it. Come back with a warrant."

Emilia held back a laugh. The guy probably thought he was being tough now. "What if a person took this with alcohol? What would happen then?"

He shook his head. "Not recommended. Of course, it depends on the amount, but mixing those two would knock out even a big guy. Dizzy, disoriented, then out cold. What's this about?"

"You know I can't tell you that." Now he could have a dose of his own medicine.

"Come on. I did you a favor. I have a date tonight. Don't force me to make up part of this story."

Emilia pulled the bag back. "Here's an idea: You keep this between you and me, and I won't arrest you for obstructing justice."

James's smile faded.

"Have a good day." She turned and left, walking back through the gauntlet of perfumes. She was bluffing, but James Schneider knew nothing about the law aside from the mandates of HIPAA.

Outside, the air was warm, with not even a whisper of a

breeze. Her belt grew heavier in the heat. She wiped sweat from her brow and climbed back into the SUV. Caleb Kilbourn was as good as caught and sentenced. Emilia had the blood work from the hospital, but she'd need the toxicology report from the Oregon State Police crime lab before she made the arrest. One more check mark on her way to taking the coach to court.

11

Seven days of back-and-forth between the hospital and the farm came to an end as Addison and Caleb pulled into the driveway. Another quarter of a mile, and the kids would be part of the new reality that had spread like antibiotic-resistant bacteria since the accident.

A large sign hung along the front porch. Addison squinted to make out the words. "Look." She nudged Caleb awake, then pointed at the childish lettering framed by beautiful drawings of flowers and birds. "The kids made you a welcome-home sign."

Caleb smiled. "I'm so glad to be here. I don't even care if they make a ton of noise and make my head feel like it will explode. I've missed them."

"Oh, honey, that's easy to say when you've been away for a few days." Addison shot him a grin. "You may have forgotten Lilly's ability to talk nonstop."

"Anything is better than that stinky hospital with nurses constantly waking me up. I'm telling you, it was worse than Connor's colicky days."

"Yeah. That's because most of the time I was the one staying up with him."

Caleb squeezed her thigh. "And we still went on to have another. That's a miracle right there."

"A surprise miracle. I don't think we would have done it otherwise." She parked the van, then let her hand settle over his. "We're blessed. I may have been taking that for granted before the accident, but not anymore." Even as she said the words, fears wove into her thoughts. They were always there, like a virus that lay dormant, waiting for the first sign of weakness. And she was greatly weakened now.

Addison brushed her palms together. They were safe, even if it didn't seem that way. There was no way Caleb, the man she'd committed her life to, was going to face a legal battle. She just needed to find a way to dismiss those worries that tried to creep into her thoughts.

"I know what you mean." His smile had an edge of sadness in it, something that had never been there before except in the days right after his father's death. Even all these months later, Addison could still smell Charles Kilbourn's hair gel when she walked into the downstairs bathroom. It was a comfort, like a hug from the first man who'd acted like a father to her.

The kids came around the side of the house, Lilly tugging Brianne by the hand.

"Looks like the welcome crew is here." Addison lifted her chin.

"No time for kissing. Is that what you're saying?"

She took a long look at her battered husband, his face a palette of bruises. "You've got to be kidding me." She shook her head. "Your people are waiting." Addison stepped out of the van and crossed to the other side. She slid the door open and retrieved the crutches, then handed them to Caleb. "Be careful, now. The gravel could be tricky."

"I'm a big boy, Mom." He stuck out his tongue at Addison.

"Daddy, that is not okay." Lilly came to his side. "I'm going to help you into the house. My poor daddy!"

Hannah rolled her eyes and opened her mouth to speak, but Addison got in a quick don't-you-dare glare, stopping her teen before she could spill any nastiness.

"Whoa. Dad, you look so much worse than Mom said." Connor's top lip curled. "Nice shiner."

"Thanks, son. All the pain is worth it if you're impressed." Caleb tried to raise his eyebrows but winced instead. "I think I'm ready for a break. Where's Grammy?"

Brianne's face twisted. "She's in the kitchen, working on some cookies. If you're all good, I'm going to head back to my house now."

"Yes. Thank you so much for the help." Addison gave her a wave.

"Not so fast." Caroline appeared on the porch, a plate of cookies in her hand. "You take these home with you. And I'll expect you to come by this Sunday for more after church this week."

An expression of pain passed over Brianne's features, but she took the plate and gave a slight nod before walking down the lane.

Caroline drew in a harsh breath. "My word, Caleb. What on earth happened to you?" She stepped off the porch, giving her son a thorough look. "There's not a spot on your body that's not banged up. You get yourself inside and lie down. I'll get the Unguentine and Epsom salts." She shook her head as she retreated into the house. "My word."

Addison leaned into Caleb's side. "I get the feeling she doesn't remember our conversation even an hour later. Once you're well enough to take care of yourself, I think we need to get her in to see the doctor. Something isn't right."

"She's just goofing with you. Trust me, Mom's fine. She's a tough old bird."

"I don't think so. Not this time."

Caleb shuffled forward on the crutches, a child on either

side to help him as Addison retrieved his hospital bag. Maybe now wasn't the time, but when Caleb recovered, she'd have to make him see the reality of his mother's foundering mental health, no matter how much he didn't want to accept it.

Inside, a six-year-old Florence Nightingale made sure Caleb was comfortable on the couch. Despite the temperature outside hovering in the eighties, she'd covered her patient with two blankets and tucked them tightly along his sides.

"I'm going to get you a cookie. It's not a normal one. This kind is medicine. It will make you all better." She stood, shook her head as if she were looking at a sick baby, then trotted off to the kitchen.

"You may miss the hospital nurses by the end of the day." Addison set Caleb's bag near the bottom of the stairs.

"Any word from the police?" His face grew serious.

Addison stalled, listening for the sounds of anyone who could be near enough to hear. She came close to Caleb and knelt on the floor beside the couch. "I don't think we should discuss this when the kids are within earshot. There's no reason to make them worry."

"Their father's being locked up all of a sudden would be more of a shock, don't you think?" New lines etched his forehead above the track of stitches. "What did my mom say?"

Addison inspected the carpet by her knees.

"Addy, are you keeping something from me?"

She wondered the same thing about Caleb. Not remembering the accident made perfect sense to her, but the entire night? Could Caleb, the first man she'd ever dared to give her trust to, be covering up something? His coming from Darlington that night left too many unanswered questions. She tried to push back the insecurities that built horrible scenarios in her mind, but they hammered on.

Pressing against the floor, Addison got to her feet. "I told her there were some concerns about the accident. She said something about Mr. Miller's boat and assured me it would all work out."

Caleb paled.

"What?"

"I dented up Mr. Miller's truck and his boat on its trailer when I was driving Dad's tractor. I was in eighth grade. I thought it was the end of the world, a mistake I'd never make it through. The fire in the old man's eyes . . . I felt so small at that moment. A lot like now."

"The moral of that story is that it turned out fine." Caroline stood in the doorway with Lilly at her side. Caroline's denim overalls were covered by a checkered apron. Lilly wore a matching one, but hers licked the ground at her feet. "Don't stew over what you can't change. Miller got his boat all patched up, and you learned how to paint a barn. And I don't recall you slamming that tractor into anything else." She shrugged. "It made you a fine driver."

"It made me paranoid, and clearly my driving is in question now too."

Caroline looked down at Lilly. "Take your daddy a cookie. That always fixes him up."

"Here you go, my daddy. Eat it all up." She handed him a cookie on a paper napkin, then brushed her palm against Caleb's stubbled face.

Caleb mimicked her, touching his hand to Lilly's cheek. "Thank you, sweetie." He took a big bite, and his eyes went wide. He coughed, his eyes growing wet.

"Did it go down the wrong tube?" Lilly tried to lift one of his arms over his head.

Caleb spit the bite of cookie into the napkin. "Mom, there's something unusual about these. They seem a touch on the salty side. Did you try a new recipe?"

"Same one I've used for the last thirty years." Caroline stepped into the kitchen, returning with a cookie in one hand

and a disgusted look on her face. "I can't even give these to the chickens. The goats, maybe. They're regular salt licks." She took the napkin full of cookie away from Caleb.

Addison ran her fingers through her hair. She had a husband who needed to recover, three children to care for, and a mother-in-law to watch. That was a whole lot to be taken on by a woman who felt every bit of her inadequacy coming to the surface.

BRIANNE SAT ON the living room floor, her legs stretched out and Amanda's file laid out in front of her. She'd avoided the paperwork the same way her brother had avoided homework. Today, she'd run dry of excuses.

She'd reread every single document, expecting answers, only to discover her carefully created notes told her nothing about what had really happened in their early meetings. An entry from the first visit said *they* made the claim that Amanda's father had touched her in an inappropriate way. Why had Brianne used the plural pronoun?

And Brianne had waited to make the report for three weeks after that initial meeting.

In her memory, she'd called it in after the first appointment, but the documentation stated otherwise. Why couldn't she remember it the way it was stated right there in permanent ink?

The inside flap of the folder had a series of pockets filled with DVDs. Brianne knew what they were. She'd recorded and burned them herself. Since she'd been new at the job, she'd kept video recordings that her supervisor could watch and critique if necessary. Most were deleted within a month, but Amanda's case was extra-sensitive, and Brianne had worried she could mess up. In the end, maybe she had.

At one point, not long after Amanda's memorial service,

Brianne had thought about destroying them. Until she'd opened this file, she thought she actually had. Her memory was like a deep and murky pool—even the simplest things were lost in the haze, and everything she thought she remembered was now in question.

What she did recall well was the reason behind the impulse to crush the shiny disks. Brianne never wanted to watch the recordings and see the sweet face, the tender eyes, of the girl she'd failed. There was no bringing Amanda back. The flat image on the screen would only give a sketch of the young teen who'd felt so lost that she took her own life.

Brianne stacked the papers in the precise order she always kept client records. While she wasn't the greatest at home organization, her clinical skills were tighter than the Army's.

Something was missing.

She thumbed through the stack again but couldn't place what it might be.

Brianne climbed up from the floor and walked back into her parents' old room, retrieving another file from the box where she'd gotten Amanda's. There in the front, along with the original intake forms, was the signed consent for recording the sessions.

She'd been new to working independently when Amanda's mother brought her in, so Brianne was sure she'd given the form for signing. As paranoid as Brianne had been the first three months of working for the county, she would have checked and double-checked the intake forms before Amanda and her mother, Leanne, even arrived at her office.

Brianne began to feel clammy with a nervous energy. Why did this even matter? She'd left the job behind, handing her clients over to a woman contracted through the state. The new therapist would have to be good enough for the community, because it was an awful lot better than having Brianne miss something that could eventually lead to the death of a child.

Whatever she missed in Amanda's case was still in the land of the hidden. Would it give her permission to walk away from all this if Brianne at least knew the exact moment in time when she had failed so fully that the consequences would never stop chasing her?

Brianne slid a DVD from the folder pocket. Her handwriting across one side indicated this was the recording of Amanda's first through third sessions. She moved the disc side to side. Light bounced off the rainbowed surface. The answers she needed were somehow trapped in this small, metallic circle.

The hum of her phone ringing carried from the kitchen. Brianne hopped up, laying the disc on the end table. Chester rose with her, bumping into her legs as she tried to reach the cell before voice mail took over. "Hello." She hadn't bothered to look at the screen.

"Hey." The voice was familiar yet distant.

"Hi." It was probably a solicitor, but if it gave her another excuse to wait on watching that recording, she'd answer every question.

"It's Seth . . . Seth Wallace. From the sheriff's department."

Brianne felt the smile burst onto her face. "And my brother's high-school best friend. Yes, Seth, I know who you are."

"Yeah. I guess that was weird."

"Is anything wrong?"

"No." He cleared his throat. "I just felt kind of bad about waking you that night last week and then dragging you into all that trouble with the coach. I wanted to say that I'm sorry. But I'm also really glad I got to see you. Not that I wanted to see you in the middle of the night like that. You looked great, though."

Brianne's mouth fell open. "Thanks."

"This is so embarrassing. Please don't tell your brother about this call. I'll never hear the end of it." His groan wove through the line, making him even more endearing than before.

"It's a deal. But you promise not to tell him I was ready to clobber you with his baseball bat." A little shared information seemed like a fair trade for his humble apology.

"Okay, then. Maybe I'll see you again . . . soon."

"I'd like that." She pinched her lips together. Transported back to high school, she dared to dream for just a moment that he'd see her as more than the kid sister of a friend.

"Bye."

The phone disconnected, and Brianne plugged it back into the charger. She cringed. All these years later, and she still had a crush on Seth Wallace.

12

Emilia jammed her boot-covered toes into the side of the truck Roger once treasured. Pain surged up her shin. Once he'd spent sunny days at home washing and polishing the metallic blue finish. She ran a finger along the side of the bed, leaving a line in the thick layer of dust.

If she could find one fundamental thing that remained the same, then she'd have something to look at, something to draw an ounce of comfort from. But even though they hadn't moved from their two-bedroom rental, there was a darkness that had moved in with the injuries. It covered all of them with a weight that made Emilia think of the beam that had held her husband down until help arrived.

Roger was angry with the world, and rightly so. He'd been a provider, a constant and loyal man, a credit to his profession. And in a blink, it was all gone, leaving him in constant agony.

Before the accident, Tally had been excited about everything. She had a stream of friends in and out of the house, always giggling, even when there didn't seem to be anything funny. That stopped when Roger took a bat to the wall because the noise was giving him a headache. At least his temper had cooled a bit with a change in medication. Still, Roger was always on the edge of an outburst, exactly what Emilia would expect from any man who bore that kind of pain.

She turned away from the truck and sat on the ground. The coolness of the earth worked its way through the fabric of her jeans as the familiar scent of motor oil wrapped around her. It wasn't the life she'd thought she was going to have, but when had she ever had that?

Roger was getting better at a pace that could be beat by a slug on a tightrope, but there were improvements. He didn't break things like he used to. His temper seemed more under control. She figured it was from the medicine, but the doctor had hope Roger was slowly regaining himself. However, the doctor didn't live in the house she now stared at. He didn't know how dangerous hope could be.

If someone else looked at her, would they notice a difference? Had the accident tattooed her the way it had Roger and Tally? Probably, but Emilia was too close to see it. There wasn't anything she wanted to look at too closely anyway. Her goal today—and every day since the accident—was to have enough energy to keep going and not lose her mind in the process.

A chain rattled, then thumping vibrated against her hand pressed flat to the ground. Before Emilia could turn, a golden retriever was on her lap, slapping her face with a warm and wet tongue.

"Gustav." Her neighbor Holly Carmen came into view. "Gustav, no." She grabbed his collar and pulled him back while continuing to scold the dog. "I'm so sorry," she said, her gaze now on Emilia. "The latch on the leash broke just as he saw you."

Emilia laced her fingers into the fur on Gustav's neck. It had been months since she'd seen him or Holly. She shook her head. "It's no problem." A tear blurred her vision before she blinked it away.

Holly shifted from one foot to the other. "How've you been?" She stared down at the dog.

"Good." The lie came easily. Emilia told it almost every day.

"Us too." She started to turn away but stopped. "I miss you. I'm not sure what happened, but I wish we could go back."

The muscles in Emilia's throat tightened. She used the truck's tire to help herself up. "Nothing happened. I'm just busy . . . work and stuff."

"I look for you at service every week. If you decide to come today, I'll have a seat for you in my row." Her bottom lip curled between her teeth. Not a sign of lying, but Emilia remained skeptical.

"Sure. It's just hard for Roger, you know. He gets tired."

A line creased the skin above Holly's nose, and Emilia could see her lie hadn't passed by Holly unnoticed.

"Well, if you change your mind."

Emilia nodded and turned her face toward the truck. "I need to get moving. I told Roger I'd wash the truck for him. You know, switching chores." She raised and lowered her shoulders, as if adding this action would tie a tight string around the ball of garbage she was tossing at a woman who used to be a friend.

"I could help."

The offer splashed cold guilt down Emilia's spine. "Thank you, but it's really nothing. I enjoy getting outside." She tucked her chin and pretended to look for something in the bed of the truck. Kindness had a way of unlocking her vulnerability. She'd tried having a good cry not long after Roger's release from the hospital. It had only served to scare Tally and infuriate Roger.

She kept scouring the area in search of nothing until she heard the jingle of Gustav's tags as the dog and Holly finally walked away. Now she'd have to actually wash the truck to give evidence to her false story.

Pulling the hose from the garage, Emilia gave up her fantasy of a nap. After screwing the hose onto the bib, she sprayed down the first side of the pickup, then moved to the other.

Through the mist of water, she noticed something in the window of her house. The water drifted away as she stared into the eyes of her husband. Then she went for the bucket and soap.

A DEEP GRIMACE etched lines into Caleb's face.

"Can I please get you the medication?" Addison sat in a chair near the couch, where Caleb writhed in agony. "It's important for the healing process. You don't need to be in this kind of pain."

"No." He bit his lower lip. "Those boys left without a mother can't take a pill to ease their grief. Why should I be able to rest easy?" Sweat dripped from his temple.

Tears fought against Addison's resolve. She couldn't think about those motherless boys, the depth of pain they must be experiencing. She had her own family to worry about. Life was simply not fair, and this accident was another example of how tragedy was always waiting to take you down when you thought you had it all figured out.

So she'd fight it, like every other time. Addison wouldn't let the fates take down her or her family. She was a force the devil wouldn't see coming. This was what a good mother did. She grew fierce when conditions warranted. Never a helpless victim. Always a warrior.

"He just needs a Tylenol and a cookie. That's always worked for my boy." Caroline came into the room carrying not one chocolate-chip cookie but an entire plate, and at eight thirty in the morning, no less. She set the treats on the coffee table beside Caleb, picked one up, and put it into his hand.

From some hidden reserve, Caleb forced a smile for his mom.

"It's time to get moving toward church." Caroline patted her silver-streaked hair, which she'd wrestled into a bun.

"Church?" Addison looked from Caroline to Caleb. "I don't think we'll be making it this morning."

"That's nonsense. Church is exactly what this family needs. Addison, you may stay home and mind Caleb, but I'll be taking the children with me. It's Celebration Sunday. There's a potluck and outdoor games." Caroline swung a hand to her hip. "And I made my fried chicken."

Addison clenched her teeth, holding back the acidic words that sprang to the tip of her tongue.

"Sounds good to me, Mom." Caleb rolled to his side and closed his eyes, the cookie still in his hand.

"May I see you in the kitchen?" Addison rose and walked that way, not waiting to see if Caroline would follow. She found all three of her children sitting at the table, faces somber, Lilly's cheeks wet with tears. Each was dressed in clean clothes suitable for church.

Another chunk broke off Addison's heart. They'd heard Caleb's words. She didn't need to ask or wonder. The grief on their faces showed their innocent child-hearts had peered into the real world this week. They needed to get away as much as Addison needed them with her, but she couldn't let Caroline drive them. She wouldn't lose them the way Georgianna Bosch's children had lost her.

"Hustle upstairs and brush your chompers. We're heading out in ten." Caroline dropped her purse on the counter, her keys hanging off the strap. She followed the kids up the stairs.

As soon as the footsteps were overhead, Addison unclipped the keys and tucked them into the breadbox. She then took her own keys and Caleb's set from the key hooks and stuffed them under a stack of towels in the laundry basket. That would buy her a few minutes to figure out what to do. It was too soon to leave Caleb on his own. He needed her, needed her reassurance, if not her care and nursing.

Maybe she could use a little church. God might be the only one who could intervene in the chaos, but would He?

It only took a moment after Caroline returned for her to notice the missing keys. "I don't get it. I always have them attached to my purse." She picked it up, looked underneath, then searched the massive interior.

Addison's children entered the room in a silence they'd never been able to manage before. They went to the door with barely a wave to their father.

Guilt twisted Addison's gut. Who was she supposed to be caring for, her children or her husband? They were all walking around as if one wrong move would bring down the house.

Caroline threw open drawer after drawer, tossing kitchen items onto the counter. "This is impossible. Did one of you kids mess with my keys?"

Hannah put her arm across Lilly's shoulders and pulled her close. For months now, Addison had been struggling with the growing sibling tension between her girls. She'd even prayed that it would resolve quickly. This was not the way she'd desired to see that prayer answered.

"Miss Brianne next door said she goes to Grandma's church." Lilly's eyes were wide, hopeful.

The mental list Addison kept of whom she owed grew another foot under Brianne's name. "I'll call and see if you all can get a ride." Addison turned to dial Brianne's number.

13

Brianne's phone buzzed, waking her from deep sleep. Her eyes fought for more, refusing to focus without a fight. All around her, files and papers were spread across the living room floor. Her neck had the beginnings of a decent kink from the way she'd twisted to fit on the couch.

Chester yawned, lifting his head from the stack of papers he'd been using as a pillow.

The phone stopped, but within a minute, its vibrations hummed through the room again.

Blinking the blur of sleep away, Brianne forced herself to search for the device, finding it wedged between the cushions. She swiped the screen and answered without checking to see who was calling. "Hello?"

"Thank goodness. I thought maybe you'd already left."

"Left?" She ran her hand across her face. Sun filtered through the front window, casting shadows of dancing leaves onto the hardwood floor littered with records of a throwaway career.

"To church. I'm sorry. I assumed you were going."

"Church. Yes. I'm going." She pulled the cell from her face and checked the time. She'd need to leave in twenty minutes to be there on time. Maybe missing this week wasn't a bad plan.

"Good. Would you be able to take Caroline and the kids with you?" A door squeaked in the background. "I don't want Caroline to drive the kids." Addison's voice had dropped to a near whisper. "I've hidden all of our keys."

"Okay." Brianne tapped her palm against her cheek. "Yes. I'll be there in a few minutes."

"Thank you." There was a weighted pause before Addison spoke again. "I really appreciate you, Brianne. I don't know how I would have managed any of this without you."

The emotion behind Addison's words was enough to make Brianne fully awake. "I'm really glad to help." Months of living alone with only her dog and her artwork as companions had left Brianne balancing on the ledge over depression. She should have seen it sneaking up; but there was a reason that therapists saw other therapists. The brain could easily play tricks on itself.

She pressed the end button and padded barefoot to the bathroom. The sight in the mirror above the sink reflected an image that would require a shower to correct, but there wasn't enough time to manage that. It wasn't like she was going to find the man of her dreams at church. Most of the other members were married or fifty years older than Brianne, and there was basically no one in town who didn't remember the time she threw up while marching in the Fall Festival parade.

As a quick alternative, she ran cold water over her hands, then slid them across her flyaway hair. She worked a brush through the mess and tied it up in a ponytail. Another cold splash of water, a little moisturizer and mascara, and the result was passable. She hurried off to find clothes and shoes.

Halfway down the Kilbourns' driveway, she spotted Caroline, all three kids alongside her, waving a large purse in the air as if Brianne were a taxi she was hailing. Brianne shivered in the already warm car. The last week had rapidly tugged her from the cocoon of her own making. She was a butterfly with wet wings struggling to unfold in the hot sun of expectations and the needs of others.

As she pulled up to the porch, Brianne evaluated the size of the group in relation to the size of her late-model Corolla. It would be a tight fit.

Lilly dragged a booster seat behind her, the pink-covered hunk of plastic thunking against the steps, then scratching through the gravel to the back of the car.

"Can I help you with that?" Brianne pulled open the door.

"No, ma'am." She stretched her tiny body. "I'm a big girl."

Brianne held back a laugh but allowed the smile. Could there be anything more precious than this child? At the thought, memories of Amanda swooped in. While not untouched by the world, she had been this precious too when Brianne first met her. Brianne's smile grew heavy. What role had she played in allowing further darkness into Amanda's life?

"Let's get this buggy on the road." Caroline climbed into the front passenger seat.

"Wait." Addison rushed down the steps and took hold of Brianne's arm, her fingers cold against warm skin. "Thank you. I really don't know what I'd do without you. I feel so horrible dragging you into this." She pressed her lips into a line. "I'll make this up to you. I promise."

Brianne covered Addison's hand with her own. "You have no idea how much I needed to help." Until she shared these words, Brianne hadn't known how true they were. Being needed had Brianne feeling more alive than she had in months. To live sometimes meant having to feel pain. The loss of Amanda hurt maybe even more now than in the beginning. But finally she was able to experience and understand the grief. Before, it had been a black cloud pressing down on her. Now there was meaning to the regret, the questions, the sadness.

The three-mile drive to church spurred flashbacks to childhood car trips with her brother. Connor could not keep his hands to himself, using them instead to irritate Hannah and Lilly at every opportunity. Lilly countered his attack with a blow of her own. Her weapon of choice was an earsplitting rendition of "Let It Go." Caroline joined right in with her warbling falsetto.

But Hannah was the one who had Brianne concerned. Adjusting the rearview mirror, Brianne glanced at the teen. She sat slumped against the door, her gaze distant as her forehead rested on the window.

There was something going on inside that girl.

They were a few minutes late, but the parking lot still had plenty of spaces. Caroline was out and slamming her door before Brianne turned the key in the ignition.

"Let's get a move on," Caroline said. Her voice carried like a foghorn. There was an edge to it that Brianne had never noticed before, maybe from the stress of Caleb's injuries. And then there was her other son. Wyatt was some kind of musician, and from what Brianne knew, he hadn't been home since Mr. Kilbourn's funeral. If her brother's stories held any truth, Wyatt had been a wild one from the beginning.

Lilly slipped her hand into Brianne's. "I wish my mom and dad were here."

Brianne smiled down at her. "Your dad will be back on his feet in a few weeks. Then you can go to church as a family."

"And you."

"Me?"

"You can come with us and be part of our family." The little girl reached down to pull a pebble from her sandal. "You don't have a family."

"My family lives in Arizona."

"That doesn't count." Lilly straightened and tugged Brianne forward.

It did count, didn't it? Lilly's words gave Brianne's life a lonely hue she wasn't comfortable with. Is that how they all saw her? Did people think of her as alone and pathetic? Brianne's stomach cramped. How had she let herself slip so far into isolation? She, of all people, should have known better.

The swirl of color near the entry chilled her. In the time since leaving her job, she'd missed more and more services, something she'd rarely done before Amanda's death. Church used to give her peace. It reminded her that her work and her life were for a purpose much higher than any reward she would see in this life. But she'd walked away from the tasks she'd once felt had been designed for her by God himself. And honestly, how could she face God now, when she'd failed so terribly?

Jeff Delmar, one of the church elders, held the door open, shaking hands with each person who entered the foyer. He held out a hand to Caroline. "Good morning. I hear lots of talk about that boy of yours being back home. Tell him to make time for an old friend, will you?"

"Of course, Jeffrey. How's your mother?"

His face grew grim. "It's hard, but she's a trooper. If you could spare the time, she'd love a visit. The pain is keeping her from leaving the house. Pastor comes by each week and gives her the Cliffs Notes version of his sermon. It's the highlight of her week."

"I'll get over there as soon as possible. Irma was always such a good friend, always the first to bring a meal to an ailing family. It's a shame to see her taken down like this."

They exchanged the solemn look of people giving honor to one who wouldn't live much longer, the intersection between grief and relief understood only by survivors.

Jeff welcomed Brianne, then squatted down to shake hands with Lilly. "Who do we have here?"

The child clung to Brianne's right leg, twisting around behind her, hands so tight on Brianne's bare skin that the movement felt as if it would tear flesh.

Brianne reached down to remove the clenched fingers from her leg and swung Lilly into her arms. She'd never seen the kid have a shy moment, much less this kind of reaction. Her first thought flew to abuse, though it was ridiculous. That was what her years as a therapist had done for her. As far as she knew, Jeff and Lilly had never met before, and Jeff had never, not once, given Brianne the feeling that he was anything but kind and honest. Clearly, she'd allowed her education and work to jade her. Maybe she'd jumped too quickly in Amanda's case too.

Caroline took charge. "Lilly. This is Mr. Delmar. He went to the same high school as your daddy."

Jeff rose and pressed fists into his side. "No way. This is Caleb's kiddo?" He looked around.

"It is. This is Lilly." Caroline pointed toward the pair who'd entered with her. "And those two are Connor and Hannah."

"Nice to meet you, little lady. Your dad's an old school friend of mine." He held out his hand to Lilly, but she shied away. "Where's the old guy?"

Brianne's stomach squirmed as Caroline moved away to speak to a friend. "He had an accident. I'm surprised you haven't heard."

"Oh man." Jeff stepped back, his eyes asking the question he didn't want to voice.

"He's okay and recovering at home. I seriously can't believe you didn't know."

"I just got back from camping late last night. Haven't even heard the church lady gossip yet. Tell him I'll come by." He rubbed his hand over his cheek as if the smooth skin was suddenly unfamiliar.

Brianne put a hand to her chest. "Did Caroline say you went to high school with Caleb?"

"Yep. Caleb and I were good buddies back then. We connected recently, even planned to get together once he was all moved in."

"But you were out of town when Caleb was in the accident?"

He narrowed his eyes. "Like I said, I've been camping. Been gone a couple weeks. We were scouting for next hunting season."

Mrs. Kilbourn and the older kids were moving toward the sanctuary.

"You should come by and see Caleb. He'd appreciate that."

Brianne nodded, her mind preoccupied with questions. "I'd better get going. Nice to see you, Jeff."

"You too." He twisted the gold band around his finger.

Brianne made her way past the hum of conversations and into the sanctuary. The volume dropped, and she could hear her thoughts. For the first time in way too long, those thoughts weren't focused on herself. She was thinking of the Kilbourns and wishing there was something bigger she could do to take some of the pressure off their family. And of course, she thought of Amanda, not as the client she'd failed, but as the young woman who also deserved to have her questions answered.

Life seemed be a long series of mysteries. It was up to each individual to uncover the truth. That's what Brianne planned to do about Amanda. Too late to save a life, but truth needed to see the light of day regardless.

Brianne to Addison, 11:02 a.m.
Did you tell me that it was Jeff Delmar that Caleb was meeting that night?

Addison to Brianne, 11:05 a.m.
I checked with Caleb. He said that's the Jeff he was friends with in high school.

Brianne to Addison, 11:09 a.m.
Jeff Delmar says he was out of town when Caleb had his accident. Any chance you're remembering the wrong name?

Addison to Brianne, 11:10 a.m.
I don't think so.

Brianne to Addison, 11:12 a.m.
Well, I'm sure there's a good explanation.

Emilia pulled the last of the frozen meals she'd stored in the freezer out of the oven. The lasagna's edges bubbled brown while the middle remained suspiciously still and pale. They could eat around the sides for now. She'd warm up the rest tomorrow.

Cooking had never been one of Emilia's great talents. She had been outdoorsy from the beginning, more interested in playing ball than in learning domestic skills. Her grandmother might have been right: She did need the basics, but it was too late now.

Setting the pan on the counter, Emilia placed three plates nearby with forks beside them. They used to eat dinner together at the table, even when it was fast-food takeout wrapped in paper.

Once Roger was healthy enough to move on his own again, however, he'd started taking his dinner by the television or in their room. Tally took that as an invitation to eat behind her own door. Emilia remained at the table for two months, hoping the others would get the hint and come back to their family tradition, but finally, she'd given up, taking bites as she cleaned the kitchen.

She tipped her head out the opening between the kitchen

and living room. "Dinner." After five minutes, when no one came, she thought about giving up another principle and texting them, but she might as well put a television in Tally's room if she was going that far.

Emilia tapped the doorframe as she opened it. "Tally, time for dinner."

"What is it?" She set down her jewelry-making supplies but didn't get up from the chair at her desk.

"That's not really relevant, is it? Dinner is whatever dinner is."

Tally's shoulders slumped. "Fine." She stood and huffed past her mother.

Knocking on the door of the room Emilia still technically shared with Roger, she listened but didn't hear a response. She pushed the door open and stared into the dark, waiting for her eyes to adjust. Roger had a hard time with sudden changes in lighting. She walked to the bed, tapping the comforter, but didn't find him. "Roger," she said in a hushed tone. "Are you in here?" Her heart began to thud. She ran her hands up and down the bed, then switched on the bedside lamp. The room was empty.

Emilia joined Tally in the kitchen. Her daughter had scooped a plate of food and was already stuffing a forkful in her mouth.

"Have you seen Papa?"

"He's not my dad." Her eyes were dark and cold. Tally had been the one to start calling him Papa shortly after Roger and Emilia were married. Now she took back the title as if it were a loaned sweater.

Emilia set her fists into her sides and stared at the girl who was once full of compassion and empathy. Would her daughter become a bitter and angry woman? Emilia debated replaying another version of the same lecture, but Tally obviously wasn't in a frame of mind to hear a thing Emilia had to say these days. "You'll clean up the kitchen tonight. No arguments. When I get home after my shift, I expect this room to be spotless." She walked away before Tally's likely sassiness could lure her into a fight.

Outside, she checked the backyard, but no Roger. He hadn't left the house without her at his side since he'd gone to work the day of the last fire.

She jogged down the block, perspiration dampening her collar and waist. He wasn't cleared to drive. He hadn't even bothered to ask if that was a possibility.

Emilia scooped her thick dark hair into a ponytail and snapped the band on her wrist around it to secure it off her neck. She'd have to call in if she couldn't find him in the next few minutes. And that would cause an avalanche of issues at the station.

At their driveway, she looked back at Roger's unused truck. There he was, behind the wheel, looking so much like the man she used to know.

Emilia took a deep breath. With a little more than a week left before the dreaded Fourth of July, sulfur and smoke already hung in the air. She approached the passenger side, curved her fingers around the handle, and pulled open the door. After a moment of hesitation, she slipped into the seat next to her husband, her heart still pounding, sweat sticking her T-shirt to her back. They both sat staring out the window, no words passing between them for a good five minutes.

"This isn't working," Roger finally said, his hands on the steering wheel.

Emilia locked her gaze on his rugged knuckles, his hands that could accomplish any task he set his mind to, hands that had been so gentle to her, offering only love and kindness. They were still Roger's hands even if Roger was hard to find anywhere else.

"I'm not happy. None of us are." His words fell from his mouth as though lined with lead.

She heard the proper responses in her head, but her mouth refused to say them again. "You're right. None of us is happy. What can we do about it?"

"That's what I've been trying to figure out. It helps being in here. I feel like I can think with all the noise cut off." He chuckled, a sound like Christmas and the Fourth of July combined. She'd missed his laugh more than almost anything they'd lost. "Maybe I should move into the truck."

She slid to the middle seat, like she'd done in their dating days, and placed one of her hands over his. "I've missed you." And she really meant it. She'd been missing Roger for thirteen months, and she wasn't ready to give up on him yet.

EMILIA SLAMMED THE department desk phone back onto its cradle.

"Whoa. What's got you all revved up so early on a Monday?" Lineman stood at the edge of the row of desks, his arms tight around a cardboard box.

She shook her head. "It's nothing."

"No one slams the phone like that for no reason. Give it up, Cruz."

He was about the last person in the department she wanted to share her frustrations with, but he was also the only one who had asked. "The crime lab says I won't get the official tox screen for a month. What exactly are they doing up there? It's been almost two weeks."

He shifted the weight of the box to one hip. "Did you tell them it's a potential homicide investigation? That should speed them up."

"That's how I got the one-month time frame. Originally, it was a *few* months, whatever that means."

"You'll get what you need. Just put the rest of the pieces in place, and present the evidence to the DA the day the results come in. Then you'll have him. You know what the lab is going to say. You smelled the alcohol. You saw the pills. It's a no-brainer. The guy is going down." He blew out a breath. "And the jerk is taking our basketball season along with him. I have a running bet with a buddy in Darlington. I hate losing." He hiked up the box and walked away.

If charges were brought before the end of summer, Mr. Kilbourn wouldn't be stepping foot in another classroom. Tally was only a year from high school. Emilia would do what it took to be sure a teacher with deadly habits wasn't influencing her daughter.

She pulled out a blank paper. What did she know for sure? Evidence that could put Kilbourn away even without the lab workup. There was the alcohol on his breath. She'd been certain of that. And the pills on the floor of the truck. The pharmacist had confirmed they were oxycodone. James was also confident that any mixture of oxy and alcohol would greatly impair a driver, and that the driver would be well aware of that impairment.

She tapped the pencil on the paper.

Emilia had two witnesses. They were young, but neither had a record, and they were both honor students and athletes. A jury would hang on the words of Ivy and Harper. That was if Emilia could get Ivy to talk without bursting into tears—something she hadn't been able to manage in the two interviews with the girl. Even if Ivy froze on the stand, the jury would see the trauma the accident had inflicted on these teens, as well as the victim's family.

The impact had taken place in Georgianna Bosch's lane, not Kilbourn's. He had been the one to cross over. Why would a man on a straight stretch of road swerve into an oncoming car? There was no reason that didn't make Caleb Kilbourn guilty of vehicular homicide, at the very least. And at best, manslaughter.

Emilia ran through the scene again, the blood, the smells . . . Every bit of evidence pointed to Kilbourn's guilt.

She had to make something right come out of that horrible nightmare. And she would. Caleb Kilbourn would not have the chance to cut another life short.

15

Brianne clicked on the fan in the living room window. The end of June, and it was already in the nineties. She couldn't imagine what August would bring. She plopped down on the sofa and dragged her cold soda can across her forehead. Too hot to do anything outside, and too hot to work with her soft colored pencils.

She fired up her new MacBook, an expense she couldn't afford but an investment she needed to enhance the details in her photographs. She opened her search engine and typed, *How long can a person put off something painful?*

What came up was a list of results ranging from how to know you have appendicitis to another question asking if pain can be felt once the brain is dead. So much for her latest stall tactic. People who said therapists were the most unstable segment of the population were on to something. Not only did most of them come into the profession because of some disturbance in their own lives, but they spent hours each day listening to patients retell horrors until peace and beauty began to feel like the stuff of fairy tales.

Brianne snapped the laptop closed. She was no longer a therapist, meaning the problems of others were no longer her concern. Maybe she should Google how long it took to accept your identity in a new profession. Her fingers brushed the computer. Avoidance was becoming as consuming as any addiction.

Opening the laptop again, Brianne clicked on the bookmark for Facebook and searched for Seth. He popped up at the top of the list—forty-two friends in common. Another click and she was staring at his profile picture as if it were Michelangelo's *Creation of Adam*. Not a bad way to procrastinate.

She set the Mac on the end table and stood, nearly falling over Chester, asleep at her feet.

Files were stacked but not straightened on the table next to her art supplies. On the very top, like a flag staking claim to Brianne's hesitation, was the DVD.

She'd tried to watch it, even taking it out of the case before realizing she didn't own a DVD player. That new laptop, the one that cost her a good chunk of her savings, was nearly naked of any ports and didn't have a DVD drive.

She was a Netflix and books kind of girl. The last time she'd rented a DVD, she'd still been in her apartment in town, and it had been an action flick, the choice of an old boyfriend.

Men were another thing she didn't need in her new life.

There were two choices. She could grab up the stack right now, toss it back in the box, and cover it with other boxes until she forgot about the letter and the doubt that kept waking her at night. Or she could man up and go into the basement, where her parents had left all kinds of things that could come in handy if the right moment arrived. There'd surely be a DVD player on one of the many Dad-built shelves that lined the cement walls.

"Come on, Chester." She scratched the fur behind his ear. "If I have to go into the dungeon, you're going too."

He lifted his head and opened his mouth, filling the quiet house with a yawn that would wake any spiders waiting for them down the rickety stairs.

Brianne tugged on his collar. "I'm not kidding. You first." She pulled him toward the basement door. The locks, all three of them added after Brianne moved back in, squeaked as she unlatched them one at a time.

Two furry feet planted on the top step while Chester anchored his backside on the kitchen linoleum.

Brianne grasped the handrail with one hand while holding tight to Chester's collar with the other. She shimmied around her guard dog, careful to plant each foot squarely on the wood stairs.

A swift tug of the collar, and it slid from Chester's neck. Before she could grab for him, the dog was gone. "Thanks a lot." Brianne tossed the collar onto the floor and edged down a couple more steps.

The air brushed across her arms, easily ten degrees cooler than the temperature upstairs. Under her feet, each plank moved at individual angles as her weight eased forward. A scent somewhere between dusty and musty pressed in from all sides.

Her palm slid over the end of the rail as her foot settled on the concrete floor. Brianne reached out, waving her hand in front of her until her finger found the light string. She grasped it and gave a firm tug. Light from a solitary swinging bulb opened up the space.

The silence swam around her. Growing up, when anything had to be done in the basement, her father had taken care of it. He'd once yelled at her when she'd taken it upon herself to open the basement door and start down the stairs. She could still hear the harsh words from her usually gentle father, warning her that she'd done something dangerous. He'd probably meant the rickety steps, but in her little mind, the basement had become the place where all childhood fears lived.

Now, at just over thirty, the fears still stuck in her mind, despite the independence she'd built up during her adult life.

Brianne forced deliberate steps toward the wall shelves, decorated by the still-moving shadows. The tops of the windows were darkened by dirt and nearly hidden by overgrown brush. Her father would never have allowed that to happen, but there was a security in hiding this entrance into her home.

Her parents had left behind some things they felt were necessary for the proper running of a home but not worth hauling to Arizona. A thick layer of dust blanketed the boxes stacked on the shelves. Even the labels had been obscured by the settled dirt. Brianne wiped a hand over the front of a large cardboard box, and the air filled with particles that wove up her nose and made her eyes itch.

Kitchen supplies.

Three boxes later, she found the one marked electronics.

Brianne tugged the heavy package forward and set it on the ground, sending more dust into the air and something running for the corner. She pulled her hands tight to her chest, doing her best to wrap herself in a protective layer as her heart raced.

Should she really be surprised to find a mouse living down here? Whether or not she should, she was, and the rodent had nearly given her a heart attack, leaving her to take her final breath in this dungeon.

She forced herself to count slowly as she breathed in and out, calming her nerves and muscles.

Brianne peeled back the tape on the box with two fingers, her gaze darting around the room in search of other tiny intruders. All this hassle so she could watch a DVD that would break her heart wide open again. She'd once felt competent to help others with their most serious problems. She shook her head. What a fool she had been.

She took one more look toward the stairs, then opened the flaps. Inside was the ancient VCR her parents had when they were first married. It was the size of her microwave and not compatible with a DVD. She slapped the box closed and shoved it to the side. Maybe this was God telling her not to relive what she couldn't change.

Above the pounding of her heart, Brianne heard a sound, like a voice in the distance.

She quickly stepped toward the stairs, climbed up five, then turned and went back down to shut off the light. The voice called again. This time she could tell it was Addison calling her name. Another mark against her guard dog.

"I'm coming." She took the stairs as fast as she thought safe and plunged through the door to the kitchen, past the dining room table with the stack still casting guilt her way, and on to the front door. On the other side, she found Addison, as expected, but the tears in her eyes were a surprise.

THERE WAS A point when the weight of daily circumstances piled so high and heavy that even the most organized woman began to bend under the pressure.

Addison stood on the porch in front of Brianne's door, having little memory of the walk that took her from Caroline's farm to the home of a woman she'd only recently met. She wasn't a crier, having learned early on that tears did not change circumstances. But somehow her emotions were pounding past her guard today, showing up in the blur of her vision.

"Addison. Is everything okay?" Brianne stepped to the side, making room for Addison to enter.

The house was simply decorated, sparse for what Addison assumed from an artist. Even as she blinked back another rush of tears, she found herself imagining what the living room would look like with a fresh coat of light sage paint and a sizable wall hanging.

A dog the size of Cujo peered around the corner of the living room before disappearing again. That couldn't be the puppy her children went on and on about. That dog was practically a horse.

"Addison?"

"Sorry. I don't even know why I'm here." She pressed her palms against her stomach, correcting her posture at the same time. "You probably think I'm here to ask another favor." Her gaze went to Brianne's deep blue eyes. "I'm not."

"Would it be so bad if you were?" Brianne's head tipped toward her right shoulder. "We're friends, aren't we?"

Friends? They were more than neighbors. "Yes. I guess that's true. It's been a long time since I had a friend that wasn't the consequence of my children's friendships."

"I get that. My mom was the same way until we were in high school. I feel horrible when I think back on that now. It's like we took everything from her and rarely did we think to say thank you."

Addison glanced to the wall behind Brianne's dining room table at a photo of what must be her parents. "I don't know how I'm ever going to make all this up to you." A heavy feeling pressed against her chest, and she swallowed hard. Debt of any kind was a burden she wasn't strong enough to carry. Debt was another term for vulnerability.

Brianne stepped onto the porch rather than invite Addison farther into the house. "Let's sit out here for a bit." She ran her fingers through her blond hair, pulling out a mess of cobwebs.

"Did I catch you in the middle of cleaning?"

A smile brightened Brianne's smooth features. "No. I was in the basement." She shook with an exaggerated shiver. "I'd like to know more about why you feel you need to make anything up to me."

"You've just done so much. You stayed with Caroline and the kids so many times while I was with Caleb at the hospital, and you even took them to church last Sunday. You've never turned me down when I've asked for you to drop what you're doing and come to my rescue." She scratched at a two-day-old mosquito bite on her upper arm. "I need to make it right."

"Hmm. That's interesting." Brianne settled into a woven metal chair and waved a hand at the matching one across the table. "Have a seat. The thing is, to me, having a neighbor or a friend help out when your hands are too full seems like life at its best. If I had surgery and needed help with a meal or two, would you keep track and want me to repay you for the kindness?"

The thought was ridiculous. "Of course not. I'd hate to think of you feeling that way." Her mouth dropped open. She'd stepped right into that little lesson.

Brianne tapped the tip of her nose with her pointer finger. "Exactly. I feel the same way. Let's wipe this scorecard clean and make a fresh start."

"Okay." Addison took a deep breath. "Let's talk about you for a change."

"Me? There's not much to talk about there."

"Well, you could tell me what you were doing down in the basement."

Brianne ran her hand over her hair again. "I was looking for a DVD player."

"Not much of a television watcher?"

"Purely a Netflix girl." Brianne pulled her foot into her seat, her knee bent near her chest. "I was hoping . . . well, I was going to watch a video recording of a session I had with a client a few years ago."

"A client? I thought you were an artist."

"I am. Now." She shifted in her seat and fidgeted with the edge of the table. "I was a therapist, mainly working with children. I left that job last year to pursue art."

"Wow. That's a big move. Do you miss it?"

"Sometimes, but not enough to go back. It's just too hard." Her gaze drew down to her lap.

"But you loved it?"

She nodded. "I did."

Despair seemed to filter through the air. Brianne had a story, but she was holding it close. If they were friends, did that mean Addison should ask about it, or was it more of a friend thing to let the subject go? "I'm sure you were very good. I see the way you talk with my kids. They're so comfortable with you."

"I love them. See, it's like you're doing me a favor. I spend way too much time on my own." She dropped her foot back to the decking.

"If you're no longer doing therapy, why watch the video?"

Brianne leaned back in her seat. "I think there may be some answers there that I need to have. But it really doesn't matter right now. There wasn't a DVD player in the basement."

"We have one still packed in the shed. And I know exactly where it is." Addison stood. "I'll get it out this afternoon. You can use it as long as you need." It was a small gesture, but finally, she could be on the giving end. She stepped down from the front porch, her flip-flops snapping along the wooden planks. "Thanks for the visit. I think it helped."

Brianne lifted her hand and waved a good-bye, the dog resting across her feet, a stick torn to shreds hanging from his mouth.

As Addison walked away, she drew in a deep breath. How different from only a short while ago, when her lungs seemed to have seized up in response to the stress at Caroline's. She stretched her arms overhead, enjoying the moments of peace before the next crisis.

An unfamiliar vehicle sat parked near the front of the farmhouse. She picked up her speed. It might be borrowing trouble, but Addison did not have a good feeling about this.

She didn't have a great feeling about much of anything since the move. *Blessings. You have blessings. Count them.*

By the time she reached the house, she was nearly jogging, something Addison made a point of never doing. She swiped the sweat from her forehead as she threw the door open and entered the living room.

Two sets of eyes snapped up at her, her husband's and another man's.

The look on Caleb's face only heightened her fears. "Addison. This is an old friend . . . Jeff Delmar."

Jeff rose and extended his hand. "Nice to meet you. Caleb speaks very highly of you."

She wiped her palm along her denim jeans and shook his hand. "Nice to meet you too. When was the last time you and Caleb saw each other?" She couldn't look back to Caleb as the words spilled out.

"I think we exchanged how-do-you-dos after a game last year, but I'm thrilled he's back here full-time. We need to get the families together. I have five boys, ages three to eleven. They're a rowdy crowd, but my wife is a regular diamond."

"That sounds wonderful. Our son would enjoy hanging out with other boys." Addison tugged on the hem of her T-shirt. "I'll let the two of you get back to your chat." She swept her gaze over Caleb, his face expressionless, his jaw set in a firm line.

16

"Are you kidding me?" Emilia slammed down the phone. Still no movement on the tox screen from the state lab. Apparently, harassment wasn't the way to speed up the process, especially with the one guy stuck in the lab on a national holiday. Didn't they understand the importance of these tests? Lives were on the line. Other people could be injured or killed. Imagine the tragedy that could take place in the time consumed by a simple blood test. Yet there was no way, even with the additional evidence, that the DA would issue charges before the official test results came in.

Emilia stood and shoved her desk chair out of the way. The clock on the wall ticked louder than necessary. She needed to be on patrol by now. The Fourth of July lit the fuse on bad decisions. It usually started before noon and continued into the early morning hours of the fifth.

She cringed as she entered the parking area for the sheriff's department vehicles. She was stuck with the oldest in the fleet today, a car that looked like it was straight off an episode of *The Dukes of Hazzard.*

The door squeaked as she opened it and sat on the plastic seat, one side starting to split. Seriously, what kind of budget did this county expect they could get away with and still keep their employees safe?

She drove up the hill that led to the exit and turned right onto Gifford Street. A trip through the city park was her first task. Kids had been hanging out there, vaping. Last week an empty cartridge had landed in a sandbox two feet from a toddler. If his mother hadn't been right there, the little guy could have picked it up and put it in his mouth—leading to a seizure or other medical complications.

A small play area stood at the entry to the park. From there, a paved single-lane road circled the property, past fields, the skate park, and shelters.

Emilia slowed to manage the dips without scraping the bumper, her eyes scanning the surroundings. The play area had been filled with parents and children, but once she moved past it, she saw few people gathered.

It was another hot one. Soon the kids would be taken inside too.

She drove toward the second shelter and spotted a rapidly dissipating vape cloud just as a group of kids ducked behind the dumpster. Emilia thought about staying in the air conditioning and driving on. Her uniform responded to the sun like a fur coat at the equator. But this was her job, and no one else was going to do it.

She pulled up tight to the dumpster and put the car in park, then stepped into the heat. "Come on out. There's no point in running. I'll recognize you and take this to your parents if you do."

Three pale faces emerged from behind the dumpster. Cami Whittle, Sydney Frank, and Tally.

Emilia's heartbeat hammered in her ears, and her neck broke out in a sweat. Tally was supposed to be at home, cleaning the trash heap she called a room. Emilia had scrimped and saved to pay for programs to keep her daughter busy throughout the summer, but the week of the Fourth, not even the boring camps were available. A few days of freedom, and here she was with the two girls Emilia had forbidden her to spend time with.

Next year, Tally was getting a job.

"Where is it?" Emilia rested her hand on the grip of her gun, more out of need to keep herself from strangling her daughter than from any desire to intimidate.

Cami shrugged, her eyebrows doing a jig. "What? We weren't doing anything. And you can't prove we were."

Emilia's hand gripped tighter. Her gaze shifted to her daughter. "Tally?"

Tally's chin dipped to her chest. At least she had the decency to look ashamed. But she didn't offer an answer.

"Get in the car, all three of you."

Tally lumbered toward the passenger side. She reached for the handle.

"I don't think so." Emilia opened the back door and motioned with her head.

Tally's eyes went round, as if she were going to cry. It took about a second for the tears to be replaced by fire. "No way."

"Now. All three of you." Emilia pointed. "Don't make me read you your rights and take you to the station."

The girls shuffled in without another word.

Emilia slammed the door, then walked back to the place where she'd first spotted the three delinquents. A vape pen lay on the cement floor of the wooden structure. Emilia picked it up and brought it to her nose. Nicotine flavored with strawberry.

Heat washed over her as she looked at the back of her daughter's head in the rear window of a squad car. They were probably working out their stories right now, but it wouldn't matter. Tally had been given a chance. And another. Cami and Sydney were the same girls Roger had been worried about the night of his accident. Thanks to those two, she'd live the rest of her life with guilt over the harsh words she and Roger had parted with that night, hours before he nearly died.

A shot of love drove through Emilia for the man she married and the guy she still caught glimpses of. How could Tally think, even for a moment, that they should walk away? Roger had been the greatest father Tally could ask for, and he could be again. They just had to have patience.

Or faith.

She wanted to go home right now and give him a hug. When had she last done that?

Emilia opened the door and sat in the driver's seat.

Cami pounded a fist on the divider. "Where are you taking us?"

Emilia took a deep breath and buckled her seat belt.

"You have to tell us. We're not your prisoners."

Actually, they kind of were. And she didn't have to tell them anything. Emilia pulled forward and drove out of the park, leaving the parents and toddlers in the playground to enjoy the years they had no idea were the easy ones.

Four blocks down the road, Emilia pulled up to a sprawling yellow ranch-style house with plaster elves peeking out of the well-manicured bushes. She opened the back door. "Come on, Sydney. Let's go have a visit with your grandma."

"You can't leave us here in the car. It's not safe." Cami's shoulders swayed with her words.

Tally had the sense to stay quiet.

"Vaping isn't safe. Being locked in the back of a police car—with the air conditioning on—is only bad for your reputation, which you clearly don't care about anyway." Emilia slammed the door and walked toward the house with Sydney.

Emilia rapped on the frame above a *No Solicitation* sign.

A gray-haired woman in a floral muumuu opened the door.

"Sydney?" She pressed her fingers into her soft chin. "What in the world?"

"Sydney, why don't you go on to your room." Emilia gave her a slight nudge, and the girl immediately obeyed.

"Mrs. Walters, I found Sydney at the park with Tally and Cami. They were vaping." Emilia pulled the pen out of her pocket, showing it as evidence.

Sydney's grandmother shook her head. "Not my Syd. She doesn't do that."

Emilia couldn't help but wonder if Mrs. Walters had given her daughter that same kind of unearned trust. Sydney's mother was in and out of jail for drug possession. She'd recently been busted for selling. Sydney's grandparents had taken custody of their granddaughter, keeping her out of the foster-care system.

In the background, a man coughed, adjusted his oxygen mask, then turned up the volume on his game show.

"Actually, she was, and I'm positive this wasn't the first time. Pardon me for saying so, but you need to get some help with that girl before she's completely out of control."

"Oh, Emilia, you know girls. They go through a bit of a wild streak. Even you had your time." Her head tilted as it bobbed up and down.

"That may be true, but please, keep an eye on her. I can't have Sydney hanging out with Tally. I hope you understand."

A sad shadow crossed the older woman's sunken eyes. She released a breath. "Thank you for bringing her home."

"No problem." Emilia turned back to the car, where Cami pressed an unpleasant hand gesture against the window.

Emilia climbed in, already dreading the next stop. "Cami, is your mom at work?"

"How would I know what that woman is doing? She took off on us a month ago. Good riddance." From the rearview mirror, Emilia watched Cami hug herself with crossed arms. It was a bigger deal than the girl cared to admit.

"And your sister?"

"No way. She bolted after that friend of hers offed herself."

Emilia tamed the expression of shock before it hit her face. How could Cami be so callous? She'd gone from concerning to downright dangerous in a year. Roger had been right to keep Tally away. "So it's just you and your dad, then?"

She nodded.

Emilia pulled away from the curb. She'd known Cami's dad since she and Tom were in kindergarten. He'd been a bully and a cheat even then. Cami didn't stand a chance with Tom as her only parent.

They drove to the edge of town, Cami filling the car with threats and complaints, and stopped at a long gravel drive off the side of the highway. A quarter mile of potholes led to a broken-down, possibly nice at one time, double-wide manufactured home.

Emilia parked beside a truck with no hood or tires and more rust than paint. A scrawny cat peeked out from under the half-attached running board. "Come on, Cami. This is your stop."

Emilia let the girl out of the back.

The eyes that had been flaming earlier now looked down at her shoes. She licked her lips but seemed to have run out of words.

Emilia laced her fingers together. This wasn't fair. Everyone in Cami's life had ignored or abandoned her. There was a time when Emilia would have welcomed a kid like Cami into her home and done whatever she could to help the girl. Now she could barely keep the three people already there from drowning in the muck of day-to-day life. "Come on, Cami. Let's get this done."

Rotten wood made up most of what had been the steps and porch. Emilia started up, but Cami stopped her. "We go in and out the back now."

"Thank you." At least she'd stopped Emilia from breaking a leg.

Around back, a dog was chained to a tree, his reach not quite to the door. He barked and foamed at the mouth, running after them again and again, only to be yanked back by his collar.

Cami slid open the glass door patched with packing tape and disappeared down a dark hall.

"Tom? You in here? It's Emilia." She leaned her head in the door to hear over the dog's raspy bark. "I brought Cami home. I'd like to talk with you."

Bottles lined a table covered with car parts and long-abandoned food containers. The floor hadn't seen a broom, much less a mop, in years. A lightbulb hung bare from wiring that draped from the ceiling. And the smell—a mix of filth and stale beer. How could anyone live like this, much less raise a child in these conditions?

"What in the world do *you* want?"

Emilia spun around, taking a step away from the voice.

Tom stood too close for comfort, his skin sallow and pale. He was thinner than the last time she'd seen him and smelled of sweat and motor oil, with a touch of rotten coming from the blackened teeth that filled his sunken mouth.

"Tom. Long time." She didn't finish the sentiment. "I brought Cami home. She was hanging out at the park, vaping."

Tom sniffed, then spit, barely missing Emilia's boot. "So? What's the problem?"

"The problem is her age. She's what? Thirteen?"

He shrugged one shoulder. "If you say so."

"You've got to keep an eye on her. Underage vaping is a crime. I could have hauled her in; then you'd be dealing with a whole lot more than me." She shimmied to the side. "Take care of your daughter, and keep her away from mine."

"Oh, your precious little princess is too good for our kind, is that it?" A bubble of brown tobacco spit gurgled down his chin. He slapped it away.

"It's not a matter of too good. It's a matter of keeping my kid safe when you have no intention of doing the same for yours." Emilia rounded the house before Tom could manage another insult. She'd call in Child Protective Services this time, not that it would do much good. They were understaffed and overworked, plus Tom's aunt ran the call center.

There was a time when Emilia would have packed Cami up and brought her to live with them. Time had gotten away, leaving Emilia in a world with no choices.

17

Brianne laid out a picture on the clipboard she used to hold other photos steady. She examined the portrait of Hannah, lost in the world of a book, lying in a hammock between two black walnut trees behind Caroline's house. This one was perfect from the beginning. Brianne didn't usually color photos of people, but Hannah had caught her eye that day, the way her face lit with expectations born in her own imagination.

Hundreds of colored pencils, some short from use, some nearly new, stood upright in rows built into a box. Brianne ran her finger along the line of green, finding a Kelly green that would highlight the edges of the leaves. With golden yellows, she lit up the lighting behind Hannah, giving the setting a look of fantasy, as if the story had come to life around the reader.

"Hey there." Addison walked past the white picket fence, a DVD player under her arm.

Two visits in a week. Brianne had gone from a hermit with little contact, to being stalked. Well, not stalked, but two visits were double the company she usually had in a month. And Addison had brought the DVD player that would force Brianne to pick up the next piece in a puzzle she wasn't sure she wanted to solve. She let a smile replace her shock, remembering how her mother insisted guests feel welcome in their home. "Where did you come from?"

"I think the real question is, where were you? I said your name three times."

Brianne rested her hand against her collarbone, the pencil still woven between her fingers. "I get lost in my mind sometimes."

"What are you working on?" Addison climbed the steps.

Insecurity attacked, and Brianne held the clipboard to her chest. "Nothing. I'm just getting started."

"Oh, please let me see. I have no artistic ability, but I love to look." She scrunched up her nose. "Please."

Brianne's stomach wobbled as she lowered the picture to the table. "Remember what I said: I'm just getting started."

Addison covered her mouth with one hand and reached for the clipboard with the other. "This is amazing. You've captured my daughter. Not just her appearance. It's like her soul is on display." She looked at Brianne. "I'm so impressed. I mean, I knew you were an artist, but this is so subtle yet also powerful."

"It's colored pencil on a picture. Anyone could do it." Brianne pretended to arrange the pencils by color from light to dark.

"Not a chance. You have an eye for detail. This is beautiful."

It was easy to impress a mother with the image of her flesh and blood. She'd seen parents hang on their child's every accomplishment, taking the success as somehow an award to themselves. Parents were powerful people in a child's life. They could boost a child, let her go to soar, or they could crush her before she had a chance to bloom.

She was starting to wonder if that's what Amanda's mother had been doing. It was Brianne's responsibility—her job—to protect Amanda, but she'd failed.

"Please show this to Hannah sometime."

Brianne looked up. The skin between Addison's eyebrows had formed two lines. "What?"

"The picture. I hope you'll show it to Hannah. I think she doesn't see her beauty. I guess that's a thing with thirteen-year-olds. Maybe if she sees this, she'll see a bit of what I see in her."

"Everyone needs to see themselves through their mother's eyes once in a while." Brianne took the picture back, setting it on the table in front of her and covering the image with a protective sheet of parchment.

"Not me." Addison took the chair across from Brianne and rested the DVD player on her lap. "I know exactly how my mom sees me. I'm a waste, the person who ruined her life by being born, and her greatest disappointment. Let's not make a portrait of that, okay?" One side of her mouth cocked in a crooked smile.

"How did you figure out how to parent your kids with that kind of childhood?" Brianne leaned back in her chair.

"Watching other women. It's probably closer to spying." A self-deprecating laugh buffeted the delicate link between them.

How had Brianne missed this vein of insecurity Addison had running through her? "It sounds to me like you developed great coping skills. What did you learn from these other women?"

Addison pulled the ponytail holder from the end of her braid and drew her fingers through her thick hair. "Everything, really. I watched how they dealt with toddler tantrums, organized their purses, how they dressed. I was starting to feel like I might finally fit in when we moved. It's crazy how different life is in West Crow. It's only thirty minutes from home, but it feels like another world."

"You use the word *home* to describe your old place often.

Do you wish you'd remained there?" Brianne brushed the unsharpened end of a pencil along her chin.

Addison blew out a breath, lifting her long bangs. "No. I'm glad we moved. Caroline needs us, and it was a brutal commute for Caleb. What about you?" She smiled at her joke.

But Brianne froze, her heart stalling at the question.

"Will you ever go back?" Addison leaned forward, her forehead a series of waves.

The question peeled a layer of fresh scar from Brianne's heart. She'd wanted to hide her past in a closet, never thinking about the people she'd worked with, the kids who'd been through so much. Would she do it again? There were aspects she missed. And there were the places in her heart that were still so raw and damaged, she wondered if they'd ever heal. Instead of helping her patients, Brianne had left with her own trauma to work through.

Addison should have been a therapist herself, the way she waited quietly for Brianne to answer, the pressure pushing against Brianne's better judgment. Much like Brianne had done with clients.

"I miss the kids. The job was just too much. I guess my parents were right. I'm not suited to handle other people's problems."

"Why would they say something like that?" Addison's head tipped, and Brianne could easily imagine her watching the other mothers, taking in every detail. "You're such a great listener. It seems like you would have been wonderful at your job."

"It was mainly my dad. He thought I was too sensitive to handle other people's trauma." She looked down at the edge of the table, examining the design in its top.

Addison didn't speak right away. They sat in silence, Brianne waiting for the next question that would reopen her old wounds.

"Do you think there's something wrong with Hannah?"

Brianne dropped the pencil. "Why do you ask?"

"I don't know. She's been so quiet since we moved here. And now there's the accident. She's never been a big talker, but I have no idea what's going on in her head. Isn't a mom supposed to have long talks with her daughter? That's what it looks like on the Hallmark Channel. I guess . . . I'm afraid."

Common sense told Brianne to abandon this line of conversation altogether and to make it clear to Addison that she didn't wish to be her therapist. But Addison had also awakened the same part of her that led her to practice child and family therapy. "What are you afraid of?"

Addison tugged her hair over her face. "I don't want to end up like my mother."

"Do you think you're like her?"

"I don't think so, but how would I know?" She looked up, pinning Brianne with desperate eyes. "My mother used to tell me she was a good mom. I think she still believes that. What if there's some kind of genetic component? What if I'm destroying my children and I don't even know it? What if my husband is making a fool of me? I know he said he was with Jeff that night, but he wasn't. Caleb lied about who he was with. What if that lie goes even deeper?"

"I'm willing to make a deal with you. If I see that you're doing anything harmful to your kids, I'll let you know. I promise. But honestly, Addison, you seem like a great mom. I think Hannah is just a normal girl entering her teens. She's likely to struggle a bit for the next few years, but that doesn't mean she's not okay."

Addison wiped a lone tear from her cheek. "Thank you. I can't understand why you'd change careers. You're so caring and understanding."

"I'm not giving you therapy. I'm just having a conversation with a friend."

Addison's smile was so innocent it triggered Brianne's guilt reflex.

"Why don't I spend a little time with Hannah. Maybe we could have a small art class." Brianne held out a hand. "But, Addison, I'm serious, this isn't my career anymore. I won't make any diagnosis or suggestions. I can be a friend to her, and I can be a friend to you. Are you comfortable with that?"

Addison stood and squeezed Brianne around the shoulders. "I'm more than comfortable. I'm blessed. Without you, I would have come undone these past three weeks. Thank you."

Brianne returned the hug, but the sentiment was something else. Did she even know how to be a friend anymore? Amanda had taken far more than her own life. She'd taken a piece of Brianne's too.

"Oh." Addison covered one eye with her palm. "I nearly forgot. Would you come over this afternoon? We're not doing much because Caleb is still moving slowly, but we thought we might have a picnic together before I take the kids for fireworks."

"That sounds perfect." Brianne's face warmed. She hadn't even realized today was the Fourth.

Message to Seth Wallace:
Brianne Demanno has accepted your Facebook friend request.

18

By five o'clock, the sun was still blazing hot in the cloudless sky, but West Crow was turning up the volume. Pops, snaps, and sizzles filled the air, along with the acrid scent that came with fireworks.

Emilia pulled up in front of her home and got out of the squad car. She drew her forearm across her face, wiping away accumulated sweat. The air conditioning in the museum-worthy car wasn't up to the challenge of a July day.

In a couple of hours, the masses would make their way to the park where the evening's show could be seen over the river. That's where Emilia would be, still in uniform, along with every other person who'd sworn an oath to protect even the thankless of West Crow and the surrounding areas.

Roger and Tally wouldn't be at the festivities. Roger couldn't handle the noise, and Tally could stare at her wall for the rest of summer. It served her right. She knew better than to hang out with those girls and vape.

Emilia thought back to the fight she and Roger had had the night of the accident. It had been about Cami. Emilia, still naïve at that point, thought Cami would be okay as long as they gave her what she was missing at home.

The past thirteen months had changed everything about

Emilia, including her ridiculously hopeful attitude. People were nasty, selfish creatures. They destroyed whatever got in the way of their desires. If Emilia didn't stop this thing with Cami, in a few years she could be visiting her daughter in prison or in a home like the one she'd returned Cami to today.

Inside, Emilia's house was dark, the blinds pulled. The window air conditioner pushed out cold air at top speed, blowing away the money that she would make on today's overtime.

Emilia stood for a moment in the icy stream of air, letting it send a chill over her skin. She had half an hour to stop at home for dinner and make sure Tally knew that leaving this house tonight would mean a loss of privileges until the next time Mount St. Helens erupted.

She pulled a watermelon from the fridge, cutting it into slices, then dropped a few hot dogs into a saucepan, covered them with water, and set them on the burner.

Hot dogs, buns, and watermelon. That would have to do for the Cruz's Fourth of July celebration. It would be as festive as they'd been in months.

Emilia tapped on Tally's door as she opened it. Tally stood by the mirror. Cutoff shorts cut three inches higher than anything Emilia would allow her daughter to wear and about two sizes too small stretched across Tally's slight hips. A tank top stamped with the image of the American flag hit halfway between Tally's belly button and rib cage.

"What do you think you're doing?" Emilia's pulse raged. She'd been a thirteen-year-old girl once. The question didn't need to be asked. But it was out there now, ready for any lie that might follow.

Tally pressed her lips together and narrowed her eyes. "This is my room. What do you think you're doing in here?" She put her hands on her hips and cocked her head, chin high.

Anger and adrenaline buzzed through Emilia's arms. The

cool of the air conditioner was gone. "Phone. Now." She held out a hand to her daughter.

"You don't have any right to my phone. It's mine." Tally's cheeks colored.

"Oh, I see. I must have forgotten that you're paying the bills around here." Emilia spotted the cell on Tally's unmade bed. She snatched it up and punched in the security code.

"How do you know my pass code?"

Emilia looked up with her own smug look. "I just do."

Sure enough, Tally had been texting with Cami, and they had a plan for the night that didn't include reading books and enjoying the sunset. The cell phone meant to keep Emilia in touch with Tally had backfired. What had happened to her daughter? How could she have been lost so quickly? A year ago, she had been a little girl who wanted to do little girl things. Now Emilia was balancing a new teen who was trying to change the spelling of her name to r-e-b-e-l.

"I'm keeping this for now." Emilia held the phone over her head. "And I'll be talking to Cami and her father. On top of that, you'll be seeing me, as well as a multitude of my coworkers, driving by all night. I suggest you don't make any crazy moves, young lady." A knot pulled tight in her stomach. She sounded like one of those out-of-touch, doesn't-understand-her-own-kids mothers. But she and Tally had been so close, like sisters.

She took in the girl in women's clothing, makeup applied too dark around her beautiful brown eyes. Emilia had to reach her before it was too late. She picked at what was left of her thumbnail and turned toward the door. "And get rid of those clothes."

The walls shook with the slam of the door, followed by sobs. Emilia had once wanted a large family. Seriously, what had she been thinking? One ninety-five-pound girl was doing her in. And without Roger's help, she no longer had the advantage of numbers.

Emilia tucked the cell phone into the pocket on the outside of her leg. She switched on the fans around the house in hopes that the noise would soften the thunder of the fireworks display. The scent of salty hot dogs circulated in the air.

Emilia got to them just in time to take them off the burner before they were too overcooked to eat.

"Dinner?" Roger's voice seemed stronger than it had been in months.

"Yes." She turned toward him.

A sad smile lifted his lips. "Thanks for doing that." He pressed his palm into his right eyebrow.

"Are you doing okay? Can I get you an ice pack?" Emilia moved toward the freezer.

He held out his other hand. "No. You do enough for me already. I got this." There was a tremor in his arm. A new symptom. Something she hadn't seen before. After more than a year of hospitals, grueling rehab, and frustrating doctor visits, they'd pushed off further testing until they'd caught up on the mountains of paperwork and red tape. But maybe it was time to make an appointment—if she could even get Roger to go.

Emilia pulled up behind Seth Wallace's squad car and flipped on her lights. Blue and red flashed in rhythm with the lights on the other two squad cars. "You need any help here?" She sidled next to the deputy, who had a shirtless man draped over his hood while fastening flexi-cuffs to the man's tattooed wrists.

"I think we got it. His buddies are already on the way to the station. They can continue their party in the county jail." He tugged the man upright and guided him toward the back seat.

Matted hair swung away from the guy's eyes with a flip of

his head, revealing a glassy, bloodshot glare matched with a sneer and rotten teeth.

A woman sat on the curb, blood curling from a cut below her eye, a rip along the neck of her T-shirt.

"What about her?" Emilia tipped her head toward the woman.

Seth shook his head. "She's the wife of the other guy. Took a hit to the face but refuses to give a statement against him." He shook his head. "Could you give it a try? Maybe she'll respond better to a woman."

Emilia stretched her fingers, then bent them in one knuckle at a time. She'd try, but this was a familiar scene that didn't seem to come with alternative endings. "All right. I'll let you know if I can get one."

Seth shut the back door, his lips quirked in a tight smile. "Good luck with that."

"Hey, there's got to be hope, right?"

"Right." He signaled the other deputy, then slid into his seat.

A large *boom* dwarfed the spits and sputters of the other fireworks around and drew the gawkers' attention away from the arrests. In the dark sky, an explosion of red and blue lit the night. Couples snuggled on blankets in the grass, their heads tipped toward each other.

She and Roger had never done that. With the jobs they both worked, the Fourth of July was a time to save lives, not savor their own.

Emilia approached the curb as the fireworks took on full force. Lights flashed across the woman's face, her mouth tight, eyes moist.

"How are you doing?" Emilia spoke loudly enough to be heard over the music and thundering entertainment.

"Can I go now? I want to get my man out of jail." She stood, her stance defiant, though her face didn't match.

"Let me be straight with you: There are other choices. You don't have to live like this."

"Like what? What makes you think you can judge me?" Her lower jaw jutted forward.

"I'm not. Listen, he hit you tonight, and I'm guessing that wasn't the first time. No one deserves to be treated that way. You have value."

An ache spread across Emilia's chest. Tally's dad had once told Emilia that she was nothing more than a dog. She could have stayed in that life. She nearly did. "I understand what you're feeling far better than you think. I know he tells you this is what you deserve. And I know he'll say he's sorry and it won't happen again. But it always does." She slipped her hand into her breast pocket and pulled out the tiny wallet where she kept resource cards. Unfolding it, she found the one with information on domestic violence help and support. "Here. Just take this and promise me you'll consider calling."

"If I take it, you'll leave me alone?"

"You haven't committed a crime. Take the card, and I won't bother you again until the next time he hurts you."

She pulled the card from Emilia's fingers and shoved it into her brightly colored woven purse. Then, without a word, she turned away and started down the sidewalk.

Emilia's shoulder radio squawked in her ear. "We have a call for a medical at 841 North Nineteenth. Deputy Cruz, do you copy?"

Emilia gasped, nearly falling as she stepped back into the curb. Her heart hammered as she pressed the button to respond. "I got it. On my way."

They were heading to Emilia's house.

19

Brianne coughed into her arm before returning to the task of plugging the DVD player into the back of the television. It's not like she prided herself on her housekeeping skills, but the layer of dust there was enough to label the place a hazard. How embarrassing to have her house burst into flames because it had never occurred to her to clean the electronics.

But at least there'd be firemen, and maybe a handsome deputy.

Of course, since today was the Fourth, the first responders would probably be too busy to save her. Through her open windows, she could hear the distant *booms* of the county display. Addison and the kids would be watching the show, hopefully making new memories.

Brianne thumped her forehead with her palm. She'd never been one of those girls to fawn over guys, but it had been over a year since her breakup. She really did need to get out more. The last meaningful conversation she'd had with a single man was with the guy who'd come out to pump the septic tank. He easily had ten more years than her father under his belt. If he'd bothered to wear a belt, that was. Brianne sure wished he had.

She pressed the plug into the outlet, and the player whirred in response. Brianne turned on the television and selected the right input. *Toy Story* played on the screen. Brianne pushed Open and removed the disc, carefully placing it on the television stand.

At some level, Addison's leaving a movie in the player gave Brianne a touch of satisfaction. Addison seemed like the kind of person who didn't mess up often. This made her a tiny touch more human.

Brianne pulled open the jewel case marked as Amanda's first visit and placed the disc on the tray as if she were depositing a butterfly onto a leaf. With a nudge, the disc slid into the machine, and an image appeared on the screen.

Sliding back on the floor until she was up against the front of the couch, Brianne pulled her knees to her chest and watched herself on the television, adjusting the camera. Six years ago, she'd looked like a child. How had anyone taken her seriously? But they had. They'd listened to her advice, and decisions were made based on her expertise.

She hadn't even been a parent.

The scene shifted to a shot of the empty room; then Amanda entered. She rushed forward toward the castle set up on a table in the corner of the play therapy area. A grin spread across her face as she picked up the princess and held it out for all to see. Her mouth moved, and Brianne realized she hadn't adjusted the volume. She lunged for the remote, somehow no longer willing to wait another second to hear Amanda's eight-year-old voice again.

"Good morning, Amanda. I'm Brianne." A younger Brianne knelt beside the girl with two lopsided brown braids. "How are you today?"

"I'm good." Amanda picked up the throne and set it in front of the castle. She turned for a moment, her eyes facing the camera, a sweet smile brightening her face. "I think the princess would rather sit outside in the sunshine."

The hour went on with Brianne and Amanda playing and

talking. Leanne, Amanda's mother, sat in the stuffed chair at one end of the room. She didn't interfere or even participate in the interaction.

"Amanda, can you tell me about your family?" Brianne reached for a large drawing pad, sketching a picture of Amanda in the center of the page.

"Is that me?"

"It sure is."

Amanda smiled up at Brianne.

"Let's draw a picture together of all the people in your family. Who should we start with?"

"My baby brother." Amanda shifted her focus toward the paper, the princess still held protectively in her hand.

"What's his name?"

"Cameron."

"Can you tell me a little about Cameron?"

"He's tiny. He has no teeth. I really like to hold him." She brushed a hand against her upper arm.

"Okay, where should we put Cameron?"

Amanda pointed to her middle. "I want him in my arms."

Brianne drew a baby where Amanda had indicated.

"Who's next?"

They continued through Amanda's three-year-old brother, her mother, and her father. The children were all close together, but she placed the mother a bit to the side and the father at the edge of the page.

"Can you tell me why you put your dad way over here?"

Amanda looked down at the doll in her hand. She shrugged her shoulders.

"Amanda, do you remember that this is a safe place to talk?"

She nodded.

"Why do you think your dad is all the way over here?" She pointed to the dad picture. "And you and your brothers are way over here." She indicated the group.

Amanda began to pick at some peeling skin on her thumb. "He's scary sometimes."

Leanne leaned forward in her chair, her arms resting on her thighs.

The pencil shook for a moment in Brianne's grip.

There was no disclosure of abuse in the session. No indication as to why Amanda found her father scary, only a blanket of dread that Brianne remembered as sharply as if she were back in that room again. And a mother who had ultimately seemed desperate to have charges filed against her husband.

Brianne pushed Off on the remote, turning the screen to blue. She needed time to process, to see this like someone from the outside, but all she could do right now was feel the wickedness, the darkness, the fear that this little girl, as precious and innocent as any human had ever been, could be the victim of terrible and evil acts.

What Brianne needed was some time outside of her suddenly claustrophobic house.

TWO HOURS EARLIER, Addison had been determined to do everything in her power to give her kids the normal holiday they deserved. Two hours earlier, Caleb had suggested she take Brianne along. Two hours earlier, Addison had felt the sting of doubt in his words, as if she weren't perfectly capable of caring for their children on her own.

Addison sat on the red, black, and blue plaid blanket, wishing she'd brought another to cover her legs. Hannah had pulled the corner over her feet and lay watching the sky as fireworks took over the darkness, exploding into colorful blooms of light.

Connor dug a stick into the dirt with one hand while his other kept a steady stream of potato chips traveling from the open bag to his mouth.

"Lilly, would you please sit down?" The child hadn't set herself on the blanket once since Addison laid it out to protect their space, a spot that turned out to be about twenty feet away from an altercation between a woman, her clearly high boyfriend, and some other guy. "Lilly, I'm serious. Sit down." Her voice had an edge she recognized with a shiver.

Regardless of what the harsh tone cost Addison, Lilly finally minded and took a seat on the blanket.

Being out here with people milling around, music pounding right along with the fireworks, and the stench of sulfur, cigarettes, and marijuana revealed just how vulnerable Addison and her family were. At any time, the world could tip, taking away the pretty pieces Addison had worked so hard to put together. Someone could snatch Lilly. Connor could fall in with a group of lawbreakers. Hannah could be seduced away by someone claiming to love her. Life was dangerous.

Caleb could be arrested.

Every moment, Addison was aware that her husband could be taken away without her ever understanding what had really happened that night. Their pretty lives were already splattered with dirt. How much farther down would they go?

Maybe they'd been heading downward for a long time, and she just hadn't noticed. Her mother had had a way of seeing exactly what she wanted to see, regardless of the truth. Maybe Addison was like her after all, and running away from that relationship wasn't enough to keep her own family safe. Addison was exactly what her mother had said she was—stupid. What kind of woman missed the clues that her husband was lying?

Paranoia took over as her controls fractured. They'd moved here from Brice. Did Caleb have reasons beyond those they'd discussed? Was it to be closer to another woman, or to keep the women in his life separate?

How long before this woman showed up on their doorstep? Did she have children too?

Addison's paranoia dove deeper. What if the other woman had been someone she'd known back in Brice? Could one of her children have shared a classroom with a half sibling? There was that boy in Lilly's kindergarten class who looked so much like Connor at that age. His mother was a gorgeous blonde, not an extra ounce of weight on her Pilates-trained body. She sure didn't mind letting everyone see just how fit she was, wearing yoga pants around as if they were a pair of jeans.

And she was single.

Addison wrapped her arms around her knees, which took a bit more effort than it used to. The weight she'd gained with Lilly hadn't all disappeared in the six years since that pregnancy. There was a mound of rounded flesh where she'd once had a flat stomach. Caleb never seemed to mind, but maybe he did and hadn't said anything. Maybe Addison's aging, inflating body wasn't a problem for him because he had someone else.

Sweat broke out across her forehead and chest, quickly cooling in the night breeze. Where was she supposed to go if her marriage ended? She had no job and lived in her mother-in-law's home. She couldn't support the children on her own.

"Mom!" Lilly stomped her foot, catching the toe of her cowboy boot on Addison's shin. "I'm talking to you."

Addison straightened, pulling herself out of her over-the-top pity party. "And not in a very nice way, either."

"Why didn't you do something about that boy?" She pointed down the walkway, where families, couples, and teens were pushing along toward their homes. "He stepped right on our cookies." She jutted her hand out toward the paper plate of cookie crumbles as if presenting the jury with Exhibit A.

Connor came from the right, kicking the plate off the blanket with the side of his foot. "Goal!"

Lilly clapped both hands over her face and howled.

Addison climbed to her feet. "Why, Connor?" She shook her head.

He shrugged his shoulders but picked up the plate, which had landed ten feet from an overflowing garbage can.

Parenting was about a million times harder than Addison had thought it would be. Maybe it was her fault that her own mother had gone off some mental wellness cliff. Yet even if Addison did feel like her sanity was sometimes a millimeter out of reach, she would never blame her children. Hannah, Connor, and Lilly were a blessing. A hard blessing sometimes, but the harder the work, the better the reward, right?

And Caleb—even though it looked bad, he couldn't have done all the things that her anxious mind was capable of cooking up.

Addison shook off the blanket and bundled it into the West Crow High School canvas bag she'd bought from the booster club during last year's basketball season. They probably hadn't even known that she was the wife of the coach. They sure would now, and she'd certainly be the low man on the small-town gossip food chain.

Lilly's face was flushed red in the light of the streetlamp. All around, parents were carrying sleeping children on their shoulders, probably hoping for the miracle of getting them home and into bed without waking them.

Addison took one of Lilly's fisted hands in hers and started to lead them on the hike to the car. She motioned for Connor but didn't see Hannah. Addison froze. "Connor, where is your sister?"

He gave a lazy nod toward the river.

Hannah stood near the railing, looking anywhere but at her family. Thirteen was no laughing matter. Anything could mortify Hannah. Addison's heart broke. Her daughter with the sensitive soul and the endless teen insecurity was about to be the new kid at school. As if that weren't bad enough, she was the daughter of a basketball coach who could be on his way to jail for vehicular manslaughter.

No matter how much Addison loved Hannah, it wouldn't make up for that.

20

Glass shards still littered the carpet as the paramedics gave Emilia one more questioning glance before walking out the door. "Thanks, guys."

"You got it. If anything else happens, give us a call. Or take him in to the ER." The younger one—Emilia had forgotten his name—hefted the large bag of medical supplies as he left.

By now, even the late-night partiers seemed to have quieted down, probably more curious about the ambulance than the fireworks they usually would be abusing.

"Are you sure you're okay?" Emilia reached toward Roger but didn't touch him. Sometimes even the slightest contact seemed to cause him pain.

"It's just a migraine. I wasn't paying attention, and I fell into the lamp." Bandages covered small cuts along his neck and the side of his face. "I'll be fine in the morning." He stood slowly, his left hand holding the edge of the couch a little longer than usual, then offered her a sad smile and ambled off toward the bedroom.

It wasn't the first time he'd fallen, but something didn't feel right. The instinct she used on the job told her there was more to the story. Emilia opened the hall closet and pulled out the tank vacuum she'd inherited from her grandmother.

It felt like a hundred pounds on the end of a giant leash, but she couldn't afford to replace it with a newer, lighter model.

She pulled the garbage can into the living room from the kitchen and carefully deposited the larger chunks of what had been the last beautiful thing she owned. As she dropped the final piece, she noticed Tally standing in the doorway. She was wearing an old T-shirt from last summer's soccer camp, something Emilia had forgotten to sign her up for this year. Maybe she'd catch a break, and it wouldn't be too late.

"Hey. I'm sorry you were alone for this. Are you okay?"

Tally shrugged.

"It's okay if you were scared. I would have been." Emilia stood, brushing away the carpet lint from her uniform.

"Right. I kind of doubt that."

"Well, it's true. I've been scared a lot this last year." Emilia collapsed onto the couch and patted the cushion next to her. "Come sit with me for a minute, please."

Tally's jaw set, but she moved forward like a stray dog examining a treat in a stranger's hand. She sat, pulling up both legs and tucking her feet underneath in a position only young girls and yoga masters can manage. She clasped her hands in her lap and kept her gaze on them. "He lied about what happened."

Brianne's throat tightened as she gripped the handle to the front door of the county health department. After viewing the last of the recorded sessions over the past week, she'd come to the place where it all began, hoping for answers instead of more nagging questions. Her office had been in this building. Though she'd often traveled to visit clients in their own homes, Amanda's mother had preferred the office.

A small sign hung over a door to the left. *County Mental*

Health. It was almost a joke. Two offices were behind that door. The one she'd used and the one used for administrative work. The counselor from up north would be using Brianne's old office now.

Brianne pulled the door open and was met by the belly of a very pregnant woman. It took a moment for Brianne to cast her eyes at the woman's face rather than at her bulging middle. "Excuse me."

The woman grinned. "It's shocking, isn't it? I had no idea a body could stretch like this." She rubbed a hand in a circular motion around the gigantic bump that looked as if it could hold triplets. "Is there something I can help you with? I'm on my way out." She gave her messenger bag a nod.

"Is Beulah around?" Brianne bit at her lip. This was the replacement, and she didn't seem long for the job.

"I'm sorry. We had a baby shower and going-away party. I think she's still cleaning up. Did you have an appointment?" She stole a glance at the face of her cell phone.

"No. I . . . I used to be the counselor here. I just wanted to check in with her."

The woman's eyes brightened. "Brianne Demanno. I've heard amazing things about you. And you left everything in such great order. I wish I had time to talk, but I have an hour's drive to get home and a doctor's appointment I'm barely going to make."

"Oh . . . well, I don't want to hold you up."

The woman propped the door open. "Go ahead and wait for Beulah in here. She should be back any moment."

Brianne nodded her thanks and walked into the darkened room. She flipped on the lights like she had a hundred times before, the familiar action calming her nerves. The scent of citrus cleaning products brought back the feeling that this was the place she'd once belonged.

She'd felt that sense of purpose wash over her almost every

day until the call had come in about Amanda. That terrible moment changed everything. The reality that Brianne's mistakes could cost lives weighed on her till she could scarcely breathe. It was too much responsibility for any person to handle. It brought her father's concerns and warning to the front of her mind, where they nagged at her until she could no longer do her job. That terrible day stole her vision, her hopes, and her dreams, replacing them with doubts and fears.

In one moment, a life could be forever altered.

Brianne stepped toward her office door. She wrapped her hand around the cold metal knob and tried to turn it, but it was locked. Peering through the window, Brianne could see the outlines of the room she knew so well, its desk on one side almost invisible. A few toys had been brought in, but it looked nothing like the way it had before, when Brianne had given life to the sterile space, filling it with hope and possibility. At least that was what she'd told herself when she was new to the job and full of hope and possibility herself.

A sound behind her sent her heart racing and the memories—both sweet and bitter—flew from her mind. She swung around, expecting Beulah, with her mound of hair straight out of a salon magazine from the seventies. Instead, a girl stood with one hand on the doorframe, the other on the knob. Her bottom lip, puffy and red, slipped between her teeth. Her walnut brown hair was pulled into a messy bun. She opened her mouth to speak but shut it as tears welled in her eyes.

"Are you okay?" Brianne stepped across the room, making the smallest contact with the girl, a hand on her upper arm.

She tipped her head and looked into Brianne's eyes. "I remember you. You came to my school. You said we could always come by to talk." The statement held the anticipation of a question. And deep need.

"That's true, and I meant it, but I don't work here anymore."

Brianne looked around at the two dark offices, closed and locked. When would another counselor be available?

"I shouldn't have come here. This was a huge mistake." The girl turned toward the door.

"Wait." Brianne tightened her hold. "Are you okay? Safe, I mean?"

The girl's eyes narrowed, then realization hit. "Oh no. I'm not going to hurt myself or anything. You don't have to call my parents. I just had a problem. It's a friend thing. No big deal. I should go. I have dinner with my parents." The fake smile she forced made her look more desperate than before. "Thanks."

"Hey. Call tomorrow. I'm sure they can arrange something for you."

The troubled girl nodded as she hustled down the hallway and out the door into the dark world.

Emilia stepped into the front doors of West Crow High School. Just prior to the Fourth, she'd interviewed the principal and come away with nothing she could use against Caleb Kilbourn. She'd waited the two long weeks since, and now the athletic director was back from his vacation. He would certainly shed some light on the coach. If not, he would look awful when she arrested Kilbourn during the school year.

A woman she recognized but didn't know walked past, her arms heavy with folders. Emilia opened the office door for her, letting the other woman enter first.

The front desk was piled high with papers of varied colors, a box of manila envelopes at the end of the line.

"Officer Cruz?"

Emilia shifted her belt and looked toward the voice coming from the hall behind the desk. Sherm Corman had aged fifty years since Emilia's graduation. His dark hair had shifted to mostly white, with some black remaining along the curve of his oversized ears. Wiry gray hairs shot from his bushy eyebrows, and thick fuzz grew from just above his lobes, making it look like he'd stuffed moss in there.

She cocked her head at him. Did he seriously not recognize her?

"Come on back to my office. I understand you have some questions."

Emilia's belt jingled as she followed Mr. Corman through the staff kitchen to a line of offices tucked out of the way. They entered the third door.

"Have a seat." He skirted the desk. The office wasn't overly small, but his abundance of plaques, photos, and trophies clogged the space.

Emilia sat in the small chair on the door side of the room. "I'd like to ask you a few questions about one of your employees." She pulled out her notebook and uncapped the pen.

Corman eased back in his desk chair. "You can ask away, but our teachers and coaches have the expectation of privacy, and I don't intend to disappoint them."

"Mr. Corman, this is a case of a serious nature. It would be better for you and the district to have this settled as soon as possible, before school starts, leaving you without a teacher and coach and with a ton of uncomfortable questions to answer."

He crossed his arms across his chest but didn't say a word.

"At any time have you known Caleb Kilbourn to have an issue with drugs or alcohol?"

"Ha. Not a chance. Caleb is a great man. A solid coach. And he's a dependable teacher."

"I didn't ask if he was good at his job. Have you ever known him to use drugs, even prescription drugs?"

Corman unfolded his arms, leaned forward, and rested

his forearms on the desk. "Let me be crystal clear with you, Emilia. Caleb is a good man, and if you think for one minute that I'm going to be part of this witch hunt, you're mistaken." His eyes narrowed as his lips tightened.

He did recognize her, and it wasn't to Emilia's benefit. Some things never changed. Men stuck with men, even when the other guy was in the wrong.

Emilia rose and slapped her card down on the desk. "Call me when you grow some courage."

She turned and left the office, wondering if he'd already rung up the sheriff. She'd be hearing about this interview.

On the other side of the kitchen, the woman who'd come in earlier with Emilia motioned her toward the nurse's room. Once inside, the woman closed the door. "Do you know who I am?"

Emilia shook her head. "You look familiar, though."

"I'm Tawny, used to be Tawny Brown. I was in your brother Tyler's class."

She nodded, the face coming into her memory now. "Is there something you need?"

"Well, I heard you talking to the principal a couple weeks ago. She doesn't know anything about what really happens around here. I assume you came to talk with Sherm about Caleb too."

Emilia nodded. "Do you have information?"

"Indirectly." She ran a hand over her hair, checking the shape. "Do you remember Wyatt Kilbourn, Coach Kilbourn's younger brother? He was in my class too."

Emilia struggled to remember. Her brother was five years older than her. He'd been out of high school before Emilia started. The only people she really knew were the ones he'd been close with. Wyatt wasn't on that list. "Not really."

"Well, Wyatt was a real piece of work. He spent most of junior and senior years drinking under the grandstands. He wasn't what you would call a good influence. My parents forbade me to be seen with him. You know the type." She cocked her hip. "Well, I haven't seen him in a decade. I hear he ran off and joined a band. Lives on the road." Her eyebrows rose so high that they disappeared underneath her bangs.

"What does that have to do with Caleb?"

Tawny sighed as if explaining her story to a preschooler. "You know the expression 'the apple doesn't fall far from the tree'?"

Emilia nodded, hoping this was leading to something she could actually use.

"Well, there you have it: Caleb is clearly the same kind of rotten apple as his brother. And the mother, well, she's a complete loon. I wouldn't be surprised to find out she's a closet drinker. I spoke with her a couple days after the accident. She didn't seem to think anything about the situation, as if Caleb had bumped another car in the parking lot rather than killed a woman." She shook her head, *tsk*ing.

"And?" This woman had to have something more than overblown gossip and farfetched assumptions.

"From what I hear, the coach's wife didn't seem surprised about the accident. Looks like she had plenty of reasons for concern, if you ask me."

Emilia hadn't asked her, but that didn't mean there wasn't a crumb of helpful information somewhere in Tawny's gossipy ramble. She slid another card out of her breast pocket and handed it to the woman. "If you remember anything specific that would indicate an issue with Mr. Kilbourn, please give me a call."

Outside, the sun drilled down on Emilia as she made her way back to the squad car. No one who had any usable information was talking. She'd love to think there was something to Tawny's theory about rotten apples, but Emilia's own brother hadn't turned out great, either. Even Emilia was at best a bruised piece of fruit.

21

Brianne bundled an assortment of colored pencils, clipboards, and simple photographs. She packed it all in her backpack and climbed onto her teal beach cruiser, a birthday gift from her parents, who clearly didn't know her that well. The bike had left the garage a total of twice in the past six months. One of those times was so she could get to some boxes stored behind it.

She pushed off and pedaled toward the Kilbourn farm, a tickle of nerves dancing in her stomach like they had when she was a child going to a friend's house. These nerves went deeper than social anxiety, though. The Kilbourns were invading her life at every turn, and the result was disorienting.

Could she settle into a happy routine, like an aunt or distant relative? She'd be invited to join in family events, but always a fraction of a degree disconnected from the rest of the group. People would talk about how lucky she was to have Addison and Caleb's children checking in on her from time to time, until they got too busy caring for their own parents.

The bike bumped along, gravel spitting out from under the tires with pops and snaps.

She made the turn into the driveway and was greeted by a goat with a mouthful of wildflowers. "Whoa, buddy. I don't think you're supposed to be out here."

The goat responded with a tip of the head but kept chewing, then dipped for another bite.

Brianne stepped off the cruiser, flicked open the kickstand, and took a step closer to the escapee. "Come on, boy. Let's get you home."

Keeping one eye trained on Brianne, the goat continued feasting until she came within an arm's length. The goat hopped away about ten feet, still watching her.

"I'm not going to hurt you. And I don't think you want to hurt me, either, do you?" Had she ever been this close to a goat? Didn't they ram people or something like that? This was her brother's kind of thing, not Brianne's. She'd been determined to live her life in the city until a few years ago. Goat herding was definitely out of her comfort zone.

She pulled off the backpack, unzipped the side pocket, and removed her last peanut-butter granola bar. "You'd better like this, because if I give up my snack and you don't come with me, someone—and I mean you—is going to pay. Got it?" She tore open the package and slipped the bar out.

The goat stretched his neck, his nostrils wiggling as he tried to get a good sniff at the bait.

"Come on. You know you want this."

The goat inched forward, nudged the granola bar with his nose, and took hold, trying to pull the entire thing from Brianne's hand.

She lunged, snagging the goat's orange collar on her way to the ground.

A throaty bleat rang in her ear.

"Ha. You didn't think I could do it, did you? I can hold my own with a four-legged beast." She pushed up from her knees, now stained by grass and dirt, her hand tight around the collar.

"Why are you playing with Thor?"

Brianne swung around to face Lilly, a chicken wearing a doll tutu under one arm. "I'm not playing. I found him out here eating the flowers."

Lilly cocked her hip. "Thor! You bad boy. You know better than that. Let's get you back to your pen." She snagged the collar from Brianne's hold and started walking toward the house, the goat following like a scolded child.

Maybe goat master wasn't Brianne's thing, either. What took her a death-defying leap and her favorite snack could be handled by a fifty-pound little girl with no effort at all.

Brianne slipped on her backpack again and walked the bike behind the odd parade in front of her.

At the house, Addison greeted them. She smiled at Lilly, shaking her head. "You're something else, little one."

Lilly responded with a wink that looked like it took every muscle in her face to accomplish.

"Thanks for coming by. You're just in time. Caroline is making lunch. I hope you'll join us. It's great to have you here."

"No arguments from me." Brianne tipped her head toward Lilly and her pal. "The goat ate the food I packed, so . . ."

"It sounds like we owe you—not that we didn't before." Addison stepped down, joining Brianne in the yard.

"How's Caleb doing?"

"Much better. He's supposed to stay off that leg, but he seems to think that traipsing all over the farm on his crutches is acceptable. It's all I can do to keep him away from the work site. They were supposed to pour the foundation today, but I called and canceled. That will easily put us six months behind schedule."

Brianne leaned her bike along the railing and dropped her

bag at her feet. "I brought over some art supplies. I thought the kids might like to give it a try."

"Wow. I'm sure they would, if we can get Connor and Lilly to sit still long enough. Come around back. We can set up on the picnic table."

A weeping willow embraced the backyard with thousands of drooping arms. In the shade of the tree, a long table made of thick beams and a set of matching benches looked like the site for filming a commercial, complete with a happy family relishing their blessings.

The view of the fields from behind the house was breathtaking. Brianne wished she had packed her camera. The light glowed on the grass, a slight breeze moving the stalks in a gentle wave.

Addison pointed to a clearing on the right, about a quarter of a mile away. "That's where the house is going."

The ground dipped down beyond the yard, making Caroline's house feel like a castle on the hill. The new place would be beautiful too. Brianne imagined the way fog filled the valley in the fall, how it would engulf the home with maybe only the peak poking out above the cloud. "You must be very excited."

"Yes." Addison looked back toward the house. "But Caleb is still . . . unstable. He can't remember us moving here. He says he has no recollection of the night of the accident or any of the days leading up to it. But . . ." She pressed a hand into each cheek. "I feel horrible, but I can't help wondering if he's lying about remembering . . . or maybe something bigger. Especially when I know he wasn't with Jeff."

"Memory loss is common with concussions. It's usually temporary. Give him some time, and I'm sure he'll remember, though maybe not the actual accident. The brain has a fascinating way of protecting us from things we can't handle. I imagine a head-on collision falls in line with that for most people. And just because he wasn't with Jeff doesn't mean he was with another woman." Brianne scrambled to come up with another explanation, but she had none. If she were in Addison's sandals, she'd have the same fears.

Addison's head didn't move, but her eyes shifted to Brianne. "He's never been the kind of man to give me any concerns about his faithfulness. But how many times do you hear women say they didn't see the signs? Or maybe it's not a woman, and he lied for some other reason. What if he's covering up something else? Something even worse."

"What makes you think that? Do you have any other reason to suspect Caleb is lying to you about his memories?"

"I can't put my finger on it. The night of the accident, it seemed like he was avoiding me, like he didn't want to talk. I brushed it off, but now it really has me scared."

"Did you ask Caroline? Maybe she heard something."

Addison tipped up her chin. "Caroline has been even worse since then. I can't get a straight answer out of her, and she talks in circles and zigzags." She twisted her hair along her right shoulder. "I flat out asked her, 'Where did Caleb tell you he was going that night?' Her answer was 'Caleb is a good man.'"

"I don't understand."

"Exactly. That's what I'm working with." Though the temperature was in the near nineties, Addison rubbed her arms as if she were cold. "If I push her, she gets agitated. Or she goes to Caleb, which makes me look like a lunatic who's attacking everyone with crazy questions. I'm not kidding you, I feel like I'm living in one of those old asylums."

Brianne nudged Addison's side. "You're doing better than that. I mean, the food is enough to know you're living in the free world."

"Well, I hope you like what Caroline's cooking up for lunch."

"As long as it's not laced with sedatives, and I don't wake up to find myself undergoing electroshock therapy."

Addison grinned. "No guarantees."

At the sudden sound of a smoke alarm, they both turned toward the house.

22

Addison burst through the mudroom into the kitchen. Black smoke hovered like a cloud near the ceiling. On the stove, a pan crackled, its contents long dry.

In five long strides, she reached the source of the problem, snagged the handle, and dropped the pot and remains into the sink. Without thinking, she twisted the faucet, sending a stream of water onto the overheated metal. Steam billowed up, joining the smoke.

Addison blinked and coughed, eyes stinging as she opened all the windows and doors while Brianne snagged a magazine from the table and waved it near the smoke detector.

After several minutes of airing out the kitchen, they'd made it to the point where they could at least breathe, though the kitchen would wear a stinky perfume for a few days.

"This is what I'm talking about." Addison leaned back along the Formica counter. "Caroline is more than forgetful. I worry about her safety, and now the safety of my kids. Caleb doesn't seem to see it." The mention of her husband reminded Addison that he should have heard the commotion from the couch. She peeked around the corner and found his station empty, his crutches missing.

"What?" Brianne set the magazine in the center of the table.

"Caleb is supposed to be on his back unless he's making a trip to the bathroom. The concussion makes him dizzy, and his leg can't bear weight. But he won't do it."

Brianne opened her mouth, but before she could speak, a scream sounded through the open window.

Addison's heart leapt to her throat. *Hannah*. What could be wrong now? Hadn't they had enough?

Mother's instinct took over. She ran for the door, flying through the mudroom and down the steps. The yard was empty, aside from a rogue chicken, who pecked at the currants hanging from a bush alongside the house. Addison jogged through the grass toward the hay shed, where a door stood open.

"Hannah?" She burst through the door. "Are you okay? Where are you?" Her eyes took a moment to adjust to the dimly lit building. When they did, she found the five missing people staring at her like she was the one on fire.

"Mom?" Hannah took a step closer. "Are *you* okay?"

"I'm not the one who screamed." Addison raised her eyebrows. Sometimes living here made her feel like she was going crazy.

Caleb sat along the wall on a bench that looked like a dump reject, his crutches beside him. A half smile lit his bruised face. "It wasn't anything but a little mouse. Not even a fat field mouse."

Hannah shrugged. "It looked big to me, and it was fast." A shudder seemed to run through her entire body.

Lilly patted Hannah's arm. "He was so cute. You just didn't get a good look."

Hannah shook off her sister's hand, returning the kindness with her newly perfected what's-wrong-with-you glare.

Caroline raised her callused hand in greeting to Brianne, then turned her attention to the stack of hay at the end of the shed. "Where did that barn cat get to?" She shoved her hand into the hay, sending the sweet smell into the air.

Addison clutched her hands together. The thought of what could be living in those dark places made her want to run.

"Coolidge, you in there?" Caroline put her eye to a gap.

Taking a step back, Addison bumped into Brianne, who held her arms tight around her own body.

"Who's Coolidge?" Connor asked.

Caleb hoisted himself up and shuffled to his son's side. "An old cat we had when I was a boy. Grammy is just being silly."

This was the example Addison had been waiting for. She pressed her palms into her sides. How much would it take for Caleb to see what was right in front of him? Caroline wasn't messing around. She was seriously looking for a cat that would have been at least thirty years old. "Let's go inside and find some lunch." Maybe the remnants burned to the pan would help her convince him.

"Ahh." Caroline reached in and pulled out a skin-and-bones, half bald, nearly toothless orange-and-white cat. *Guinness Book of World Records* should be notified about this ancient feline. She laid the scrap of a cat on a hay bale.

Coolidge looked around, then dropped his head and closed his eyes.

"You lazy old cat." Caroline scratched behind his head. "No treats for you until you get your chores done around here."

The cat responded by lifting his head, licking his paw, and wiping it across his face.

"You can be replaced, you know." Caroline wagged her finger.

"Maybe we can hire an assistant for the old guy." Caleb's face registered his shock as he leaned closer. "Sorry, Cool." He patted the cat's head. "I figured you were long dead."

"Are you sure he's not?" Connor cocked his head, his lip raised in disgust. "That's the ugliest thing I've ever seen."

"Respect your elders, young man." His grandmother bumped him with her hip.

Addison bit down on the side of her index finger. No one told her this relocation would be more like a jump off Wackadoodle Pier. "Let's get lunch going. Brianne is staying to eat with us. And, Caleb, you're supposed to be on the couch, resting."

"Don't fuss over me. I'm fine, and I think Mom already had a plan for food."

Addison rubbed her hand over Caleb's, firmly gripped on the crutch. "I've saved her plan just for you. The rest of us will have sandwiches."

He gave her a questioning stare, but Addison wanted him to wait and see with his own eyes what her words could not do justice describing. Caroline was slipping big-time. Maybe this move had come at just the right moment. The woman was capable of burning her house down around herself. "Kids, be sure to wash your hands when you get inside. And, Connor, use soap."

Brianne smirked in a way that broadcasted sympathy. At least someone understood. If not for Brianne, Addison could have been convinced that this craziness was something her imagination had cooked up.

The first thing Addison did once she was back in the kitchen was to pull out the ancient address book that Caroline kept in the drawer under the landline. She found the doctor's information in the front with the emergency numbers.

The phone rang seven times before a man answered, "Hello?" He sounded as if he'd been woken from a nap.

"I'm trying to reach Dr. Campbell. Do I have the right number?" Addison tapped the ballpoint pen against her front teeth.

"You certainly do."

"I'd like to make an appointment for my mother-in-law, Caroline Kilbourn."

"Dear me. Carrie isn't ailing, is she?"

Addison hadn't heard anyone call Caroline by this nickname since her Charles had passed away. "No, sir. She just needs to get in for a checkup."

"Oh, well, I don't do that kind of thing anymore. They say I'm getting up there in the years, but I'm still licensed. And you know what, experience makes a good doctor. You can't get experience without putting in time out here in the real world, treating real problems. Don't you agree?"

"Sure. I see your point."

"And the bedside manner. Well, there is none. All these young guns care about is the almighty dollar. Give 'em a buck, and they're happy, no matter how the patient feels. Do you see what I mean?"

"Yes. Can you tell me who I should call for Caroline's appointment?"

"I suspect the clinic is about the best you're going to find in this area. They took it over when I stopped practicing a while back, but don't make any judgments about my character based on the know-nothings there. I could write her out a scrip if that's all you need." A hard sigh filtered through the line. "It's just a shame. Hold on, and I'll get you the number."

Addison shook her head at Brianne. This guy needed to have his license revoked. At least three minutes passed before the old man was back on the line, reciting the clinic's phone number.

"Thank you." Addison ended the call.

"What was that about?" Brianne undid her ponytail, smoothed her hair, then banded it up again.

"Caroline's doctor. If I didn't know better, I'd think they both were drinking from the same batch of whiskey."

Brianne cocked an eyebrow and laughed.

"What's all the ruckus about in here?" Caroline looked around the room, her gaze stopping on the charred meal.

"Aw. You think that's a hoot, do you? Well, you're welcome to do the cooking around here. I'm sure you never have a flop." She shot a high-powered glare at Addison before wrinkling her nose and marching out of the room.

"Caroline, that's not what we were laughing about." Addison spoke loudly enough to be heard throughout the house but was relieved when Caroline didn't return to the kitchen. Joking about her mother-in-law throwing back liquor with a kooky doctor might be worse than insulting her cooking ability.

23

Tally insisted she'd seen Roger's eyes roll back before he collapsed into the lamp. But how many times had Emilia spoken with witnesses who were positive about what they'd seen, only to find out that version of their story wasn't even possible?

She'd asked Roger again if there was any chance he'd lost consciousness at the time, but he remained insistent. He remembered it all with such clarity, giving details down to the moment he fell into the lamp. Whom was she supposed to believe?

Eyewitness testimony was not as reliable as the general public believed. In fact, it was the most common factor in wrongful convictions. Translating that to her home life might seem off base to some people, but didn't butchers bring home meat? If Emilia were a doctor, she'd surely evaluate her daughter's symptoms when she became sick.

Choosing whose side to take was the issue. If Tally was right, Emilia should get the neurologist involved, which was a solid connection to more paperwork and more hoops to jump through for workers' comp. Based on the experience she'd had already, nothing would change.

If she let Roger's version of the story continue to win out, they'd keep moving along like they'd done for months. No new tests, no long meetings with doctors who had differing opinions, and no new hopes that would end in disappointment.

Either way, Tally was frustrated.

She knocked on her daughter's door, giving her more privacy than her cop mind felt necessary.

"What?" Tally's words hammered through.

Emilia opened the door and stepped in. For the first time that summer, the floor was clear of layered dirty clothes, papers, and dishes complete with dried-on leftovers. "Wow. What happened in here?"

"Seriously? You're on me all the time about my room, and now that it's cleaned up, you have a problem with that too?" Tally's upper lip lifted to one side. "There's just no winning around here."

No kidding. Emilia and Tally finally had something they could agree on, but Emilia couldn't and wouldn't share that with her daughter. Hope was a fragile thread, and reality cut like the blade of a knife. There were so many things Tally didn't have to know about at thirteen, so many she'd already seen, and so many Emilia would do anything to protect her from. Once hope was torn, it was nearly impossible to repair the fiber. "I meant that as a compliment. It looks great in here."

The cocked lip dropped back into place, but Tally continued to stare her down with narrowed eyes. "I'm still grounded. What else am I supposed to do?"

"Hmm. You're making discipline seem enticing from my perspective. Are you sure you want to do that?" Emilia winked.

Tally fell back onto the mound of pillows at the head of her bed. "Whatever."

"Here's the thing." Emilia eased down onto the mattress beside her daughter. "I called in a favor at the parks and recreation department. I got you signed up for soccer camp. It starts Monday." Her voice flew up an octave, as if her tone would dictate Tally's reaction.

Emilia braced herself for the smile she'd finally see on her daughter's face, but instead, Tally rolled her eyes.

"Don't I get a say?" She crossed her arms against her chest.

No way. That ridiculous camp had cost Emilia seventy dollars, two hours, and a favor she'd rather still have available. "Girl, you are going to soccer camp. Dig out your shin guards." Throbbing pounded in her jaw. No matter what she did lately, she lost. Parenting had turned from her greatest joy to a thankless daily encounter. She cut her losses and left the room, hoping to escape before the next sassy comment made it to her ears.

"What was that about?" Roger sat in the corner of the sofa, his hand gripping the armrest. His eyes held sincere interest, something that hadn't been there since before the accident.

"I signed her up for soccer camp, and apparently, she didn't want that." Emilia eased down on the other side of the couch, being sure to move slowly and not upset Roger's balance.

"She loves soccer. Is something else bothering her?" He turned his head in her direction, but his gaze seemed to stare through her the way cartoon ghosts glided through walls. He blinked, then covered one eye with his free palm.

"I'm sure it's just hormones. She's a teenager." There was so much more to it, but Roger's shoulders were not the place to set her burdens. They held enough with his efforts to make it through each day.

His head jerked in an awkward nod. "I suppose . . . you're right." He tipped forward, then stood. "Going to lie down." The eyes that once simultaneously gave Emilia comfort and hope now turned away. They were strangers living in the same house. But every once in a while, she sensed Roger in there, like a prisoner fighting to break free. If only she could find the key to getting her husband back.

Roger moved across the room, his right leg almost pulled along, as if it had grown heavier. Was that new? Emilia searched through her memories, trying to remember the last time she'd paid enough attention to her husband to notice something like that. She found nothing.

Emilia pulled her cell from the pocket of her jeans and searched her contacts until she found the one for the neurologist, then made the call.

"You've reached Mountain View Neurology and Memory. We're serving another client. Please hold. Your call will be answered in the order it was received. If this is an emergency, please hang up and dial 911." An instrumental version of an eighties ballad played through the phone.

"Mom?"

Emilia looked up to find Tally standing in the last place she'd seen Roger. She tipped the phone away from her mouth, keeping the earpiece pressed to her head. "Yes."

"I'm really sorry." Tally's eyes glistened. Her gaze dropped to the floor. "I shouldn't have been so mean."

Emilia pulled the cell away from her face and terminated the call. Her chest deflated like a balloon that had been blown up too tight. The space gave her heart room to ache for her daughter. She patted the cushion beside her on the couch.

In a second, Tally was there, warming Emilia's side, the weight of her daughter in her arms reviving hope and peace. Tears dampened Emilia's T-shirt. She pulled Tally tighter and ran her hand over her daughter's dark hair, the scent of coconut so familiar on her girl.

Until last year, Emilia had spent time each day running a brush through her daughter's hair, savoring the familiar freshness the shampoo left behind. Memories poured over her. Tally as a toddler, streaking through the house Emilia had shared with her grandmother, Tally's dark curls transformed into wet ringlets from her bath. The sound of her little-girl laughter had swelled Emilia's heart until she felt she would burst with the pressure of so much all-consuming love.

She hadn't thought anyone could ever understand that kind of love until she met Roger. He had fallen in love with Emilia, and that transferred to her daughter. How many times had she watched him as he watched Tally, the sparkle of fatherly affection in his eyes, pride for a daughter he didn't create but loved as if he had.

"Tally, I love you more than you can ever understand."

"I know, Mom."

24

Addison had managed more than a month of skipping church for the sake of Caleb's care, but her pardon had come to an end.

She rolled over on the full-sized mattress, rubbing the spot where her hip pressed into a spring all night. Caleb had promised to bring their queen-sized bed with the pillow-top mattress into the house, but then the accident happened. Somewhere out in the shed, her perfectly delicious night's sleep sat in storage while she fought the canyon that pulled her body into Caleb's all night.

She'd managed to wake up with a stiff back, a dull headache, and the scent of coffee and bacon in the air . . . and no Caleb. He'd somehow succeeded in getting out of the squeaky bed and out of the room on crutches without waking her. Not even Howard's crowing at half past nowhere-near-time-to-wake-up had roused her enough to open her eyes. Maybe country life was sinking in.

She scratched her toenail along the rough edge of the floor plank while a grumble of rebellion worked its way up her throat.

No, she wouldn't become bitter like her mother. This was the phrase she'd been repeating internally since she was

Hannah's age, long before she truly understood what bitterness was. Back then, she'd heard people use the word to describe her mom. That was enough. Whatever it meant, she wanted nothing to do with it.

Straightening, Addison shook her arms and slipped her feet into a pair of Caleb's too-big slippers. She was blessed to have three healthy children and a husband who had lived through a horrific accident and would soon be back to building her a beautiful home at the end of this gorgeous farm.

Her attitude would be far better with enough sleep. Wiping the last remains of slumber from her eyes, Addison headed out of the room and toward the waiting day.

In the kitchen, she found Hannah, a book in one hand and a piece of bacon in the other, sitting at the table, her gaze glued to her story.

Caroline rinsed a plate and balanced it in the dish rack while a perfectly good dishwasher, a gift from Addison and Caleb last Christmas, sat unused. She turned, wiping her hands on a dish towel. "Good morning. How did you sleep?"

"Later than anyone else, it appears." From the window, Addison watched Lilly twirling from the tire swing while Connor picked at a piece of bark. She turned and ruffled Hannah's hair, then placed a kiss on top of her head.

"That's good for you. Moving is exhausting. Can I get you an egg?"

"I don't think I can blame the move any longer. We've been here over a month already." Addison's stomach wobbled, a victim of her growing anxiety. "No thank you to breakfast. I think coffee is enough this morning." She pulled down a mug with a scripture scrolled across the front. "Are you sure it's okay we're here? We could rent a place close by if it would be easier for you."

"Nothing doing. I can handle a few kids, and you and Caleb too. No biggie." Caroline pulled a pan back onto the burner, turned on the gas heat, and cracked two eggs, dropping them onto the cast-iron surface. "It's a pleasure to have noise in this house again." She sounded like the loving mother-in-law Addison had looked up to.

Please don't let her slip away.

The warm scent of sourdough toasting filled the room, making Addison regret her decision to skip breakfast.

"Tell me again." Caroline flipped the eggs over like a culinary professional. "When do you expect to be done with the new house?"

Addison tucked a strand of untamed hair behind her ear. "Late fall was the original plan, but with Caleb laid up and all . . . plus you know how construction is." She pulled a carton of half-and-half from the refrigerator door and poured a long stream into her coffee, then slid into the seat next to Hannah.

"Here you go." Caroline placed a plate of eggs, bacon, and toast in front of Addison. A kindness, though probably laced with either control or forgetfulness. But what a luxury . . . to be cared for.

Just as she took the first bite, she heard a piercing scream from outside. Addison jumped to her feet.

Lilly pounded up the steps and threw herself into her mother's arms. "Connor ran me right into the tree."

Addison held her back and pulled the hand away from her temple. Light scrapes lined her face along her cheekbone. "I'm sorry. Should we get you all cleaned up before heading out to church?"

"Yes. And I think you should punish him." She pressed her tiny hands into her hips, her lips forming a straight line. "I don't understand why God made boys. They're horrible."

"Hey now." Caleb's voice boomed through the room, finally sounding like it had before the accident. "I'm a boy."

"I'm sorry, Daddy. You're okay." She left Addison and flung her arms around Caleb's good leg. "I'm just dealing with my feelings."

"Huh. That's a new one. Where'd you learn that?"

"Miss Brianne told me it's okay to have feelings as long as you deal with them right. She knows a lot for someone without kids."

Addison nodded. "She sure does."

Connor slammed the door. "I don't know what she's telling you, but I didn't do anything wrong. She's been nagging me all morning to push her. You take a risk when you sit in a tire swing."

Caleb's eyebrows rose. "And she's a little girl, so you should know not to push her too high."

Connor tipped his head back, his mouth wide open, and moaned, "I'm sorry." His tone contradicted his words.

"It's time to load up for church." Caleb placed a hand on Addison's shoulder. "I really need this today." His eyes said more than his words ever could. Caleb Kilbourn was still hurt deeper than any of his physical injuries. He needed healing a doctor could not provide.

A HEADACHE THROBBED behind Addison's eyebrows as she pulled their green minivan into the parking lot of her husband's childhood church. It's not that she didn't believe in God. She did. In fact, God was one of the only things she was certain of. Church was the struggle.

As if wrestling three children into clean and appropriate clothing wasn't enough, it was followed by an hour of keeping them quiet and seated or face the piercing eyes of disapproving people. A dramatic *dum-dum-dum* played in her head. It was a no-win situation for a mom who couldn't even get a meal on the table without something having gone cold while another dish burned.

"Oh look." Caroline pointed to someone entering the

church. "That's the sweet young woman from down the lane." She tapped her forehead. "I can't come up with her name right now, but she's a treasure. She brought some of her homemade strawberry jam a couple weeks ago. It was as good as my own."

"Brianne," Addison said.

"What?" Caroline cocked her head.

"That's the woman's name. Brianne. She had lunch with us a few days ago."

"No. I think it's Diane or Luann."

Addison's mouth hung wide open. Caroline had known Brianne most of her life. She was the only friend Addison had made in West Crow, and with the constant work of keeping her kids from killing themselves on the farm, helping Caleb heal, and being sure Caroline didn't bring the place crashing down, Brianne had been a frequent presence lately.

Lilly slid open the van door and popped out, almost running into the car parked beside them. "Come on, Mom. I want to see if any of my friends from school are here this time."

Caleb used his arms to set his casted leg on the gravel, then adjusted his crutches. "It's not real likely, kid." He gave Lilly a wink. "Most people here live in West Crow."

Her smile faded.

"But you're so sweet, you'll have a ton of new friends by the time school starts, too many to count."

"Daddy, you're crazy." She stepped between his crutch and good leg and reached up to squeeze his face between her hands. "But I love you a bunch."

Caleb formed fish lips and kissed her nose, making Lilly burst into laughter.

"Let's not get her all wound up before we even get inside." Addison pulled her daughter into her arms, kissed her forehead, then took Lilly's hand and led them all toward church. A look back at Connor caught a glimpse of a tablet being pushed under his buttoned-up church shirt. "No way." Addison held out her hand, tipping her head to make her seriousness clear. "Hand it over."

"What?" Connor's mouth turned down as his eyes widened into a not-me stare.

"You know exactly what." Addison leveled her hand in front of him and tapped the toe of her pinching pumps into the parking lot.

"Ah, come on." He tugged the device free, leaving his hem hanging half out.

Before Addison could say anything about that, Caleb gently touched her elbow, refocusing her on the door.

"I can't believe he tried that," Addison whispered next to her husband.

"I can't believe I didn't think of it myself." Caleb smirked. "The kid is a genius."

She shook her head. "Would you feel the same way if Hannah snuck a book in under her shirt?"

He didn't have a response for that.

At the door, Caleb and Addison waited to enter until the rest of the family caught up. Caroline and Hannah seemed to be deep in conversation, which slowed their pace.

The doors opened, and Jeff Delmar, with his round belly and even rounder cheeks, thrust a hand toward Caleb. "Hey, buddy. Finally back upright, huh? You're looking a whole lot better than the last time I saw you."

While balancing the crutches, Caleb grabbed the extended hand like a boxer claiming his win. "I'm coming along. Still throwing your pole in the water along with the hook?"

"You bet. And I'm counting on you joining me as soon as you can toss those crutches." The man's deep chuckle was swiftly followed by a soft slap on Caleb's back.

"Now, Jeff Delmar, you settle down." Caroline stepped up

and poked a finger in the towering man's gut. "This is not the place for roughhousing, understand?"

"Yes, ma'am." His circular cheeks flamed red. "Caleb, I sure am sorry you're going through this." He stood back and held the door as they entered.

Caleb's face flushed. He looked Addison square in the eyes as he muttered, "I wouldn't lie to you."

"He was out of town." She kept her tone hushed. They didn't need every churchgoer in the neighborhood privy to their challenges. And there was no reason to go over the same information again.

Caleb shook his head. "If I could tell you why, I would."

She held her hands up. This wasn't the place or time to try to find the missing pieces of that night.

The foyer smelled of scorched coffee and flowers. People milled about, concentrating at two tables where blank stickers were laid out with felt pens.

Caroline leaned close. "It's name-tag Sunday. When I was younger, I despised this, but now it's my favorite. Names just don't stick in my noggin the way they used to." She nudged her elbow gently into Addison's side.

From what Addison had observed, it didn't seem like much was sticking in Caroline's *noggin* these days. Hopefully her appointment with the doctor would help Caleb to see what Addison was seeing.

A woman with a name tag that read *Tawny* stood at the entrance to the sanctuary. As they approached, her eyes went wide, her gaze at an angle. "Addison," she said without a look at Addison's name tag as she handed her a bulletin. "Good to see you here." The chill in Tawny's voice was enough to warrant a sweater.

"Thanks." Addison took the paper, her mind jumping back into the loop she couldn't avoid for long. Everyone she came into contact with felt like a threat to her family. Every situation seemed dangerous. Addison's lungs tightened as she struggled to remember if she'd ever met Tawny before.

They moved forward to the row Caroline had shared with her family for decades, all but Addison seemingly unaware of the eyes boring into them.

Her heart raced and her legs ached to run from the building, but this was a church, a place where people were supposed to be welcomed, accepted, loved. Could it be her imagination? Maybe the lack of sleep was making her paranoid. Or the worst of all possibilities, maybe she was slipping into whatever mental illness had taken her mother. She'd read about how stress could trigger imbalances.

Addison placed a hand over her chest and felt the pounding behind her rib cage.

"Hey. Do you mind if I sit with you?" Brianne put a hand on Addison's shoulder.

"I am so glad to see you. Please do." Addison motioned for Brianne to join her. "Do you know Tawny?"

Brianne nodded. "She's hard not to notice."

"Should I know her?"

"Maybe. She works at the high school."

Addison clasped her hands together. She *was* paranoid. Of course they'd met before.

A man on the other side of the sanctuary made eye contact with Brianne, and her face flushed pink.

"Who's that?" Addison nudged Brianne.

"Seth Wallace. The deputy who came to your house." She dropped her gaze to the bulletin in her lap.

Addison looked again. She didn't recognize the man without his uniform. "I didn't know he went to church here."

"He doesn't. Usually." She fiddled nervously with her loose hair. "I think he goes to Grace."

"It seems you know him better than I thought."

"He was a good friend of my brother's." Brianne stared at the pages of calendar items and nursery needs.

The music started up, and Caleb set his hand on Addison's knee. For a moment, she let herself remember those first moments together when the thought of him looking at her had put a blush on her cheeks. Where had the time gone?

25

Brianne took advantage of the quiet Sunday afternoon to skim the books still packed away in boxes and stored in one of the spare rooms. Directly after Amanda's death, Brianne dove into research on the causes of suicide in young teens. Now that she'd watched all the DVDs once more, she could see Amanda's hesitation, the way she looked to her mother for the right answers. That, along with the letter, was enough for Brianne to face facts: She'd made a horrible mistake.

She pulled out another stack of books, looking for two in particular. One had been written by an FBI expert on how to detect lying. The other was about the formation of false memories.

At the bottom, she found one of the two, the book on deception. She flipped through the pages, cringing at her notes, which documented signs she should have or could have noticed in Amanda's mother. Signs she could see in the videos now but had missed in real time.

Back then, she had believed that a child would never lie about abuse. What she hadn't counted on was the even stronger desire children have to please their parents. When pushed to believe something had occurred, Amanda had only two choices: She could have disagreed with her mother and faced the disappointment of the most important person in her life, or she could believe her mother was telling her something that was true. Eventually, that story had become part of her memory and her reality—even though the event had never occurred.

Brianne pushed the heavy box against the wall and tugged the tape off the next one. Cardboard fibers drifted into the air. Book after book about the mind of a child, reconciliation of the family, healthy relationships—she'd studied all of these, highlighting as she went, preparing for a career that, it turned out, a college education couldn't completely prepare for.

It was possible that Caleb was telling the truth and he really didn't remember the events of that day or the two weeks before. But what if Addison's fears weren't unfounded? How could she ever be sure? And even if he had told the truth, would he find it hard to trust his memories if they did return?

The one thing Brianne knew for sure was that memories had a way of lying to people. She thought about the last time she had been with both her brother and cousin at Thanksgiving. Craig and Riley were talking about the year Riley had joined the family on a vacation to Yellowstone. Craig remembered being hungry and hoping Dad would catch a fish after a bear had eaten the family's food supply. Riley remembered it raining through the tent. Mom said it had been a squirrel, they'd had plenty of food, and Riley had wet the bed. Three different recollections, probably none of them fully correct.

She stood and placed the FBI agent's book on the empty bookshelf. This was more of an investment in her own memory than Brianne was ready to handle. She nudged the sleeping dog curled up on top of her tennis shoe. "Come on, Chester, let's get out of the house."

The dog went from sleeping to running around in circles in under ten seconds.

Brianne slipped her feet into fuchsia flip-flops near the front door. Movement caught her eye through the picture window. She peered closer and caught a glimpse of Hannah walking near Brianne's fence, a book in front of her face.

Brianne had been that kind of girl, lost in another world, hoping her future would play out like a story line in a fantasy novel. But instead she'd trudged through the plot of a psychological thriller with no romantic thread to ease the tension. It turned out she didn't have the heart for that much conflict and suspense.

If her story were playing out in a book now, no one would read past the first chapter.

Brianne ran her fingers down her face. For a second, she caught herself giving a therapist's evaluation of her life. And she didn't like the thoughts that sprang to her mind. Was she hiding? Was it possible that Brianne was like so many women she'd counseled who had experienced trauma and then tucked into themselves, afraid of the next thing the world might throw at them?

Brianne knew better than to get stuck in an unhealthy coping pattern. She was trained, educated. And she hadn't been the one traumatized. If anything, she had taken part in the abuse by missing the signs.

Brianne opened the door, letting the fresh summer air wash into her stale living room. "Hannah?"

The girl started and looked back at Brianne.

"Hey. I had something to show you the other day, but I didn't get a chance. Do you have a moment?"

Hannah lowered her book and glanced back down the gravel road toward her house. "I guess."

"Come on over here." Brianne waved her toward the porch. "I'll be right back."

Inside, she snagged her backpack, lying on the floor near the couch and still stuffed with art supplies. Her stomach tightened. Children had a way of making her feel as if she were about to step on a land mine. There were so many ways to fail them. They depended on adults, and adults were only older people who sometimes didn't know much more about right and wrong than they had as kids. Life didn't get easier nor everyone wiser.

Life wasn't like that.

Brianne stepped back out and dropped the bag beside the small table. "Have a seat. I want to show you one of my current art projects."

Hannah glanced down the road again.

Brianne pulled out the half-colored photograph of Hannah and slid it across the table to the girl. "This is a picture I've been working on. It's actually the first time I've done this with a person in the photograph."

Hannah leaned closer. "Wow. That doesn't look anything like me. I mean, I know it is, but . . ."

Brianne cocked her head. "Sometimes we see ourselves very differently than others see us. I look at that picture, and I see a perfect replica of the beautiful, intelligent, and imaginative young woman I've just started to know."

Hannah's nose wrinkled. "I'm not beautiful." Her words were just above a whisper.

"I think your filter is blurring your view of yourself."

"My filter?"

"How we see the world. Everything we've experienced helps build a lens. But the filter doesn't necessarily show us an accurate picture."

Brianne ran her finger over her bottom lip. "When I was in third grade, a boy told me my hair looked like bugs lived in it. I washed my hair every morning and night for two years. I combed it obsessively and spent way too much time keeping it neat and styled. And still, I thought my hair was ugly. All because of something a rude boy said, probably without even really looking at me."

She paused to gauge Hannah's reaction. Nothing showed. "I was looking at myself through a filter that was warped and distorted. Not the true picture. That's what happens when we look at ourselves through the words and actions of others."

"Did he treat you better after you started taking care of it?" Hannah's gaze remained on the grass in front of her.

Sorrow pinched at Brianne. Why did kids so need their peers' acceptance? If she could understand that, she'd change her life plans and go back to work. "Hannah, my hair wasn't messy to begin with. It was fine. Just because someone tells you there's something wrong with you doesn't make it true. Have you ever said something you didn't mean, maybe to your brother or sister?"

She shrugged. "I guess."

"Did saying it make it true?"

One side of her mouth tipped up in a slight smile. "I don't know. Do *you* think Connor's face looks like the backside of a monkey?"

Brianne couldn't help herself. She chuckled. "No. I don't think there's even a slight resemblance, but if you'd said that to someone who was already concerned about their looks, they might have taken it as at least partially true. Do you understand what I mean?"

She nodded. "You were already sensitive about your hair, so what the boy said made sense to you. It seemed real."

"Exactly. The thing is, when we're in middle school, and sometimes into high school, we can be sensitive about almost every part of ourselves, so it's easy to let bad filters affect the way we view ourselves."

"Then how do you know what's true and what's not?"

Hannah turned her head, and for the first time, she looked Brianne directly in the eyes.

"Great question. We all need people we can trust, who we go to when we're uncertain or insecure. People like your mom and dad. They'll tell you the truth. And God. And if you don't mind, I can be one of those people too."

Hannah's lips curved into a smile. "I'd like that. Thank you."

26

Addison ran her finger down today's date in her planner. It bumped over a frog sticker someone had stuck onto July 23. She bit her lower lip as she tapped a fast rhythm with her toe. She was fastidious about her calendar. Every little appointment and reminder was handwritten in the appropriate place. Why did it feel like she was missing something?

"Mom . . ." The name came out long and pained, as only Hannah could express it. "Do I really have to go to this soccer thing?"

"Um, yes. I feel like we've covered this question maybe a hundred times." Addison kept her gaze on the calendar. There was something else. Something important.

"But I don't know anyone there." The kitchen chair screeched against the linoleum as Hannah flopped down.

"That's the point." Addison raised a finger above her head. "You can meet some people your age." She added a second finger. "It'll give you a head start on school."

"Okay, okay. Please spare me the list."

Oh, the tiny moments when a parent wins a battle.

Addison grinned. Hannah was turning into a beautiful young woman. Each day, she watched as her daughter fumbled around, searching the world for the kind of person she'd become. Hannah was and would be amazing, if only she could see herself the way her mother did.

Addison brought her hand back to the planner's page and pulled at the sticker. That frog gave her orderly list a haphazard look. Gently tugging, she peeled it away without tearing or damaging the paper below. What was underneath sent a surge of adrenaline through Addison's chest. Today was Caroline's doctor appointment. The one that had taken so long to convince Caroline she needed.

Initially Addison had felt a tiny twinge of guilt as she pulled back the sticker, thinking Lilly must have placed it there as a sweetness. The truth tasted bitter. Addison slammed her fist down on the book. *Caroline!*

Seriously, she'd gone from half of a parenting team with three children, to a woman managing five on her own. Where was the book on this arrangement? None of the parenting manuals or magazines had mentioned this as even a possibility.

"Caroline?" Addison stuck her head out the kitchen door. No one was in sight, a rarity that produced more concern than peace. She'd expect this kind of behavior from Connor when he knew there'd be vaccinations, but Caroline was well past being a grown woman. Didn't Addison have the right to expect a bit of maturity?

She tapped her watch. There was no way to be at Hannah's soccer camp in time and still get Caroline to the doctor. Addison's shoulders slumped. She'd called the win too early. Hannah would get her wish and stay home to mind Lilly while Addison escorted her runaway mother-in-law to the doctor.

"Caroline, I'm going to give your kitchen mixer a spin. Thought you'd want to know." Addison let the words float out into the warm summer air, baiting her trap.

Caroline scooted around the corner, her speed indicating

her physical health was in prime condition. "Addison, were you calling? I was out with the goats. Sometimes it's hard to hear with all their bleating and such."

There wasn't a sound in the air. If those goats were bleating, they were using sign language to do it.

Hannah stepped into the kitchen. "All right. I give in. But I want an hour of uninterrupted reading time as my end of this deal." Both eyebrows raised, as if daring anyone to disagree.

"You've got it." The words were out of Addison's mouth before she'd given them a thought. How would she be in two places at once? Addison stared out the kitchen window while both Caroline and Hannah stood behind her. In the distance, the corner of Brianne's house showed through the dense rhododendrons that bordered her yard. How many favors could Addison ask before she destroyed the one friendship she had in West Crow?

Hopefully one more wouldn't be the breaking point.

"Caroline, please get ready for your appointment. We're leaving in twenty minutes." She didn't need to turn. She could imagine the gaping mouth of her mother-in-law. Chalk that up to two wins for Addison—if Brianne was on board.

She pulled the cell phone from her pocket and tapped the last contact she'd called.

"Good morning." Brianne's voice was lighter than usual. It almost made Addison rethink her request.

"Hey. I hate that most of our conversations start the same way, but I have a favor to ask."

"Go for it. I slept like a baby last night. Today I can take on the world."

Addison stopped herself before pointing out that babies don't sleep through the night. "Could you take Hannah to soccer camp? And would you mind taking Lilly too? I'd leave you my van—you wouldn't even have to move Lilly's booster seat."

A crash broke through, and the other line was silent.

"Brianne?" A vision of the phone flying across the room and smashing against the wall filled Addison's imagination.

"Sorry." Brianne's breathing was hard. "Chester landed on my lap, and I dropped the phone. I can do that. In fact, I could use the fresh air."

Leave it to Brianne to make a favor sound like she was getting the good end of the deal. "Thank you so much. I have to leave with Caroline in a few minutes."

"I'll be right down as soon as I do something with this puppy."

"Hey." Addison tucked a clump of hair behind her ear. "Why don't you bring Chester here? Connor is staying with Caleb. He'd love some puppy time."

"Really?"

"Yes!" Connor hollered from the living room, where he was playing a video game with Caleb.

"Did you hear that?" Addison asked.

"I did. I'll be right there."

Addison ended the call and turned back to her daughter and mother-in-law. The looks of resignation on their faces highlighted a family resemblance she hadn't noticed before.

EMILIA FISTED HER hands and held her smile under tight restraint. July 23, and the results were finally in. The medication in the blood matched the medication in the baggie. Though the levels weren't as high as she'd hoped, mixed with the alcohol, she had him. Caleb Kilbourn was impaired. He was guilty.

Kilbourn was going to pay for his crime.

The printer hummed, spitting out a hard copy that Emilia added to the file of evidence she'd been gathering. She stacked it on top of the collision report—a large X marking the point of impact, sketches for skids and scrub marks, some probably not even relevant to this collision. Nothing in there was as important as the numbers on the new sheet of paper, a detailed analysis of Kilbourn's blood on the night of the MVA.

Emilia snagged the compilation of her investigation and headed for the door. She'd sit in the DA's office all day if that's what it took. As she rounded the corner, she came face to face with the sheriff, reminding Emilia of her promise to run the case by her before asking for the state to file charges.

"Where are you off to in such a hurry?"

Sweat dampened Emilia's neck. "Your office. If you approve, I'd like to take the Kilbourn file to the DA myself."

Sherriff Commons motioned Emilia toward her office. "I saw the toxicology report. This is going to be a hard sell. Are you sure you want to push this one?"

"He killed a woman. We live in a town that's overrun with drugs and alcohol. If we allow the basketball coach to get away with driving under the influence, what does that tell teens?" Blood pulsed in Emilia's neck. She couldn't let this go. Not until Caleb Kilbourn paid for the death of an innocent woman.

Brianne pulled up to the soccer field in Addison's family van, feeling like a fraud in mother's clothing.

"Do I really have to do this?" Hannah's head lay back against the seat.

"Don't you want to meet some new kids? It will certainly make things easier when school starts." Brianne used the same reasoning she'd heard from Addison.

Like a puppet, Lilly's head popped up beside Hannah in the back. "I wish I was going to soccer camp. Look." She pointed toward a group forming near the side of the field. "They've got those orange hat markers Daddy uses."

"They're called cones, and you're not supposed to wear them." Hannah's shoulders slumped further.

"Whatever. I think I'll still call them hats, 'cause Daddy says I can." She flopped over the seat, her right foot nearly crashing into Hannah's head. "Can we get out?" Lilly wriggled next to Brianne. "I can't wait. Maybe some of the other girls have sisters." Her chin jutted forward.

"Okay, but, Lilly, you stay on the side of the field where I can see you at all times. Do you understand?" Brianne tried to make her voice convey the seriousness of her statement.

Lilly nodded as she slid the door open and jumped to the sidewalk, nearly colliding with a mom and her toddler.

"Would you just tell Mom I'm fine. I don't need to spend time with my peers. And I *don't* need to talk out my feelings. I get it. Bad things happen."

"They do." Brianne twisted in her seat to face Hannah. "And good things happen too. It's important for you to remember that life is a mix. Maybe soccer camp will turn out to be one of the good things."

Hannah pulled hair over her eyes. "You sound just like Mom." She sighed, but she unbuckled her seat belt and climbed out the door.

Outside, the air smelled of freshly mowed grass and new bark mulch. A group of twenty girls clustered together as if reuniting after months apart.

A girl with a dark ponytail biked up the sidewalk. She stopped near the group and dropped her bicycle onto the grass. Instead of joining in with the others, this kid picked up a soccer ball and held it tight to her stomach, like a boundary she dared any of them to cross. This was not the kind of kid Hannah needed in her life. This girl looked ready for a fight, and Hannah really needed to make a friend, someone she could share secrets, jokes, and dreams with.

Brianne searched the group and found Hannah standing

on the edge, her mouth curved into a smile that looked as fake as an actress's eyelashes.

Brianne's stomach squeezed into a ball. Hannah's discomfort was so palpable. Was this how mothers felt all the time? Did they go around beaten by the fears, emotions, insecurities of their children? How was a mom expected to survive the childhood of her children?

A woman, tall and thin, her blond hair gathered into a braid so tight it yanked at the corners of her eyes, blew a whistle and motioned for the girls to join her on the field.

Hannah and the girl from the bike held back a few steps behind the others.

The coach hollered out instructions, ending with the brutal command to "find a partner."

Girls paired off and started kicking balls back and forth.

Brianne bit her bottom lip as Hannah watched, eyes round, as everyone started warm-ups.

The coach went to Hannah and pointed out the girl from the bike, the only other player without a partner.

It took every muscle in Brianne's body to stop herself from running out there, grabbing Hannah, and leaving. This favor to Addison was bigger than she'd anticipated.

At one end of the field, just beyond the goal, Lilly stood with the attention of four other children directed toward her. From the cock of her hip and the way she wagged her finger, she was handing out her own list of instructions and forming her very own team.

Addison must have been like that as a child—direct and in command. Hannah was more like Brianne had been—introspective, fragile. Why Brianne had ever thought child psychology was a good field for herself was a mystery with a missing chapter. Her father had mentioned this concern about the time Brianne was entering grad school, wondering if her sensitive nature was compatible with this line of work.

She'd grown up with amazing and supportive parents. They'd attended every event Brianne and her brother had been a part of. With all the love and understanding they'd given, why hadn't Brianne listened to her father's reservations?

A faint tinkle of laughter drew Brianne's attention away from Lilly's forming army.

Hannah held her hand over her mouth, a smile on her face.

The other girl grinned and kicked the ball back to her.

By the time the coach called the team together, it was clear a bond was already forming. Hannah and the bike girl were becoming friends.

27

"She'll have to fill out this new patient information form." The receptionist handed a clipboard to Addison, a pleasant smile on her still-young face.

Addison slowly returned the smile. "But my mother-in-law has been coming to this office since before her boys were born. She's hardly a new patient."

"I understand what you're saying, ma'am, but Mrs. Kilbourn was a patient of Dr. Campbell. He's retired, so she will be a new patient to Dr. Larson."

Addison licked her lips. The stress was getting to her in weird ways. She'd nearly chewed a hole in the delicate skin, leaving her chained to a tube of ChapStick. "How long ago did Dr. Campbell leave?"

The woman cupped her hands together. "Let's see. It was just a bit before I started working here, so at least five years ago."

"And Caroline hasn't been in since then?"

"I'm sorry. I can't tell you that. It's considered private information. I can tell you that Dr. Campbell still took house calls for some time after leaving, but I can't speak to Mrs. Kilbourn's medical care."

"What do I need to do to have access to that kind of information?"

One of the receptionist's eyebrows lowered. "You'd need to have Mrs. Kilbourn sign a waiver with your name on it."

"And what if she was unable to consent?"

The woman looked past Addison to Caroline, still thumbing through a copy of *Women's Health*. "I don't understand. Do you mean if she were unconscious?"

"Like that, or unable to make decisions for herself because her mind was . . . foggy."

"That would have to be confirmed by the doctor." She nodded, and this time her smile was as fake as the dog poop Addison had found under Connor's pillow that morning.

Addison stepped away, thanking the woman but leaving before the receptionist called the people with the special white coats to take her away.

Caroline lowered her magazine. "Did you get all the scuttlebutt you wanted?" The tone of her voice had a bitter edge.

"I'm not trying to pry. Honestly, I just want to help you out."

"I don't know what makes you think I need help. I'm a grown woman. I raised two amazing boys and take great care of our farm and home. I even took care of my husband until . . . well, you know."

Addison laid her hand over Caroline's thin forearm. "It's just a checkup. We want you to live a long and healthy life." And Addison didn't have the reserves to care for Caroline while dealing with Caleb's depression and recuperation. It was a fight with her tongue to hold back a snarky comment about the absentee approach of Caleb's self-centered brother.

"Mrs. Kilbourn?" A nurse in seafoam green scrubs stood in the doorway to the left of reception.

Caroline got up, and Addison joined her. There was a quick flash of question in Caroline's eyes before resignation took over. She didn't stop Addison from joining her.

"Let's get your height and weight."

Caroline lifted her chin toward the ceiling. "I'm an old woman, not a child. I don't think I've had a growth spurt."

The nurse beamed, even adding a genuine chuckle. It must be easy to see Caroline as charming and quirky when you didn't live every waking moment with her.

Addison tried to take Brianne's advice and let the tension slide away. She drew in a purposeful breath, filling her lungs to capacity, then let the air out slowly as she mentally counted to ten.

"What on earth are you doing?" Caroline poked one finger into Addison's shoulder. "You're not going to get all woo-woo on me now, are you?"

Addison sucked in more air, then blew it out in one hard puff.

The nurse made a note before ushering them down the hall and into an examination room. A couple months ago, the interchange she'd just had with her mother-in-law in a public area would have mortified Addison. Now it was just another moment on just another day spent looking over the brink of the crazy cliff. If things didn't change soon, she'd jump.

The nurse settled them into the room, taking Caroline's blood pressure, temperature, and pulse.

Addison would soon need a checkup of her own. The last weeks had her blood pulsing a hip-hop beat behind her eardrums. That couldn't be healthy. Neither could the wash of cold numbness that poured down her arms every time she thought of the investigation.

A few minutes after the nurse left, there was a tap on the door, and the doctor entered. She was slim, only about as tall as Hannah, and wore her dark blond hair in a bun anchored at the base of her skull.

Caroline's eyes swept up and down the woman as if she could evaluate her competency by sight alone.

"Good morning. I'm Dr. Larson. I don't believe we've met before." She held her thin hand out to Caroline, who scowled at the gesture just long enough to make the room swell with tension before she took the doctor's hand.

The examination moved quickly through the normal routine. Caroline appeared to be in better shape than Addison had been in her twenties.

Dr. Larson tapped a few keys on the computer, then swiveled her chair to face Caroline and Addison. She laced her fingers together and leaned forward. "Mrs. Kilbourn, I understand you've been having some memory issues. Can you tell me about that?"

Caroline's back went ramrod straight. "I don't know what you're talking about. I'm just fine. As sharp as a farmer's pitchfork."

"Are you on any medications?"

The second hand on the clock ticked past three numbers.

"No. Don't need anything either."

Addison cleared her throat. "Caroline, I've seen you taking pills."

Caroline's face turned away from Addison.

"Is that true, Mrs. Kilbourn? Can you tell me what you're taking?" Dr. Larson slid a notepad from the desk. "It may help me to help you. I can't prescribe anything if I don't know what you're already taking."

"Vitamins. That's all." Caroline picked at the edge of her fingernails. "Oh, and the Tylenol for my hip. It gives me an awful ache, but my memory is fine. I'm just tired, is all. I've got a mighty full house right now, and I'm not sleepin' too well. That's the hip again. It causes a great deal of pain in the night."

Dr. Larson looked back at the computer screen and scrolled through information. "I don't see any mention of your hip here. When did this start being a problem?"

"About the time my son and his crew moved in. It's the nerve. I've messed it up before. A ram got me full force. Threw me right into the fence." She looked down at her feet. "Dr. Campbell gave me some sort of pain medication back then, and it cleared up."

"Do you remember the name?"

"Nope. Big white pills. They did the trick. I wouldn't mind getting some of those again, you know, just for bedtime."

"I'm willing to prescribe a mild muscle relaxer if you'll come back in two weeks so we can see if there's been improvement."

"I think a pain pill would be better."

"You can take an over-the-counter pain medication with this prescription. Trust me. It should do the trick."

Caroline opened her mouth as if she were going to protest once more, but shook her head instead. "All right, then."

Dr. Larson proceeded to give Caroline a thorough physical, without digging any deeper into the cause of the visit. When she finished, she washed her hands and gave a list of wellness advice.

The printer hummed, and Dr. Larson handed Caroline the printout. "If there's nothing else, please make a follow-up appointment at the front desk."

Addison made the next appointment while Caroline grumbled her disapproval of the new doctor. She was not a child. It was clear to Addison that everyone in the office had a firm understanding of Caroline's feelings on this matter.

The drive home was nearly silent. If tensions hadn't been at a level next to dangerous, Addison may have actually enjoyed the fifteen minutes of quiet.

As they approached the driveway, the sight up ahead punched Addison square in the stomach. A patrol car was parked near the front of the house.

Addison pressed her foot farther down on the pedal and

took the corner fast enough to cause her mother-in-law to grab for the dash.

"What on earth?" Caroline's scolding halted as she too saw what was ahead.

Fear beat at Addison's heart. Her son was in there. What was he hearing or seeing? Had they come to make an arrest or to apologize?

Addison pulled up behind the squad car, shoved the truck into park, and swung her door open. Without waiting for Caroline, she jogged up the steps and rushed into the house.

Caleb sat on the edge of the sofa, his elbows pressed into his thighs, his face in his hands. Beside him, Connor clung to his father's waist, eyes wide.

"Mrs. Kilbourn." Deputy Cruz shoved her notepad into her vest pocket. "I'm glad you're here." She motioned toward Connor. "I think it would be better if we handled this with just the adults."

Caroline shoved past Addison, taking hold of Connor's arm. "Come on, now. We have chores to get to."

Connor tugged back. "I want to stay with my dad."

"You listen to your elders." Caroline gave his arm a firm shake. "Come along."

Caleb unwrapped Connor's fingers from his flannel shirt. "Everything is going to be just fine. Go on with Grammy now. Give us a chance to work this out." A tight-lipped smile etched Caleb's face.

Connor rose, looking to Addison for help, but she nodded and pointed toward the back of the house, a piece of her heart ripping open as her son left the room, his shoulders slumped and head down.

Addison typed a quick text to Brianne. *Police here. Don't come back yet.*

A moment later, the back door slammed, giving emotion permission to hit Addison square in the face. She sank onto the cushion beside her husband, tears flushing her eyes. "What's happening?"

Caleb's arm drew her close. "They say they're here to arrest me. I'm going to jail."

"No. You can't do this." Gripping Caleb's free hand in both of hers, she made direct eye contact with the female deputy. "It was all a terrible accident. Please. Don't do this."

"Mrs. Kilbourn, we have solid evidence to the contrary. And it's well beyond enough for an arrest. Let's not make this harder than it has to be. Mr. Kilbourn, you have the right to remain silent. . . ."

The words blurred until Addison couldn't distinguish one from another. She knew this life, and she'd left it behind. She'd tossed the good, her sisters, along with the bad, to be sure her family could live free of trauma like what they faced this very minute.

Suddenly, she longed to have a sister, or someone as close, to take her in her arms and say everything would be all right.

Caleb groaned as he rose to his feet, sounding as if he'd given himself over to guilt.

Addison's family was shaken to its foundation, but Deputy Cruz didn't seem to have any reservations or trouble picking her side. For her, it was as if this were another traffic citation. Pay the fine and move on. But these were their lives, their children's memories, the security Addison had worked so hard to establish.

The deputy placed a hand on Caleb's upper arm and guided him toward the door.

"I'll be right there to post bail. We'll be home before the kids are even aware you're gone." Addison reached out for her husband, but he shrugged away.

"It doesn't work that way." Deputy Cruz opened the door, ushering Caleb outside. "He needs to be questioned, and the judge will decide what happens after that."

"Can I be with him at least?"

"No. I'm sorry." For a fleeting moment, compassion shone in her dark eyes. "I truly am sorry for what your family will have to go through."

Addison shook her head. "How can you even say that? This is all up to you."

The deputy opened the back of her squad car and guided Caleb into the seat. "No. This was all up to your husband. He made a choice that killed a woman. If he had been the one killed by an impaired driver, I guarantee you, you'd be begging me to bring the driver to justice."

Addison's arms fell heavy at her sides. Nausea roiled through her middle. And her carefully planned and cultivated life collapsed.

28

The soccer coach blew her much-used whistle again, gathering the girls around her.

Brianne scanned the field and found Lilly at the top of the play structure, yelling to the kids below. She gripped a bar and swooped onto the slide, gliding down to the ground like a mix between a superhero and a fairy.

Parents called their younger ones over, and Lilly followed, arriving at Brianne's side with flushed cheeks and grass-stained knees. "That was exactly what I needed."

Brianne cocked her head toward the woman still trapped in a child's body. "It was, was it?"

"Yes. I've made a pile of new friends. I'm going to be very popular when school starts." She brushed her hands over her blond hair.

Brianne blew out a breath. "Life is not about being popular."

"Then what?"

"I don't know." Brianne chewed the side of her lip. "It's about finding your special people, I guess. The people you can help and who can help you. It's like a team, but no one is the boss."

"Like you and my mom?"

"Yes. Like me and your mom."

Brianne's phone buzzed in the pocket of her shorts. She pulled it out and opened a text from Addison, ready to reply with Lilly's observation. Then she read the message. Her heart skipped a beat. *No, Lord, no.* Brianne's eyes brimmed with tears before she could halt the reaction.

"What's wrong?" Lilly tugged on Brianne's T-shirt.

She forced back the tears. "Nothing. I was just surprised." Brianne looked out at the field, buying a minute to think.

Hannah and her new friend broke away from the group, walking toward the van and Brianne.

"Thanks for being my partner." Hannah waved as the other girl picked up her bike from where she'd dropped it when she arrived.

"Looks like we've got some extra time. How about ice cream?" Brianne tucked loose hair behind her ear.

Lilly exploded in a burst of bouncing and squealing.

"Can I invite Tally?" Hannah looked over her shoulder at the other girl.

Brianne shrugged. "If it's okay with her parents." Let them be the out.

In the first bit of enthusiasm Hannah had shown since Brianne met her, the girl ran toward the bike as Tally settled her foot on the pedal. The two giggled as they spoke too far away for Brianne to understand.

Lilly's hand curved into Brianne's as Hannah and Tally walked toward the van, Tally pulling her bike along beside her.

Where were they supposed to put that thing?

"Tally said she'd love to come with us." Hannah's eyes sparkled.

Brianne cocked her head to the side, truly sorry to ruin the fun. "Girls, we can't put the bike in the van." Addison kept everything as neat and tidy as possible. Today of all days, Brianne couldn't return with tire marks in her car.

"No problem." The dark-haired girl had turned from sulking to excited. "I live only a couple blocks from here. Can you pick me up at my house?"

Brianne nodded. "But you'll have to check with your folks."

"I will. My dad's home. He won't mind."

They climbed into the van and followed Tally's fast figure around a corner and up to a small cottage in a neighborhood that looked to be struggling.

Tally tipped her bike against the side of the house, popped inside for a moment, then ran toward the van, her drawstring pack flapping on her back.

"Shouldn't you lock your bike?" Brianne looked around for an adult before she drove off with a kid she didn't even know.

"It's not a problem." Tally buckled in next to Hannah.

Brianne's phone buzzed again. Addison confirmed that they were making an arrest.

Over the weeks, Brianne had seen the man Caleb Kilbourn was. No matter the circumstances of that horrible night, Caleb was a loving and caring husband and father. She couldn't even force herself to believe this was a man who could callously fail to value the lives and safety of others. But she'd been terribly wrong before.

Would it be easier to envision Caleb as guilty if he weren't a confident, middle-class, well-thought-of man? If Amanda's mother had brought her in with an allegation against someone like Caleb, would Brianne have still missed the signs of deception?

Life really wasn't fair. It wasn't fair that Brianne had Amanda as one of her very first solo cases. It wasn't fair that Amanda was born into a family with serious levels of dysfunction that began well before Brianne had met with Amanda and her mother. And it wasn't fair that young girls had to take on the weight of the misery around them.

Whatever happened to fresh starts and new beginnings? Were they even a thing?

Tally and Hannah burst into giggles about something they'd been discussing.

Lilly rolled her eyes, then smacked the palm of her hand on her forehead. "Teenagers. I'll never understand them."

"No worries, Lilly. We're two minutes from the ice-cream shop, and you can escape from all this crazy fun." Brianne reached back and tickled Lilly's leg.

Little Miss Drama giggled in spite of herself.

A parking spot emptied right in front of the large window with the words *Carmichael's Creamery* curling across the top. Brianne pulled in Addison's forest green van, edging close to the curb in front. She'd never driven a minivan before, and by the looks of her love life, she'd be sporting her little Honda Civic for a long time yet. No need to give up a good thing, right?

Before she could pull the key from the ignition, the van's side doors slid open, and the three girls headed for the shop. As they reached it, a boy, perhaps thirteen or fourteen, his silky blond hair falling loose over one eye, came out. He held the door while the girls entered.

By the time Brianne caught up, Hannah and Tally were whispering, their heads tilted close.

"What's that about?" Brianne took Lilly's hand and walked toward the long display of ice-cream varieties.

Lilly faked a deep gag. "It's the hormones."

The melodramatic gesture brought a scowl from her older sister, new teen though she was. Children really were growing up too soon these days.

"All right, ladies. Pick your two favorite flavors." Brianne licked her lips in exaggerated anticipation. She caught the attention of the teen behind the counter. "Could I please get a double cone, mint chocolate chip and chocolate caramel swirl?" When in doubt, she went with something chocolate.

Tally and Hannah were quick to choose, ordering identical cones, but Lilly paced up and down the display.

The boy behind the counter, not much beyond Hannah's age, passed the cones to the older girls. This time it was the boy who blushed while the girls seemed to hardly notice him, aside from the ice cream. He looked to Lilly. "Would you like to sample any of the flavors?"

Her posture went straight. "I can do that? For free?"

"Yep. Just let me know what you'd like to try."

She cocked her head to the side. "Is there a limit to this offer?"

The boy looked from Lilly to Brianne.

Brianne pulled Lilly up onto her hip. "How about keeping it to two samples. I'm sure this nice young man has other things to do today."

Lilly's mouth tightened, and her forehead wrinkled. She pointed to a deep purple ice cream with chunks of chocolate. "I'd like to try that one, and the lemon kind."

He scooped a small helping of each onto tiny pink spoons and handed them across the counter to Lilly once Brianne set her down.

Holding one in each hand, she scrutinized her take, then looked up at Brianne with questioning eyes.

"It's just a taste. Try them and let this nice guy know which ones you'd like."

Lilly slurped the purple sample first. Her eyes brightened. Then she tried the lemon, which wrinkled her nose. "I'd like one scoop of chocolate and the other one strawberry."

Brianne rested her hand on Lilly's shoulder. "I thought you liked the—" she searched the display until she found the purple ice cream—"Purple Storm."

"I did."

"Then why didn't you order that kind?"

Lilly's eyebrows scrunched. "I was just trying something new. Daddy says that's always a good idea. But I like chocolate and strawberry. I always get chocolate and strawberry."

They joined the other girls at a table in the corner.

"Do you have a cell?" Tally pulled hers out from her soccer bag. "We can text."

Hannah's face flushed bright red. "I don't have one."

"That's okay. I just got mine this year, and the only reason my mom got it for me is so she can track me. She's a stalker that way. Maybe we can hang out after practice tomorrow." Tally looked to Brianne. "Would that be all right?"

"I wish she could answer." Hannah smiled at Brianne. "I'll have to ask my mom. She'll be driving me tomorrow."

"This is so good!" Lilly swished around the brown and pink ice cream until the colors swirled into each other, forming a putrid puddle in her paper bowl.

29

Maybe defiance would have made the arrest more satisfying.

Emilia led Caleb Kilbourn from the back of her car through the maze of cement and metal that was the county jail, his walking boot clumping with each step of his right foot. Mr. Kilbourn hadn't even asked for an explanation when she'd cuffed him and read him his rights at the house. It was like he'd given up. Maybe the victim's family wouldn't even need to go through the heartbreak of a trial. Kilbourn looked like he was ready to fold.

He needed to fold.

Emilia ground her teeth together. The DA was essentially doing this because she'd made a good argument about the merits of charging someone in leadership—and there was evidence, though not overwhelming. She'd sold the woman who'd campaigned on a platform of ridding the county of drug crimes on the importance of making this a public stand. *Whatever it takes.*

Yet Emilia found herself avoiding Kilbourn's eyes, which looked defeated rather than dangerous.

They ran through the procedure with little conversation, only an occasional order from Emilia. When they'd finished, she sat him down on the other side of a table in a room with nothing to distract from the issue at hand.

"This conversation will be recorded."

Kilbourn nodded, his expression still numb.

Emilia clicked the button to start the digital audio/visual recorder. "I want to remind you of your rights." She ran through Miranda again, not taking a chance of losing due to a technicality.

He nodded once more, his shoulders slumped, his eyes moist.

"Please state your agreement verbally."

"I understand my rights."

"Mr. Kilbourn, where were you the night of June 12, 2018?"

"I was in an accident on the Darlington-West Crow Highway."

"Prior to that collision, where were you?"

He scrubbed his hands through his hair. "I don't know."

"Can you elaborate on that?"

"I have no memory of where I was. I don't remember getting up that morning. I don't even remember the accident."

"So you're saying you don't remember drinking and taking prescription medications?"

He shook his head.

"That's awfully convenient, isn't it?" Emilia's heart rate sped up. She checked herself to ensure she wasn't emanating her discomfort.

"No. It's not at all convenient." With his right hand, Caleb massaged the muscles at the back of his neck. "As much as you'd like to know what I was doing that night, I'd like to know even more."

"Mr. Kilbourn, why should I believe you? What's to stop you from just saying you don't know? Let's get serious here. You have something to hide, and I'm fully planning to find out what it is. When did you start taking oxycodone?"

"I took it when I broke my leg in college. It made me feel horrible, so I stopped after a few doses. I've never taken it again since."

"Then please explain to me how it showed up in your blood work." Emilia tapped her pen on the edge of the table. This guy was really something. Willing to lie right to her face about a proven fact. The possibility of a guilty verdict grew more certain with each statement that leaked out of his mouth.

If only she could erase the image of his young son.

Kilbourn crossed his arms on the table and leaned closer. "I have no idea. Trust me. This is more frustrating for me than anyone else. I know a woman is dead. I just can't believe I did it. I don't remember, but I can see the evidence." He blew out a breath, perspiration beading on his forehead.

This guy was about to make a statement he couldn't take back, and Emilia was recording it. Her chest expanded with satisfaction.

Someone pounded on the door; then it swung open.

Emilia let her shoulders hang. She scowled at Deputy Seth Wallace, standing in the doorway with a lawyer pushing past him. Two more minutes was all she'd needed. Two more minutes, and Kilbourn would have admitted his fault in the death of Georgianna Bosch. Two more minutes, and guilt would have been established, locking away Caleb Kilbourn.

ADDISON PACED BACK and forth in the tiny waiting area of the county jail. Molded plastic seats were bolted into place on the cement floor. The cinder block walls had been painted yellow at some point many years ago. The whole place looked like it could be hosed down for cleaning without doing any damage, but by the smell of stale cigarettes and body odor that clung to everything, no one had cleaned in here for a very long time.

Camden Howell was just another name from someone she had no history with or knowledge about, but he was an attorney, and he had agreed to take Caleb's case. Desperation made for quick decisions. Hopefully, Mr. Howell wouldn't be a mistake.

Addison's body ached with the agony of being here, in this place meant for criminals and their families. They weren't these people. They were the kind who followed the law, made good decisions. She'd escaped the life her mother tried to sentence her to. But here Addison was, as if all that work had meant nothing.

A beep sounded, then a door clanked open, producing a deputy. Every inch of the man seemed to hang with weaponry.

A chill ran over Addison, followed by the tingle of growing numbness. There was nowhere to run. No way out of this mess. They'd be looked down on by everyone in the community. They'd have to move away, start fresh. But how far would the story of the coach arrested for vehicular homicide carry?

And her children—they would be labeled forever. Addison was supposed to be the one to defend them from any shame, but it had made it past her guard to attack her kids. They wouldn't even see it coming. They didn't have the skills she'd acquired from birth. They were innocent and sheltered, unprepared for silent stares and backward whispers.

"We only do visits by appointment between five and seven today. If you'd like to schedule one, you'll have to call it in." The deputy hooked his thumbs above his belt.

"I'm not here for that. Well, I would visit, but my husband was just brought in. His attorney is back there. I hoped maybe I could pay his bail." She opened the purse hanging over her shoulder.

"Who is this for?"

"Caleb Kilbourn." She kept her gaze on the inside of her purse.

"The coach. Yeah. I heard they were taking him over for arraignment."

She pressed her fingertips into the flesh above her right eyebrow, where pain had begun to throb.

"You'll have to wait until the judge sets the amount. All that's taken care of in the courthouse."

"Should I be over there now?" Her pulse sped up, somehow beating directly under her collarbone.

The man glanced at his watch. "You've got a bit of time. You should talk to the lawyer. He can help you out." He nodded, punched in a code, and exited through another door.

The slam and clank echoed throughout the room. Caleb might face this kind of restraint for years if the court found him guilty. It would strip the sanity from her husband, a man who thrived in the outdoors, who loved his children with a fierceness Addison had never seen from a father. Would she bring them to visit their dad in prison? Would they even want to see him after his choices destroyed their lives?

Addison was always aware of the possibilities. Growing up, she'd never seen a marriage last longer than a few years. Charles and Caroline were the first long-term couple she'd known. But even though Caleb came from the kind of family that stuck it out, she didn't. In many ways, she'd always known that Caleb could change his mind, replace her with someone better, younger, less demanding. But she'd neglected to imagine the scenario they were facing right now. Not only was there a chance her husband was possibly cheating on her, he was going to jail. Yet she still loved him. She definitely hadn't expected to still love him.

In the corner, a plexiglass window divided two facing counters. Old-style telephone receivers hung on the walls.

She walked closer, taking a hard look at her future. Filthy comments were etched onto the surface, and this was on the visitors' side. What must be on the prisoners' side? She could never bring her kids here. Ten minutes, and her skin already crawled with invisible germs, as if a layer of something dirty had attached itself to her body.

Addison hugged her arms around herself. She needed a shower, with bleach. Mostly, though, she needed to wake up and find out this was the worst dream of her life.

Rolling her hands into tight fists, Addison looked up at the pockmarked ceiling tiles. *Lord, why are you letting this happen to us?* The words screamed though her mind so loudly, she wondered if she'd yelled them out loud. Tears she wouldn't shed here in this waiting cage pounded behind her eyes. Pressure built inside, growing with each fear that wove into her thoughts, like a demon coming to take her down to the pits where she belonged.

She'd gotten too comfortable.

The punishment would be the loss of her family's security.

ADDISON DROVE DOWN the country road with Caleb in the passenger seat and tension filling the pickup like a pressure cooker.

"I can't believe you did that." Caleb set his jaw, his face turned away from his wife as they traveled away from the courthouse and toward home.

Anxiety was taking over her body, pulsing along to the rhythm of her increased blood pressure. "What did you expect? Should I have gone home and told our children that you were in jail? That you were just giving up on them? It's not that easy. You will not drop this on me."

His eyes flashed her way, catching her attention in her peripheral vision. "I'm doing the best I can."

Addison slammed on the brakes and pulled the pickup to a stop along the country road. "Where were you? Where did you really go that night? And don't you dare tell me that you don't remember." Her fingers curled tight around the steering wheel, making her joints ache. "Maybe you still don't remember the accident, but the whole night and what you were doing in Darlington . . . I don't buy that. Who were you really with? I want to know the truth."

The truck cab was silent aside from the *tick-tick-tick*ing of the blinker she'd bumped somewhere along her rage. It clicked out an uneven beat punctuating the wait. Weeks of wondering . . . Addison couldn't keep it up, couldn't question her husband's loyalty and remain a rock for her children. The edges were starting to crumble away. Something had to give.

Caleb threw the door open so hard that it bounced back at him. With all the speed he could manage, his leg still held tight in the walking cast, he extricated himself from the truck and stumbled into the ditch. He yanked a stone from the ground and chucked it full force at the deer-crossing sign. It pinged off the metal, leaving a dent before crashing to the ground.

Addison dropped her forehead onto the steering wheel. There was an urge inside her to pull the pickup back onto the road and leave her husband in that ditch to get his story straight. But for the sake of her children, she wouldn't do that. She wouldn't repeat any of the choices her own mother had made and take her kids down with her in order to preserve her pride.

A red sedan passed by, slowing to check out the scene.

Addison ducked her head, but the car came to a stop, then shifted into reverse. Another humiliation.

A man, baseball cap shading his eyes, leaned across, waving his hand out his passenger side window. "Do you need any help?"

Tears tried to use the distraction as a means of escape, but Addison held firm. She forced a smile into place. "No.

But thank you. We're fine." Without waiting for his response, she pressed the button and the glass slid up, cutting a border between them.

The guy shrugged and drove on. How long until the next Good Samaritan came their way? This was exactly how rumors got a footing.

Addison stepped onto the pavement, heat radiating from the dark surface and soaking through the soles of her sandals.

In the ditch, Caleb sat on the dirt, his hands cradling his face. Either he was a great actor or a man who really didn't know what was happening. How could she trust it was the latter? Until Caleb came into her life, she'd never met a man she could trust. Her mother's words still haunted her. *"He may look like he's going to take care of you, but don't get comfortable. They all cheat eventually."* That voice was getting louder every day. It had started waking her in the middle of the night. Those words drew her back to the cab of the truck and held her to the seat, forming a wall between her and Caleb that she couldn't climb over.

She wouldn't leave him, but she wasn't going after him, either.

30

Brianne did her best to keep the mood light, but Connor had met them at the van and news of the scene they had avoided came tumbling out of his mouth. Brianne hadn't even unlatched her seat belt before it was too late to buffer Hannah and Lilly from the story.

Connor seemed oblivious to the shock on his older sister's face and the panic of the younger one. When Lilly started to sob, he paused, looked her way, and told her it was no big deal. "Mom said she'd go get him and straighten everything out."

He still believed his parents could fix any wrong. Brianne prayed this wouldn't be the time he found out he was mistaken.

For hours, Brianne took the role of comforter while Caroline took out her fears on the kitchen. Fried chicken, fresh bread, and a variety of cookies filled the house with the scent of deception. Everything was not all right here. There was a giant problem, and until someone was willing to be straight with these kids, their fears were certain to grow.

Lilly came out the front door, a plastic plate piled with untouched cookies stacked on a matching tray. She sat next to Brianne on the top step and leaned into her side.

"How are you doing?" Brianne put her arm around Lilly's slight shoulders.

She shrugged. "Do you really think Daddy is going to be okay?"

"Well." Brianne pulled stray strands of golden hair away from Lilly's eyes and tucked them behind her ear. "I think he will. This may be a tough time, but in the end, he's a survivor like you."

"I'm afraid. I told Grammy that, but she said I need to trust God. She said that to me when Grampy was sick too, and he died." A tear glistened in the corner of her eye.

Brianne nodded. "I can see why that would be a big worry for you. But your daddy isn't sick. No matter what happens, you know that he loves you, and he'll do whatever he can to be with you. I think what Grammy means is that, even though sometimes we go through hard times, we can trust that God loves us and will make it all work out in His time."

Lilly sighed, no doubt disappointed in Brianne's assurance.

There weren't always words to fix a bruised heart. Sometimes, the hurt had to happen before the healing could begin. Lilly's summer was bound to hold some tears.

The advice Brianne had been given early in her job as a counselor rose to the surface of her memory. She'd been working with three siblings who'd been removed from their mother's care. The state was hoping to place them with an aunt who lived on the coast. Even before the kids came in for their first meeting, her supervisor told her to beware of hope. She said hope could be a dangerous thing for children in the midst of trauma.

But how could anyone survive without hope? It was what spurred people on toward the future. Maybe if Amanda had known there was always hope . . . maybe Amanda would still be there.

LILLY HAD SPENT the entire drive to the soccer field catching Connor up on the procedure. Somehow, Brianne's taking them to ice cream on Monday indicated they would do it again on Friday. It wasn't a great idea to overindulge kids like this, but with all the Kilbourn children were going through, a bit of extra sugar and fat wouldn't be the worst thing.

Brianne pulled up to the curb, turned off the minivan's ignition, and opened her door. Doing the mom thing wasn't as awkward as she'd assumed it would be. Sure, she was tired by the time she gave the kids back to their parents, but it was nothing like the look of absolute exhaustion that hung on Addison's drooping shoulders.

This was a little thing Brianne could do to help. She used to tell clients that, sometimes, serving others was the best way to feel better about their lives and circumstances. Not that the other person had it worse—though many did—but the act of helping someone else simply lifted the spirit. Brianne's heart was experiencing a bit of that healing.

Today, Brianne had brought along a camp chair and one of the books on memory issues. She'd seen the other moms sitting on the sidelines while the girls raced up and down the field. In this new world, reading was something she could do to avoid the oddity and not call attention to whose kids she was bringing. She'd bury her face in a book, and no one would even notice her.

Brianne lifted the back door of the van to retrieve her chair and bag. She slammed the rear hatch shut just in time to see a jogger jump to the side to avoid a collision with Lilly as she bounded from the side door. He staggered, then landed on his side.

So much for not drawing extra attention. "Oh, I'm so sorry! Are you okay?" Brianne dropped her things on the grass beside the sidewalk. Her face flushed hot as the jogger turned her way. Seth. Again.

"Well, you were the last person I expected to be with this

little hurdle." He smiled at Lilly. "No harm. I should have been paying better attention." He hopped up.

"Solving crime while exercising?" She heard the flirty tone in her voice and cringed. "I'm really sorry. I hate having my runs interrupted." She brushed her hand over her hair before she realized how that must look.

"I was about to stop anyway. My house is just around the corner."

Brianne nodded. "I'm a few miles out of town."

He smiled, obviously waiting for her to see the ridiculousness of that statement.

A sigh oozed out of her mouth. "You caught me unprepared."

"It seems that's the only way we see each other."

She thought back to the middle of the night visit, the news of Caleb's accident. The way Seth had handled the situation, comforting yet serious. He had great people skills. Brianne . . . not so much.

"So, you said you run?" Seth wiped sweat from his forehead with the edge of his sleeve.

"Yep. Almost daily. It keeps the crazy away."

His eyes lit with amusement. "Maybe we can get out there together sometime."

The silence stretched on too long, further paralyzing Brianne's tongue.

"I think she'd really like that." Lilly pulled the basket of snacks from the passenger seat. "Brianne doesn't get out much. Grammy says it's a big waste of youth."

If it was possible to turn the heat up higher, that statement did it. Perspiration dampened Brianne's hairline. Her mouth sagged open, no words willing to try and save this conversation from humiliation.

"Let me help you with all this stuff." Seth picked up the bag and chair.

Brianne scanned the soccer field and spotted Hannah kicking a ball back and forth with another girl. Hannah's gaze darted down the road after every second or third kick, no doubt watching for Tally to come around the corner.

Connor looked from Seth to Brianne, rolled his eyes, and headed toward the basketball hoops, his ball tucked under his arm.

Lilly tugged on the hem of Brianne's shorts. "Can I go now?" She pointed toward the playground.

"Yes, but remember, stay in my sight. Understand?"

She nodded as she ran toward the kids she'd bonded with over the week.

"There's no way those are your kids. Who'd you snag them from?"

"Ha. They belong to the Kilbourns. I'm helping them out. It's been rough." Could he talk about the case? Was it impolite to even bring it up? She hadn't been this nervous since middle-school dances.

"I'm sure. It's hard to see this kind of thing happen. They're good people."

But bad things happened to good people. They happened all the time, and no one could stop those horrible seasons from coming or predict when they'd arrive. "I was wondering about something."

"Yeah."

She pointed to a place along the sideline, and Seth set down the bag and pulled the chair from its case. "Do you remember Amanda Tanger?"

"The suicide last year. How could I forget?" His eyes clouded.

"Do you remember her dad and the charges against him?"

He nodded. "He was just in the office last week, registering."

Brianne swallowed hard. "He's out of prison?"

"A day or two before he came in."

"What did you think about all that? Do you think he could have been innocent?"

Seth's eyebrows raised. "Innocent is not a word I would ever use along with Clyde's name. I can say the sex-abuse charges surprised me, but that's generally true with that kind of thing. You can't tell what's going on in a person's mind. It's one of the hardest parts of my job."

He shook his head. "But Clyde wasn't a nice guy. It's public record, so I don't mind telling you that we'd been out to the house quite a few times on disturbing-the-peace calls. His wife never filed charges, but the thought was that he beat her pretty regularly."

Brianne's arms grew heavy. Why on earth did it feel so important to uncover possible innocence in a man who was anything but guiltless?

Addison's life had become a series of unanswered questions. There were the questions that stalked the corners of her mind, keeping her awake at night and fighting waves of fear during the day. And there were the questions from others. The ones she knew were out there but that would only be asked in hushed tones behind her family's backs.

How many people had seen them duck into the offices of Howell, Steves, and Goragie? For that matter, how many had watched them slink out of the county jail a few nights before?

Addison was too new in this community to hear the gossip fresh from the mouths of old men and bored housewives. She didn't work outside the home, so she missed out on the water-cooler talk. Her kids hadn't even started school, so the jabber of parents didn't reach her ears. But summer was in its final weeks, and she couldn't stay anonymous much longer.

A letter from the school district had arrived via certified

mail, letting them know of Caleb's suspension until all legal matters and investigations were concluded. The whole thing was humiliating. Addison found herself not wanting to leave the safety of the farm.

Yet here they were. She and Caleb sat in matching chairs, side by side, as if this were a simple dentist appointment instead of a meeting with her husband's defense attorney.

Caleb placed his hand on top of Addison's, curling his fingers around hers.

That gesture had once brought comfort and security. Addison's stomach swirled with sickness at what their lives had turned into. Deep inside, some layer of her trembled. She kept her fingers straight, not acknowledging the tenderness of the man sitting to her left. Did she really even know him?

"Hey there, Coach." Camden Howell stepped into the room, offering his hand first to Caleb, then to Addison. "Come on back. We have a lot to discuss."

Addison studied his face, looking for a hint of news, but Mr. Howell's expression remained an impenetrable mask of neutrality, a trait that probably served him well in the courtroom, though it felt like a form of torture here.

He ushered them down the hall, stopping at the door to his office, only entering after she and Caleb had. The room was large but not overly furnished. A couple of framed diplomas hung on the wall to the right. Behind the cluttered desk, a window took up most of the space, revealing a view of the historic Corban County Courthouse. The room smelled of men's deodorant and Bengay. Bookshelves housed books but no pictures.

Addison checked the attorney's ring finger. Empty but dented, as if he'd been married a long time but wasn't anymore.

Mr. Howell pointed to the client chairs, then eased himself into a desk chair with worn armrests. "I'm kind of expensive, so let's get to business. There's both good and bad news. I think we've got a solid chance at this thing, but don't take that as any kind of assurance. These cases can be highly unpredictable. Unless we negotiate a settlement, the jury will decide the outcome. Juries are just people. Their thoughts and experiences differ as much as any other group of folks. That makes them a risk."

"Are you saying we should settle?" Caleb leaned forward and clasped his hands together.

"I'm saying it's something to consider. Right now, we don't have an offer from the state, but I expect we'll get one. It may or may not involve jail time. I think the best we can hope for is a reduced charge, perhaps criminally negligent homicide with a suspended sentence. What I can almost guarantee is that taking a deal will mean admitting guilt, and that will cost you your job. But going to a trial has costs too, and not only my fees. The longer this stretches out, the more it becomes a public trial with the citizens of our dear town electing themselves judge and jury. Even an acquittal comes with consequences. There's no free pass."

Caleb shook his head. "I don't want a free pass. I don't deserve that."

Howell held up a hand. "Let me stop you right there. I'm not your priest. If you have something to confess, please, do us both a favor and don't do it here. It's my job to make sure your side is heard—your very best side. I'll be bringing in expert witnesses and people who will testify to your great character."

"What should we be doing?" Addison dug her fingernails into the faux leather of her purse.

Mr. Howell shrugged. "Come up with a list of people who might be willing to testify to Caleb's character." He leaned back. "The thing is, there's evidence. We know you were drinking. There was alcohol in your system. And we know you took oxy. However, we might be able to argue that the amounts weren't enough to cause impairment." He tipped his chin, eyes on Caleb. "Do me a favor and eat up. We don't want you looking like a lightweight. What we have going for us are the metabolites. It doesn't appear that oxy is a habit. If I'm wrong, don't tell me."

Addison's heart pounded as it did every time drugs in her husband's system came up. There was concrete physical evidence that said Caleb wasn't the man she thought he was. He'd preached about the dangers of getting involved with drugs, even prescription drugs, warning the kids how easy it was to slip off the path. Was that because he, himself, had fallen?

July 27, 2018

Dear West Crow School District employees and staff,

As many of you may have heard, Coach Caleb Kilbourn was arrested recently on charges of driving while under the influence. Our district takes these kinds of allegations very seriously but wishes to remind all that Mr. Kilbourn is innocent until proven guilty. The district will run an independent investigation once the official police investigation is complete. Please understand that we wish to protect the privacy of our staff members and will not discuss this case now or at any point in the future.

Sincerely,
Marijo Taylor
West Crow Superintendent

31

Emilia retrieved her personal belongings from her locker and started toward the parking lot. This was supposed to be a week of great victory, but something kept pulling her down. She couldn't do anything to make the people who'd hurt her husband and taken that loving father away from Tally pay, but she'd done something to help the Bosch family. They would have closure about the senseless death of their mother. They'd have someone to blame and restitution to collect.

A haze blurred the view of the mountains that surrounded their rugged valley. Off in the distance, she could see where wildfires had destroyed and devoured the landscape. Two years ago, Roger had been gone for three weeks fighting a blaze that left only charred spikes where towering trees had once shaded the forest floor.

When he'd finally returned, even his skin held the scent of smoky finality. She'd felt true fear for her husband during those weeks, yet she'd taken his safety for granted here in town. In the end, it was a local fire, one nearly routine in its beginning, that could have killed him. And in some ways, it did.

Tally sat on the front porch, her bicycle on its side in the yellowed grass. She held a worn copy of *The Horse and His Boy* in her hands. "Hey, Mom. How was work?"

Emilia caught herself before she let the shock play out on her face. "Good. How did soccer camp turn out?"

"Great." Tally looked up, making eye contact with her mother. "I got to know a new girl. We had ice cream on Monday. Sorry I forgot to tell you."

Relief filled the places worry had recently claimed. A new friend, and Tally was willing to mention her. That was a great sign. "Was she at the soccer camp too?"

"Yep. She didn't want to be there, either, but her mother thought it would be a good way to make friends." Tally's face lit up the way it used to. "Would it be okay if we hung out sometime?"

"I'd like to know a little more about her. What's her name? What are her parents like?"

Tally fastened her fists to her sides. "I'm not a baby, you know. I get the right to make my own friends without it being a police matter."

"Yes. But I'm still your mother, and I have the right to know who my daughter is spending time with." Emilia crossed her arms in mock sternness.

"Whatever. Her name's Hannah. She was with her neighbor Brianne when we had ice cream. I don't know anything about her parents because, believe it or not, normal girls our age do not find our moms and dads to be fascinating conversation."

Emilia let her mouth drop open. "I'm shocked."

"Sure. Whatever."

"Why did the neighbor bring her to soccer?"

"I don't know."

"Where does she live?"

Tally shrugged.

"What do her parents do for a living?"

"I don't know, Mom. But she's nice. She likes to read. She has an obnoxious little sister who I guess is better than her little brother, but I didn't get to talk to him. She's in my grade, and she didn't actually want to play soccer, but now she's thinking about joining the team."

"All right. I understand." Emilia ran her hand over her daughter's hair. "Maybe I can meet her mom soon. Does that sound fair?"

"In your uniform?" Tally covered her face with her hands.

Emilia couldn't help wondering if her work attire would have been half as humiliating if she'd been a man. "I guess that depends on the when and where of our meeting."

Tally shrugged. "Hannah doesn't have a cell phone, so it's not like we can easily get together until school starts."

"No cell phone, huh? I think I might like these people."

BRIANNE'S FEET POUNDED in rhythm with Seth's along the asphalt path. Beside them, the river flowed, its current seeming to push against her body. Brianne raised her hand in defeat. She slowed to a jog, then a walk. "Okay, Seth. You're killing me. I give."

"Ha!" Seth wiped his arm across his dripping forehead. "Thank you, Lord! I couldn't have kept that up for another minute."

She leaned forward, stretching her hamstrings. "What exactly was this torture for?"

"I didn't want you to think I couldn't keep up with you." He tipped his face toward the sky. "Why can't it start raining right now?"

"Um. I think because it's late July." Her body was in a delicious state of fatigue, the kind that left her feeling tired but satisfied. She'd pushed her legs and lungs to their limit and survived. Wasn't that what life was about?

"Why are you grinning?"

"Chalk it up to endorphins."

"You're one of those girls, huh?" Seth ambled to a grassy area along the riverside and sat, his legs extended.

"What's that supposed to mean?" How could he possibly be so much more attractive now, with sweat making his shirt cling to his chest and his hair glued to his face?

"You like the runner's high. I admit I don't understand. I run because it gets the job out of my head, and I like to eat a lot of pizza."

"I get that. Or at least I used to. When I worked for the county, running was my key to sanity." She sat down beside him and nudged him with her elbow. "And I like pizza too."

"How about I treat you to Pisano's tonight? I feel like I may have a crazy appetite after that run."

Brianne thanked God that her face was already flushed from exertion, covering the blush his invitation would have surely produced. She had some sketching that needed to be finished by early next week. The gallery in town was running low, and she had to restock the cards she sold at numerous establishments throughout the county as well as online, but maybe it would be okay to let that wait one night. "All right. That sounds great."

"I'll swing by your place at six, if that's okay." He grinned, revealing a delicate scar beside his upper lip.

"Perfect."

Seth was seven minutes early.

Brianne snuck a peek out the window. He was dressed in khakis and a soft blue polo shirt. Even his shoes were nice. She looked down at her jeans and black T-shirt, then rushed into the bedroom.

His knock startled her even though she knew he was there.

Chester, for once, took up his role as guard dog, whining and barking at the closed door.

She yanked off her clothes and slid into a black cotton dress, brushing it straight. She kicked away her Converse and drove her feet into a pair of sandals. A one-minute change. Not bad.

It took all the strength her tired body had to pull the dog away from the door and get it open without Chester tackling Seth. This was as bad as the way her brother greeted her dates in high school. He liked to tell them to be careful not to let her have spicy food because it gave her diarrhea. It wasn't true, but she'd seen more than one boy blanch at the comment. "I'm so sorry," she said as she gripped Chester's collar. "I should have put him in the bedroom."

Chester's barks of warning turned to wiggles and begging.

She chose to interpret Chester's response as evidence of Seth's good character, but likely it was a fault in the dog's protective instinct, of which he had very little.

Seth scrubbed his fingers through Chester's thick fur, earning the mutt's loyalty forever. "I love him. How old is he?"

"Nearing five months."

Seth stood straight. "You're kidding me. He's huge."

"No kidding. I thought he'd be good protection, living out here on my own, but he's more coward than warrior." She tugged Chester back by his collar and stepped out onto the porch, slipping the door closed between the dog and them.

"Wow." Seth took in her appearance. "You look amazing."

She shrugged, feeling as though she'd gotten away with something, thanks to her last-minute clothing change. "It's easy to impress when you've seen me in the middle of the night and after a long run."

A dimple appeared on the right side of his face, and his gaze lingered until she found herself forced to look away, reminding herself that he was the same guy she'd grown up with. Isolation was probably messing with her mind.

She looked back toward Seth, who held out an arm for her. It would take a lot of convincing for her brain to believe the story she was selling. She couldn't find a trace of the jock who didn't look her way. The man who walked beside her carried himself with confidence and humility. If she could talk to anyone about the concerns in Amanda's case, it was Seth.

They pulled up to the pizza place. Already, many of the outside tables were filled with families or couples. Hanging bulbs glittered in the dimming light. The scents of oregano, basil, and garlic drifted on the warm night air. Something about Pisano's gave Brianne the feeling that she was on vacation, transported to another country.

Seth grabbed a menu from a rack by the cast-iron fence that bordered the outdoor seating. "What do you think? Inside or out?"

She started to answer with the typical *I don't care* but thought better of it. "Outside."

"My thoughts exactly. We don't get enough of these perfect summer evenings. It would be a shame to waste one."

Brianne's heart raced. Those were her very thoughts whenever she sat on her porch watching the sun slip behind the mountains, listening to the frogs take up their songs.

Seth led her to an open table and handed her the menu.

It took only a moment to settle on the chicken pesto pizza and two iced teas. But once they'd finished, silence stepped between them.

Brianne listened as other couples laughed and joked, wishing she were the kind of woman who had adventures to relay. But she found it easier to chat with Hannah about books than with a man about any subject.

"Did you think any more about the Tanger guy?"

Brianne swallowed hard. If she was right, an injustice had occurred. An innocent man had spent years in prison for a crime he didn't commit. But those thoughts slipped away more easily now that she knew he was out of prison. Wasn't that enough? Clyde may have paid for a crime he didn't commit, but by the sound of it, he had gotten away with others. She sighed. "It's complicated."

"Sure. Anything that involves people is. Would talking about it help?"

A server delivered two tall glasses of iced tea and set straws on the table.

Seth reached for the sugar and poured at least a tablespoon into his glass.

Brianne's eyes grew wide. "Wow."

"Hey." He winked. "Don't judge."

The awkward silence drifted away on their laughter.

She took a long drink, then set her glass back onto the circle of condensation it had already formed on the table. "I'm not sure what to do about the situation. I've reviewed my notes and rewatched the sessions, and I'm convinced I was wrong. I screwed up, and a man went to prison."

He held up his hand. "Wait a minute. You're pretty impressive, but I've been a cop for a while. You made the initial report to Child Protective Services, right?"

She nodded, wishing she liked even a little sugar in her tea so that she'd have that to stir.

"Doesn't CPS have some responsibility too? What about the investigating officer? And then there's the mother. She needs to carry some of this weight. It was your job to make a report. You were a mandatory reporter. It wasn't your job to declare innocence or guilt." He reached across the table and laid his hand over hers. "Give yourself a break. You're not God."

"Ouch." She cringed.

"I know. My brother gave me this same talk a couple of years ago." He squeezed her hand, then looked down at it, seemingly shocked to find their fingers intertwined. He pulled back. "I'm sorry. That was very presumptuous of me.

You obviously know how I feel about you, but I shouldn't have crossed that line."

"How you feel about me?" Her heart thundered. "What do you mean?"

"Well." His face flushed. "I like you . . . a lot."

Brianne felt her eyes start to burn. She couldn't cry. No one cried when a handsome man told her that he liked her. She blinked hard, begging them not to spill over. What kind of fool would he think she was?

"And now I've totally put you on the spot. I'm sorry." He thunked his forehead with the heel of his palm. "Nice one. I hope I haven't ruined our friendship."

She grinned. In what dream could she have come up with Seth sitting across the table, thinking she wasn't interested in him? She'd had a crush on him for as long as she remembered knowing him. Brianne reached across the table and wove her fingers between his.

32

Emilia bent over, picked at another weed, then tossed it back to the ground. What was the point? She wasn't ever going to be one of those bring-home-the-bacon-fry-it-up-in-a-pan kind of women. When left to be the head of the household, she felt like her talents were limited to just getting by.

Tally flipped another page in her book. August 15. Summer break was into its final weeks, and for once, Emilia could send her daughter back to school knowing she'd completed the requested reading hours. With her back pressed up against the siding and her ankles crossed in front of her, Tally looked like the sweet girl Emilia knew was still in there.

"I love you, Tally." Emilia curled her lips inward.

She looked up from her story, eyes narrowed as if she was evaluating her mother's words for errors. "Okay. Thanks."

Something thunked inside the house. They both turned toward the door as if the source would show itself.

Two more deep thumps; then they came in a rhythm. *Bang. Bang. Bang. Bang.*

Emilia jumped to her feet, her hand on her weapon out of training and habit. She threw the door open. *Bang. Bang. Bang.* "Roger?"

No answer. *Bang. Bang.* The hollow thumps continued, maintaining their beat. She followed the sound toward the bathroom, where it reverberated off the walls. The door wouldn't move. Something heavy held it shut. Emilia pounded on the door. "Roger? What's going on in there?"

Again, no answer.

"Tally. Call 911, then bring me a screwdriver." Emilia turned to her daughter. The color had faded in her face. "Hurry."

Bang. Bang. Bang.

"Roger, I'm here! We're getting help. Hold on." Emilia slid to the floor, one eye against the gap between the door and the linoleum. A foul smell and the jerking movements of her husband pushed her back. She could be losing him right now. No matter how many times she'd wondered if death wouldn't have been better, right now, she wasn't ready. "Stay with me, Roger. Hang in there. I'm coming around to the window."

Emilia jumped up and found Tally with a screwdriver in her shaking hand and a cell phone to her ear.

"Talk to him. I'm going to see if I can get in."

Tally dropped to her knees. "I'm here, Papa."

Emilia shook her head, dismissing her tears for action. She jogged through the house, grabbing the step stool as she ran through the kitchen. Outside, the hot sun scorched down on her as if in punishment. She pushed through brush, then edged along the narrow space between the side of their house and the weathered old fence that separated their property from the neighbors'.

At the window, Emilia attempted to balance the stool on the uneven ground. She climbed to the top step and popped the screen out of the way. The pounding had stopped, and Roger lay motionless in a pile on the unswept floor. Drool formed a ribbon from his mouth to his arm. His eyes were shut. Perspiration dripped along his brow.

Emilia took hold of the windowsill and launched herself

forward. Her belly landed hard on the edge of the windowsill, while her head and shoulders made it partially through the opening. The stool flew back, clanking into the fence. She shimmied and scooted, rough surfaces scraping at her skin, until she got both arms and her chest through the tight opening.

Sirens blared in the distance, but she couldn't take time to evaluate how far away they were. Emilia hung forward, her fingers catching hold of the counter, and pulled herself through, her legs crashing down on the toilet.

Without missing a beat, she crawled to his side. "I'm here, Roger. Stay with me."

There was no response.

Voices boomed through the house, followed by Tally's cries of relief.

"We're in here!" Emilia yelled. She threaded her arms under her husband's and slid him away from the door.

Paramedics squeezed into the tiny room, and life went blurry. Beeps and thumps. Orders called out. Someone helped Emilia from the bathroom. Someone checked her leg, where blood flowed freely. Then they put her husband in the back of the ambulance, and he was gone.

33

I'm calling in Aunt Maria." Emilia slid her cell from her pocket and scrolled through the contacts.

Tally groaned. "Why? I'm not a little girl. I can handle myself. Besides, Maria is far less mature than I am."

She was probably right about the last part, but Emilia knew the dangers that lurked in the shadows of West Crow, and Tally was balancing on the line. One wrong move, and her daughter could be in trouble. She wouldn't be the first officer to have a kid frequent the court. "I'm calling her." Emilia pressed the call button.

"Long time no talk, sis." Maria sounded like she'd just gotten out of bed.

"Hey. Roger is in the hospital. It's getting late. Can you help me out? I need you to come get Tally and take her home."

Tally rolled her eyes.

"Seriously? What's going on with him now?"

Emilia willed herself to ignore Maria's tone. "Can you do it?"

"Sure. I'll see if I can borrow Trevor's car. I can be there in a couple hours. At the house?"

"Come get Tally at the hospital."

"Got it." Maria yawned, then disconnected.

"I can't believe you hate me this much." Tally crossed her arms, her jaw tight. "You treat me like I'm a useless baby."

If only Emilia could go back to Tally's baby days. What she thought was tough then was nothing compared to now.

Emilia walked to the door of the private family waiting room. How long would it take to get some answers? Her mind drifted back to that night fifteen months earlier. She'd gotten the call and rushed to the hospital after dropping Tally at the neighbors' house. That night had stretched on, leading to weeks in the hospital followed by a rehab facility. And just when she thought her husband was coming back, Roger had started drifting further and further away, until she now lived with a complete stranger.

How could this night be any worse than that one?

He could die.

The possibility was just as strong now as it had been then. At any minute, a doctor could come around the corner, a somber look on his face, and declare Emilia a widow.

Would that be worse or better than the way they'd been living?

Emilia pressed her palms into her face. She was a monster. That was the only explanation for a wife who wondered if she and her husband would be better off if he died. How would she ever be able to forgive herself if he did?

The grim-faced doctor entered and walked toward her, and Tally's hand slipped into Emilia's.

"Mrs. Cruz, I'm Dr. Harrison." His eyes were deep with sympathy. "This must have been a horrible scare for both of you." He motioned to a set of chairs.

They sat, Emilia's gaze never leaving the doctor's mouth. Her profiling gifts didn't always come in handy. "What's happening?"

"We have Roger stabilized. And we're running tests. I've also made a call to a specialist who will be consulting on this case." Dr. Harrison laced his fingers together. "Roger has been through a lot this year. I'm afraid it looks like we may have another battle to fight with him. I want you both to take good care of yourselves. He's going to need you."

JUDGMENT CAME IN many flavors. The judgment of the court was just the vanilla. There was public judgment, like the recent letter to the editor calling for Caleb to be fired, and the hidden kind that found its spice in whispered secrets and exaggerated rumors. Addison had grown full of all of it.

Had no one in this town ever made a mistake?

She should have let Brianne come along like she'd offered, but taking her up on it felt like failure of another kind. It was Addison's job to keep her family on track, to keep them from sinking into the darkness. She had to stay strong.

"Come on, Mom." Hannah tugged at her arm. "I want to see if Tally is here."

They took those first steps into West Crow Middle School, a place that, by definition, would leave her daughter with scars under the best of circumstances.

Addison shivered as she remembered her own eighth-grade year. She was sure she'd fallen in love with a boy who played the trumpet and who had hair that floated on the wind when he ran. Her heart raced and her palms sweated. At home, she wrote her name with his last name over and over, until she mastered her future signature. Her hopes had all come crashing down during lunch in the cafeteria. The girl she thought was her best friend told the boy, and the boy stuck his finger deep into his mouth, miming his need to vomit at the thought of the two of them together.

If that had been the only humiliation, maybe she wouldn't have such fear for her daughter now. On top of the normal drama, Hannah was the new girl—the one whose father had just been arrested.

They followed signs directing them down the hall and turned into the gym for registration. Where the halls had been calm, the gymnasium was buzzing. Teachers were stationed along the wall, with lines of students and parents in front of each of them. In the middle, another table was set up with a *Start Here* sign.

Addison and Hannah did as the other sheep, stepping into the line. Eventually they reached the front of the short line, where a rounded older woman with tight curls and a welcoming smile asked for Hannah's name.

"Hannah Kilbourn," Addison said.

A gasp turned Addison and Hannah around.

The woman behind her, blond and too tan, put her hand over her mouth. "Sorry. I just remembered something." Her eyebrows twitched.

Prickles dotted Addison's arms and legs. She'd just witnessed one of the worst liars in the state, and the woman didn't appear to have an ounce of regret. She was starting the year with a thirty-something middle schooler to contend with.

The woman behind the desk tapped Addison's arm with a stack of papers.

"Oh, thank you." Her voice shook.

"This is very simple. Read over the schedule. We already have Hannah in our system, and her school records have been transferred. We did our best to anticipate which classes she would like, but kids this age are hard to predict." She winked at Hannah. "If you don't like your classes, look through what's offered during that time slot and request a change with the counselor. And take some time to meet the teachers. It's going to be a great year." Her smile was like a reassuring hug.

"Thank you." Addison held one hand to her chest.

"It's my pleasure. Caleb spoke so highly of you all. I'm glad we finally get to have one of your kids in our school. Call me at the office if you have any questions."

Addison took her first deep breath of the day. "Thank you. That means a lot." Addison waved good-bye as the woman next in line let out another exaggerated sigh.

"There she is." Hannah pointed to a slender girl with straight dark hair and hurried over to her. The pair thrust their schedules toward each other, then got down to the business of comparing.

All that worry about Hannah withdrawing from others and not finding a friend—what a waste of time that had been. Worry wasn't the answer. Addison knew that. Taking control and deliberate action, those were the qualities she needed to employ now more than ever. "You must be Tally." Addison pasted on her best fun-mom smile.

Tally nodded. "Nice to meet you."

The girl had good taste in friends and manners. Perfect. "Is your mother here?" Addison looked around as if she could spot a woman she'd never seen before.

Tally's smile faded. "No. My dad's in the hospital. My aunt Maria is here instead. She's staying until . . ." Tally pointed at a woman leaning on the wall of the gymnasium, her gaze glued to her cell phone and her long red nails texting at breakneck speed.

"I'm so sorry, Tally. Please let us know if there's anything we can do to help." Addison's heart ached. No wonder she and Hannah were connecting. They were both in the middle of family trauma.

"Thank you."

"How about a playdate at our farm? I can pick you up and bring you home."

Hannah rolled her eyes. "Seriously, Mom. We're in middle school. We don't have playdates."

"Okay." Addison reached to brush Hannah's hair away from

her face but caught herself just in time. *Bad choice.* "Tally, would you like to come over tomorrow and *hang*?" She cocked a hip.

"I'd love that. Let me check with my aunt." She trotted over to the woman and tapped her arm to get her attention.

A moment later, the aunt waved their way and nodded, her bright lips a red that matched her nails.

Tally returned. "She said tomorrow would be fine. Hannah knows where I live."

"That sounds perfect." Addison would make a meal for Tally to take home with her, offer to help with back-to-school shopping, whatever they needed.

Then she remembered the attorney appointments. The hearing coming up. The money it would cost to defend her husband for a crime he very well might have committed. She'd do it all. Somehow.

EMILIA STARED AT Roger's closed eyes. They had hardly opened since he'd been admitted to the hospital. And when he did seem somewhat conscious, he was impossible to understand and didn't appear to know where he was. She needed one last chance to tell him that she loved him, that he'd made a difference in her life and in Tally's, that she wouldn't trade any of their days together, not even considering the hardships they'd faced.

With every moment that ticked by, she felt like her chances of ever having a conversation again with her husband were slipping away. Her last memories with him would be covered with the bitterness she'd allowed to invade their home. She was guilty, and she wouldn't get a chance to be forgiven.

A tap on the door startled her.

Dr. Harrison stepped in. "Good morning, Emilia. Did you get home to sleep last night?"

She shook her head. How could she go when any minute could be his last?

The doctor walked to the head of Roger's bed and laid a hand on his shoulder. "Roger, it's Dr. Harrison. I'm going to go over your test results and the plan we've developed for your treatment. I know you're having a hard time waking up. That's to be expected, but I'll try to cover everything, so hopefully any questions you may have will be answered."

Emilia slid her hand into her husband's.

His fingers pulsed against hers. Whether the action was voluntary or not was something only God and Roger knew.

"So, after consulting with some specialists in Portland, we feel confident that Roger's aneurysm is a result of the original accident. The symptoms you've been describing tell us this problem has been coming on for a bit now, but it's reached a very serious point."

"Why didn't anyone notice this with all the scans he had? I don't understand." Emilia's heart hammered, its rhythm an echo in her ears.

"I wish it were that simple. It actually didn't exist then. Likely the wall of the artery was damaged in the initial accident, but the aneurysm formed much later."

Emilia grabbed the collar of her T-shirt with her free hand. She hadn't brought Roger in for the last follow-up appointment. *She'd* done this to her husband. An alcoholic had taken the first shot, but she'd finished the job.

"Are you okay?" Dr. Harrison came around the bed, his hand grasping her shoulder as the other took her elbow. He eased her into the chair at Roger's bedside. "Can you take a couple of deep breaths for me?"

Her lungs hardened, only allowing puffs of air while tears flushed her eyes. "Neither of us could deal with any more medical stuff. I needed a break from the paperwork and all of this, just for a little while." She covered her face with her hands.

"Emilia, the cost should be covered by his workers' comp. And if it isn't, the hospital will work this out with your personal insurance."

"No." Her voice shuddered. "I was so overwhelmed with everything . . . I didn't bring him in for the scan in June."

"Okay. I see the problem." He patted her shoulder like a grandfather would. "Emilia, even if you would have come in, I doubt this would have shown up. It's new. To the best of our knowledge, the aneurysm only formed over the last few weeks."

She lifted her face out of her hands, her breaths shaky. "What happens now?"

"Well, now we can try to correct the problem, or we can let it be. There's a choice to be made." His graying eyebrows pushed together.

"If we do nothing?"

"The nonoperative measure would be to do nothing. The mortality rate is about forty percent, and with what we know about the stage of Roger's condition, I believe it could be much higher. Left completely alone, the aneurysm will likely continue to enlarge and finally rupture, and Roger will pass away."

Fresh tears streamed down her cheeks. How could she have ever wanted this?

"But there is another alternative." The doctor patted Roger's leg. "We can go in and attempt to clip the aneurysm. It's risky too, but our odds of losing him go down to about twenty percent."

"One of five?" Her voice was a raspy whisper.

"That's right. This is your choice. But, Emilia, you need to make it soon." He dipped his head and closed his eyes for a few seconds as if he were praying.

That was exactly what Emilia needed to do.

34

Addison squinted into the brightly lit backyard where Hannah and Tally kicked a soccer ball back and forth. The light pinged off the nerves behind one eye, causing a pulsing above her left eyebrow.

"Mama, do you have a headache?" Lilly rubbed her little hand gently over the exposed skin on Addison's arm.

"Yes, baby, I do." She scooped the child into her embrace. The days she would still be able to carry her youngest were swiftly coming to an end. "Thank you for being such a caring girl."

Lilly placed a hand on either side of Addison's face. "Let me get you something for that." She wriggled out of her mother's arms and tiptoed to the junk drawer. Stretching her arm out, she maneuvered her fingers until they reached the farthest point in the back. She pulled out an acetaminophen bottle and tried the lid. "I can't get this."

Addison held out her hand. "How did you know there was medicine in the back of the drawer?"

"Grammy got it out for Daddy before he went to town."

Something clicked in Addison's brain. Caleb still wasn't cleared to drive. "When was this, Lilly?"

"Before his accident. His head hurt, so she told him to take it just in case."

Addison twisted the lid, lining up the arrows, and popped off the top. She dumped the contents into her palm. Five large oval-shaped tablets. She scooped them back into the container, then took down the bottle of prescribed medication that Caleb kept refusing. The bottle was light. When she opened it, a handful of round tablets spilled into her palm. These weren't the pain pills that had been here before. These were plain acetaminophen.

Nausea swept over her as her mouth went dry. "Caleb!" She shouted the name as if he'd come running. "Caleb, come in here!"

"Mama, what's wrong?" Lilly's hand grasped hers.

"Nothing. I just want to talk with Daddy. Can you take some soda out to the girls?"

Lilly froze.

"You can have a can too."

Her daughter might be curious, but she also knew better than to give up an opportunity for a pop. Lilly swung open the refrigerator door, retrieved three cans of Coke, and jogged out the back door.

Addison leaned over the sink, her stomach swaying. What did this mean for that night?

Caleb clomped into the kitchen, his walking cast sending nails through Addison's throbbing skull. Behind him, Connor carried a remote-control car and controller. "Did you just holler for me?" Her husband was out of breath, and sweat beaded along his temples.

"Yes. Connor, can you head outside?"

He peered out the back door. "Hey, the girls have pop."

"Get one and go, please." She heard the demand in her voice, but this wasn't the time to berate herself for a parenting fail. She could do that later.

He threw open the fridge and grabbed a can. "Whatever." He tossed the word back at her as he left the kitchen, leaving a wave of guilt behind.

"What in the world is going on?"

She slapped both bottles into his hand, then turned back to the sink, pulling up the faucet until cold water cascaded into the basin. She cupped her hands, filling them with the icy liquid from the deep well and splashing it across her face.

"What's this?"

"Open them." Addison repeated her procedure with the water.

"I don't understand."

She grabbed a kitchen towel and blotted it along her face.

Caleb set the bottles next to each other on the counter. "What am I supposed to be getting from this?"

She rolled her eyes. "That's the oxy the doctor prescribed you." She pointed to the brown bottle. "Except it's not. The pills in there have been replaced with acetaminophen."

"Why would anyone do that?" He lifted it up, reading the label. "Where did they go? Did one of the kids—" His face paled.

Addison shook her head. "The other bottle came from the drawer. It's where you got the oxy the night of the accident."

"You know I don't take that stuff." His voice grew demanding. "I'm telling you, I don't know why the police think I took it. I didn't, and I would think my own wife would believe me."

"Don't you dare turn this on me." Her jaw throbbed with tension. "You are the one with missing hours, positive drug tests, and a manslaughter charge."

Caleb slammed his fist down on the counter. "I don't use oxy."

Addison shook her head and leveled her gaze at her husband. "But your mother does."

Caleb took three steps back and collapsed into a kitchen chair. His fingers formed a tent against his mouth.

"Lilly told me Caroline gave you some pills from this bottle the night of the accident. You took them with you."

"Oh no. But that's not acetaminophen." He ducked his head and covered it with his arms.

"You need to face it. Your mom has a problem." Addison touched his shoulder. "It's been a hard year. She misses your dad, but she's not one to talk about her grief. Maybe this is how she's dealing with the loss."

"I hear you." He sat up and pulled her into his arms. "But I just can't believe Mom could be an addict."

"Either way, you need to take this to your attorney."

"It would humiliate her. And how does this bring Georgianna Bosch back to life?" He rubbed at the base of his neck.

"It doesn't, but it might keep you with your family."

"I doubt it." He shook his head. "I need time to think. Just give me some time, okay?" Caleb limped from the room.

Time was one of the many things they no longer had.

THE CELL PHONE was cold in Emilia's hand. "Maria, I need to talk with Tally. Could you bring her to the hospital?" She tapped her fingers along the bedside table. Roger was waking more frequently, though the doctor was keeping him on morphine to reduce the pain of his headaches. She'd decided to go forward with the surgery, but first Tally needed a chance to see him for what could be the last time.

"Hey, sis. Yes, I'm doing well. Thanks for asking." Maria's words smacked as if she had a mouth full of gum.

"Knock it off. Roger's situation is serious. I need Tally here." She turned away from her husband and walked into the hallway. "He's going into surgery soon. There's a twenty-percent chance he won't make it through."

There was a momentary silence, then "I'm sorry to hear that. Roger was always decent to me."

"Could you put Tally on the line, please?" Her pride had

sent her to her sister for help instead of asking one of the neighbors or any of their old friends. If pride went before a fall, Maria was like diving off the edge of the Grand Canyon.

"She's not actually here."

"Okay. Where is she?" Emilia rested her head on the wall. Behind her, the nurses' station beeped and hummed with constant monitoring and movement.

"I'm not sure exactly. She went to a friend's house."

"What friend?" The answer had better not be Cami. If Tally missed seeing Roger for the last time because of Maria, that would be the last straw.

"I don't remember. It's not like she's a baby. The mom picked her up this morning. She said she'd bring her back this afternoon."

Emilia glanced at her watch. Lunchtime. She should eat, but that could wait until after Roger was in surgery.

"The friend's a new kid she met at soccer camp. See, I was paying attention. And the mother drives a green minivan with one of those ridiculous stick-figure family bumper stickers."

Alarm shot through Emilia's system. "How many children?"

"What?"

"I said, how many children? How many on the bumper sticker?" Emilia caught a warning glare from one of the nurses, so she stepped a few paces closer to the elevator.

"I think it was three, and the dad had a basketball. Do you want me to remember the license plate too?" Maria huffed. "I'm your sister, not your babysitter or one of your work buddies. Tally went to a friend's house. What's the big deal?"

Emilia ground her molars together and punched the down button for the elevator. "You want to know what the big deal is? That car belongs to the wife of a guy I arrested for vehicular manslaughter. You let Tally go to his house! And I have to leave my husband, who may have only a few more hours to live, in order to get my daughter and bring her back to say good-bye!" She pulled the phone away from her ear and tapped the end icon so hard, the tip of her finger ached.

How was it possible for any human being to be so thoughtless?

The elevator door slid open. Emilia stepped inside to wordless eighties tunes and gripped the railing as if it were the only thing that could possibly keep her safe. When the elevator finally hit the bottom floor, a bell dinged and she was released.

Emilia called Tally as she jogged to the parking lot, found her car, and hopped in. Her call went to voice mail. The sun had heated the seats to scorching, and her thighs felt the burn even through her denim jeans. She flipped on the air conditioner to full blast, a tiny stream in comparison to any other car made after 1975, and took off toward the farm where she'd recently arrested Caleb Kilbourn.

How would this family treat her daughter when they found out who she was? Or did they already know? Were they using Tally to get Emilia to back off? A new friend who wasn't a troublemaker—why was that too much to ask for?

Pavement turned into gravel, and dust billowed out behind the little Honda, but Emilia didn't slow down, even as the road became deeply rutted. She held tightly with both hands, willing the car to stay steady on the road.

In a split second, she spotted a boy on a bicycle and slammed on her brakes. The sedan skidded sideways, turning as the gravel carried the locked-up tires. When she came to a stop, the air was dense with dust. Emilia's heart pounded. Had she hit him?

She popped open the door, waving her hand in front of her face until the air cleared enough to see the bicycle riding away from her. She'd missed him. By some power, the grace of God maybe, she'd missed hitting the kid.

Emilia's heart pounded, and her head swam. She could have

killed someone's son because she wasn't paying attention. She could have been one of the people she sought to condemn.

And it only took a second.

Tears welled in her eyes. This was all too much. Didn't everyone have a breaking point? What if she was hitting hers?

Tally would need someone who had it together. But Emilia was no longer sure she could be that person. A tear ran down her cheek. She wiped it away. "Why, God? Haven't we been through enough? Don't take Roger now."

She climbed back into the car, her nose running and tears flowing as fast as a river. She pressed her palms into her eyes, forcing herself to gain control. The boy on the bike was fine. He had gone on like nothing had even happened. She couldn't let this get to her, but it was. She could have killed him.

Emilia's arms ached. She turned the car around and continued toward the house at the end of a long lane, the one she'd been to in the name of justice. She pulled up the collar of her T-shirt and wiped her face with rough motions, then turned off the engine.

The scent of jasmine filled the air, and a light breeze filtered through the leaves on the willow tree in front of the house. There was a peace she hadn't noticed before and didn't expect to find at a defendant's residence, like life kept going, and everything that happened here didn't revolve around Georgianna Bosch's death. There should be a shroud over the farm, a darkness that hovered like a low cloud, but the sky was clear and birds sang in the trees.

Emilia took the three steps to the front porch and knocked on the door. Her confidence suffered a hit without her uniform, leaving her with the nerves of a middle schooler as she waited for Addison Kilbourn to answer.

Time ticked by. Time Emilia didn't have to waste.

She knocked again, this time louder.

The door creaked open. "Sorry. It takes me a while to get

across the house." Caleb Kilbourn raked his hand through his hair. He smiled at her until the realization of who she was hit him.

She watched the man's friendly expression grow serious and distant. Cold washed over her skin.

"How can I help you?" The smile had melted into a deep frown. The greeting was surely meant to acknowledge the person on the other side of the door more than to display his actual feelings.

"My daughter." Those tears she'd been fighting chose an awful time to return. Emilia blinked hard, avoiding eye contact. "She's here with your daughter. I need to pick her up."

"Tally is your daughter?"

She nodded, looking over her shoulder as if there was something there that demanded her attention. "Could you get her, please? I'm in a hurry." She tapped her foot on the wood decking.

"She's not here. My wife took the girls to pick up school supplies on the way to take Tally home. She thought it might help you out."

Emilia swung around. "I don't need your help. Nothing your wife does for my daughter will change your legal situation. Do you understand?"

He held up his hands. "I didn't even know she was your kid until I answered the door. Honest."

How could she believe him? This was the man who'd told her over and over again that he did not and had not used prescription drugs, yet two blood tests showed a very different story. She tried Tally's cell again, but it went right to voice mail. Probably a dead battery. Emilia jogged down the steps. "Can you get ahold of your wife and have her drop Tally at the hospital? It's important."

"I'll call her right now. I'm sorry about your husband."

She didn't turn back. He didn't deserve her thanks.

35

Addison eyed the register belt stacked with school supplies for four children. It looked like she was starting her own district.

The scanner beeped like the monitor on Caleb's heart had that first day in the hospital. She'd begged God to let him live. She'd pleaded for the life of her husband and the father of her children. And God had granted her his nearly full recovery. For what? Caleb still claimed he didn't remember a thing from that night or the days before. And he certainly wasn't ready to make the leap to his mother having a drug problem, though he'd agreed to have a conversation with Caroline that night.

Beep, beep, beep.

Addison rubbed at her temples. She'd grabbed the kids and left the house without her supply lists with the items they already owned carefully marked off. The result was a very expensive escape from a certain fight.

"Mom." Lilly tugged at her arm. "Can I get an L.O.L. Surprise doll? All the other girls will have them at my new school, and I'll be the only one without." She tipped her head as far back as it could go, her mouth open in a silent beg.

"No. Those are the most ridiculous toys ever. I'm not spending another cent today." As Addison shoved her credit card into the slot, her phone rang out Caleb's ringtone. She silenced it and pasted a smile on her face.

The checker sighed as she put the last binder in the bag. "It's a spendy time of year." She punched a few keys and waited. The smile faded. "Let's try this again. Can you take your card out of the reader?"

The second try wasn't any better. She made the mistake of glancing Hannah's way and caught her thirteen-year-old's horrified expression. Addison's neck burned as she retrieved their debit card and tried that.

The debit card saved the day, or at least it got them free to leave the store.

Before they could reach the freedom of the parking lot, her phone began to buzz again. "You four take this stuff to the car. I'll be right with you." She unhooked her keys from her purse and handed them to Hannah, then gave the cart over to Connor. "Watch Lilly."

"Ugh, Mom." Lilly put her hands on her hips. "I'm not a little baby."

Addison answered the phone. "What? If you're calling to apologize for questioning me about what should be obvious to you and anyone with a clear mind, I'm not ready to hear it yet."

"Well then, you won't have any argument with why I'm calling. Something happened. Tally's mother came by."

Addison covered her mouth with her hand, then brushed it through her hair. "Did something happen to Tally's dad?"

"I don't know. I assume so, but there's another issue. Tally's mom is Deputy Cruz. How did you not know that?"

Addison choked on her breath. "What?"

"You heard me right. You brought home my arresting officer's daughter. Didn't you find out anything about that girl before bringing her to our home?"

"Stop right there." She caught the looks of a couple of shoppers and lowered her voice. "I don't think you have the right to question my parenting right now."

"Whatever. She wants you to drop Tally off at the hospital." He blew out a breath so strong, it sounded like a hurricane. "Hey, let's not do this, okay?"

"Whatever." Addison ended the call and stuffed the phone into the bottom of her purse.

BRIANNE STOOD AT the counter in the county courthouse clerk's office. All around her, cherry-stained wood was polished to a shine. Though the room was in the basement, light shone through the shallow windows near the top of the far wall, competing with the electric glare of overhead fluorescent lighting.

Two women worked at computers along that wall. Both looked as if they'd stepped out of a women's magazine from the seventies. Neither acknowledged her presence.

Brianne cleared her throat, but they might as well have been holograms.

"Excuse me." Brianne leaned over the counter. "Could I ask a question?"

The woman closest to her turned her chin but kept her gaze on the screen. Her mahogany hair was pulled into a bun in the back, while the top pouffed out like a show poodle's mane. "What do you need?"

"I'd like access to some court records. I was told I could get those here."

"Fill out the form on the counter and drop it in the box. You'll get a call when the documents are available."

"Yes, I have the form." Brianne held up the clipboard. "But I don't have the case number. Is that necessary?"

The woman blew out a sigh. She clicked around with her mouse. "What's the name and the date of the trial?"

"I don't have the exact date, but it was April of 2015 and the defendant had the last name Tanger."

The woman's head turned. She dropped her computer glasses down to the tip of her nose, examining Brianne. "Get ready. I'm going to read you the number."

Brianne waved her pen in the air.

"It's case number 1548695. Drop your form in the box. We'll get back to you." She shifted away, ending the conversation.

The form slipped out of Brianne's fingers and into a locked box, where she couldn't retrieve it if she'd wanted to. At least that was done. In a few days—or possibly decades by the look of that office—she'd have the details of what went on in the trial. Then she'd know—or at least she felt that she'd know—what had really happened and if she was guilty of putting an innocent man in prison.

Brianne scrolled through social media as she entered the hallway, desperately looking for a distraction from her own worries. All of her high-school friends seemed to be having babies. Tons of babies. And they were busily documenting every single new tooth, taste of food, and haircut as if they were raising royalty.

A few posts down and there was a new one, fresh from the womb. Bethany Sawyer's baby looked like something from a horror movie, but the comments below his squished newborn face were all about how lovely, handsome, and precious he was. Did the entire country need glasses?

Someone grabbed her arm, and Brianne threw the phone in the air and lunged back.

Seth snagged it just before it would have hit the wall. "Whoa. What's going on in your head?"

"Um . . . babies."

He took a step back.

"No, not like I want one. Kind of the opposite. I think I need new Facebook friends who post something other than wedding and baby pictures." Her heart resumed a somewhat normal rhythm.

"But you're not morally opposed to those things, right?" His gaze studied her in a way that made her feel as if she were on trial.

"Not morally opposed. Just not in a huge hurry, that's all." Her mother asked each week on their Sunday afternoon phone call if she'd met anyone, as though the one goal a woman should have was to find a husband and reproduce. She'd managed to keep this thing she and Seth had to herself, but how long would it be until small-town gossip reached Arizona? "What about you? Are you in a rush to have those things?"

"Not a rush, but I don't see any good reason to drag out dating and engagement if you've found the right person. Is that what you mean?" His pinky finger grazed hers.

Brianne swallowed. "I guess not. I don't know."

"Then we'll have fun figuring it all out together." He placed a soft kiss on her forehead.

The room dipped and turned as she took a long look at his blue-green eyes. If anyone could get her to change her mind, it would be Seth.

"We're going to have to take him to pre-op in the next ten minutes." The nurse tucked the bedding under Roger. "I'll be back."

"Thank you." Emilia grasped her husband's hand. "I'm sure Tally will be here any minute."

Roger nodded, his eyes narrow slits. "Tell her . . . tell her I love her. And I love you." He licked at his dry lips.

A tear—how there could be any more she didn't know—ran down Emilia's cheek and landed on Roger's forearm. "I should have been a better wife. I really messed up the *in sickness and in health* thing."

Half of his mouth curled up in an attempted smile. "You're perfect."

"Mom?" Tally stood in the doorway, a woman beside her with a hand on Tally's shoulder.

Emilia motioned her daughter toward her.

"What happened? Is Papa okay?" She took one hesitant step forward.

"Papa has an aneurysm. It's a problem from the accident. They need to go in and fix it."

"Just a simple surgery?"

Emilia's lungs hardened. "No."

The tan tone of Tally's skin turned pink.

Standing, Emilia reached her arms out to her daughter, who fell into them, silent sobs jarring her shoulders. "I wanted you to get here before they took him. You just made it."

Tally pulled her head back. "Can I talk to Papa alone?"

Emilia rubbed a hand over her daughter's hair. "Of course." She went to Roger and kissed his forehead. "I'll see you as soon as they let me. I love you."

"You too, sweets."

Emilia's vision blurred. He hadn't called her that since the morning of that last fire. Was it a good sign or a bad one? *Lord, let it be good.* She walked away, keeping that prayer on her breath and in her heart.

"I wanted to tell you I'm really sorry about what you're going through, and I'm sorry about not realizing Tally's your daughter."

Emilia's head shot up. Kilbourn's wife. She'd barely registered her in the room. Now in the hall, it felt as if they were chained together. "Thanks for getting her here."

The woman handed Emilia three plastic bags. "These are Tally's school supplies."

Emilia stared down at the binders, pencils, and folders. "You didn't need to do this."

"I wanted to. I know what it's like to have a hard time." She turned to leave, then came back. "Listen . . . we really like Tally, and Hannah is new in the district. Please don't punish Hannah for whatever happened with Caleb. It's not her fault. I really don't want the girls to pay the price here."

Emilia nodded. "We'll see."

"I'll be praying for your husband."

For a moment, Emilia almost offered to pray for this woman's husband in return.

Almost.

36

A horn honked in the front of the house. Caroline wiped her hands on the kitchen towel, grabbed her Bible, and shuffled toward the front door. "That's my ride. Don't wait up for me. You know how wild the church choir can get after practice." She slapped the side of her leg.

"See you, Mom. Don't get into too much trouble." Caleb reclined on the sofa, a soda in one hand and the remote in the other.

"Where's the fun in that?" She shut the door and hollered something at the woman waiting in a Suburban.

Addison gave Caleb a frustrated look. Their little talk with Caroline had come to an end with Caroline denying any knowledge of the medication. Didn't she understand how serious this was?

A moment later, the SUV crunched down the driveway.

Hannah was in her room, probably reading. Lilly had fallen asleep right after dinner, and Connor was glued to the game on the television alongside his dad. Caroline's absence left Addison free to do what she'd been planning since her lunchtime discovery. She pulled open the junk drawer, giving each item a look. The pain-reliever bottle was gone, but she wasn't surprised about that.

Addison proceeded to rifle through every drawer and cupboard, coming up with no additional evidence to justify her suspicions. In the pantry, she found toy soldiers lined up on a back shelf, covered in a thick layer of dust.

"I know what you're doing," Caleb called from the living room.

Fine. It wasn't a secret. At least it wasn't something she should have to hide from him. If he had his head on right, he'd be in here helping. The concussion seemed to cement him on the path of denial.

Addison went through each shelf in the hall closet. She shuffled through the bill basket, which jogged her memory of what had happened earlier at the store.

At the top of the stairs, she turned left and entered the room she and Caleb shared. She'd set up a mini workstation at his old desk. On the corner was a file she put their personal bills into when she sorted the mail. Since the very beginning of their marriage, Caleb had been in charge of the finances. In a way, giving over this little bit of control had helped Addison to trust him.

Addison pulled the file from its holder and laid it open on the desktop. Two bills from the credit card company. Caleb hadn't even opened them. Was she supposed to take on this job now too? Since he seemed to have no intention of fighting for his freedom, maybe it was his way of transitioning her to single parenthood.

She ripped open the envelope with the newest postmark. Red letters stared back at her as if making a public accusation. Addison was failing. Even the marriage she thought was rock solid had cracks running across the surface.

Growing tension ached across her shoulders and upper back. She hadn't worked outside the home since Hannah was a baby. How would she support her kids, especially with the added burden of a substance-using grandmother? She couldn't leave Caroline alone with them.

Addison flipped to the detailed list of purchases. They'd have to cut back now, get used to living on a strict budget. She ran her finger down the list, evaluating each line with the eye of an accountant. After ripping open the other envelope, she did the same.

Her finger paused on a place she didn't recognize: Virtue. There was a twenty-two dollar charge there. Maybe it was a mistake. She punched the name into her phone's search. Virtue was a restaurant in Darlington, a nice one by the looks of it. It was the kind of place she and Caleb would only visit on special anniversaries, racking up a bill much higher than twenty-two dollars.

She went back to the bill and checked the date so she could refer to it when she contacted the credit card company. June 12. Addison lowered herself into the hard resin chair. This was the missing piece, the place Caleb had gone the night of the accident. She dropped the phone and the papers onto the desk and wrapped her arms around her body. Virtue wasn't the kind of restaurant where you met a buddy to catch up. It was the kind of place you met a woman and, by the size of the bill, left before the main course.

THE CLOCK TICKED so loudly in the waiting room, Emilia wanted to rip it off the wall and crush it under her foot. Each tiny click made time move slower and Roger's surgery last longer. What were they doing in there? She lifted Tally's head off her lap and laid it on her folded sweat shirt. Stress always put her daughter out while it kept Emilia from sleeping at all.

The doctor had said two hours. Two and a half had ticked away on the horrible clock. How hard could it be to cut a hole and attach a clip? Aside from the risk of death, brain surgery didn't look like that big of a deal when she'd Googled it. *Right. No big deal.*

Emilia poured a cup of coffee into a Styrofoam cup about a quarter of the size she'd typically use. She took a sip. It burned with both heat and acid.

"It's better to stay away from that stuff."

Emilia turned toward the woman who'd sat quietly in the corner knitting for at least an hour. "Sounds like you've been here before."

"Many times." She lowered the blanket she worked on to her lap. "My husband has brain cancer."

"I'm so sorry." Emilia swallowed the sour taste in her mouth.

"Don't be. He's a fighter and a man of faith. If the Lord takes him, I'll see him again when my own time comes."

Emilia dumped the coffee into the sink and tossed the cup in the trash. "You make it sound so simple."

"It is and it isn't." A tear twinkled in her eye. "I've been married to that man for forty-seven years. We raised five kids together and weathered all sorts of storms. I can't imagine life without him, and I really don't want to, but I know better than to question God's timing."

Emilia's jaw twitched.

"Have a seat here." She patted the other side of the couch. "I'm Ginger. My mother wanted a redhead, like her side of the family." Ginger brushed a hand through her salt-and-pepper hair. "I take after my Italian dad."

There was something about Ginger that made Emilia want to obey, while at the same time, she ached to fight against this woman's resolve to accept whatever came her way. She eased into her seat, gripping a pillow in her lap. "I'm Emilia. Tally over there is my daughter."

"What brings you here, Emilia?"

"My husband, Roger. He has an aneurysm."

"That must be frightening. How are you doing with that?" Ginger touched Emilia's hand.

"I'm . . . I'm doing okay." Muscles constricted across her chest. "We've been here before. Roger was in an accident over a year ago while fighting a fire."

Ginger nodded her head. "I think I remember reading about that. Praise God, he survived."

Emilia clutched at her neck. Had he survived? Really? Her head grew heavy. "Maybe. He wasn't the same after." A warm hand rubbed circles on Emilia's back. "I miss him."

"Sounds like you've been grieving and caregiving at the same time. That's a lot to carry on your own."

Grieving. Maybe that's why she'd wondered if they would have been better off if Roger had died. At least then, the world would give her permission to grieve the loss of her husband rather than force her to pretend to be grateful for the outward shell that remained.

Ginger pulled Emilia into her arms, where Emilia's tears flowed once more. She'd lost her edge and turned into an endless storm cloud. Emilia hadn't even cried the night of the accident. She'd held it together for her husband and her daughter. This last battle was too much for her to fight alone.

"Emilia, give it all to God. He can handle your disappointment, your grief, and your anger. You can't. It will sour you from the inside out if you don't let it go."

For the first time in months, Emilia found herself longing for the fellowship, comfort, and surrender that she found in church.

She sat partway up, wiping her face on her sleeves. She nodded. It *was* killing her.

Through the blur of her tears, Emilia recognized Dr. Harrison standing in the doorway.

Emilia and Tally walked alongside Roger's bed as they wheeled him to his room from recovery. His head was covered in bandages, and his eyes remained still and closed. The pink that usually colored his cheeks had faded to an orangish hue under dark-circled eyes.

Once inside, the nurse reattached his monitors, filling the room with the comfort of his steady heart rhythms. "He should be more aware within the next hour or two. They've still got him on quite a bit of pain medication, but we'll be cutting that back soon." She patted Roger's leg. "You did great, Roger. I'll be in to check on you." She looked to Emilia. "Press the call button if you need anything."

Tally hovered in the corner.

Emilia motioned her to the side of the bed. "He's going to be all right."

Two steps closer, Tally stalled again. "What does 'all right' mean? Will he be like he was last week or before the fire?"

Emilia's shoulders drooped. Tension had tightened her muscles as she worked to keep that same question pushed down. There was painful relief as Tally took the fear out of the darkness and gave it words. "Tally, I just don't know. Probably better than last week, but not as good as before."

"What happened last week?"

They both turned to the bed.

Roger blinked and cringed as if the simple act brought back the searing migraines.

"Nothing. We were just waiting for you to wake up. How are you feeling?" Emilia touched her hand to his arm.

"There was a fire. Did everyone get out?"

Emilia nodded. "Are you talking about the fire on Fernridge?"

"Of course. What happened?"

"You saved the child, then went back in. A beam fell on you."

"That explains this headache." He slowly reached a hand to the side of his head, running his fingers over the bandage.

"Papa, it was—"

Emilia held up her hand to stop her daughter's flow of words. "Let me tell the nurse that you're awake. They'll want to check on you."

He grasped her hand and gently tugged her toward him, kissing her lips. "I love you, sweets."

She stood, pulling away. "I love you too. Tally, keep an eye on your papa. I'll be right back. The nurse will want to see how he's doing after such a terrible accident."

Tally's eyes were wide, but she nodded, having understood the hidden meaning: *Do not tell him about the last fifteen months.*

"Come over here, kid." Roger took a deep breath. "You're growing up too fast." He held Tally's hand, and his eyes drifted closed.

Emilia eased out of the room and sucked in deep gasps of breath. Her chest tightened with each hammer of her heart. Roger had been in there. The real man, instead of the imitation she'd lived with for over a year. Her legs were weak as she fought back tears. Something told her this might not be permanent. She had to get back to him quickly and take in every bit of him while he was here.

Emilia sped to the nurses' station. They hummed around like worker bees in a hive, no one noticing her until she waved a hand and cleared her throat.

"Mrs. Cruz. Is Roger waking up?" The night shift nurse tucked her long braid under her collar and rose from where she'd been typing away at a computer station.

"He is, but something is . . . weird."

Her eyes went wide. "Let's take a look. His vitals on the monitor have been steady, but I don't want to miss anything."

Emilia touched her arm as the much taller woman rounded the desk. "He doesn't seem to remember the time between the accident fifteen months ago and now. Is that normal?"

The nurse paused before speaking. "Well, these delayed aneurysms are extremely rare. I don't think we have a normal in this situation. I'll call in Dr. Harrison and see if he can come take a look."

Emilia gazed back at the closed door of room 214. If she could keep even a tiny bit of the man she'd lost, she'd praise God every day for the rest of her life. But what if she lost him again? Would God be in that too?

Brianne and Seth held back while the crowd made its way from the sanctuary to the foyer. On the way out, Tawny tipped her head toward another woman and said something. Then they both looked back toward Brianne. There was no stopping the talk now that they'd made the move to sit together at church.

"Did you see that?" Brianne discreetly pointed Tawny's way.

"What?"

"They're talking about us."

A smile crooked one of Seth's cheeks. "So. Am I too embarrassing to be seen with in public?" He mocked shock.

"Cute. No, I just don't like people talking about me."

"Maybe they were talking about me. Some people have called me awkwardly handsome." He straightened his collar and winked.

"I think I'm the awkward and you're the handsome. I bet that's exactly what they're saying. 'How did she get him to sit with her?'"

"Brianne, that's a lot of pronouns. Who cares what they're saying? I'm thrilled that people know we're whatever it is we are. I love spending time with you. You're gorgeous, kind, and you've got the biggest heart. And . . . you're just weird enough that I feel comfortable with you."

She nudged him with her elbow. "Weird, huh?"

"Oh, watch out." He grabbed her by the shoulders and turned her body toward the platform. "I think that sound guy is planning our wedding music."

She shook her head. "You think you're so funny."

His grin grew, lighting his eyes.

Addison walked up the aisle toward them. "I guess this relationship is public now."

Brianne covered her face with her hands. "See. Addison understands."

"I think it's wonderful." Addison wrapped her arm around Brianne's shoulders and looked at Seth. "You better be good to her. She's a treasure."

"I fully agree." Seth took one of Brianne's hands, pulling it away from her face. "She's amazing."

"Any chance this amazing couple could join us for lunch? Caroline's making her famous fried chicken, and I'd like time with my friend. You've been hogging her." Addison cocked one eyebrow and leaned forward as if desperate for Brianne and Seth to accept the invitation. "Caleb could use the company of a man too. That's okay, isn't it? I don't mean to put you on the spot."

Seth rubbed his palms together. "I've heard things about this chicken. If it's cool with Brianne, I'm in."

"Sounds great to me. I'm trying to avoid Seth eating my cooking for as long as possible." She twisted her fingers into his. "What time and what should we bring?"

"We should be ready about one, and just bring yourselves. Consider it my first payment of many. I owe you so much."

"You owe me nothing. We're friends."

Addison looked to Seth. "See? She's great. I'll look for you both in a couple of hours."

They walked out, Seth shaking hands with what felt like every man on the property while Brianne ducked her head, wishing the church hadn't seen so much growth in the last few years.

Outside, she stopped by the passenger side of his car. "Would you mind looking at the court records with me before we go over to the Kilbourns'? There are a few things I don't understand."

"Sure. I'm not a lawyer, though. I may not be able to help much." He closed her door once she was seated and walked around to the driver's side. "Thanks for letting me drive." He buckled his seat belt and placed a hand on hers. "I can't believe I didn't notice you in high school."

A pleasant shiver went up her spine. "So, Mr. Perfect, why haven't you gotten married yet?"

"If I give you the *I'm waiting for the right girl* line, would you believe me?" He pulled out of the parking lot and onto the highway.

"Nope."

Seth scratched at the back of his neck. "I was engaged a few years after high school. But it didn't work out. She decided a couple weeks before the wedding that the best man was a better man for her."

"Ouch."

"Yep. You can probably understand why I didn't date for a while after that." He squeezed her hand.

"I'm so sorry."

"Don't be. I felt sorry enough for myself to count for everyone. Then it occurred to me that if I wasn't the right guy for her, she couldn't be the right one for me. And if I'd married her, I wouldn't have gotten to know you." He glanced over, then returned his gaze to the road.

They rode in silence until he pulled into her driveway. "Let's take a look at those records."

Inside, Brianne pulled the papers from a manila envelope. "I don't understand why they convicted Clyde Tanger. There wasn't any solid evidence that I can see."

Seth took the stack, skimming through page after page. "The testimony of the professionals must have been convincing to the jury, but none of that is specific to this case. It says that Amanda refused to answer the attorney's questions about the abuse. That was one tough girl."

Brianne nodded. "I think that's one of the reasons her suicide shocked me so much. I didn't see it coming. She seemed stable . . . settled."

"I understand your worries, but they just show how much you care. You have so much to offer.'" Seth put the papers down and took Brianne's hand. "There are kids out there who need you."

His words settled on her, but not like the weight she would have expected. Instead, it was like a burden was lifting.

Addison set fresh potato salad in the middle of the picnic table already covered with a red-and-white tablecloth. The scent of frying chicken drifted through the screen door and into the backyard.

Connor positioned himself in an old tractor tire while Caleb braced the weight between his arm and good leg, then gave it a shove down the hill.

Addison jogged over, her heart thumping in her throat.

The tire bounced over a bump before tumbling to its side, expelling Connor.

"That was awesome." Connor jumped up and down, pumping his fist in the air.

"Didn't I tell you?" Caleb hollered back.

Addison huffed. "You'd better be careful. I don't have the patience for another injured body around here."

Caleb mumbled something under his breath.

"What was that?"

"Nothing, ma'am." His mouth was a firm line.

Addison stomped toward the tables.

The screen door slammed, and Lilly propelled forward. "Brianne!" She lunged into Brianne's arms. "Do you want to see my new frog? His name is Mr. Green. I'm taking very good care of him."

"Why don't you show Seth, and I'll help your mom. I'm more into frogs after I've had my lunch."

Lilly shrugged and grabbed Seth's hand, pulling him toward the shade under the black walnut tree.

Brianne picked up a stack of plates at the end of the table and started setting them out. "Any news on the case?"

Addison placed a fork beside each plate. "Yes . . . so much. I think Caroline is a drug addict and Caleb is having an affair."

Brianne laughed until she looked Addison in the eyes. "You're not serious."

"I am. I found oxy in an acetaminophen bottle. Lilly said Caroline gave him some to take with him the night of the accident. And the bottle Caleb got from the doctor is nearly gone, yet he hasn't taken any."

"You're sure it's Caroline and not Caleb who's hiding the issue?"

Addison stood straight and rubbed at her lower back. "I don't know. I guess it could be him. He hasn't exactly been honest with me."

"Being dishonest is not the same as having a relationship with another woman. What makes you think he's having an affair?" Brianne's voice was just above a whisper.

"Our credit card statement. I found out where he was that night. He was at a fancy restaurant, Virtue. Have you heard of it?"

Brianne's face went pale. "I wouldn't call it fancy. It's convenient. They have music and people . . . they meet up there."

Addison's mouth dropped open.

"I'm sorry. How about I take you there and we ask the management if they remember him? Maybe it's a simple mistake, or he was helping someone out."

Addison looked over at Caleb, now talking with Seth as

if they'd been best friends their whole lives. "Would you? I think I need to find out what's going on for myself. It's hard to believe anything from a man who has a convenient gap in his memory and wasn't with the person he claimed to be with."

Brianne's hand warmed inside Seth's grip, but the discomfort wasn't enough to warrant pulling away.

"Wow. You are blessed to have that kind of fried chicken just down the road." Seth licked his lips. "I can see why you moved back into your parents' house. I'd give up easy access to restaurants for that any day of the week."

She shook her head. "I hope you're not thinking it's a typical talent around here. I have never once fried a piece of chicken, unless you count eggs. I can do that, if you don't mind a broken yolk."

"It's not your cooking skills I'm interested in."

A wave of heat rushed over her. She swallowed.

"I like your heart. I can't believe you're not into kids. I saw the way the Kilbourn children love you, and you obviously care a great deal about them."

"I didn't say I don't like kids. I just don't get all gushy over baby pictures. And I'm not sure I'd make a very good mother. Mothers can't walk away. They're stuck, every single day, and if they make mistakes, they have to stick around to watch their children pay the consequences." Her dad had said she'd have trouble with the pressure of the work she'd chosen; motherhood was ten times more consequential.

"You're selling yourself far too short." He released her hand and put his arm around her shoulder, still maintaining his stride as they passed by the towering cedar that grew on the border between Brianne's property and the Kilbourns'. "Seriously, you're a trained counselor."

She leaned into his side. "I had a professor who came right out and said our training would make us horrible parents."

"What did he mean by that?"

"I think he meant we'd know too much about what could go wrong, all the places and ways a child could be damaged before they were even out of elementary school. And we'd understand how adverse childhood experiences would play a part in the rest of our children's lives and in their future health." More than anything she'd learned that semester, those words made an imprint in her mind. But even so, she'd still dreamed of a large family, of adopting children from the foster-care system and giving them a home where they could flourish.

"You should talk with my sister sometime. She and her husband adopted two siblings. It's been hard, and the kids have been through all sorts of horrible things, but their family is very happy and the kids are doing so well. It's not all tragedy and heartache, even in the hardest situations."

They turned the corner to her house, where Chester whined behind the door. Brianne felt the need to run, not just for exercise, but to put distance between herself and this man who kept dragging out her old desires. She wasn't that same girl with the big dreams anymore. Brianne was a realist, and reality was not unicorns and rainbows. It was so much darker than that.

BRIANNE PULLED INTO Addison's driveway, thoughts from her earlier conversation with Seth still replaying in her mind. He reminded her of the person she'd been before she took the job she'd once loved, a job that had ultimately revealed her for who she was beneath the surface.

The sun was dimming as it neared the horizon, an orange hue in the filter of smoke from distant wildfires.

Addison appeared from around the house, walking at a gait that seemed at once sneaky and determined. She climbed in beside Brianne. "Thanks for driving. I feel like I've become everyone's chauffeur lately. Caroline is the only one cleared to drive in that house, but I think I'd take my chances with Lilly behind the wheel before I'd ride with her."

"It's my pleasure." Brianne shifted into reverse and turned the car around. "Are you sure you want to do this? I hope my thinking out loud didn't pressure you to do something you don't want to do."

"Of course not. I need to know what happened—if Caleb's lying to me. We'll be in court in a few weeks, and I don't know if even I believe my husband. How am I supposed to hope a jury will?"

"Let's break it down. Why do you think he's lying?" Brianne turned onto the highway, her headlights clicked on.

Addison stared out the window. "He wasn't with Jeff. Before this, I've never caught Caleb in a lie. Maybe he finally realized I'm not good enough for him. Maybe he wanted out, and he doesn't remember it now."

Brianne tapped her index finger against the steering wheel. It was hard to recall how to be a friend versus being a counselor. The two relationships overlapped in the adult world, and she hadn't had much practice in either type in the last year. "Did he give you a reason not to trust him?"

"Caleb has asked me that same question hundreds of times." She leaned her head back on the seat. "No, he absolutely hasn't. Until now, he's been as good a husband as anyone could ask for."

"Stop me if I'm being too personal. Was your dad trustworthy?"

Addison shook her head. "I don't know. I never knew him."

"Did it bother you?"

She shrugged. "It's like he never existed. The way my

mother talked about men, I guess I assumed he wasn't worth missing."

They drove along the outskirts of town, then climbed the hill that separated West Crow and Darlington.

Brianne unrolled her window and let the sweet mountain air drift across her face. "Maybe you should talk to Caleb about how you're feeling. I'm guessing he's frustrated by this too."

Addison turned toward Brianne. "What do you mean?"

"I just wonder if Caleb is every bit as bothered by not being able to pull his true memories out of the rubble." Brianne bit her bottom lip. She'd taken a risk that wouldn't be such an investment if Addison were a client, but she was a friend, the closest one Brianne had at the moment.

39

Addison's mouth dried as she sat, stunned by the hit she'd taken from Brianne's words. How was she supposed to balance her feelings of possible rejection and infidelity with the very real possibility that Caleb might truly not remember what had happened?

Did an indiscretion that wasn't remembered still count? It did to her.

Brianne parked in front of a white building with gold-painted trim. The entrance was decorated to look as if it were a walkway into a luxury hotel, but no one stood outside to greet them. Though the paint gave a bright look to the outside, the lighting seemed almost muted.

The car door pinged as Brianne opened it, nearly forgetting her keys in the ignition. "Do you still want to do this?"

"I do." Addison climbed out. "I at least need to see where he was that night. The not knowing and not understanding are more than I can handle."

"Are you prepared for the worst or even the best?"

She shrugged. What was the best she could hope for? It's not like they would walk in and find Jeff Delmar standing in the foyer with a surprise note admitting he'd actually been with Caleb all along. The best-case scenario still had her husband lying to her about who he was meeting that night. Even good was bad.

Brianne pushed the door open.

To the left was a lounge with dark lighting and red velvet everything. The scent wafting from the kitchen reminded Addison of a Chinese restaurant her mother would take them to when things were good. The place had served fried rice, fried shrimp, and Shirley Temples. As an adult, Addison would be horrified to eat in an establishment that dark, especially with children, but at the time, it had seemed glamourous to her and her sisters.

"Did the bill indicate if he was in the restaurant or the lounge?"

Addison shook her head. "It just said Virtue."

They moved forward through an entryway and approached the stand where a maître d' would be present in a more posh establishment. To the right were tables with white linens, water glasses already at each setting.

Addison ran her tongue over her lips. She hadn't realized how thirsty she'd become until she watched a waiter pour ice water for a new customer. "Let's get a table. They might be more helpful if we're customers."

Brianne nodded. "I'm not sure I want to eat anything, but an iced tea would be amazing." She looked around, then pointed her elbow toward a couple in the corner sharing a hot fudge sundae. "Okay, maybe one of those. But no sharing." She grinned.

Why had Addison let so much time go without investing in a good friendship? Brianne had a way of bringing out the funny in life, even when everything else pointed toward tragic. "We'll see."

Finally, a man with a belly the size of an opera singer and a dozen hairs slicked over his bald head approached. "Ladies, how can I help you tonight?" He stretched his upper lip as if his overgrown mustache was tickling the inside of his nose.

"Table for two." Addison looked back at Brianne. "And I was wondering if you could help me with something."

"I'd be delighted." His nose twitched like a nervous bunny's.

Addison pulled the credit card bill from her purse. "My husband was in here a couple months ago. Unfortunately, he was in an accident, and he's unable to remember what happened that day." She pointed to the charges. "We can see he was here. We were wondering if anyone might have seen him that night."

The man tipped his head back. "Ma'am, if your husband has a question about this, I'd feel better talking to him. We do not go around spreading gossip about our customers. It's one of the reasons people continue to return to us."

Brianne leaned in close to Addison. "And I thought it was the charming employees."

Once again, Addison went from frustration to holding back her amusement. "I'm not asking you to divulge a great secret. Just a little information." She scrolled through her phone and held it out in front of his face. "This is my husband. Do you recognize him?"

The man shrugged. "It could be anyone. Please follow me to your table."

They were seated as near to the door as possible, but it gave Addison a view of the lounge, as well as the dining area.

He set a menu in front of each of them. "Barbie is your server this evening. She'll be right with you. And I assure you that she takes the privacy of our patrons as seriously as I do. Thank you for visiting Virtue." He moved away in a kind of side-to-side amble.

"Well, *I* feel welcome." Brianne lifted the menu. "I suppose he's the manager."

Every other employee was dressed in black pants or skirts

with a white buttoned-up shirt and a thin black tie. "He must be. I hope the tips are at least good here. I can't imagine working for that guy."

"Good evening, ladies. Can I get you a drink from the bar before you order?" Barbie filled both water glasses.

Addison ran her finger down the menu. "Let's say I had just twenty-two dollars to spend for maybe myself or myself and my friend. What would you suggest? A drink would need to be included."

Barbie tapped the side of her head with her pen. "If you're getting drinks from the bar, that would pretty much do you in, after tip, that is. You might have enough for an appetizer depending on what you ordered."

Addison punched the code into her cell and slid it toward Barbie. "Do you remember this man coming in a couple months ago?"

The server looked around the room. "Listen. I know you must be in an awful spot to ask like this, but I need this job. I have a kid to support. Can I get you anything to drink?"

Brianne shook her head. "I'm not feeling so hungry. Thank you, though."

Reaching into her purse, Addison pulled out a five-dollar bill and laid it on the table. "We appreciate your situation."

Barbie pocketed the bill. "You'd be surprised how often we get wives in here with questions. I hope you find what you need." She slipped her old-style order sheet into the pocket on the front of her black apron and stepped to the next table.

Brianne got up first. She waited as Addison checked the contents of her purse, finally rising.

Addison bit at the inside of her cheek. There had to be something to gain from this visit. When they'd pulled up, she'd been overcome with a confidence that some key to that night would be found inside these walls. As they walked out, desperation slowed her pace.

"Do you mind if I pop into the restroom before we go?" Brianne pointed down a long hall.

"No problem."

After emerging from the restroom, Brianne turned and ran into the side of a man with a tub of dirty dishes. "I'm sorry." She looked up, and her face paled.

HE LOOKED HER square in the eye. "Do I know you?"

Brianne struggled to gain enough control to speak. He was the same man he'd been, but thinner and stronger. Yet at the same time, there was a weakness in his eyes, a vulnerability. "We've met."

He shifted the weight of the tub and tipped his head to the side. "I'm afraid I can't recall where."

"I was Amanda's therapist." She blinked hard. "I'm so sorry for your loss."

Clyde Tanger's face grew red and splotchy. His chin dipped, and his gaze dropped to the floor. "Thank you. No one has ever said that to me."

There were so many things to ask, to say, but Brianne's mouth was paralyzed by the shock of the encounter.

"Well. Thanks." He nodded, still not able to look at her eyes, then left the hall through a swinging door. Clanks and crashes of dishes and silverware escaped from the room he'd retreated into.

Brianne braced a hand on the rough-textured wall.

"Are you okay? Who was that?"

She swallowed, tears forming in her eyes. "That was Clyde Tanger . . . Amanda's father."

"Oh, Brianne." Addison pulled her into a side hug.

"I need to talk with him, but not now, not here." She wiped

a hand across the back of her neck. "I need to hear his side of the story."

"What good does that do anyone now? He served his time. He has a job and probably a new life."

"And he registers as a sex offender every time he moves. What if I saddled him with that forever, and it's not even true?" Brianne picked at the peeling cuticle on her thumb. "I feel like I took part in destroying his life."

"Listen, I'm not Caroline's biggest fan right now, but there's something she's said to me many times that makes a lot of sense, and I think you could stand to hear it." Addison turned Brianne around and started guiding her toward the exit. Low country tunes hummed from the lounge, where a band had started playing. "She says we're too big for our britches when we take responsibility for things that are ultimately out of our control. If we trust God, we trust that He can work through even the most upside-down situation. Then she always tops it off with this whammy: 'You are not God.'"

40

No. I really don't think the school secretary will be much help on the stand. She's a behind-the-back kind of person, not the sort who's willing to make a public statement."

Seth Wallace stood next to Emilia's desk, waiting for a chance to speak.

"I'll get back to you as soon as I gather some more information." Emilia hung up the phone. The DA had fully bought into the angle she'd given her, and though politics generally made Emilia's stomach ache, they could be used on occasion to get criminals off the streets. "What's up? I only have a minute. I need to get back to the hospital."

"How's Roger doing?"

Emilia felt the grin rise on her face. "Actually, he's doing well. There's some odd memory loss, but he's closer to his old self than he has been since the accident."

Seth nodded. "That's great news."

"Is that what you wanted to talk about?"

"No. Not all of it, anyway." Seth took a seat on the edge of her desk. "So, listen, I've been seeing Brianne Demanno. Do you know who she is?"

"The therapist who left after that girl killed herself, right?" Emilia had never met Brianne in person, but she'd found herself wondering about the character and strength of a woman who gave up so easily.

"Yes. But she's also the Kilbourns' neighbor. She and Addison have become good friends."

Emilia leaned back in her desk chair, crossing her arms tight against her chest. "And?"

"And, well, I think you may have missed something."

She rolled her eyes. "Give me a break. You're not the kind of cop to come in here trying to sway a case because your girlfriend blinked her eyes and asked you to. Have some self-respect, Seth."

Seth held up a hand. "No way. She didn't ask me to say anything, and she doesn't know I am. This is for your benefit as much as anyone else's. It turns out—and please do not say this information came from me—that the older Mrs. Kilbourn may have a problem with oxy."

Emilia shrugged. "That stinks, but I don't see how this changes the case."

"Addison and Brianne are wondering if Caleb might have taken the medication by accident."

She pushed the chair back and got up. "Sure. By accident. I bet that would make all the difference to Georgianna Bosch's children."

WHO DOESN'T KNOW the difference between oxy and over-the-counter pain relievers? No one over the age of twelve, that's who. Emilia couldn't shake the conversation with Seth. Had he really thought this would make a difference?

Emilia ticked off the evidence against Caleb Kilbourn as she drove toward the hospital. The testimony of Harper and Ivy would go a long way to that end. How could a jury possibly acquit with their stories? Eyewitnesses who'd seen it all happen. Ivy's emotional state could actually help the prosecution's case.

She parked in the patient pickup area behind a gigantic Ford F-150. Her engine sputtered to a stop. The last few nights without Roger at home, she'd gotten to sleep in her own bed. There was no tension, fear, or nervous energy, but she'd missed his presence. Almost losing him made having him so much more precious, even though he'd changed. Emilia rededicated herself to the commitment of in sickness and in health. She'd choose to love in times of illness and hope for health to return.

The smell of the hospital always made her stomach swim. It brought back the fear and horror of the worst night of her life. It teased her heart with the hope she'd had when the doctor had said Roger would survive, and the disappointment when the man admitted a couple weeks later to a rehab facility was a shadow of the one she'd married.

Today wasn't any different.

She rode the elevator to the second floor and walked down the corridor to Roger's room like she had every day for the past week.

The nurse met her at the door, a file folder under her arm. "There you are. Roger is ready to go, I just wanted to talk over a few items the doctor wants you to understand."

Emilia blew out a breath. "Okay."

She opened the folder and pulled out the top paper. "First, Roger is doing well. He's struggling with headaches, but that's to be expected. Dr. Harrison is concerned that the oxycodone may be causing rebound headaches. He feels it might be better for him to come completely off opioids."

Emilia's shoulders ached as if the burden on her back had grown by another two hundred pounds. "He's been dependent on those to survive the last months."

"I understand, but Dr. Harrison feels this will lead to a better long-term outcome."

It was so easy for people on the outside to determine what was best for their family. Would any of them be there when Roger was heaving and crying out in pain? Emilia would be able to hear the animal-like sounds that haunted her memories into her old age. That sound was something she could never escape.

"My advice to you would be to give this a try for a few weeks. If he really can't get by on the levels of ibuprofen Dr. Harrison suggests, bring it up to him again."

Emilia nodded, but inside, she started to die again. A little at a time, Roger's pain was taking away her will. She took the folder from the nurse and entered the hospital room.

Roger slumped in the wheelchair, his head in his hands.

The migraines were back. And her husband was gone again.

Caleb stood at the edge of the lawn, looking down to where the ground dipped away from his feet.

For a few moments, Addison just watched. She watched the sun as it sank below the horizon, painting the sky with colors that made her think of Brianne's amazing artwork. She watched as the bats came from wherever they spent their days to dip and dive in the fading light, collecting their dinner of mosquitos. And she watched as her husband took in the freedom that hung in the balance of justice.

She watched the man she'd always loved, the one who'd taught her she could trust another person. How easily she'd walked away from that trust when he couldn't or wouldn't answer her questions.

Now Addison approached with caution, as if he were a stranger and not the man who'd slept next to her for fifteen years. She laid her hand on his upper arm.

Without turning to look at her, Caleb covered her hand with his palm. "It's beautiful out here."

"It is."

"This was why I wanted to move here now, rather than wait for the house to be finished." He held out his arm toward the sky. "I didn't want any of us to miss another summer of this. But we have. We lost the time because I did something stupid."

Her stomach fluttered as if she hadn't eaten in weeks. Every joint took on the pain her heart could not contain. The breaking was starting before his confession.

Caleb turned to her, took her chin in his hand. "I don't remember, Addison. I'm not lying about that, but I obviously wasn't with Jeff. I somehow took the oxycodone. I drank. I can almost see myself cheating too. But at the same time, I can't believe I ever would. I've never wanted anyone other than you. I want you to know that, even though I can't tell you exactly what I did, I'm so sorry, because, at the very least, I lied to you. You deserve so much better than this."

She'd thought this would be the moment when she'd walk away, take the children, and start a new life somewhere else. But she knew she would feel like a coward if she left without untangling the mess. Their vows had been for better or worse. This was worse than anything she'd imagined, but her children still needed their dad, and Addison, for whatever reason, still loved him. She leaned forward, her forehead on his chest, and Caleb covered the back of her head with his palm.

Waves of guilt crashed over her. She pulled away. "Last weekend Brianne and I went to Darlington, to a restaurant named Virtue."

His eyebrows furrowed. "That sounds familiar. Have we been there before?"

"It was my first time, but . . ." She wrapped her arms around herself, holding back the night's chill. "I should have told you.

You were there the night of the accident. It was on the credit card bill. I thought I could go and find out who you'd been with. I'm sorry. I didn't handle this well."

He grabbed her arm. "Did you find out? What did they say?"

The look of utter desperation on his face was so genuine, she knew this man truly didn't remember.

"We weren't able to find out anything. The manager thought we were up to something, and he wanted to protect his customer's privacy."

"Then I'll go." He started toward the house.

She grabbed the back of his T-shirt. "You're not cleared to drive, and I can't leave the kids with your mother."

He looked to the left, and she followed his gaze. In the distance, a light was on in Brianne's house. "You said Brianne used to be a therapist, that she had a lot of knowledge about memories, false and otherwise. Maybe she'd go again. With me this time."

Addison stared at Brianne's place. "If the attorney is okay with it and Brianne is okay with it, then I'm okay too."

There had to be a time to jump, to let go and let God take control, to trust. Addison chose this moment. She took a step closer, wrapped her arms around her husband's neck, and pressed her cheek to his.

Emilia shut the door to their darkened bedroom in slow motion. She twisted the knob back in place, releasing the smallest click. Then she rested her forehead against the wall and let the exhaustion that raged through her body melt into the rough surface.

Once again, the pain was severe for Roger, but now she had nothing to give him besides a few ibuprofens. The helplessness added to the burden of her agony.

Her gaze swept to Tally's closed room. She'd grown increasingly distant with Roger slipping back into pain, but that wasn't the real issue, and Emilia knew it.

She made the five-foot trek to Tally's closed door and knocked.

"What?"

Emilia eased the door open.

Tally sat on her unmade bed, her back against the wall, her arms crossed and face firm.

"Do you want to talk about it?"

Tally's eyebrows shot up. "About how I can't have any friends? About how I finally met someone exactly like who you wanted me to hang out with, and now I can't see her, either? Um, no. I don't want to talk about it."

"Can you try to understand where I'm coming from?"

"Like how you take the time to understand my side?" Tally grabbed the pillow from the head of the bed and stuffed it into her middle. "I don't want to talk about this or anything else. Would you please leave me alone? I have to get used to it since I'm not allowed to have friends."

Emilia eased out of the room.

A knock on their front door startled her.

She rushed through the living room, whipping the door open before whoever it was could reach for the dreaded doorbell.

Her neighbor Holly Carmen stood there, eyes wide, arms laden with tinfoil-covered baking pans. A grocery bag hung from one arm. "Don't try to stop me."

Emilia gripped the side of the doorframe.

"I've made a decision, and I'm not going to let you stop me this time. I'm here to help." She raised her chin and took a step closer, invading Emilia's personal space.

Emilia stepped back.

The neighbor walked right through the living room and into the kitchen. "Can you help me out?"

"What?"

"Make some room on the counter and take these casseroles. They're getting heavy."

Emilia stacked last night's dishes in the sink. "What is all this? What's going on?"

Holly set down the pans. "I saw the ambulance, and I talked to your sister. She told me about Roger's surgery." She hung the bag from the handle of the silverware drawer. "I stayed back and respected your need to do this on your own when Roger got hurt, but it didn't end. You never let me back in. Please don't get mad at me for saying this, but you have a whole lot of pride."

Pride goes before a fall.

Emilia rubbed her hand on the back of her neck. She'd fallen hard. So had Roger and Tally.

"I talked with a few of our friends at church. We'll be back this afternoon to help you get caught up around the house."

Emilia looked around, seeing the place through the eyes of a visitor. Dust decorated every horizontal surface. A drip of something red had dried along the outside of the refrigerator. The book she'd been reading before Roger's accident peered out from under a stack of bills on the table. But she couldn't let other people come in and see the mess she hadn't been able to handle. "It's fine. Thank you, but we've got everything under control."

"Is that food?" Tally pushed into the kitchen and peeled the foil off the top casserole.

"That's enchiladas, and the one below is mac and cheese. I figured you could choose what you want for today and freeze the other." Holly retrieved the bag, pulling out a two-liter bottle of soda and a bagged salad.

Tally launched into her arms. "This looks so good. Thank you!"

"So what do you say about accepting some help?" Holly smiled over Tally's shoulder.

Emilia nodded. "Thank you."

EMILIA ROLLED UP to the curb in front of West Crow Middle School. Tally had barely allowed her the honor of dropping her off for the first day of class. The reward for this inconvenience had so far been paid in eye rolls and sighs.

Tally reached for the door, but Emilia held out her arm. "Wait a second."

Another sigh. "What? I don't want to be late. I have to find a seat near the back, where no one will talk to me and I won't run the risk of making a friend." And an eye roll.

Emilia breathed in deep, filling her lungs, then released the air while mentally counting to ten. "Okay. I understand your frustration, and I'm working on ways to compromise with you."

"Does that mean I'm allowed to eat in the cafeteria with everyone else, or should I find a nice, safe place in a closet somewhere?"

"Hey. I'm trying. It would be great if you could try too." The next breath didn't do the trick. It trickled out like a deflating balloon. "Hang out with Hannah at school. I can't say that I'm okay with you going to her house, or her coming to ours. Absolutely not her coming to ours. But her father's legal issues aren't her fault."

Tally tipped her head. "Really. That's it? Like I wasn't going to do that anyway." She shook her head and got out of the car, the sound of another acidic sigh drifting behind her.

It was time to get a referral to a therapist. Tally was falling off the cliff, and she wasn't even in high school yet. What had made Emilia think she could usher her daughter through the upheaval of the last year and expect that Tally would come out better for it in the end? Emilia didn't even recognize herself anymore. Yet she'd thought Tally would be okay. Denial at its finest.

A car honked, and Emilia pulled away from the drop-off area. Dr. Harrison had called in a prescription for Zofran this morning, and Emilia had every intention of pounding on the door until the pharmacist answered and got the drugs that should at least allow Roger to hold down a glass of water.

Roger's migraines were back with the force of a semi and showed little sign of stopping. The pain drove him to the point of vomiting in the early hours of the morning. Against Emilia's wisdom, Roger's wishes, and her pride, Emilia had allowed Holly to stay at the house while she took Tally to school and went to the drugstore.

Emilia pulled into a space around the back of the store, knowing this was where James and the other employees parked and entered. She cut the engine and stepped out. Opening wasn't for another hour, but this was an emergency and there wasn't another drugstore in town.

James Schneider's two-door sports car, painted the red of middle-age desperation, sat in the spot closest to the door.

Emilia pounded on the solid wood. She spotted a doorbell camera above her head and jammed her finger into the button, waving at the lens with the other hand.

The door swung open. "What's your problem, Emilia?" James ran a hand through his thinning hair. A crease line etched the side of his face.

"I need to pick up a prescription."

His head jutted forward. "We're not open." He started to close the door, but she blocked it.

"Listen. It's important. I need this right now."

His voice grew quiet. "Some kind of opioid, I'm assuming."

"No." She pushed past him. "It's for my husband. Zofran. You should have gotten the order from Dr. Harrison."

"Okay, then. Why don't you come on in?" His voice carried a sharp edge of sarcasm.

She turned back to him. "How about I don't tell anyone that you're sleeping in the store, and you get Roger's medication ready?"

He scratched at his scruffy chin. "That seems fair."

Twenty minutes later, she had the pills and a two-liter of stomach-calming lemon-lime soda. She hurried down the streets of downtown West Crow and finally returned to her house.

The front yard looked off. She grabbed the soda and pharmacy bag and got out of the car. Flowers were planted along the foundation, pinks and purples, even a Russian sage, her favorite. And the faded Christmas lights from two years back had been removed from the gutters. Even the sidewalk seemed lighter, as if someone had actually washed it. Had that happened since she'd left, or was Emilia too busy this morning to notice? How many other kindnesses had she missed in her self-inflicted prison of pride?

Zofran was a miracle. Thirty minutes after the first dose, Roger had stopped vomiting. An hour later, he was able to drink some water.

Tally had returned from school ready for whatever dinner Holly's group of warriors had provided, and Roger asked if he could have a plate. Lasagna might not be the best choice for a man who couldn't keep air down that morning, but he had an appetite and he kept saying how good dinner smelled. He hadn't said that in . . . she couldn't remember the last time.

Emilia dished a small plate of the thick lasagna and poured a half glass of lemon-lime soda. Roger didn't like having much light on, so she'd learned the hard way not to fill a cup too full. It was easy to miss your aim in the dark.

As she turned, she nearly dropped the dinner and the drink. Roger stood in the doorway, a bandage still engulfing the side of his skull, his face unshaved and his eyes blinking. "I was just bringing this in to you. Go on back to bed."

He shrugged. "I'm not contagious. I thought it might be nice to sit out here for dinner. Where's Tally?"

"She usually eats in her room." Emilia heard the words and tasted the shame. She'd let their relationship go, much like she'd watched Roger drift away. "It's easier than fighting with her."

"That doesn't sound like you." He leaned hard against the doorframe. "Would you mind asking her to join us tonight?"

"Of course not. I mean, I'll try."

Roger eased himself into a dining room chair.

Papers were stacked where they used to savor their time together in the evenings, talking over the events of their days. Emilia pushed the mountains to the side and set Roger's meal in front of him. "You should get started in case you get tired."

"I'll wait." He leaned forward on his crossed arms.

Emilia knocked on Tally's door, then walked through, closing it partway behind her. "Hey, Papa wants us all to sit down together for dinner. Can you come out here?"

Tally rolled her eyes, then pointed to her empty dinner plate. "Too late."

Emilia stepped closer. She ground her teeth together and hardened her expression. "I don't care that you've eaten. Get yourself into that dining room and sit at the table. Have another slice of lasagna or just sit there, but do it now."

Tally's eyes were as round as her plate and her mouth wide open, as if waiting for a response to show up.

For all these months, Emilia had held it together, used proper parenting language, assessed the difficulties Tally was experiencing, and gave her daughter the room she claimed she needed. But none of that felt as good and right as laying down the law just had.

Fire raged in Tally's eyes, but she got up, collected her plate and fork, and walked out of the room.

Emilia passed her sullen daughter, obediently sitting at the table, and dished herself a plate of food. Taking a seat, she felt like she was returning from a year-long journey of epic failures. She lifted her fork and cut the corner off the square of lasagna.

As he cleared his throat, Roger reached his hands out, one to Tally and one to Emilia, indicating the start of their prayer. The last one they'd shared was the night before life had changed. One of the first things that had drawn Emilia to Roger was his deep faith. Had his slipped away during the hard times? Or had she just been too blind to see it? And how weak was Emilia's own faith for her to have abandoned prayer in the midst of trial? At first she'd prayed by herself, but soon it had become little more than her begging God to fix their lives. She'd been as surly as Tally during a fit, turning her back when she didn't get her way.

"Amen." Roger's hand pulled from hers before Emilia was ready. "This looks really good. Thank you."

"I didn't make it." Emilia swiped at her chin with a paper napkin with a fast-food logo.

"You warmed it up and set it on the table. You work and take care of us. You deserve many thank-yous that you never get." His eyes shone over a sweet smile that said so much more than his words ever could.

Emilia had to look away before her family caught her with tears in her eyes. There was a time she'd actually thought about giving up, walking away from her husband and her marriage. Thank God she hadn't been crazy enough to do it. She could have missed this moment that made every struggle worth living through.

"So, what have you been doing at work?"

Emilia choked on a chunk of garlic bread. No one had asked her about her job for so long, the question felt foreign. She took two swallows of soda and wiped her face.

"She's very busy"—Tally leaned back in her chair—"trying to put my best friend's dad in jail for murder."

Lasagna set like cement in Emilia's stomach. "That's not fair."

"Funny. I bet Hannah doesn't feel like it's very fair that she's about to lose her dad because he was in an accident. I thought police went after people who hurt others on purpose. I sure hope no one trips over my bike. You'd have me sent off to juvie."

Emilia looked to Roger, expecting him to question her, but the interchange had washed the color from his face. His fork rested on the side of his plate, a chunk of pasta still stuck to the tines.

"I'm feeling kind of tired. I hope you two won't mind if I excuse myself for a nap." He ran a hand over the top of his head.

"Of course not." Emilia shot a scowl at her daughter. "I'll save your plate for later."

"Thanks." He got up from the table as though the effort to join them had aged him forty years. A few minutes later, the bedroom door clicked shut.

"What was the meaning of that?" Emilia's voice was a harsh whisper. "He's doing his best to bring this family back together, and you pull that stunt?"

"Oh, so we should have our family, but Hannah doesn't deserve to have hers? Nice, Mom. Or should I say, Deputy?" Tally rose from the table. She was growing quickly and stood eye to eye with Emilia.

"Of course she does. And I'm not about to discuss this case with you."

Tally's eyes narrowed to angry slits. "I wouldn't expect you to. I'm just a *child*." She flung a napkin onto the table and stomped away.

Exhaustion weakened Emilia's legs. She dropped into the chair. From the moment she found out Tally had made friends with Caleb Kilbourn's daughter, she'd known it would lead to trouble, but she hadn't expected the guilt that wouldn't let her go.

42

I wish you could go with us." Brianne held tightly to Seth's arm. Her car already hummed beside them. "This feels weird, just me and Caleb."

"I don't think Sheriff Commons would stand for my being involved in that way. And Emilia is already steamed about my bringing up her case."

"Thanks for trying."

He pulled her into a hug. "For you, of course."

"Whatever. You're starting to love the Kilbourns as much as I do." She stretched her head back so she could look at him eye to eye.

"Lilly's a pretty great ambassador. I can't say no to that kid." He gave Brianne a squeeze, then let her go. "Call me as soon as you get back, okay?"

"I promise." Having someone to call, someone who wanted to be sure she made it home safely . . . She hadn't realized how much she'd missed that. Seth filled a giant void in her life. But she had to use caution, take each step with a careful measure. Time after time, she'd counseled couples who'd jumped too quickly because of those initial sappy feelings. There were serious items to check off, things she and Seth needed to understand about each other.

He opened her door, and Brianne took her place behind the wheel. "I really hope you can help them find some answers."

"Me too." She dropped her sunglasses over her eyes before he could see just how much she was falling for him, then put the car into reverse.

As she drove away, she watched him climb into his Jeep, the car that was parked in her driveway so often now, it seemed like it belonged there.

Caleb and Addison were waiting on their porch.

Addison came to Brianne's window as soon as the car stopped. She blinked faster than usual. "You're a great friend. I'll help you plan your wedding to start making up for all of this, okay?"

"We'll probably be attending Lilly's wedding before mine."

Addison waved toward the road, and in the rearview mirror, Brianne could see the billow of dust left behind Seth's vehicle.

"We'll just have to see what happens." Addison nudged her arm.

Caleb wriggled and squirmed as he found the right position in the car. His jaw was set as if he were heading for the guillotine instead of a restaurant in a neighboring town.

"This won't be too bad." Brianne headed away from the Kilbourn farm. "I can talk about baseball and basketball, and I'm a decent football fan."

"With everything you've done for us, I'm willing to chat about men and the opera if it makes you happy."

Brianne held a hand up. "Please. No."

"Tell me what you think the chances are this will help."

"That's hard to say. The brain's complicated. What I don't want you to do is try and force the memories. That gets into a dangerous area. People are capable of creating memories that feel as though they're real. What we're interested in is what actually happened that night."

"With the trial later this week, I'm feeling a lot of pressure." He started digging at the hem of his shorts with his fingernails. "But I think I understand what you mean."

"Try to relax and just experience what's around you."

He unrolled his window halfway and tilted his head to the outside.

They drove through the twists and turns. Caleb said nothing as they passed the site of the accident. Even as they pulled close to the restaurant, he remained silent.

"How are you feeling? Is this all okay for you still?"

"I recognize roads and places, but only because I've been through Darlington a hundred times before." He rubbed his palm on his forehead. "How could I forget doing something so wrong that I'd lie to my wife about it?"

"Remember what I said before? You can't make assumptions about what happened." Brianne parked the car and grabbed her purse.

It was still early in the day, before any lunch rush, and there were hardly any other cars in the lot. In the daylight, the exterior of the restaurant looked shabby, in need of a paint job.

A poster advertising the night's entertainment hung in a display case. Caleb stopped there. He tapped his finger on the plexiglass.

"Does that look familiar?"

"Yes and no." He blew out a hard breath. "It's like I've been here before, but so long ago that everything's changed. Let's try inside."

The lounge was the hue of blood from the little bit of light reflecting off the velvet interior. A man stood behind the bar, pouring a drink for a customer who slumped as if he'd already gone past his limit.

Caleb clenched and unclenched his hands, and Brianne watched the line of his jaw tighten.

"What are you feeling?" she asked.

"Anger. I don't know where it's coming from, but I'm angry." He stepped farther into the room.

Brianne flinched against the scent of beer and too much aftershave. It hung like smoke used to in places like these, before city ordinances prohibited smoking inside.

Caleb slipped into a booth in the corner, Brianne following suit. He tipped his head back. "That ceiling tile."

"What about it?"

"The remnants of a water leak," he said. "I've seen it before. I've been here."

"Oh, Caleb." Brianne couldn't imagine what was going through his mind.

The bartender approached. "Can I get you two anything?" His voice was gruff and impatient.

Caleb rambled off the name of a drink Brianne had never heard of. "I'm not much of a drinker," he explained, "but my father saw drinking as a rite of passage, and that was his favorite. Unappealing as it is, on the rare occasion I order it as a way to honor my roots . . . the men who came before me."

The bartender raised his chin. "Yes. You mentioned that when you were here before. I don't have much of an eye for people, but I remember their drink orders. Glad to see you have company with you this time." He glanced at Brianne. "And what can I get you, ma'am?"

"Lemonade would be great. And can you tell us anything about the last time my friend was here?"

"All I remember is he ordered the same thing—actually two—during happy hour. You'd have to ask Squirrelly if you want to know more than that. He's the one who would have been on the floor." The guy sauntered away with a slight lean to his left.

Brianne eyed Caleb.

"I wasn't lying about seldom drinking. It seemed like the

thing to do when he asked—like I was on autopilot, I guess. But I'd never order two."

"Apparently that's what you did that night. I think we're getting somewhere."

Caleb laced his fingers together and set his hands on the table, leaning forward. "All I know is I did drink then. And I know it must have been for a reason." He stretched his shoulders. "I think I'm building a case for the prosecution. They'll have a slam dunk in court."

Brianne leaned back in her chair.

"I deserve the court's judgment. But my wife and kids? How can I pay the debt I owe without them taking a huge chunk of the punishment? That's not fair to them."

A dark-haired man approached the table with a tray holding two full glasses. He slid the whole tray onto the table, then placed a drink in front of Caleb.

"Are you Squirrelly?" Caleb fingered the glass of amber liquid.

"Clyde. They call me that 'cause I squirrel away my tips. I don't party or anything like that." He pressed his hands into his pockets. "Ms. Demanno . . . it's nice to see you again." His gaze seemed magnetically pulled away from Brianne.

Caleb dipped his finger into the drink and touched it to his tongue. He grimaced. "Do you remember seeing me in here before?"

"Sure. I've got a good memory for those things. At least I seem to, now that I'm clean." He shook his head as if pronouncing judgment on himself.

"Was I with anyone?"

"No. You sat down right here and ordered two of those." He pointed to the glass. "You said someone was meeting you, but they never showed. I remember that well because it was also the night the talent skipped out. People had come to watch, and we had no band."

Clyde Tanger stood waiting as Brianne watched Caleb lift his glass, letting it brush his lips but not drinking. "What are you feeling, Caleb? What are you remembering?"

Caleb closed his eyes. "Frustration. Irritation. Utter disappointment at my . . ."

"Say it."

His eyes opened wide. "The other drink. It was for my brother."

BRIANNE WATCHED COLOR rise in Caleb's cheeks. He was remembering, but she couldn't tell if what he felt was relief or another blow.

Brianne looked at the man who still stood beside their table. "Mr. Tanger . . . thank you so much. Would it be possible for me to talk with you sometime about your daughter?"

Tears flushed his eyes. "There's nothing more to say. It's time to let Amanda rest in peace." He walked away with the tray in his hand and exited out an employee door at the side of the lounge.

Everyone said the same thing: *"Let well enough alone."* But if that was right, why did the possibility of Clyde's innocence nag at her soul?

Caleb slapped a twenty-dollar bill on the table. "I'm ready to go." The tone in his voice had dropped to a depth that warned her not to interfere with whatever was happening in his mind. He'd walled himself off, separating himself from her and the surroundings. Was he frustrated with his brother?

They drove toward home in near silence, the day turning to afternoon as they entered the stretch of highway that connected the two communities. This time, when they emerged from the curves, Caleb held up his hand. "Stop. Please."

She pulled to a safe shoulder once the road straightened.

He jumped from the car and stood on the white line staring toward the mountainside that bordered the opposite side of the road.

No trace of the accident remained as far as Brianne was able to tell. A sedan sped by, honking its horn as it passed, a welcome breeze following in its wake.

Caleb remained still, his gaze not straying, his body so near motionless that he seemed like a movie image frozen on the screen. Until that one tear.

Brianne lowered her head, processing the emotions that must be assaulting the heart of her best friend's husband. In a moment of bad and careless decisions, Caleb had made a huge mistake. And that had cost a woman her life.

Even in the late-summer heat, a chill washed over Brianne's skin. Where were grace and mercy in the face of justice?

43

Addison twisted the flip-flop she'd found sticking out from under the couch. Brianne's car was making its way down the drive, Addison's hopes and fears riding in the passenger seat.

Flinging the shoe into the basket by the door, she stepped onto the porch.

The dust settled, and Caleb maneuvered his way out.

Without any words, Brianne waved and pulled away.

Even the air was heavy with humidity and dread. The look on Caleb's face said the trip wasn't a waste, but it also looked so much like the grief he'd worn after his father's death.

They stood, facing each other, only the haze of pollen and distant wildfires separating them. Addison eased down onto the top step.

Caleb dug in his back pocket and pulled out a slip of paper. He hobbled up to the porch and pushed it into her hand.

"What's this?" An unfamiliar name was scrawled in handwriting she didn't recognize. She handed it back to him.

"It's the name Wyatt's using. He was in Darlington the night of the accident. I think I was trying to talk with him, get him to come home and patch things up with Mom. He didn't show. In typical Wyatt fashion, the guy even ran out on the bar he was supposed to be playing that night."

Addison covered her mouth. Her chin quivered with the release of repressed emotion. Each muscle in her body ached with the surrender of held tension. They were okay. Their marriage wasn't the broken frame she'd feared. Her husband wasn't looking for someone new.

He was looking for his brother.

"I don't know why I didn't tell you." He shook his head. "I should have."

She lifted her hand and placed it into his.

Caleb leaned into her. His presence soothed her in a way she hadn't allowed it to during the months of doubt.

"I'm sorry about Wyatt." She laid her hand on his chest. "Do you know where he went after Darlington?"

"Not a clue, and I'm not going to search for him. I've come to the end of that trail. When Wyatt is ready to come home, he'll get here on his own."

"What was that?" Caroline stepped from around the corner. "Did you say Wyatt is coming home?" Tears filled her eyes.

"No, Mom. I don't know where he is. I remember where I was the night of the accident. I was trying to talk with him, but it didn't happen. I'm sorry."

She held up a gloved hand, waving it in tiny motions as she stepped back, disappearing again behind the house.

Caleb raked both hands through his hair. "What seems like good news for us is horrible for her." He tipped his head toward Addison. "When did my not cheating become good news instead of something that's a given?"

The mother's heart within Addison crumbled for Caroline. She'd never given Wyatt's absence much thought. In some ways, she didn't think of what he'd done as much different than the way she'd walked away from her own mother. But there was a difference: Caroline loved her boys. She cherished everything about them. Addison's mother had never known how to love. Leaving her was like leaving behind a neighbor with whom you'd shared a fence but no real relationship.

"How could Wyatt not come visit your mom? How could he leave her to grieve your father like this without even seeing if she's okay?" She squeezed Caleb's leg, then got up. "I'm going to check on her."

In the mudroom, Caroline's garden shoes were slung against the wall, a smear of dirt streaking the yellow paint where one had hit. There was no sign of her in the kitchen. Addison stuck her head into the living room. Nothing.

Something pounded the wall in the hallway.

Addison went to Caroline's bedroom door and tapped. "Caroline? Can I come in?"

"No. I'm resting." Her voice sounded ten years older than it had that morning.

"I'd like to talk for a minute. Please."

"Not now, Addy."

Addison stepped back until she bumped into the wall behind her. She'd failed her mother-in-law. She had to do better.

Brianne pulled up to her house and found a rental car parked in her normal spot. She cut the engine and stepped out of her car, carefully skirting the other vehicle.

Sitting at the table on the front porch was her father, in plaid shorts and a blue polo shirt. His head leaned against the side of the house, and his eyes were closed.

"Dad?"

His eyes popped open. "Wow. I must have dozed off. This cool weather is relaxing after an Arizona summer." He got to his feet and pulled her into a giant hug. "I've missed you, sugar."

"I've missed you too, but what are you doing here? I wasn't

expecting you." She unlocked the front door, and Chester bounded out, paying no attention to Brianne or her dad as he lifted his leg to the bottom step, the nearest upright object.

"Your mother's been worried. She says you seem low, and she wanted to be sure the furnace was in good working order before the cold weather sets in." He grabbed hold of the stair railing and gave it a tug.

"You don't have to come all the way up here to check my heater. Really, Dad, I'm an adult." She grabbed a pitcher of lemonade out of the refrigerator, then retrieved two glasses.

"You'll never be an adult to your mother. Don't fight it." He grinned and held out one of the glasses while she filled it. He nodded toward the vase of daisies on the counter. "So who got you those?" His eyebrows lifted.

"Who says I couldn't have gotten them for myself?" She poured herself a glass and returned the pitcher to the fridge.

Her dad took a long drink, set the glass down, and folded his arms. "But you didn't, did you?"

She couldn't look him in the eye, never had been able to when the topic was guys. She shook her head.

"You know if you told your mother you're seeing someone, she'd probably worry less."

"And you?"

"I'll worry more, but I can be contained."

The lemonade sent a chill through Brianne's body. "Do you worry because I'm too sensitive?"

He chuckled. "Why would you think that? Bri, I think you have just the right amount of caring and compassion, and enough good sense and wisdom to make great choices. I have complete trust in you. This boy, however . . . I don't know him."

"He's hardly a boy."

"At my age, they're all boys."

"So you don't think I'll get hurt for the same reason I

shouldn't have become a therapist?" She sat her half-full glass in the sink.

Her dad rested a hand on her arm. "Bri, you're a great therapist. I loved seeing how you glowed in that job. Helping others is part of who God made you to be. Your mother and I pray that you'll get over this hurt and get back to where you belong."

Tears rushed into Brianne's eyes. Her father brought out the soft spots in her, made her vulnerable and weak.

"You've been hurt. And that's okay. But, Bri, you were meant for that job. Your mom says we can't push you, but enough time has passed already." He took hold of her by both shoulders. "Pick up your life."

"I thought you'd be happy that I'm doing something safer." Chester bounded in, jumping up, with his paws nearly knocking her over.

"Safer? Nah. You're a tough girl. You've got this."

"But you always said I was too sensitive." She pushed the dog down.

Dad gave Chester a firm scratch. "You *are* sensitive. But whatever gave you the idea that I thought that wasn't a good thing? You're full of empathy and compassion. I wouldn't want to talk out my problems with someone who wasn't those things."

Brianne knelt, burying her face in Chester's fluff. Maybe she'd made her own assumptions, thoughts that gave her an excuse to walk out when the job got hard. Another obstacle blew away on the summer breeze.

"DO YOU THINK we should check on her?" Addison leaned against the cold stove. "She's been in there an hour."

"Maybe she's tired." Caleb's mouth pinched in that way that told her he didn't buy what he was saying.

"The kids will be home in less than an hour. I really think we should talk with her now." Lilly had barely met Wyatt. Connor and Hannah probably didn't remember him well. To them, Wyatt was just a guy in some old family pictures, no relationship to go along with the image. Addison and Caleb had made the hard decision years ago to stop helping Caleb's brother. Wyatt had been a wild teen who turned into an out-of-control adult.

"I'll do it." Caleb walked away, leaving her with the feeling that she wasn't part of this. Not now. She followed her husband into the hall.

Caleb knocked on the door with a firm rap. "Mom, we'd like to talk to you."

Caroline didn't respond.

Addison nudged him to try again.

This time, Caleb pounded on the wood.

Again, no response.

He reached his fingers to the top of the doorframe and came away with a key-like tool. Inserting it into the hole in the knob, Caleb popped it open. "Mom, we're coming in, like it or not."

Addison cringed. This was a great way to lose their free housing.

A still lump lay along the bed in the darkened room.

Caleb touched her arm. His gaze shot back to Addison.

Each breath Addison took shuddered in her chest. Caroline was far too still. "Caroline? Can you hear me?" Her voice was nearly a shout.

A low moan escaped the older woman's lips, then silence again. Her breathing had little rhythm, as if the next one might not come.

Caleb forced his mother up, holding her weight with both hands. He winced as his healing arm took the brunt of the movement.

Caroline's eyes rolled back, her head flopping to the side.

A bottle lay open on the nightstand beside a picture of Caroline, Charles, and their two little boys. The label said OxyContin, prescribed by Caroline's retired doctor just last week. "How many of these did you take?" Addison held his mother's head upright. "We need to get her to the hospital. I'll pull the van around to the back door."

Caleb nodded, his eyes fierce pools of regret.

She grabbed her purse on the way out the door, unclipping her keys from the strap and finding her cell phone as she moved. Addison punched Brianne's number, then held the phone between her shoulder and jaw as she started the van and drove it as close to the door as possible.

"Hey." There was a lightness in Brianne's voice that hadn't been there before.

"I hate to ask this, but can you do me a big favor?"

"Of course. What is it?"

"The kids get off the bus at 4:40. We're taking Caroline to the hospital. Can you be here?"

"On my way."

Addison beat her head on the steering wheel twice, a luxury she wasn't sure Caroline could afford, but life was dealing out too much.

Caroline hadn't improved by the time they pulled into the emergency department's entrance. Caleb had called ahead to say they were on the way. Two people in scrubs waited at the door with a stretcher.

Time flashed by as Caroline was rushed away, the bottle from Caleb's hand taken with them. Then Caleb collapsed onto the van's running board. "What's going on?"

"Your mom has a problem." Addison scooted in next to him. "And we're going to help her."

"I can't do much from prison."

Addison wrapped her arm around his uninjured one. "Then we have to fight this."

44

Morning came with a crisp chill that wove into Addison's bones. She waved as the bus pulled away from the end of the driveway, tugging her sweater a little tighter. The bus was a new adventure, a relinquishing of sorts, letting someone else deliver her children safely to their school.

The dust cleared behind the retreating vehicle. What had happened to December, to Christmastime, to grand plans? What happened to the perfection she'd sewn into the lives of her family? It was fleeting, like the plumes that rose behind the bus as it drove away. It couldn't be controlled or contained. The wind blew it away and left the present clear and open yet filled with threats.

They'd returned from the hospital in the early morning hours, just as the sun cast the first glow over the mountains. After taking Brianne back to her house, Addison and Caleb had settled on the couch for a nap before waking the kids and getting them out the door for school. Coffee and prayers. They'd survive on both today.

Her feet crunched over the gravel as she strolled back toward the house, a beautiful vision in front of her, with flowers blooming and fog floating away across the field behind the barn. Soon there'd be smoke rising from the chimney. Soon they'd have the answer to the question that bound her heart: Would Caleb be with them this Christmas?

Dew collected on the toes of her Converse as she walked through the front yard, then up the steps.

Caleb held a hand on either side of his leg, the orthopedic boot empty against the couch. He pointed and contracted his foot.

"What are you doing?" Addison reached for the coffee mug she'd left on the sideboard.

"I'm counting my blessings." He lowered his foot and patted the seat next to him.

"And . . . what did you come to?"

"Six. You, of course." He reached for her hand and pulled her down beside him. "The kids. Mom didn't die. She's shaken up, but now she can start to heal from this. And I get rid of this awful boot today, just in time to meet the jury."

She leaned her head on his shoulder. There was a peace in having the house to themselves, calm in an otherwise turbulent time. The relief was laced with guilt. How could she enjoy time alone with her husband when it meant Caroline had spent the night in the hospital?

Caroline had been given a dose of naloxone, an anti-opioid, when they arrived at the emergency room. Though she'd seemed to recover well, the doctor wanted to keep her there while she completed the detox process due to her age and potential health problems.

"I think things will be better with your mom now, don't you?" She wove her fingers between Caleb's. "The doctor was optimistic that her memory problems will resolve with the medication out of her system. They'll keep a close eye on her, and so will we."

His head nodded against hers. "I'm sorry about doubting you. It could have cost her life."

"I've learned a lot this summer about perceptions and reality." She curled tighter into his warmth. "It's easy to see what we want to see, or even what we expect to see. It's much harder to stand back and see the truth."

He nodded. "This is going to be a tough road for her. What if I can't be here to help her?"

"I'll be here. And so will the kids. We're a family."

Caleb kissed the top of her head. "You're so much more than I deserve."

"That's exactly what I was thinking about you."

BRIANNE WOKE TO the sound of pounding. She stretched and looked at her phone. August 29. Today would have been Amanda's fifteenth birthday. The date had stood out to her when reviewing the girl's files.

The time had come to let Amanda rest in peace, to put the anguish aside and turn the loss of that sweet girl into something that could stop other children and teens from facing darkness alone.

Brianne stretched and slipped on her flip-flops. The air was growing cooler every day, making her thankful that her father had come to visit. Though she could handle the furnace on her own, trips to the basement were a task she'd gladly give up.

The scent of coffee and the gurgle of the maker delighted her as she walked into the kitchen. She could have this every morning if she, for once, remembered to set up the machine the night before and put on the timer. Living alone was an endless series of responsibilities.

For a moment, she let her mind wander to what it would be like if she and Seth did get married someday. Maybe he would get the coffee and deal with the furnace maintenance, and she could walk the dog and cook pancakes.

"What are you all smiles about this morning?"

Brianne nearly jumped. She raised her hand to her chest. "Just deep in thought."

He wagged his eyebrows. "Does that deep thought have anything to do with Seth Wallace?" He shrugged. "I'm asking purely for your mother, of course."

"The news made it to Mom, huh?"

The twinkle in his eyes gave the answer.

"I might be thinking of him." She pulled down her favorite Disneyland mug, added an embarrassing amount of creamer, then poured in the rich coffee.

"That is one seriously lucky boy." Her dad wrapped her in a hug. "I'm so proud of my baby girl." His breath warmed the top of her head where he planted a kiss.

She pulled back a bit. "Then I think you might like this. I was up half the night thinking. And not about Seth. Okay, not *just* about Seth." She grinned. "I'm going back to work. Helping the Kilbourns, getting to know their children, and understanding more about Amanda's case has reminded me why God put me in that position to begin with."

He pumped a fist in the air. "That's my girl."

"But I'm not going to do it in the exact same way. I've decided to open a private practice. I think I can provide better service if I can include my faith. I've emailed a colleague to help me get started, but I think I'll offer a sliding-scale fee to accommodate clients with little income. It won't make me rich, but it's where I belong."

He placed a hand on each of her cheeks. "You're my hero." Then he kissed her forehead. "Before you go off and save the world, would you give me a hand with that railing out front? Don't want anyone breaking a leg out there."

She took a good swig of fresh coffee and followed him out the door.

Addison and Caleb spent the morning in Caroline's hospital room. She'd stabilized, but the real work was about to begin. The doctor had serious concerns about her heart and decided it was best for her to spend a couple more nights in observation before he would consider discharge.

Inside Addison's purse were pamphlets with further information on what they could expect for the coming weeks and months. Yet that material was lacking the answers she really needed. How was she going to support her mother-in-law, protect her kids, and fight for her husband's freedom all at the same time?

They approached the offices of Howell, Steves, and Goragie, attorneys at law. A familiar feeling hit Addison every time they entered this building, stealing her balance as it cut away her ability to breathe. Passing through these doors, Addison couldn't deny the reality of their tenuous position.

She reached for Caleb's hand to steady herself and found his palm clammy and his grip shaky. In her entire adult life, she'd never allowed herself to feel this much vulnerability, and it was washing over the only person who could hold her up.

Mr. Howell was in the waiting room, ready for them. "Is there anything you'd like to go over before we head to the courthouse for jury selection?"

Caleb looked to Addison, his eyes pools of resignation. "Yes."

"I'm not going to lie. Your tone has me worried." His two eyebrows joined together in a furrow. He turned and led them back to his office. "What's going on?"

"There are a couple of things that might come up. My brother is a real piece of work. He's been estranged from the family for about eight years."

Mr. Howell nodded. "We can work with that. It's not like you have regular contact with him. I'd say that matter is irrelevant."

"I agree, but it turns out Wyatt isn't the only family member struggling. My mom has a problem with oxy. She's in the hospital, detoxing. And . . . I went to see my brother the night of the accident. That's where I was, and that's where I apparently had a drink." He held up a hand. "Honestly, I would never touch the stuff otherwise. It's a family tradition of sorts."

The lawyer leaned forward, placing his arms on his desk, his fingers interlinked. "Ouch. You've just made a connection between your family and both substances found in your blood. It's not great, but it's not a death sentence."

Caleb cringed.

"Sorry. Bad choice of words."

"The oxy was an accident." Addison clung to her purse. "He didn't know. What about the fact that our daughter saw Caleb's mother get the medication out of an acetaminophen bottle? She put it in a baggie for him in case his headache got worse. Doesn't there need to be some kind of intent for him to be found guilty?"

"How old is that daughter again?" Mr. Howell grabbed a pencil and opened his file.

"Six."

He shut the file. "We can bring it in with your testimony, but it's hearsay unless we put your daughter on the stand. I'd be shocked if the DA doesn't object. Most six-year-olds don't do well in the courtroom."

Howell sat back. "Listen, I fully expect the state to bring a deal to me this evening. They're very predictable that way. I'll introduce this information, try to make it sound as compelling as possible. Maybe it will help with negotiation if you decide to go that direction."

"But he didn't mean for any of this to happen." Addison ached to run into court and make everyone listen. "How can they do this?"

"I get it, but the DA is running for reelection on a platform of ridding this community of drug and alcohol offenses. Don't give up now. We weren't able to interview the eyewitnesses, thanks to one having an attorney for a father, but that might not be a bad thing."

Caleb leaned forward. "How's that?"

"I understand one of them is very nervous. I'm not advocating for the harassment of a witness, but if she falls apart on the stand and her testimony doesn't line up with Miss Hampton's testimony or her prior statements, that's good for us."

"But Georgianna Bosch is dead no matter what the jury decides." Caleb scrubbed his hands through his hair.

"True. And that's horrible. But you serving time doesn't bring her back. If we don't win, I believe all the circumstances we've talked about today will influence the judge when he decides on a sentence." He tapped his watch. "We need to get going."

BRIANNE BREATHED IN the delicate scent of the wild flowers she'd bought at a florist. It wasn't the right season to pick them in the hills like she would have preferred. She stepped out of the car at the hillside cemetery and started down the path to the place she'd visited many times before—Amanda's grave.

The marker was simple but fitting, a picture of a dove with an olive branch carved into the stone. Brianne reached down and removed dead flowers, setting them in a pile to discard on her way out. Then she arranged the new bouquet in the tiny vase provided by the groundskeeper.

She stood back and clasped her hands. No child should ever be here.

Her mind started to replay her last visit with Amanda, and along with the memories came the rebuke. Brianne shook her head. Not this time. Yes, she could have done better. But it was so easy to see mistakes when looking back. If there was one thing she'd learned this summer, it was that every single person on earth was in need of grace. She needed it more than she could put words to.

Closing her eyes, she let the stillness fill her, let the pain and the self-punishment go. Addison would try to find a way to turn this to good, and that was exactly what Brianne was doing. When she left here, the next stop would be West Crow High School, then on to the high school in Darlington. She was on a mission to bring depression and suicide out of the shadows. Teens and preteens needed to understand the warning signs and know how to get help. Once that was established, she'd expand her reach to senior citizens, another group with high rates of suicide. They needed somewhere to turn. This was the place and the cause God had designed Brianne for, and she wasn't about to back down.

Footfalls interrupted the peace. Brianne turned around to see where they came from.

Clyde Tanger stood ten feet behind her, his head bowed, a bunch of flowers in one hand and a small teddy bear in the other.

Brianne stepped to the side, leaving him room.

"Take your time. You were here first." His voice was thick with emotion.

"I need to tell you something." She looked down at the grave, then back to Clyde. "Somehow this seems like an appropriate place."

He looked up with bloodshot eyes, pain etched into the grooves around his mouth.

"Amanda left me a letter the day she died." Brianne pulled the envelope out of her back pocket. "She said you were innocent. Is that true?" She handed the letter to Clyde.

He placed the flowers and teddy bear at the head of the grave before taking the letter. Unfolding it, he pinched his lips and scanned the words. "There are a lot of ways to be guilty, Ms. Demanno. No, I didn't do what I went to prison for, but I was by no means an innocent man."

A chill ran over Brianne's skin. She looked toward the parking lot.

"You have no reason to be worried. I've changed. Prison gave me time to sober up and see the mess I'd made, the people I'd hurt. There isn't a sentence long enough to make it all right. My wife—my ex—she did what she had to. She was trying to protect our kids."

Brianne looked down at the grave beside her feet. "That wasn't protection. It was manipulation."

"Call it what you will. She was scared."

"How can you give her so much grace but allow yourself none?" Brianne crossed her arms, hugging herself in an effort to retain heat.

"Because I was there, and I know the depth of hurt I unleashed on my family. I'm a horrible, angry drunk. I deserved what I got, Ms. Demanno. I deserved so much worse." Taking two steps forward, he kissed his hand and touched the spot where her name was engraved. His gaze settled back on Brianne. "I need to feel the weight of this for a bit longer. Maybe forever." He nodded, turned, and started to walk away.

"Wait."

Clyde stopped, offering the letter back to Brianne.

"Keep it. When you're ready, you can give it to your attorney. I'll testify to its being from Amanda."

His eyes clouded. "Thank you." He held the paper to his heart, then left.

Cold air whipped through the trees of the cemetery, rustling the branches, still heavy with leaves. A sprinkle of rain misted her face as Brianne watched the retreating form of Clyde Tanger walk away.

45

Emilia waited outside the office of the DA until the woman finally appeared, a tablet in one hand and a cup of coffee in the other.

"I was hoping to talk with you before the trial." Emilia stepped into pace beside her.

"We have everything we need." The DA punched the elevator button.

"The older Mrs. Kilbourn—the mother of the defendant—was hospitalized recently with an oxy overdose. She's apparently the one in the house who was using it illegally. I think this throws some light on Mr. Kilbourn's assertion that he did not take the medication knowingly. Maybe it really was accidental."

The DA shifted, giving Emilia her full attention for the first time. "How is that my problem? The man killed a woman. You pushed for this to be prosecuted. Exactly how do you think it would look if I dropped it now?"

"I just thought you should know."

The elevator opened, and the DA got in. She held the door. "Are you coming?"

"I think I'll take the stairs."

There'd been an unease in Emilia's chest all morning. Something wasn't right, and she was the one responsible for this case. She really had let her anger and fears get in the way of her job. Yet at the time, she was sure she'd maintained tight boundaries between her family and her work, not letting one bleed into the other. Prickles darted up and down her arms. Right was still right, wasn't it?

Emilia adjusted the collar of her uniform and took the stairs at a slow pace. Georgianna Bosch was dead. That was the point Emilia needed to remember. That was why they were here today: to find justice for a woman who had needlessly died.

Addison and Caleb sat in a conference room on the first floor of the Corban County Courthouse.

At the head, Mr. Howell sat with Caleb's file in front of him on the polished wood table. He rested his hands on the surface. "This is a new one to me. The DA didn't offer a deal."

Tears pricked Addison's tired eyes. She'd hoped maybe there'd be a chance of community service and no time in prison. That maybe the DA would have compassion on a man who'd never had a run-in with the court system before. That hope was getting crushed.

Mr. Howell rose. "We want to show the judge that we see the seriousness of this situation and that we respect the court, so let's get in there." He straightened his tie.

Addison brushed at the shoulder of Caleb's best suit, removing the tiny specks of lint that remained after she'd gone over him with the fabric roller before leaving home.

Benches lined the hallway. Already a group of people huddled outside the door to courtroom number two. Three boys, teenagers, stood close together, their height working down by their apparent ages. These would be the Bosch boys.

Weakness filtered through Addison's body. For the first time, she truly understood what Caleb had been saying. No one could possibly win in court. Those boys were without their mother, no matter what caused her death. Would seeing Caleb behind bars help them to work through the grief that must still be powerfully present? Or would this continue to bring up a loss that no one could change?

HARPER PACED THE conference room where she'd been placed with Ivy and their mothers, as well as a few other people she didn't even know. This was boring. She'd thought a day off of school to come to court could be interesting, but her mother hadn't even let them stop at Dutch Bros. on the way over. It wouldn't be so bad if Ivy hadn't become so basic.

"Mom." Harper let her arms hang. "I need my coffee."

Her mother pointed to the stand at the end of the room.

"I can't drink that." She flopped down on a rolling chair and started twisting back and forth.

Her phone vibrated, alerting her to a text from Ivy. *I can't stand this.*

Harper typed back a quick reply. *You probably won't even testify. I think the lawyer thinks you cry too much.*

Ivy cast a glare across the room, hitting Harper square between the eyes.

Wow. Chill, will you? Harper returned.

You're seriously heartless.

Harper shook her head. Ivy was a wreck, so typical these days. *Not heartless. Smart. And you better be too. Driver.*

"Harper and Ivy." A woman dressed in a suit with no personality at all stepped into the room. Her hair was a shade darker than the camel-colored fabric. "They're almost ready for you downstairs."

Harper's mother stood, gave Ivy's mom a side hug, and ushered Harper toward the hall.

Holding her phone high, Harper snapped a selfie and posted it to her Snapchat story.

"Seriously?" Her mother snagged the phone and dropped it into her purse. "Do you realize a man's life is on the line here?"

The woman in the boring suit looked back at them, her face a series of lines that would definitely lead to premature wrinkles.

By the time they got to the courtroom, Harper was distracted by the buzzing in her mother's purse. Being cut off from the world didn't seem fair when Harper wasn't even the one on trial.

"Ivy, you'll need to have a seat out here. The DA will call you after Harper is done." The assistant looked through the small window in the courtroom door, nodded, and then pushed it open, ushering Harper and her mother into the room.

Addison took a deep breath.

Brianne patted her leg, a reassurance Addison not only needed but greatly appreciated. Brianne had been teaching her ways to calm herself under this kind of stress. She'd given her breathing techniques, positive thoughts to turn to, and a few verses from the Bible. Nothing she'd given could top the gift of her being there, though, right at Addison's side in the bench behind Caleb and his attorney.

After a day of witnesses for the prosecution, it didn't look good for Caleb's future. There'd been testimony about the amounts of alcohol and oxy in his system. There was a specialist who spoke of the seriousness of mixing these two substances. And James Schneider, the local pharmacist, brought in the typical acetaminophen tablet, comparing it to the oval oxy pills. The difference was obvious.

Addison had spent the day watching witness after witness

as they shoveled the hole her husband and family were to be buried in. Fear buzzed through her veins, riding on a current of caffeine and no additional nutrients. Sipping coffee was as much as her stomach could manage today.

Harper Hampton took the stand, her face blank of any expression unless boredom qualified. She yawned three times while replaying the way Caleb's truck had crossed the line, running into Georgianna Bosch's car. It wasn't new information. Everyone in the courtroom knew he'd done it. That was not the question. They were there for the judge to determine the extent of his responsibility in that death.

Harper left the bench and plopped down next to her mother, her palm up as if waiting for some kind of payment.

A moment later, the DA called the other witness, Ivy Smith. It was hard to imagine these two girls riding along in a car together as friends. Ivy was thin to the point of frail. Her dark hair was tied loosely at the base of her neck. If she wore any makeup at all, it was subtle enough to not be visible. Her steps were slow, as if she'd been battling some sort of disease and was weakened.

Brianne leaned in toward Addison. "I know that girl."

"From where?"

She shook her head. "I can't place her, but I've definitely seen her recently."

The bailiff came forward to swear in the witness.

The DA brushed at her skirt, taking her time before circling the table and approaching the witness, who seemed to be disappearing into herself. "Ms. Smith, you were driving that night, is that correct?"

Ivy's head shot up, her eyes wide. She nodded.

"Please answer the questions out loud." The judge adjusted his robe and leaned in, as if anticipating a whispered response.

"Yes . . . I was." She looked out at the people watching,

her gaze stopping on Brianne. She held there, tears pooling in her eyes.

"Can you tell us what happened the night of June 12?"

Ivy's face crinkled. She covered her face with her hands. Sobs echoed through the room.

In the bench across the aisle from Addison, Ivy's mother leaned forward. Her ache to comfort her child was as evident as the pink designs woven into her white blouse.

"Your Honor"—the DA approached the bench—"I'd like to excuse this witness. Clearly recalling that night is too traumatic for her."

Caleb's attorney stood. "I object. The witness has been sworn in. The defense has the right to question the witness."

"He's right. Mr. Howell may still question your witness. I would have thought you could anticipate this problem and make your decision prior to bringing it into my courtroom."

"I'm sorry, Your Honor." The DA paced in front of the witness box. "Thank you, Ms. Smith. That is all." She took a seat behind her desk.

Mr. Howell approached Ivy. He crossed his arms. "Ms. Smith, please tell us what happened that night." He leaned in close to the teen.

A bench squeaked, calling Addison's attention to Harper, her eyes like missiles targeted on Ivy.

Ivy shuddered as she looked back at Brianne. "We were driving home."

"And where is home?"

"Darlington."

"You were driving toward Darlington?"

"Yes."

Mr. Howell rubbed a finger along his jawline. "According to the police report, you were driving toward West Crow." He moved to his desk and pulled out a paper from a large file. "It says here you were going back for a sweater. So again, could you tell us which direction you were driving?"

She straightened a tiny bit. "East. Toward Darlington."

Mr. Howell looked back at Caleb, his eyebrows wrinkled. "Okay. Please tell us why you told Deputy Cruz that you were driving west?"

Harper coughed three times, but Ivy's eyes stayed focused on Brianne. "We were heading home. Harper wanted to take a selfie to post on her Snapchat story." She shook her head. "It all happened so fast. I was looking at the phone, and I just kind of got into the other lane for a minute."

Mr. Howell nodded and turned back to Ivy. "What happened when you swerved?"

"I didn't see him because of the curve . . . and the phone. Harper kept saying to tip my chin up. I didn't see him coming."

Brianne's hand tightened on Addison's. She nodded toward the girl.

There was some kind of connection happening between Brianne and Ivy. Addison breathed as softly as she could, trying not to move and break the delicate threads that seemed to be pulling the story from the trembling teen.

"He . . ." Ivy pointed toward Caleb. "He swerved to miss me. I thought just for a tiny second that we'd been saved . . . then everything exploded." Tears washed down her face. Ivy's cheeks flushed, and her eyes crinkled. "It was me. I did this." She buried her face in her hands.

The judge tapped his gavel. "I'd like to see both attorneys in my chambers. We'll have a fifteen-minute recess."

Addison's heart pounded. She turned to Brianne, who was still watching the teen as she stepped away from the witness chair. "What's happening?"

"That girl, Ivy—I met her at the counseling office. She made a horrible mistake, but she's making it right the best way she can." Brianne wrapped her arm around Addison's shoulder.

THE JUDGE PRONOUNCED the case dismissed and gave his gavel a final bang.

Turning to Addison, Brianne watched the happy tears pour over her friend's cheeks. Months of agony, fear, and questioning, all gone in a moment of truth.

Addison leaned into Brianne. "Thank you."

"I didn't do anything. This was God. Go see your husband."

The grin on Addison's face could have lit the room. She squeezed Brianne's hand and went to the defendant's desk, hugging Caleb, who still stood like a man in shock.

All around the courtroom, people buzzed, unfolding the new information and starting the gossip chain all over again. Still in the same seats, Ivy huddled next to her mother, her face buried in the white blouse.

Brianne's heart was torn in two. She rejoiced with her friends but grieved with the young woman who'd held onto this painful secret all summer. There would be harsh consequences to follow: the loss of friends, the loss of respect, and the possible loss of freedom. And Ivy would need people to stand beside her.

With a prayer flowing over her heart, Brianne made her way to the bench on the other side of the room. She scooted in next to Ivy and gently brushed the hair back from her face. "I remember you."

Red blotches colored the face of Ivy's mother. Another woman in fear for her child.

"I'm a counselor. Ivy and I met when I was visiting my old office. I'd like to help, if I can."

Ivy covered her face with her hands. "I don't think you can. I've ruined everything."

"No, you haven't. You came forward when it counted."

"But now my life is over." Her words weren't laced with teen drama. It was a natural assumption for a girl Ivy's age.

"It may feel that way, but there are still amazingly beautiful days in your future. One step at a time, okay?"

Mrs. Smith touched Brianne's arm and mouthed a thank-you.

This was where the healing could begin. Not in the secrets and regrets, but in the moving forward, trusting, and truth.

46

Addison and Caleb stepped out into the sunlight in front of the Corban County Courthouse. Colorful blooms lined the edge of the lush green lawn, while a breeze hinted at autumn's approach. Along the street, a group of people held signs protesting the city's plan to change West Crow's traffic flow. Brianne waved out her window as she drove by on her way to pick up the Kilbourn children from school.

It seemed like a fully different day from the one it had been when Addison and Caleb walked up these steps that morning. Even the seasons seemed to have changed in the hours they'd spent in the courtroom. They stopped under a maple tree.

Caleb picked up a stray scarlet leaf and twirled it between his fingers. "I don't know what to do now."

"Well, there's Hannah's first soccer game. I'd like to be there for that, since we're done early."

"No. I mean now that this is over." His gaze drew back to the white courthouse. "The judge dismissing the case was outside of anything I could even think to pray for."

Addison scooped her hand around his upper arm. "How are you feeling?"

"I don't know. I wish I could remember the accident clearly." He turned to face her, tears in his eyes. "The thing is, it was still my truck that hit her car. What if I hadn't had that drink? What if I hadn't taken that pill? Maybe I would have been able to avoid her car too."

Addison's face tingled as the blood rushed from her cheeks. The Bosch boys were leaving the courthouse, their eyes red and swollen. Caleb's innocence did nothing to help those boys. Instead, they were now saddled with the knowledge that their mother had been killed because of two careless girls from their hometown.

"I heard they're about to lose their home. Their mother didn't have life insurance, and with the oldest just turning eighteen, they've chosen to stay together as long as they can. The social security payments aren't enough to pay the bills and the mortgage. I can't imagine having to give up college at that age to care for my little brothers."

"That's horrible. I wish we could do something."

His silence drew her attention to his face. "I think we can."

Her shoulders slumped. Their dream home across the field was still slipping away. They'd given a chunk of savings to the attorney, and that had felt wrong, but what Caleb was suggesting was different. It rang with a tone of freedom and honor. And they'd continue to save. "Let's help them out. We can keep saving, and we can build on to your mother's house if it's okay with her. My dream house is anywhere my family lives."

Caleb grinned and pulled her into his chest. "I love you so much."

Emilia returned from the car, the bowl of sliced oranges on her hip, just in time to see the girls run back onto the field after halftime.

Her heart stalled at the collision of worlds happening directly between where she stood and the soccer field.

Roger lifted himself out of a camp chair. Although still moving tentatively, he'd made great strides forward. There was a smile on his face as he reached his hand out to Caleb Kilbourn. They shook, Caleb pointing to Tally as she advanced the ball down the field toward the goal.

Emilia kept going forward, though her pace was substantially slowed.

At ten feet behind the men, she could just make out their conversation over the crowd of cheering and encouraging parents.

"She's a great kid," Caleb said. "You must be proud."

"More than you know. And she loves your family. I've heard many great things about you all." Roger's speech still lagged and slurred, but his mouth formed a lopsided grin that took any cares out of Emilia's reach. He looked back and caught sight of her. "Emilia, come meet this man."

She stepped up next to Roger, not doubting for a second that her husband knew exactly what he was doing.

"This is Caleb Kilbourn. He's Hannah's father. I was just thinking we should get to know each other, seeing as how the girls have become such great friends. And then Caleb came on over and introduced himself."

Emilia set her spine in a rigid stance, ready to take what Caleb was about to throw at her.

He held out his hand. "It's so great to meet you, Emilia."

She took his hand. "It's an honor. And I want to say I'm sorry."

He shook his head. "No need. We're just two parents on the soccer field, potential friends."

Their gazes connected for a moment, saying more than words could.

"Let me get my wife over here." He motioned for Addison to join them.

Addison's face was pale, but she smiled as she came toward them, Seth and his girlfriend tagging along.

"This is Addison. We've really enjoyed getting to know your daughter. How about we all get some dinner after the game?" Caleb looked back at Seth. "What do you think?"

"Every one of my favorite people in one place? I'm in." He put his arm around his girlfriend. "What do you think, Brianne?"

"Absolutely."

"Brianne?" Emilia took a deep breath. "I've heard a lot about the new practice you hope to set up. There's a girl I'd like to refer to you. Can we talk sometime?" Cami deserved to have someone in her corner too. Emilia might not have the reserves to help the girl, but she could help her find people who could.

"Of course." Brianne pulled a card from her back pocket. "Give me a call any time."

Tally kicked the ball into the goal, sending the crowd into thrilled hysteria.

And Addison placed her hand on Emilia's arm. "It's so good to meet another mom."

Author's Note

Much like life, a book is the combination of many people and their experiences. Thank you to everyone who supported me as I spent hours trying to uncover and unravel this story.

Thank you to God, who blessed me with this wonderful career, my amazing family, and a whole lot of beautiful friends.

My family puts up with so much as I try out ideas and pound away in my office instead of making dinner. They are patient and supportive, loving and encouraging. The older kids take the time to care for the younger ones when I'm working. My husband picks up extra household chores so we have clean dishes and can walk through the house without getting lost. Without all of them, I wouldn't have the motivation and material to write books.

A big thank-you to the Benton County sheriff's office, which let me ride along with one of their deputies. I discovered more than the answers I needed for this novel; I found a love for speeding down the highway.

Debi Friedlander graciously explained and demonstrated her colored pencil photo fusion art techniques. I first saw her work at an open studio event, and I knew right away that I wanted to bring this art form into a story. Thank you, Debi, for sharing your talent.

Thank you to my dear friend Pete Dunn, who should have the title of technical advisor and who never teases me about asking the same question over and over again. Thank you, Mari Bacho, for explaining a bit of your photography magic. Jen Cooper, thanks for giving me a better understanding of the paperwork side of counseling. I have truly talented friends.

Raela Schoenherr, thank you for believing in this project, believing in me, and welcoming me into the Baker/Bethany House family. I'm honored.

Rochelle Gloege, your keen eye and ability to see flaws in my timeline made this story what I had envisioned. Thank you!

I'm so amazed by Cynthia Ruchti. First, she was one of my favorite authors. Later, she became my agent. Now Cynthia is also a dear friend, a sounding board, a prayer warrior for my career and my family, and someone I respect, admire, and cherish. Thank you, Cynthia, for taking on this project, believing in me, and being the beautiful woman of God you are.

Thank you to my sister, Kaitlin, who reads anything I send to her, even when it's unpolished, and tells me it's better than I know it actually is.

Thanks to those dear women who take my work and tear it to pieces. Karen Barnett, Marilyn Rhoads, and Heidi Gaul are the best critique partners any writer could ever have.

Jodie Bailey, you are a blessing. You remind me regularly how to eat an elephant: one bite at a time. Thank you, sister.

And to all my friends, the ones who take my little ones so I can stay sane, go to conferences, and make deadlines, thank you for letting me be that friend who, for this season, needs more than she gives. Thank you for loving me even when I don't respond to texts until they're outdated, when I forget to return your dishes, and when I beg for help at the last moment. I'm so blessed to have you. You are my people, and I love you more than I can say.

Sign Up for Christina's Newsletter!

Keep up to date with Christina's news on book releases and events by signing up for her email list at christinasuzannnelson.com.

You May Also Like . . .

After the rival McLean clan guns down his cousin, Colman Harpe chooses peace over seeking revenge with his family. But when he hears God tell him to preach to the McLeans, he attempts to run away and fails, leaving him sick and suffering in their territory. He soon learns that appearances can be deceiving, and that the face of evil doesn't look like he expected.

When Silence Sings by Sarah Loudin Thomas
sarahloudinthomas.com

BETHANYHOUSE

Stay up to date on your favorite books and authors with our free e-newsletters.
Sign up today at bethanyhouse.com.

facebook.com/bethanyhousepublishers

@bethanyhousefiction

Free exclusive resources for your book group! bethanyhouse.com/anopenbook

More from Bethany House

Famous author Josephine Bourdillon is in a coma, her memories surfacing as her body fights to survive. But those around her are facing their own battles: Henry Hughes, who agreed to kill her for hire out of desperation, is uncertain how to finish the job now, and her teenage daughter, Paige, is overwhelmed by fear. Can grace bring them all into the light?

When I Close My Eyes by Elizabeth Musser
elizabethmusser.com

In the wake of WWII, a grieving fisherman submits a poem to a local newspaper asking readers to send rocks in honor of loved ones to create something life-giving—but the building halts when tragedy strikes. Decades later, Annie returns to the coastal Maine town, where stone ruins spark her curiosity and her search for answers faces a battle against time.

Whose Waves These Are by Amanda Dykes
amandadykes.com

BETHANYHOUSE